Dark Is The Broken Heart

Dark Is The Broken Heart
Part one of the Substitute Trilogy

By Phil Thorpe

**Published by:
Little Nell Publishing at The Old Curiosity Bookshop
2020**

Little Nell Publishing at The Old Curiosity Bookshop
2020

Copyright ©2020 by Phil Thorpe

All rights reserved. This book or any portion thereof may not be reproduced or used in any manner whatsoever without the express written permission of the publisher except for the use of brief quotations in a book review or scholarly journal.

First Printing: February 2020

ISBN 978-0-244-56042-3

Little Nell Publishing at The Old Curiosity Bookshop
115 Loughborough Road, Hathern, Leicestershire LE12 5HZ

www.oldcuriositybookshop.co.uk.com

Ordering Information:
Special discounts are available on quantity purchases by Bookshops, associations, educators, and others. For details, contact the publisher at the above listed address or email: hello@oldcuriositybookshop.co.uk

U.S. trade bookstores and wholesalers: Please contact Little Nell Publishing Tel: (+44) 773773-8018; or email hello@oldcuriositybookshop.co.uk

Copy available from the British Library Records

Dedicated to
Eunice

Introduction

A note from the Publisher...

If you enjoy reading this, look out for his second book or contact us to buy a copy.

You can contact the Author via the Publisher – Little Nell Publishing, or talk to us about publishing your book at: Old Curiosity Bookshop, 115 Loughborough Road, Hathern, LE12 5HZ.

Tel: 0773 773 8018,
Email: hello@oldcuriositybookshop.co.uk
Website: www.oldcuriositybookshop.co.uk

CHAPTER 1

Hot, hot, hot. It was unquestionably hot in the office. The ancient fan was to be read the last rites and consigned to the scrapheap. Or, more likely, the storeroom, gathering dust, to be hauled out again later, sworn at, and thrown away. Jim, attention totally focused on the report before him, absentmindedly reached out to open a window behind him. He needed fresh air or otherwise he'd fall asleep into the thick pile before him.

The window latch, however, had other ideas, refusing to yield. Tipping his chair back like a naughty schoolboy, Jim tore his attention away from his report to wrench the window open. Disastrously, the window flew open, a gust of hot air breathed in, and blew Jim's report all over his desk. The chair toppled over backwards. Attempting to save himself, Jim grabbed at whatever was available to grab but only succeeded in pulling his office phone, a blotter, assorted items of stationery and a small picture frame to the floor with him.

An attractive woman entered the office. Long dark hair framing a pretty face wafted up in the breeze. She stood there, hands on hips, trying not to laugh at the sprawling mess.

"What are you doing?" She laughed.

"Practicing for the riot squad?"

"Stop standing there and give me a fucking hand here!" Jim, normally taciturn, rarely excitable, and never foul mouthed, shouted from his impossible tangle of chair, jacket, phone cables, pens, pencils, stapler, blotter and picture frame. Rachael Read sidled around the side of her bosses' desk, picking up the silver picture frame first, handling it delicately because although she had never seen what the subject was, she had on several occasions seen her boss looking at it wistfully. It contained a photo of a woman somewhere in her mid-twenties smiling directly into the camera, in her arms a little baby, wrapped in a white shawl. Rachael wondered who it was- Jim's sister, mother, even wife? She placed the frame back in its usual place and turned to help her boss.

Jim had managed to slide his back partially up the wall, seemingly sitting on an invisible stool. He had managed to entangle the phone cord around his leg and ankle. Rachael bent down to release him from his telecommunications tangle, still wondering what had happened. Maybe Jim was getting senile. She stopped in the middle of unwrapping Jim's leg and looked up into his face, blushing, ashamed at her own thoughts. He mistook the blush as something else completely, and so said, quite huffily, "Yes, OK, that's enough now. Could you concentrate on my report?"

"Of course, Sir." Standing, she straightened her skirt and went back around the desk to retrieve what she could of the report. As she bent over, retrieving page after page of neatly drafted notes, she was grateful that none had torn, or crumpled too badly. That would tip the old bastard right over the edge.

"On second thoughts, DC Read, just put it on the desk. No, don't sort it, I'll do it later." He looked around at what the mess. "We'll do it later. Leave it. If anyone comes in, they can just assume we were fighting."

"Or...worse". Rachael smiled, and blushed again.

Jim smiled, not a dirty smile, like a pervert looking at schoolchildren, nor yet a smile one would bestow on a favoured child. Perhaps somewhere in between. Maybe there was life in the old dog yet.

"Pub." That strange, enigmatic smile again. "It's almost lunchtime, it'll be open."

He picked up and shook his jacket. He locked the office on his way out, so no-one would see the mess. Turning, he hustled along the corridor and out towards the front of the station.

Nerveless, implacable. His chosen path. It wasn't his fault the women had rejected him. He was normal, they were the abnormal ones. They were the weirdoes, and they would pay. He smiled and laughed out loud. It wasn't just the women who would pay. It was the others as well.

He strolled down the street, not even looking at the house. Instead he was looking for cars that weren't normally here. Of course, there could be any number of vehicles that wouldn't ordinarily be here- sisters or mums or daughters visiting their family; carpenters or decorators sizing up jobs; but he felt that the kind of car that he was looking for would stand out like a sore thumb. He was walking at a normal pace, sauntering almost, face emotionless. Inside he was a maelstrom of emotion. Trepidation, of future success or failure. No, scratch that, he thought, of course he would succeed. There was no alternative. He'd put far too much in so far. Excitement, soared in him like an eagle above a mountain, spying out his prey below. Regret was futile. A wrong word here, a touch there, then the feeling of crushing hopelessness as his world crashed around his ears yet again. There certainly were no regrets about the deaths of the women. Maybe the families and friends of the others; but God had chosen them for a specific reason. Or so he thought. Pre-ordination. The parents of the others had met, fallen in love, coupled, and named their children. Maybe not even that far. A quick fumble outside a discotheque, maybe, but with the same end result. Were the parents the ones who were really to blame?

He shook his head to clear it. Thirsty after his walk around the streets, he looked for a pub. It didn't really matter which one, he thought, not at this end of the town. He hadn't socialised in these parts for years, it was the middle of the day, and he was virtually certain that anyone who had known him wouldn't recognise him any more anyway. After a quick final check around him, he pulled open the door of the White Lion and entered into the smoky surroundings. Only one bar in here, no divide between lounge and saloon bars. He confidently walked up to the bar, quietly asked for a pint of lager, mentally picking a table. Not at the back, that was for sure, or the front, but somewhere in the middle, where he would be quickly forgotten. For now. He sat down and took a large swallow of the cooling amber liquid. Fishing around in his pocket for his lighter, he glanced up at the door to see two more punters come into the pub. Watching them as he lit his cigarette, he wondered about their dynamic, their relationship. Judging by the relatively smart clothing, and the difference in age between the forty-something man and the woman with him, who looked about mid-twenties, he reckoned they were a boss and his secretary. He looked at the man. About 5'8", with short salt and pepper hair, smallish face, his main features were equally spaced. Slightly careworn, but with a distinguished look about him; dignified and authoritative. His suit was looking a bit crumpled, but at least his quality patent leather shoes were highly polished. An office manager, or an accountant, maybe? He studied her closer. About 5'10" in height, she was quite pretty in an austere way. She was wearing a maroon skirt, white blouse and sensible flat shoes. Her handbag was over one shoulder.

Stupid, he thought. He figured they were police just as the woman glanced over at him, checking him out. He immediately looked away, out of the window, cursing himself inwardly for doing anything to attract attention.

Charming, thought Rachael, looking at the handsome man sitting by the table smoking. Just one look at me is all it takes to show no interest nowadays. Although she was in work clobber, with minimal make up on, she thought she didn't look too bad. She wasn't wheeling a double pram around, fag in mouth, with a can of Special Brew on the go, pizza stains and god knows what else staining her pink shell suit. She scowled at the man, but he had already turned his attention elsewhere. So she focused on her boss, who had evidently just asked her a question.

"Sorry, sir, what was that?" she asked.
"I was asking what you wanted to drink." Jim said.
"Oh, lemonade, please." She replied. "Shall I get us a table?"
"Why, expecting a rush?" Jim laughed. "Go on then. Crisps?"
"Err, yes please. Cheese and onion. Thanks." She walked over to the table directly behind the man who by now had finished his cigarette and was now nonchalantly drinking his lager. As she was going to sit down, the man stood up, making his way to the toilet. They almost touched as they swerved to avoid knocking into each other.

"Sorry." The man, who appeared to Rachael to be about her age, maybe two or three years older, apologised to her. Brushing a strand of fair hair out of his eyes, Rachael noticed that they were a lovely blue-grey, and warm, eyes to get lost in. He smiled, as he stopped to let her sit down. A lovely smile. Not for the first time that day, Rachael blushed.

Now, that was better, as he headed to the gents. She had been put at ease. She would probably forget him immediately. He finished his business, crossed to the chipped washbasin, and looked at his reflection in the cracked mirror. He laughed as he saw his face was actually made up of about five different shapes. Just like his personality, he mused. He had an ability to be what he wanted to whomever he wanted. Mostly so that people could be what they wanted him to be. But it hadn't always been that way. He had learned the hard way. Many instances of rejection floated through his mind. People like Sam, for instance.

The sun slanted its rays through the branches and leaves of the huge horse chestnut, splaying alternates of shade and light across her face. Her beauty, in that moment, took his breath away. Her long curly hair fluttered in the light breeze as they sat hand in hand on his denim jacket. Somewhere in the distance a boom box was playing Duran Duran, the Rio album. Not too loud, but just right, for the moment. Sam Taylor was staring into the distance, squinting in the bright sunlight, her lips pursed.
"Is that Sarah and Lawrence?" Sam asked, turning to him. "Over there, by the putting green, coming this way?" She pointed, where he could see his best friend strolling along, hands entwined with his girlfriend. Sam jumped to her feet and started waving her arms in attempt to gain her friends attention. Sarah was her best friend, and he thought darkly that perhaps Sam had 'engineered' this encounter, so that she wouldn't have to be alone with him for the entire afternoon. It was something she seemed to be doing with increasing regularity recently. When they had gone bowling

the other day, it was Sam that suggested that they tag along. And at the cinema the week before. Not that he resented their company, but sometimes... sometimes he felt that it would be nice if they did something on their own. Just the two of them, together.

Sarah had obviously spotted them because she was enthusiastically waving back, tugging Lawrence off the path in their direction. As they were heading towards them, Sam turned back to him, and said, "You don't mind, do you?"

"No, not all." He replied, meaning the exact opposite.

"Hiya, babe!" This was Sarah, calling out to Sam. The couple eventually reached them. Sarah looked at him. "And hello, you." This was to him. The two girls embraced as if had been two weeks since they'd been together, not the two hours or so that it had been. Lawrence caught his gaze and responded by rolling his eyes and giving a small shrug as if to say, 'sorry mate'.

"Come on, sit down with me." Sam sat down on his jacket, and Sarah sat next to her. Meanwhile, Lawrence sauntered nonchalantly over to him and whispered in his ear,

"Quiet word is in order, methinks." And then to the girls, "Who's up for ice cream?"

The two boys wandered off in search of an ice cream van. They walked along in silence before he spoke.

"So what am I doing wrong then mate?"

"Sorry, dunno." Lawrence shrugged again.

"Reckon she likes someone else?"

"Still dunno." Lawrence looked at him. "Sarah hasn't said much about it."

"Much? Then she has said something." He turned, an imploring look on his face, adding "If you know something, spill."

Lawrence shrugged yet again. "That's the whole point. Every time I mention the two of you, she either changes the subject or clams up completely." He pocketed his change and turned back.

"We'd better get these back before they melt completely."

And so, without the answers that he was seeking to the questions whirring round his brain, he trooped back to his beautiful girlfriend, hoping against hope that everything would work out fine.

Four days later, Sam dumped him.

CHAPTER 2

He stood watching shadows lengthen. It had been a glorious day, but he had hardly moved, except to replenish his coffee or go to the toilet. All day he maintained his vigil, standing by the window, watching. When the residents of the street had begun their daily rituals, bringing in the milk, sending the kids to school, going to work, he had gently pulled the net curtains back across the window, shielding him from the gaze of others.

Hour after hour he stood there, watching. He ran the plan through his head. And again. And again. From his perspective, from the perspective of others, too. When he was convinced that everything was right, he went through it again. The music played repeatedly on the stereo. Over and over. Like the thoughts going round his head. He had spent months on his research, heaps of money, hundreds of hours, travelling the country, searching through archives of birth and death, electoral rolls, newspapers. He had become a temporary member of libraries the length and breadth of the country. He rarely stayed in the same place twice. Now he was ready. He had picked the optimum time between events to instill maximum pain, fear and confusion. He sometimes suspected in his darkest moods that the police would catch him before the plan was complete. But then the power would lift his spirits and he felt euphoric and he knew that he would never be caught. Not if he didn't want to be.

Evening was slowly releasing its grip on the day and handing its charge to the darkness. The darkness where monsters slide out from under a million beds to scare a million children. Darkness, where dreams became nightmares for a million more. Darkness, where the nightmare was reality for a million prostitutes, nurses, police, firemen, cleaners, waiters, barmen. Darkness, when he would start his murderous campaign. He left the room, pausing in the hallway to put on a dark windcheater. He went out around the side of the house, checking his watch. It was just after midnight.

Two streets away was an alley, which opened onto a double row of garages. At the third garage on the right, he opened the doors. Before entering, he glanced around his surroundings to make sure the coast was clear. Inside was a transit van and inside that, a man. Bound and gagged. He climbed in, grabbing a torch. He turned it on carefully, so that the beam didn't shine out of the garage. Using it to check the man in the back, who had woken when he had heard the garage doors open. He struggled for a short while until realising the futility of his actions.

Starting the van, he moved it slowly back until it was clear of the doors and hopped out, padlocking them. He ensured that the back door of the transit was locked as well. He didn't want his quarry sliding out en route to the destination. Getting back in, he selected first gear and slowly moved off. As he drove, he thought back on how his path had crossed with the bound and gagged man behind him, gently rocking with the motions of the van.

Pete slid his pint glass along the bar towards the Old Git.
"Come on, old git, stump up, I've got a rare old parch on."
"Eh, what's that you're saying, lad?"
Pete ignored him and looking at the barmaid said, "Same again when you're ready, Shirley."
"Ok, my lover, two best coming up."
"If only you were, if only you were, Shirl." Pete cast a surreptitious glance at the end of the bar where her husband Grant was reading the Racing Post. Pete reckoned that he must've read it cover to cover at least twice by now. He rarely put it down, unless someone asked for him, or the tables needed clearing or the ashtrays emptying. Even then, he stalked round the bar with a perceptible scowl on under his beard.

Shirley placed the two pints of frothy beer on the bar, smiled at Pete, and held out her hand for the money. Shaking his head, the man known simply as Old Git put his hand in his pocket and fished out his battered wallet and sighed. "I don't know how my pension stretches to buying you all this beer, me lad."

Pete almost choked into his beer. "Pension? You're 53!"

"Well, in that case, less of the old then. And as I'm buying the beer, less of the git as well."

He took a long gulp of his beer." You could just call me by my given name, you know."

"Samuel, Samuel, Samuel, what are we going to do with you?" Pete's eyes temporarily glazed over as he stared at the mirror behind the optics. If only you knew, he reflected, you wouldn't be sitting here so amiably.

"Ok, ok, don't wear it out, as me mam used to say." Samuel Obadiah Taylor, 53, but looking 73, protested. "And don't drink my beer while I'm in the gents." He winced theatrically as he eased himself off the bar stool, shuffling off in the direction of the toilets. Pete watched his receding back and thought to himself how incredibly easy this man had been to track. Taylor was the fifth most popular surname in England, the 11th in Scotland, and the 22nd most widely used in Wales and in Lancashire, where he was now, it was very common. And as for Samuel... He returned to face the optics, aware of how crucially important this was to get right. This was the first one, and would mean nothing to anyone at the beginning, but would ultimately lead the old git to become infamous.

In the meantime, Samuel had returned from his trip to the loo. Settling himself down on the barstool again, he turned to face Pete. "So, how's the book coming along then?"

"Oh, almost done now. I'll be heading back to Edinburgh soon, Sam." Pete lied. He had never been to the Scottish capital. He had told Sam that he was a post-grad there, writing a book about modern proponents of ancient jobs: coopers, tanners, and rat-catchers, like Samuel. The old man had swallowed the bait whole, especially when his initial reticence to contribute to the project had been tempered by the offer of free beer, and lots of it. Pete wondered how upset Samuel would be if he knew he'd been totally hoodwinked. Not as upset as he would be when he found out Pete's real interest in the ageing, lonely, pest controller. The fact that he was a bachelor, with no family except for some cousins that lived on the other side of the Pennines and had nothing much to do with him, was a bonus. Even his occupation was a solitary affair, the smell of sewers and odour precluding him from making many friends. A tendency to become a boor after beer was another factor. Not too many folk would notice him gone until it was too late.

"Oh sorry to hear that mate......." Samuel was saying, but Pete wasn't listening. He was deep in thought of the next stage.

He drove around the block twice to make sure that nothing looked out of place before coming to a halt outside the rented flat. At this time of night, mid-week in this town, nothing stirred. He drove the van around the back, into a courtyard. There were no lights from the nearby flats. It didn't surprise him, as one was unoccupied, and the other seemed to house some kind of salesman who was often away. A run-down part of town that didn't seem to be going up in the world and fine for his needs.

Climbing in the back and squatting down, he placed a knife on the floor and flicked his torch on and shone it onto the chest of the man still lying supine on the floor.

"I'm going to let you into a secret. Actually, two. But first I have to know that if I remove your gag that you are not going to scream or even call out ...agree?"

He waited for Samuel to nod and removed the gag.

"Thanks." The old man's voice was scarcely a whisper. "What are you going to do to me?"

"Water?" He asked, ignoring the question. He waited again for a nod before giving him a small bottle of water. "Sorry, but it's warm."

He tilted the bottle to the old man's parched lips. When he was satisfied that he had had enough, he re-screwed the cap on the water, throwing into back onto a shelf.

"Firstly, I'm not Pete, a post-grad student from Edinburgh University researching into ancient trades, or anything like that. Although, I have done a lot of research, of a different kind, into people, like you." He picked up the knife and placed the blade directly below the eye of the helpless man on the floor, before carrying on. "No, don't ask any questions. I'm going to untie you and help you into my flat. Any false move, and you'll feel this..." He held the knife directly in front of Sam's vision, "...sliding into your ribs. And, I'm guessing that you don't want that, do you?" Sam shook his head.

"Right now, let's get you on your feet." The man that Sam knew was now not Pete grabbed him by the elbow. Gently, as if it was an elderly uncle he was helping, he pulled Sam to his feet. They waited until Sam could feel his legs.

He reached into the pocket of the jacket he was wearing and pulled out a hip flask, lifting it to the older man's lips. "Don't gulp it, just deep swallows, like beer, mate." Sam just looked askance at him and kept guzzling greedily, until most of the flask had gone. Good boy, he thought, give me five minutes and you won't know what hit you. "Come on then, let's get you inside." He opened the side door of the van and jumped down. "No funny business now. Just shuffle forward to the edge and I will help you down." The old man duly obliged and was half pulled, half lifted out of the van, and directed towards the door of the flat and then gently pushed into the darkened hallway.

The abject fear that Sam had felt when he'd first been abducted had returned. It had subsided on the long journey in the van and the even longer wait afterwards. But there was something else, a feeling like someone had wrapped his head in cotton wool. He started to feel very tired and leant against the dark wall for a rest. Just a quick rest, he thought, and then he'd carry on planning his escape. Before he knew what was happening, he had slid down into a crumpled heap on the floor.

The other man stepped over the prone Sam and along the hallway without even bothering to turn the lights on. In the kitchen he placed his keys on the side, sniffing the air, finding nothing untoward. In the larger of the two bedrooms, he closed the curtains before switching the bedside lamp on. There wasn't a lot in here apart from the bed and the small cabinet beside it. Over in one corner was a dilapidated Queen Anne chair that had seen better times; a print of the Empire State building hung incongruously on the wall. The bed was bare apart from a white sheet and a pillow. Hanging over the back of the armchair was a white duvet cover without its duvet.

Crouching down, he opened the bedside cabinet draw. He removed a syringe that was in there, checking that it was still full. He didn't want anything to go wrong now. Years of meticulous planning had led him to this very moment. Smiling to himself, he straightened up, looking around one last time. Satisfied, he went back into the hallway. Sam was still lying as if comatose just inside the door. Going up to the prone body, he smiled to himself; no turning back now. Not that there had been even before he had tricked Sam into getting into the back of his van, on the pretense of giving the old drunk a lift home the previous evening. At least, he reflected, the three hundred miles or so he had driven since then would act as some sort of security barrier even if someone noticed that Sam wasn't at home, which was highly unlikely anyway.

He bent over Sam and gingerly felt for the back of his jacket and dragged the body along the hallway towards the bedroom. He laid him face down at the foot of the bed, pulling up the back of Sam's jacket, looking for the belt holding up his jeans. He grasped hold of it firmly and readjusted his hold on Sam's collar with his other hand. Bracing his knees, he hoisted the old man bodily onto the bed, so that he was lying face down with his head resting on one side, nestled into the solitary pillow. He gently eased off Sam's shoes, placing them neatly together at the foot of the bed. He then removed the old battered sports jacket that Sam was so fond of wearing. Making sure that only his gloved hands touched the material, he folded it neatly over one arm of the Queen Anne. Turning back to the body, he grabbed one hip and gently rolled enough of the unconscious Sam so that he could reach under and gently unbuckle the belt. When that was done, he let gravity do its job and let the body roll back again. This time, however, there was the slightest movement of Sam's chin. The sedative was wearing off. He had to act quickly now, before he revived completely.

Going back to the foot of the bed, he placed one knee between Sam's legs, catching an unsavoury whiff of unwashed feet as he did so. There was distinct moaning coming from the top of the bed now. He yanked the jeans down, swiftly followed by the underpants. He recoiled from the stench. Sam had soiled himself at least twice. Moving rapidly now, he grabbed the syringe and thrust it deeply into the anus, discharging the contents quickly into the void. He had intended to inject directly into the pectinate line, but both the dried shit and the still wet stuff obscured his vision; the stench was overwhelming. Suddenly, Sam started writhing all over the place. He knelt directly onto the old mans' calves and pressed downwards on Sam's shoulders. Gradually, the movements slowed as the contents of the syringe took effect. Then they stopped. One last shudder and it was all over. He got off the inert body, annoyed with himself that he hadn't thought of the possibility of Sam defecating all over himself. He stumbled over the shoes and fell down, putting a handout to break his fall. He rolled over onto one knee and then his bottom. He looked down at the carpet. The seventies styled Wilton carpet was a brown whorled rose pattern, browns and reds. It now looked like one of the roses had four short twigs poking out from behind a leaf.

Breathing a sigh of relief, he got to his feet and went into the bathroom. He managed, with some difficulty, to turn on one of the taps by using just his forearms. The water felt cold, even through the gloves. After a while he backed up and elbowed on the light switch. Flecks of faeces dotted the washbasin. He cupped his hands and slowly managed to clean all the debris down the plughole.

Satisfied, he wandered into the bedroom again. The room still stank. He went into the kitchen and looked in a cupboard under the sink, carefully nudging a bottle of bleach, ant killer and Windolene out of the way until he found a can of air freshener. He went around the flat, spraying until the cloying aroma of lavender overwhelmed the smell of shit. Opening a window, he inhaled the night air deeply. The faint aroma of night scented stock drifted in on the breeze. Glancing at the body, he noticed that the cool night air had dried the faeces on Sam's backside. Taking a deep breath, he pulled the soiled underwear back over Sam's bum. Looking over the body, he noticed faint smearing on both of Sam's shoulders. He left the bedroom, going to fetch the flannel from the bathroom. He rinsed it out this time under the hot tap, and returning to the body, carefully washed off the shit off the shoulders. He knew that traces would be found in any post-mortem, and that there may well be bruising there as well. He reflected that this may reduce the time to find the injection site, but he wasn't worried. As long as he was careful nothing could give him away. There was no trace of his DNA that he had left anywhere, and it didn't matter anyway because the police had no record of him on their system anywhere. He had never committed a crime – at least one which the police had solved: to outward appearances, he presented a warm, caring sensible persona. He certainly didn't present as a criminal mastermind.

He certainly wasn't going to do a full cleansing of the body. Let him wallow in his own filth, he thought. It briefly crossed his mind that the filth was from caused by panic that he had induced in the first place. He stood back, checking his handiwork. He closed the window, because the stench had lessened significantly, and he didn't want anyone or anything getting in and discovering the horrors inside. Not at least until he decided they could.

Just one last thing to do then before a final check round to make sure everything was perfect, he decided. He started shaking out the duvet.

CHAPTER 3

Rachael Read had spent the best part of two days clearing the office, with minimal help from Jim. This morning however, another bright and sunny day, had bought greater promise. Rachael had arrived to find Jim manhandling a big old leather swivel chair behind Rachael's desk. He was sweating profusely.

"Wouldn't it be more comfortable if you removed your jacket, Sir?" Rachael grinned at her superior from the other side of the desk. Nodding at the big chair, she added, "That's not police issue, is it, Sir?" She beamed at him.

"No, it's not." Jim looked at the chair. "It's from home."

"...And why is it here now?" Rachael asked.

"Well, I thought it would be really comfy." He gazed across at her. "It was my wife's writing chair." He suddenly looked worried. "I can take it back if you don't want it."

Rachael felt contrite. She tried to brave it out, however, by saying, "I'm sure it'll be lovely. Move over, Sir, so I can try it out."

"Oh yes, of course. There you go."

Rachael moved around the desk and sat down in the capacious chair. It was indeed very comfortable. She swiveled it from side to side to test it further. It was lovely. "It's great. If you're sure that you can spare it." As she as the words were out of her mouth, she regretted them.

In response, Jim looked down at his feet. There was an uncomfortable silence.

"I'm so sorry, boss." She stammered. "I meant no offence."

A sad looked crossed Jim's face. "I've been meaning to clear her study out for ages. I never really go in there. I just didn't want it to go to the skip." He added wistfully.

"How long has it been," Rachael asked," since she.um..." Her voice trailed off.

"Seven years. Breast cancer. Phoebe was twelve."

"I'm so sorry." Rachael was aware that she was repeating herself. "You don't have to tell me anything, Sir." She looked down at her new desk.

"On the contrary, Rachael. I find talking helps...sometimes." He took a deep breath. "It was incredibly sudden. Twelve weeks from finding a lump when Sandrine was in the shower till she was being lowered into the ground. We were together all through school. We even went to university in the same city. We married the year we graduated. She got a first in English and Comparative Literature. Then she worked for a number of magazines before she fell pregnant with Phoebe. Then she went freelance after that when Phoebe was at school. She was a great writer."

"Words can't really express the sadness."

"On the contrary, Rachael, on the contrary, Sandrine would've had the words to express any emotion on any occasion."

"Sandrine, Sir? Is that French?" Rachael asked.

"Yes. Her mother was from Toulouse. I have a small place down there, which she, then I inherited."

"Oh wow! Do you go there often?"

"Not as often as I'd like. I don't really fancy going there on my own."

"No, I suppose you wouldn't." Rachael sighed, imagining having a place of her own in sunny France, rather than her drab rented flat here. She couldn't ever see herself affording even the smallest place abroad. Just then the telephone rang again. Jim picked it up and began a hushed conversation before replacing the handset back on the cradle. He looked up at Rachael and then around the disarray before shrugging and saying, "I'm really sorry, but I've got to go out again. I shouldn't be more than a couple of hours."

Rachael nodded. "That's ok. I think we've done it all."

"You've mean you've done most of it."

"No... no. But thanks for the chair. I'll take good care of it."

And that had been four hours ago.

17

She had finally managed to sort the room so that there was both a professional aspect to it, but with a touch of homely appeal as well. An old mentor had once said to her that blank walls were no good for thinking unless they were padded. To that end, she had bought in a couple of prints from home and put them up on the wall. I hope he doesn't mind, she reflected, and she smiled to herself about the conversation they had had this morning. He was opening up about himself, and she was warming to him. She felt a momentary sadness about the death of his wife. But he seemed to be coping, or at least he was putting a brave face on. Maybe the old adage about time healing all wounds was right. When he came bustling in, his arms were full of packages. He plonked them down on her desk and smiled at her shyly.

"Just a little something for you." He then looked around the office in wonder. "Wow! You've done an amazing job!" He strode over to one of the prints. He put his hands on his hips. "Interesting. I hope that's not meant to be me." He was staring at a laminated poster showing a huge man in a green suit with an incredibly tiny head staring out of a pair of pink shuttered windows at a crescent moon.

"No, it's not meant to be you. It's an album cover."

"Duke."

"I'm impressed."

"So am I."

"Why?"

"Impeccable music taste, Read."

"Put that down to having three older brothers, Sir."

"Mm." He turned to her. "Open your gifts then. I can take it back if you don't want or like it." A polka dotted white bag sat on her desk. She peered inside. Contained within was a beautiful miniature lily in a pot. It had delicate white flowers tinged with pink, and long delicate leaves. It sat in a tasteful blue ceramic pot.

"That's lovely, Sir." Rachael said. "Thank you."

"Don't mention it. Just a small token of thanks for all your hard work."

A comfortable silence stretched as both police thought their own thoughts. After a while, Jim looked at Rachael and said, "Are you going to Sergeant Harris's leaving do tonight?"

"Do you mean the desk Sergeant with the salt and pepper hair? The grumpy one?" Rachael replied.

"He's not always grumpy. He needs to get to know you." Jim countered. Rachael nodded. "Took three years in my case."

"Three years just to decide that you're a nice person who he can talk to?" She asked, exasperated.

"You think I'm nice, do you?" Jim laughed.

"You know what I mean..."

"Well, if you came along tonight, then I'm sure he'd talk to you. Especially if you bought him his favourite drink."

"Which is?"

"Gin and bitter lemon."

"Really?"

"Really." There was a pause, in which both heard a van passing along outside the station was over-revving really badly. They both ignored it.

"And it's whom, not who." Jim broke the silence.

"Oh, in that case, I'm definitely coming. If nothing else, so that you can improve my grammar." Rachael smiled sardonically at her superior.

"Excellent, excellent. Let's say 8 o'clock at the Arms then." Jim checked his watch. "We might as well call it a day now." He turned and picked up his jacket. "I normally have one on the way home, but I don't think I will, because things might well get a bit raucous tonight." He actually winked at her. "And there's something else I want to run by you tonight, but it's probably best to discuss it in a more relaxed atmosphere." He shook his head enigmatically.

"Is it serious? Have I done something wrong? Am I doing something wrong?" Rachael asked, worried. She was frantically trying to remember everything that she had said and done over the last few days, but to no avail.

Jim actually stopped putting his jacket on. "Goodness gracious me; no, you're getting on just grand."

"Grandly."
"Touché."
Jim grimaced but didn't reply at once. Instead he finished putting on his jacket before eventually saying, "Don't be late."

Rachael was already deep in thought about what it was, that Jim wanted to 'talk' about, on her way. She was still thinking about it as she rooted through the fridge, found the remnants of the previous nights' takeaway, and ate that cold whilst perched at her breakfast bar.

"Damn you, Smallwood." She snarled as she undressed and climbed into the shower. However, she began to relax as the expensive French 'gel douche', that her mother had bought her last Christmas, began to work its wonders. By the time that she had finished luxuriating, she had smoothed all her worries away.

She turned off the shower and reached for the towels. She wrapped one round her hair and looked at herself in the full-length mirror. Not bad, she thought, as her reflection gazed back at her. Full breasts, flat tummy, nicely trimmed pubic area and long, slim legs left her wondering why she was still single. Maybe it was her personality? Or maybe she set her sights too high, looking for a Mr. Right that didn't exist. Picking up her towel, she found herself thinking about Jim as she dried her private areas. Nevertheless, she selected some nice lacy lilac panties and bra before sitting on her bed to paint her toenails. She thought that the cream top and jeans and open-toed sandals would be fine.

Inclining her head one way and the other, she decided her toenails were fine, so started on her hands. That accomplished, she took the towel off her head and shook her hair furiously for several seconds before deciding that she didn't need to dry it. Just a quick comb and she could wear it down for a change. She looked at herself in the mirror again. Less is more, in terms of make-up, she thought. She certainly didn't want to trowel it on, like some of the civilian secretaries at the station did.

Heaving a sigh, she reached up and turned the stereo off and carefully re-combed her hair. She realised with a start that unless she got a move on, she'd be late.

Jim, however, was in no such rush. He had got home, fixed himself a sandwich, not because he was hungry, but his mum always said he needed something to line his stomach if he was going out 'gallivanting'. He filled the bath, intending to have a quick soak. This was ignoring his mum's advice not to go swimming or have a bath for half an hour after eating. Whilst it was filling up, he switched his stereo on. Perusing his large collection of vinyl records, he selected 'Duke' by Genesis. He turned on the volume higher than he would normally have it, so that he could hear it whilst in the bath. At least living in a large, detached house afforded some privacy from neighbours.

Reflecting about his new sergeant in the relaxing bath, he figured that DC Read was shaping up quite nicely; he had heard about some problems at her previous station, but he figured not only that she wasn't to blame but that also everyone deserved a second chance. Rising from the bath he walked dripping and naked into his lounge where he poured himself a large whisky. What was he thinking about? Ah, yes, Read, he remembered. His growing fondness of her was tempered by the fact that in the long run, Rachael may be better served if she moved to one of the forces in a bigger city, like London or even Manchester. He would be sorry to see her go but given a healthy slice of luck and a following wind, in all likelihood she would return as his superior officer in about ten years' time. If he was still here, that was. He had a growing hankering deep in his soul to retire to his place in France and produce goats' cheese and apple brandy.

He selected a pair of faded jeans and a simple, striped shirt. His sense of fashion merely meant not wearing a tie. Still, he reflected, not too shabby as he looked in his full-length mirror as he put his favourite brown leather loafers on.

Just the right side of fifty, and with not too many grey hairs, he passed muster. Not that he was looking to impress the ladies. His sexual passion had died with Sandrine. Still, it would be remiss of him to look scruffy in front of his boss, his colleagues and, of course, Rachael. So begrudgingly and with a heartfelt sigh, he changed his loafers for a sensible looking pair of brogues. Stopping only to pick up his keys, wallet and a beige sports jacket from the cupboard under the stairs, he stepped out into the warm evening with a keen sense of excitement about what the evening held in store.

Standing behind the counter of the off-licence he managed, Ali Buchan spotted the familiar figure of the friendly policeman from fully fifty yards away. He fetched a packet of the policeman's favourite cigars from the racks and placed it on the counter as Jim entered the shop.
"Good evening, Sir. How are you today?"
"I'm fine. And your good self?" Jim asked affably.
In response, Ali shrugged and waved his arms around the empty shop before replying, "Slow. Sir, these supermarkets are driving me out of business." He frowned at Jim. "What is an honest merchant to do?"
Jim laughed. "I'll be sure to ask that question if I ever find one." To which they both laughed. "And how is your good lady wife? And your beautiful children?"
"Getting bigger by the day. And so are the children!" Ali replied. They both laughed out loud again, until a strange look crossed Ali's face. "Allah in Heaven!" He exclaimed. "Do you have a date, Sir?"
Jim saw that the shopkeeper was looking over his shoulder, out to the pavement. He turned and saw Rachael looking in.
"No no....she's a colleague. We're just going to a leaving do together. She's my new sergeant."
"Alas!" Ali exclaimed. "If only I was twenty years younger. I could take another wife!"

Jim was about to complain that this wasn't the best course of action, but suddenly remembered that as a Muslim, Ali could have multiple wives. Laughing, he paid for the cigars and went out to meet Rachael, still chuckling.

"Evening, Sir." Rachael beamed at him.

"Rule number one, Rachael. Tonight is first names only ."

"Yes, Sir."

"Yes, Jim, you mean." There was a slight pause.

"Yes...Jim." Rachael was struggling with the informality. Suddenly, she felt pressure on her forearm as Jim was walking off, pulling her with him.

"We've got time for a quick one in the Cross Keys before the party. There's something I want to talk over with you." After getting their drinks, they stepped through into a garden beautifully illuminated by the sun's setting rays. They made themselves comfortable before the conversation resumed.

"I think you're a great DS, Read, I really do... it's just I think you'd make an even better DI." Jim said, looking directly at Rachael, who held his gaze.

"I sense a 'but' coming, Sir." Rachael looked back at him as quizzically as he was looking at her. There was a long pause before Jim broke eye contact and looked down at his pint.

"I also think you'll make a great DCI, even a great Super. Just not here." This time, Rachael looked down at her drink.

Jim looked contrite. "I don't mean to upset you, Rachael. But if you want to fulfil your potential you're going to have to move to where the action is."

She looked again. "Have I done something to upset you? Or done something wrong?"

The inspector looked up and Rachael saw that there were infinite pools of sadness behind his eyes.

"On the contrary, Rachael." She noted how he had switched from her surname to her forename without her noticing. "It's because everything you do, have done, and probably will continue to do has been exemplary. It's just nothing ever happens here. You're not being stretched." He shrugged his shoulders. She suddenly felt a compulsion to comfort him, to hug him, smother him with sympathy. She contented herself with clasping his hands where they held his pint glass.

"You remind me of my grandfather." She said, smiling. "A much younger version. No, don't say anything yet. I completely understand what you mean. But you can rest assured that I have no intention of going anywhere else yet." She noticed that her hands were still round his, and she withdrew them swiftly, blushing, before continuing, "I want to be completely healed, completely confident in my own abilities and, well, complete, before I do anything else." She noticed that he was staring earnestly at her, a half-smile on his lips. She raised her gaze to a small white cloud sailing off into the sunset. "Thank you for your kind offer of shipping me off to the grimy metropolis, Sir, but I will tell you as and when I'm good and ready. Now, we have a party to go to."

"Jim. How many times do you need telling?" was all that he replied, before downing the rest of his pint, getting up from the table and holding the door open for her, a smile on his face.

They could hear the music long before they opened the door of the pub hosting the party. A live band were attempting a rendition of David Bowie's 'Let's Dance', with more than a little success. A fug of cigarettes, dry ice and sweat partially obscured a proper view of them. The two of them fought their way to the bar, Jim shouting to make himself heard even though he was standing less than a foot away. She shook her head, waving a five-pound note in the air to indicate that it was her round. Jim shrugged, pointed to one of the beer pumps, then nodded his head backwards to indicate that he was heading into the other bar. Rachael joined the scrum of people trying to get the barman's attention. Two minutes later, thanks to flashing a winning smile, she was carrying two pints, one of bitter and one cider. Some kind man even helped her with the door between the two bars. She saw Jim over by a group of men all sharing a good laugh together amidst a lot of backslapping and cheers. He turned just as she approached.

"Got 'er trained well, already Jim." This came from one of the Inspectors gathered round the table, maybe of one the three uniformed men of that rank the station employed. Rachael wasn't sure of his name, Telling or Thompson or something like that. She just smiled sweetly and handed the drink to Jim.

"It's nothing like that, John. She offered to pay. Equality and all that." He turned and winked secretly at Rachael, who only just managed to keep herself from laughing out loud.

"Quite right, Smallwood, quite right too." A loud voice boomed from the back door of the pub. All the men at the table scrambled up to their feet, as the loud voice belonged to no other than the ACC, Nathaniel Parker. He waved them down quickly, an affable look on his face. His huge moustache quivered when he had spoken. Immaculately dressed in a pin stripe suit, he stood well over six and a half feet in his socks. He carried the air of a military brigadier from one of the World Wars. "Evening, men." He nodded to Rachael, before adding, "And ladies, too." He appeared to assess her for a moment, as if noting everything from her shoes to what she was wearing, how she had her hair, even what she was drinking. She evidently passed muster, for he gave her another nod, before turning his attention to the table who had seated themselves again. He addressed them all. "You must forgive the suit, men, I've just come from a meeting at Division." He looked round the room until his eyes settled on Sergeant Harris, whose party it was. He called across the room, "Robert! A word if you may!" He strode across the bar and clapped the retiree around the shoulders, pumping his hand up and down energetically. Rachael smiled to herself and turned back to the bar.

"Gin and bitter lemon, please." It was time to ingratiate herself with the soon to be ex-sergeant.

Crossing over to the small knot of people sat sharing long tales of the custody sergeant's most famous exploits, she quietly put the drink on the table in front of Sergeant Harris, with a shy smile. She was rewarded with a huge guffaw of laughter from the entire table and the exclamation from the sergeant, "SMALLWOOD! You fucking bastard!" Rachael taken aback, looked over her shoulder at where her boss was sitting with his mates, all creased up with laughter. She realised then that she had been the victim of a massive practical joke. Worse than that, a private, in-joke. Sloping back to the bar, Rachael was laughing to herself. Instead of being upset at being the victim of a schoolyard prank, she believed because it signified acceptance. She was still chuckling to herself when a young, worried looking uniformed WPC rushed into the bar. Hurrying over to Inspector Smallwood, she bent over to whisper in his ear. A brief conversation, but with an immediate effect. He stood up, shrugging himself into his jacket. He motioned to Rachael, who put the remnants of her drink down untouched. Exiting the bar, he waited for her to catch up. She asked, "Sir?"

"We have a body. A dead body."

CHAPTER 4

It was two in the afternoon and the louts at the bar were almost drunk. "Shur round," one of them muttered to his mate, shoving his glass towards his pal before staggering to the toilet.

He was too inebriated and lost in his thoughts to hear the door open and close behind him. He didn't hear the pulling of a zip open, or the light tinkling sounds of the man next to him. He didn't register anything until he suddenly started when the man spoke to him.

"Hey, you're Seamus, right?" The shock caused him to piss against the fly of his jeans. Annoyed, but not prepared to reveal what he had done, he carried on as nonchalantly as he could. When he had finished, he casually replied, "Who wants to know?"

"To be sure, to be sure, people know me as Connemara Col." The man known as Col turned to face Seamus and stuck out his hand. "Be glad to be making your acquaintance, wouldn't you know?" Before Seamus could say anything, he carried on, "Would that be a Galway City accent you be having there?" Col beamed at him. His hand was still hand out. Seamus looked at him, then his hand, then back to his face, a face full of smiles surrounded by curly fair hair.

"Connemara, you say. What part would that be?" Seamus still eyed both the man and his outstretched arm with suspicion.

"To be sure, I'm Letterfrack born and bred. Ma and I used to live right next to Molly's Bar. Do you know it?"

"Molly's? I've heard of it, yeah." Seamus was convinced of the man now, so offered up his own hand to shake Col's. They shook and smiled. Seamus indicated the surroundings and said, "Though this is a strange place for two Irishman to be meeting, so it is." Col laughed, and went to the sink to wash his hands, saying over his shoulder, Well, when I've done this, I'll be buying a drop of the black stuff. And I'd be delighted if you be joining me." Col turned, smiled once more and indicated that Seamus should leave the toilet first. "After you, Seamus, after you, but hurry up as I've a rare thirst on, so I have." Seamus traipsed out of the toilet with a happy look on his face, whilst behind him, Col's expression was one of pure contempt. The smile had vanished to be replaced with grimly set teeth and a hard glint in his eye. They walked to the bar, and roused Lucky from where he had been picking at his dirty fingernails, lost in a world of his own. "I made a new friend, Lucky, so maybe you can slope off now."

"In the toilet? You a faggot now?" Lucky sneered.

"Go on with you, eejit. This man here," he said, turning to put an arm round Col like he was his long-lost brother, "This man here is a proper Irishman, not a plastic paddy like yourself." Lucky looked at Col, up and down, and turned back to his lager, distinctly nonplussed. Col intervened at this point by saying to then both, "Now, lads, why don't you be getting yourselves comfortable in those chairs over there whilst I get the beers in? I may be in the way of being able to offer you something that you'd be wanting now?" He winked conspiratorially at them both and turned to the barmaid."Good afternoon, sweet lady, could I be getting four pints of Guinness and three large whiskies, and one for yourself, perhaps?" He gave her another of his broad smiles as well as handing over a twenty.

By the time that the barmaid had finished pouring out the round, Col had already finished one of the pints of stout. Carrying the tray over to where Seamus and Lucky were sitting, he boomed, "Now aint this grand, lads?" He handed out the drinks before settling himself into a chair. He drained half of his second pint in one gulp, picked up his whisky and tasted that too.

"Now, am I right in supposing that you two lads would not be in the habit of having proper jobs?" He looked at both of them.

"How did you know my name?" Seamus asked in reply. Col looked at him for a long while, as if considering his options, before leaning back in his chair and exclaiming, "To be sure, I understand. Caution, is it?" He smiled before leaning forward again. "Well, your friend Pete is a friend of a friend of mine, and when I was putting out feelers for this wee job, your names were mentioned. "He looked at each in turn before adding, "In complete confidence, to be sure although I'm sure that the boys in blue know a bit about you." At this Lucky laughed, and Seamus gave a half-smile. To state that the police knew about them was a massive understatement. They were well known to be two low level criminals whose ability was not matched by their confidence. They had indeed been lucky not to serving time at Her Majesty's convenience.

"What 'wee' job is this you'd be talking about then?"

Col looked down at the table for a while before starting his tale. "Well, there was this girl, Alice was her name, and we were sweet on each other, very sweet, don't you know?" He smiled at them both, but this time it was rather a sad smile. "There was a time when I thought I'd be taking her for my wife." As he said this, he looked beyond them, out of the window at the traffic. There was a pause before he resumed. "But life has a funny way of intervening, to be sure, and we ended up going our separate ways." At this, he returned his gaze to the pair opposite him. "My mother is gravely ill, God bless her, and Alice has some stuff that I'd be mighty glad in getting back." He glanced at each of them. "I'd be in the way of needing to raise some money for her treatment." Again, the wistful look came back.

"Why can't you just be taking them back yourself then?" Lucky asked.

"You are an asshole, Lucky." This wee girl gets burgled, the police are sure to be in the way of blaming your man here. He'll be needing a cast iron alibi, to be sure." This time he looked straight at Col, who nodded back at Seamus.

"Aye, that's the craic, to be sure." He looked down again before continuing. "A while back, I was in the way of winning myself a tidy sum on the football pools. I bought my wee girl a diamond necklace."

29

"How much is it worth, then?" Asked an intrigued Lucky.

"About eight thousand pounds."

There was intake of breath from the lads. They looked at each other. Seamus was the first to speak up. "And so how much would you be thinking of giving us, if we were thinking of helping you, then?" He gave Col an appraising look.

"I was thinking of four hundred pounds. To each of you, half now, half later." As if to reinforce what he was saying, Col withdrew his wallet, extracted a wad of neatly folded notes, and laid it out on the table. He then covered it with one of his hands. He looked at each of them in turn, an expectant look on his face.

Seamus nodded at Col without even consulting his pal, saying simply, "Of course we will. It's for your mother, so it is." He looked at Lucky for confirmation, who nodded assent.

"Just tell us where and when, then."

"It's 4, Harpers Close, the ground floor flat. Entrance round the back. Spare key is usually kept under the middle flowerpot. She's not very security conscious, is our Alice." He stopped to finish his whisky. "After you've found the jewellery, anything else you can carry is yours. She's away for two days, but she's back tomorrow, so maybe about eight o'clock tonight? I'll be here this time tomorrow, to pick up the goods and pay you the rest." He took his hand off the money and held it out for them to shake. After a moment's hesitation, first Seamus and then Lucky grasped the outstretched hand and shook it. Looking them both in the eye for the last time, he nodded, and stood up.

"Be seeing you." He left the table and walked straight out of the pub. Lucky looked at Seamus, grinned, and held up his arm for a high five. Seamus, grinning himself, stretched out his arm and slapped his mates' hand.

Outside the pub, Col leant against the wall and breathed out deeply. He had most of the plans in place. He smiled to himself, and whispered under his breath, "Well done, Col, well done." The only problem: whatever his name was, it certainly wasn't Col.

Seamus squatted down by the flowerpot and gingerly looked underneath it. He saw the key gleaming faintly in the last of the summer sun and quickly palmed it. He looked back over his shoulder to see Lucky was doing his best to look unobtrusive whilst keeping a look-out, to make sure that they themselves weren't being observed. Standing up, he gave Lucky a low whistle and unlocked the door. "Are you ready then?"

His mate nodded, grinning. "Put these on then." He handed Lucky a pair of gloves that he had taken from his jacket. They were both aware that their fingerprints were on file with police. They had both been caught before and didn't want that again.

Taking a deep breath, Seamus stepped inside the flat. A hallway lay in front of him, several doors off on either side, one directly in front. He motioned Lucky to take the first on the right, while he opened the door of the first on the left. His eyes quickly adjusted to the gloom. He found himself in the kitchen. He didn't want to turn on the torch yet, if at all. He quickly established that there was nothing of value in here. He left the kitchen, quietly closing the door behind him. Glancing across the hallway, he could see Lucky moving around what seemed to be the lounge, opening drawers, looking in a sideboard. He went onto the next room, instantly recognising the smell of the bathroom. There were no windows, so he felt on the wall for the light switch. His arm brushed against a string pull, making it click against the wall. He pulled it, and light flooded the room. He was about to leave that room too but turned back as he had spotted a medicine cabinet on the wall. He was sweating slightly, for it was warm in here, and he had a big jacket on. Shrugging himself out of it, he folded it over the side of the bath, and took his baseball cap off as well, putting that on top of his jacket. He opened the cabinet, thinking that there may be some kind of drug in there, some uppers maybe, for later on. The blank back wall stared back at him. That's odd, Seamus reflected. It was completely empty: no screwed-up tubes of toothpaste, no worn-out toothbrushes, plasters, of bottles of witch hazel. A shiver sank down his spine despite the warmth in here.

Alarm bells started tinkling in the back of his head. Something was not right here.

Turning to go out of the bathroom, he almost bumped into Lucky, whom had evidently finished his search of the lounge. Stopping, he asked his friend, "Have you found anything of interest yet?"

"Nada. You?"

"There's nothing of interest so far." Seamus managed to stop himself from telling Lucky about his bad feelings about the place. It didn't do to get Lucky too excitable at the best of times; and especially not when they were out on a job. "The stuff Col wanted must be in one of the bedrooms."

"Makes sense, I suppose, if it's jewellery."

"One room each, then. Pint for the one who finds it."

"You're on, mate." Lucky headed for the door at the end of the hallway.

"Oh, that's cheating taking the large room." Seamus lamented, to which Lucky laughed. Shrugging his shoulders, Seamus put his hand on the door handle of the smaller bedroom, depressed it, and just pushed the door open. He peered into the dark room before entering it. He fumbled for the light switch on the wall, found it, and turned it on. He was presented with an average size room containing a mattress on a divan, and a wardrobe with one of its doors hanging open. Nothing else. No cabinets, no lamps, not even a lampshade to cover the bare bulb in the ceiling. There were no paintings, no cuddly toys sitting on shelves, nothing. Come to that, there weren't even any shelves. Confirming his worst suspicions, Seamus strode over to the wardrobe and yanked the other door open. He was met by the familiar jangle of half a dozen metal clothes hangers disturbed by the sudden movement of air around them. Seamus leant on the door of the wardrobe, staring at the hangers but not seeing them. The wave of uneasiness washed over him again. He shook his head to get rid of it, as if it was a fly that had landed on his head.

He called through to Lucky in the other room, "Find anything yet, mate?" He was only answered by silence. He waited for maybe ten seconds, gathering his senses, before slamming the wardrobe doors shut and leaving the bedroom, not even bothering to turn the light off. He turned to his right and saw Lucky with his back to him, standing in the doorway to the last bedroom. He seemed to be swaying slightly.

"Come on, what are you waiting for?" Seamus asked, but he received nothing except for a stony silence. So Seamus went up behind him and peered over his friends' shoulder into the room.

Lucky seemingly had managed to turn the light on but nothing else. On a first glance, Seamus was relieved that at least this room was furnished. He took in a chair, a picture, a wardrobe, a bedside cabinet with a lamp on it, a bed...

Seamus stopped and stared just as his mate had done. On the bed covered by what looked like a sheet, was a body.

Neither of them moved a muscle, neither of them spoke. Lucky had stopped swaying. His arm was still raised to the light switch from when he had first come in and turned it on. Their eyes were transfixed by the scene.

Lying as if asleep was a man whose face showed him to be about sixty. As if that wasn't strange enough, only his face showed. An oblong of material seemed to be cut out from a white sheet that was covering the man's body, just enough to reveal part if not all of his face. It gave the impression that the man was peering out from behind a pair of curtains. The hole revealed most of his forehead, his nose, and stretched to just below his lips. From side to side, the material rested on the cheekbones of the dead man, so that most, but not all, of his eyes were showing. But even stranger still, both eyes appeared to have been shut with tape. All of this both Lucky and Seamus could see quite clearly from where they still stood transfixed in the doorway.

The pair of them stared at the body on the bed, not daring to step any closer yet not wanting to leave either.

"Fuck, Seamus, fucking hell."

"I know, Lucky. I know..." Seamus knew now that he should've trusted his instinct. They had been blinded by alcohol, the promise of easy money, by greed.

"Do you reckon its Col's old man? Or that of his bird, whatever her name was?" asked Lucky.

"No, it aint." Lucky replied. "It's Col."

Lucky wrested his gaze away from the corpse to look at his friend incredulously." Col? You gotta be joking, man. That dude is well old." Lucky chuckled nervously despite the situation.

"No, you fuckhead. Its Col. The bastard has set us up, good and proper." Seamus was still looking at the body.

"You reckon? But he seemed quite genuine. Virtually a neighbour, you said."

Seamus turned to grip Lucky by the shoulders. "Look, mate, it's a stitch up. A wind-up. We've been conned."

Lucky shook himself free. "We don't know if this dude is dead yet. Maybe we should check him out, just to be sure."

"Don't go near him!" Seamus screamed at Lucky, who had started to go over to the side of the bed for a closer look. Luckily for him, the vehemence in Seamus' voice was enough to stop before he touched anything. "We've got to get out of here!"

Lucky turned with a shocked look on his face. "We can't just go, man. We gotta phone the pigs or something before we split." They stared at each other for fully thirty seconds, thinking. They could easily leave, disappear and try to forget about it, Seamus thought. That was the most prudent course of action. He was pretty sure that because they had been wearing their gloves, there were no traces that either of them were ever here. His mind made up, he traced his steps back to the bathroom where he had left his cap and jacket. His gaze rested on the empty medicine cabinet once more. Bastard, Seamus muttered under his breath before calling out to Lucky, "Mate, you seen a phone anyway? Maybe we should call the cops, anonymously, like."

Lucky put his head around the doorjamb of the bathroom. He looked really pale, as if he just seen a ghost. His Adams apple was bobbing up and down furiously. "Lounge. I think I'm going to be sick."

Nodding his head for Lucky to leave the flat if indeed he was going to vomit, Seamus crossed the hallway into the lounge, found the telephone and dialled 999, his gloved fingers slipping on the dials twice. As he waited for the call to connect, Seamus wondered why Col had set them up.

"Emergency, what service do you require?" The voice on the line pulled Seamus back to the present.

"Police, please." He managed to mumble.

"Putting you through, caller."

"Good evening, Hertfordshire constabulary, how can we be of service?" A harassed sounding voice came over the line.

"I have found a body, I mean we've found a body, and he's dead. It's well weird, man."

"Where exactly are you calling from, Sir?" The voice on the other end now seemed to be less harassed, more in control now. Seamus explained where he was, but not what he was doing there, and when he finished, he replaced the headset of the phone on its cradle. He left the flat, crossing over the courtyard to where his friend was bent over heaving his guts up. Seamus rubbed his mates' back and waited for the police. In the distance he could hear the faintest wail of a siren. Whatever he had done wrong that day, at least in the end they had done the right thing. Seamus smiled to himself.

CHAPTER 5

Jim turned to Rachael, nodding that she should go back into the party. "You don't have to come. Rachael. It's your night off. A party like that," he looked through the window," A party like that would be great for meeting the rest of the team, the bosses." He seemed to be searching for the right word.

"For networking, perhaps, Sir?" She added helpfully.

"Just the word I was looking for, Constable." Jim said, a look on his face suggesting that wasn't the word he had been looking for at all, and that he was wondering to himself what the word was that he had been trying to think of. "Networking. Mm. Americanisms are taking over our mother tongue." He was frowning as he said this. "And anyway, this may be a hoax. Get them all the time. Occupational hazard and all that." He smiled at her, now that he was back on more familiar ground.

"But you don't think it's a hoax at all, do you?" She smiled.

"No. There's a patrol car around the corner so that 'nosey' Nan Parker doesn't get wind of it. Come on, let's get a wriggle on." Rachael duly followed her boss, trying not to snigger at his use of the word 'wriggle', spotted the WPC nervously standing by the car, another officer behind the wheel.

"Do you mind if I go in the front, Joss? It's that I'm not keen about the back seat of cars."

"Of course, Sir. Be my guest- just mind my dinner." Jim got reached in, putting a burger carton on the dashboard before getting in. Settling in herself, Rachael held her hand out to Joss. "HI, I'm Rachael. We haven't been properly introduced yet."

Joss shook Rachael's proffered hand. "Joss Stafford. Glad to meet you at last." She smiled, revealing perfect white teeth. She removed her hat, revealing long blonde hair, carefully arranged in some kind of plait so that it wouldn't show when she was on duty. Rachael thought that Joss would be quite a stunner when in her civilian clothes. Long legs, beautiful skin, minimal make-up. Some girls seem to have all the luck, she mused.

"What we've got, Graham?" Jim was asking.

"Call came in calling us to a ground floor flat in Southdown. A male had phoned to say they had found a body inside the flat."

"What was this male doing in the flat? A relative? A friend?"

"I don't know the full details, Sir. We were on patrol up at Roundwood and control just radioed us to come and collect you. They knew where you were..."

"On patrol?" Jim asked, retrieving the burger carton and waving it around. Joss spoke up from the back seat.

"Sorry Sir, I missed lunch. We were just sitting down when we were called to a domestic. I hadn't had anything since breakfast, and I was absolutely famished. Sorry."

Jim handed the carton over whilst studying the WPC in the rear-view mirror. "Better finish it before we arrive then. It still feels warmish." Joss took it, a faint blush on her cheeks. She opened the plastic lid and tried to nibble surreptitiously. After a couple of bites, she decided against it, closed the lid, placed it on her lap and looked out of the window. Jim was still looking at her in the mirror, a faint smile on his face. Two minutes later Graham announced, "We're here, Sir. The entrance is round the back."

"Thank you, Graham. Can you hang on? We may be in need extra bodies if this is a suspicious death..."

"It's bound to be, Sir." Nodding through the windscreen, Graham was looking at two men talking to a constable. "That's Seamus Blockley and his associate, Lucky. Couple of low life scum if I ever saw it." He looked at the scruffy pair with distaste.

"So it is. I wonder how they're involved. Thanks."

"Sorry to spoil your party, though, Sir." Jim nodded in acknowledgement. He walked over to where the small group of men were standing, stopping about ten feet short, before beckoning PC Sharma over.

"What have we got?" He asked.

"Good evening, Sir." DC Sharma took one look at the clothes that the inspector was wearing, and at Rachael's attire, but didn't even bat an eyelid. "At 8.03 this evening control received a call from a male, later confirmed as Mr. Seamus Blockley. "Here he paused to indicate Seamus, who was standing watching them. "The gentleman indicated that they were in the ground floor flat, which is occupied, he says, by a woman known only as 'Alice', and that he discovered the body of a male in a bedroom." PC Sharma looked into his notebook before resuming. On arrival we were met by two males, the other gentleman is Lucky Ryatt...

"Lucky?" Rachael, moving closer, interrupted, one eyebrow raised. "Doesn't seem very lucky to me." PC Sharma suppressed a laugh. He gathered his thoughts. "Yes well, this other male had just been sick, so we concentrated our efforts on Mr. Blockley. He gave us some cock and bull about another Irish called 'Col', who had assured him that this was, or used to be, his place of abode. They were meant to be retrieving some items for him."

"Items?" Enquired Jim.

"They seem to be a bit reticent about that, Sir." Sharma fixed Seamus with a stare before turning his attention back to the detectives. "I thought you'd have better luck than me with that, Sir." Jim grunted, nodding to Sharma to carry on.

"I left PC Palmer guarding them, and entered the flat..."

"You entered alone, Constable?"

"Yes Sir. I know that I should've waited for back-up, but if it was a hoax, I didn't think taking two patrols off their rounds would've gone too well."

Jim looked up from the ground which he had been gazing at whilst listening to Sharma's account. He fixed the constable with a withering look. "You decided, or Sergeant Morgan decided, constable?" Sharma looked uncomfortable at being caught out and shifted his weight from foot to foot as he waited for the storm from his superior.

"I admire your dedication and loyalty to your shift sergeant, but it may help your career if try to tell the truth at all times, especially to more senior colleagues. I will be having words with Donny Morgan later. So, to cut a long story short, it was decided you should go alone into an unknown situation where they may or may not have been a crime committed." He fixed Sharma with a steely stare and their eyes locked, the junior policeman visibly quaking. Remarkable, the effect he has on people, thought Rachael. Jim spoke so quietly Rachael had to strain to hear him.

"PC Sharma, indeed, you are an extremely brave man. If I was wearing a hat, I'd take it off to you. "Sharma and Rachael stared at Smallwood with open mouths. Whatever they were expecting him to say, it wasn't that. "Close your mouth, Detective Read." This was all the more impressive to Rachael as she was standing behind Smallwood, who couldn't even see her. To Sharma, who was in front of him, he simply said, "Fine dental work, son. But if you would be so pleased to get on with it, huh?"

Closing his mouth, still somewhat shocked at this recent turn of events, Sharma gave the faintest of nods, swallowed, and whispered, "I found a body."

"Congratulations, sonny!" Smallwood barked, which made all of them jump violently in unison. Smallwood complemented this bizarre behaviour by clapping his hands, spinning round, and beaming at Rachael. "DC Read, we had better get the whole kit and caboodle down here at the double. You know what to do. Carry on." Spinning again, he arrested his gaze on the two youths who looked like they were ready to make a dash for it.

"Come here." The authority is his voice ensured both complied instantly, shuffling towards him, hands thrust deep in pockets. "I don't know how much shit you two are in, yet. It may be a little bit, "Here he put his thumb and index finger half an inch apart." Or it may be a whole world of it." He said this whilst stretching both arms wide. "But don't compound this shit stack you're in by running off." At this, he pointed at the floor and shouted at both of them, "DON'T BLOODY MOVE UNTIL I SAY YOU CAN!" He wheeled away, indicating to Sharma to keep an eye. He looked over to Rachael, who by this point had retreated to the patrol car and was using the radio to summon all the resources needed. Satisfied, he nodded to himself, and strode off around the side of the building to where PC Palmer was still waiting patiently, kicking a small pebble around.

Prince songs pumped out at near maximum volume. Three feet from a speaker, he could feel the bass and guitars blasting over him like waves crashing on a beach. The last chords of "1999' blended into 'Take Me With U'. About half a dozen girls started singing along in time, with varying levels of success. He stood, partially because bad singing always made him embarrassed, but mainly his paper cup of punch was empty again. He weaved his way through the writhing mass of teenage boys and girls all crammed into an ordinary suburban lounge. He exhaled with relief when he reached the relative calm of the hall, although there were still half a dozen or so people either leaning on the wall, the stairs, or the chairs placed next to a table which held the telephone. One couple, John and Nicky, were kissing in the little porch by the front door. He checked his watch. It was only ten past nine. He chuckled, thinking that John was a fast worker. They had only been chatting this afternoon, when John had revealed that he had feelings for Nicky. He'd only gone to chat to her about half an hour previously. Shaking his head in wonder and disbelief, he went in search of the punchbowl, and found no more than a dribble in the bottom of it, along with two oranges cut in half, squeezed and discoloured a pale red. That'll be the Martini Rosso that someone had poured in near the end, he thought. He spied the distinctive label of Thunderbird next to the fridge, three quarters full. He wasn't really surprised, for he knew it was an acquired taste that didn't appeal to too many people. Their loss, he supposed, and poured himself a cupful. He found his fags and stepped into the garden. lighting one.

 He wandered a little, enjoying the way the last of the sun reflected on the conifers at the bottom of the garden, turning the tips a lovely golden hue. He sucked deep mouthfuls of smoke into his lungs, held it awhile, and exhaled, enjoying the rush of the nicotine in his head. It complemented the alcohol, combining to give a great sense of well-being. He was enjoying himself.

Suddenly he was aware of John beside him. Giving him a sly smile, he said, "I didn't think that I'd be seeing you for a while."

John gave a cheeky smile before replying, "She said she had to go pee. Give us a quick puff on that." John reached up and took the proffered ciggie, took a quick couple of puffs and handed it back. "Cheers. See you around."

"Be careful. If you can't be careful, buy a pram."

"Yeah, yeah, whatever."

And then he was alone again. He smoked the last of the cigarette before burying the butt carefully in a flowerpot. Wiping his hands down his jeans, he re-entered the party. There were a couple of girls giggling in the kitchen, filling up the punchbowl again with whatever they could find. Picking up the Thunderbird, he filled up his cup again before putting the bottle under his arm for safe keeping. The clear liquid was far too precious to put into a bowl for general girl consumption. He headed for the stairs, intending to find a safe hideaway for his purloined bottle. They were the kind that turned in the middle, and as he reached the turn, his progress was blocked by another couple coming down. They in turn were impeded by another person who seemed to be slumped, head bowed. Long, wavy brown hair hung down over her face, but it was obvious to him from the little bobbing movements that there were crying. Forgetting about the booze, he perched a couple of stairs below her.

"Hey, are you alright?" He felt foolish as soon as he'd asked it. Here was a girl at what was meant to be a happy occasion who was obviously upset. He continued though. "I mean I can see you're not alright, but is there anything I can do for you?" He asked the veil of long brown hair, unable as he was to see anything of the young girls' face. All that happened was a slight change in the direction of the moving of the hair, from up and down to side to side as the mystery girl seemed to suggest that there was indeed nothing, he could do to assist her.

"Go away." It was spoken so softly that he strained to hear what she had said over the noise coming from downstairs.

"I will if you're sure, absolutely positively certain and utterly convinced that there is nothing I can do to help you." The head stopped bobbing, and then came up, the hands parting the hair to reveal a beautiful, if mascara lined face. Brown, almond-shaped eyes looked down over an average nose to full lips and a gently curved chin. He suspected that there may be dimples if the girl ever smiled. The sobbing had stopped, for the time being. He dug in his pockets for some kind of tissue. Failing to find one, he stood up, eased past her and ducked into the bathroom just ahead of another guy, who complained that he was 'busting'. Smiling his thanks and whispering 'emergency,' he scooped up half a dozen sheets of toilet roll and hoped the girl on the stairway was still there and that no other knight in shining armour had ridden to her rescue. She was, and still alone. Squeezing past her once again he touched her lightly and held out the sheets of toilet roll, he said to her, "Here you go. I'm sorry it's not a proper tissue, but I'm fairly sure that it's Andrex." He smiled shyly at her, and they there were- two dimples caused by the small upturning her of her lips in the ghost of a smile. She took the tissue and started to wipe away the mascara stained tears.

"Thanks." She looked up at him with that ghost of a smile returning. "You really didn't have to bother about me, though."

"Rubbish!" He exclaimed. "How could I leave a beautiful damsel such as yourself in distress? Besides," He sat down two stairs below her again, "I was looking for somewhere to hide this." He gestured to the bottle which he now tucked beside her. As he did so he noticed that she was barefoot. Her little toenails were painted an ultramarine blue. He glanced at her fingernails, which were painted in the same hue. "What a lovely colour varnish, by the way."

"Thanks, again, it's called 'lapis delight' but heaven knows why." She replied.

"Ultramarine originally comes from lapis lazuli, from Afghanistan. It was imported by Italian traders in the 15th century, and literally means 'beyond the sea'". He stopped because she was staring at him. He blushed. "Sorry," he mumbled.

"Don't be." She replied. "It's fascinating."

"No it's not."

"Yes really, it is." She held up her tissue." It's stopped me blubbing."

He held put his hand. "Phil at your service. Provider of inferior tissue and superior wisdom."

She laughed outright at this, revealing two rows of perfect, white teeth. "Chris. Well my mum insists on Christine, but my friends call me Chris." Again, that smile, the dimples deepening this time. A shudder ran through her and she frowned. "I'm sorry that you've met me when I look such a frightful mess like this."

"Nonsense, you look fine. Your fragility just adds to your beauty..." he stopped, blushing again, as he noticed she was staring at him intently, the dimples gone for now. Her eyes narrowed as she spoke.

"I can't tell if you are serious or not. Maybe you are, in which case you're seriously mistaken. I'm not beautiful."

"Contrare, madame. Beauty is in the eye of the beholder." Their eyes met, searching each other's soul. She suddenly reached her hand up and grabbed the front of his Soft Cell t-shirt, pulling him to her as she leant forward to kiss him passionately.

A fine kisser, if a little moist, he was thinking as he kissed her. He had kept his eyes open all the time they were kissing; she did not. Their lips were locked together for only thirty seconds but to him it seemed to go on forever. He was enjoying it so much that everything around him, the music, the laughter and the chatter seemed to fade away to nothing. It finally came to an end as Chris opened her eyes to stare at him with something like wonder in her eyes.

"Wow...that was ...lovely." She smiled at him, the dimples returning. She moved her hand down from where it was still bunching his shirt to take hold of his hand, intertwining her fingers with his.

He knelt on the stair below, her legs to either side of him. He leant back a bit and asked, "Do you want to tell me what it was that's upset you so much?" His face expressed concern, because he didn't want to see her cry again.

He could see the eyes begin to crinkle as they looked away from his; her lips quivered and trembled as she tried to fight back the tears. Eventually, one solitary tear welled up and rolled down her cheek. He reached up and wiped it away with a finger. "It doesn't matter, you know. Not really."

In response, Chris lifted her head above the landing rail to look down into the hallway. She sat down again swiftly after nodding with her head to the porch. He stood up and glanced to where she had looked. Sure enough, John was still there with Nicky, this time engaged in a really passionate kiss, no thoughts of their surroundings or who might see them. He crouched back down again, but Chris's head had fallen forward again, her hair shaking as she was racked by sobs once more. He put a finger under her chin and lifted her face to about six inches from his.

"I can't quite believe it. You have feelings for Nicky?" A look of incomprehension crossed her face before she realised he was gently pulling her leg.

"No, you arse. John."

"Let me tell you something about him. He's nothing but a male slag..."

"He's your mate!" Chris spluttered out.

"Yes, but that doesn't stop him from being a slut. He'll get what he wants from her and then move onto the next conquest."

Chris said nothing, but just raised one eyebrow in question. She used the already damp to wipe away the new tears before asking, "Really? You mean that?"

He nodded assent. "You've had a very lucky escape, darlin'."

Chris pursed her lips and blew out a great sigh- of relief, release, whatever. She reached up and caressed his cheek. "Rescued by a Soft Cell fan. Who'd have guessed it possible."

According to Jim's watch, it was a quarter past nine. The last vestiges of sunlight had gone, and the streetlights were coming on.

He desperately wanted to enter the flat that he had his back to at present, to confirm what he feared. On the other hand, he didn't want to compromise what was a crime scene by stomping all over possible evidence in his size nines. In the end, curiosity overcame prudence, to stay put.

"Come here Palmer, will you?"

Edging towards the senior policeman, it was evident both in his slow movement and the look on his face that he really had no desire to go in with the Inspector. His mate PC Sharma had gone in and he swore that his colleague had turned pale beneath his Indian skin. He stopped two feet in front of the shorter man.

"COME HERE!" Thundered Smallwood. Reluctantly, Palmer shuffled forward again. Jim reached up and grabbed his arm. Palmer breathed a huge sigh of relief, for the Inspector was just using him for support as he removed his shoes.

"Hold them, then, if you're not coming into party." Without waiting, Jim turned abruptly and padded up to the door, removed a handkerchief from his pocket, and used it to open the door with. Palmer was impressed.

Inside, Jim put the hankie back into his pocket. He noticed that someone, presumably Sharma, or the thieving cretin Blockley, had left the hallway lights on. Well, if they've left prints on the switch, that would be one more nail in their coffin.

Jim stopped after he had closed the front door and waited thirty seconds before sniffing the air. Strange smells assaulted his senses, but he'd be damned if he could distinguish any one thing from another. Sherlock Holmes I'm not, he reflected ruefully. Straight in front of him through an open door he noted a corner of a bedside cabinet, so he slowly headed towards it. He was just to push the door fully open when there was a commotion at the front door. He spun around to see three men in white suits rushing in, the front door crashing back against the wall.

"Stop right there. Please, don't move another inch." A man in a white suit breathily exclaimed. Smallwood held up his hands as if in surrender, and looking past the two men, noticed Rachael standing behind them, one hand on the door frame. She was wearing latex gloves and overshoes. She took one look at her boss, from his stretched arms down to his socked feet, and burst out laughing. The leading white-suited man spun round.

"Funny, is it, DC Read? Inspector Smallwood is in the middle of contaminating a possible crime scene, and all you can do there is stand and laugh?" He shook his head, and Rachael suddenly appeared contrite, head bowed. The man in the white suit turned back to face Smallwood, but the inspector could see that Rachael was still trying to suppress a giggle.

"Hold on, Bernie, don't go taking it out on her. Everything here is my fault, and I unreservedly apologize."

"Well, yes, at least you haven't come running in like a bull in a china shop, I suppose." Bernie Went pulled his face mask down. "I'm just peeved to have missed the party. I liked Harris."

"He hasn't died as well has he?" Smallwood smiled at the scene of crime officer.

"Ha fucking ha, Jim." Bernie gave a sardonic smile. "You know what I mean."

"Yes. Yes... and I'm sorry again."

Bernie nodded. "Well, between you, that young constable, and those two louts I'd be surprised if we find anything..."

Jim stepped into the lounge. "After you, gentlemen. I'll come back, suitably attired, to see what you have. "Bernie nodded once more and headed off to the bathroom, a large silver metallic case held up in both hands in front of him like a shield.

Jim found Rachael in conversation with Pc Sharma. They broke off when they saw him, looking for news with hushed anticipation. Jim shook his head to say he didn't know anything, and asked, "Where are those two idiots?" He held his fingers as though his words should be in parenthesis. He wanted to call them much worse.

Rachael was the first to answer." Pc Palmer has taken them down to the station, for now at least, Sir."

"Are they under arrest?"

"For what, Sir? We don't really know if they've committed any crimes for certain yet." Jim just grunted.

"What else have we got, then?"

"A couple more uniforms doing crowd control, and two more SOCOs here. We're still awaiting confirmation of a suspicious death, aren't we?" Rachael gave the ghost of a smile, as if to suggest that everything was under control.

"Carry on then, constable, carry on. I'll alert you if anything comes up." Feeling satisfied that all bases were covered, the Inspector went back to the flat. He stopped in the same place as before, this time listening for anything unusual. Silence stretched as far as the occasional car going past out on the road; inside was deathly quiet. Even the pathologist and the SOCOs were quiet. He advanced as far as the door to the bedroom, which was slightly ajar. He hesitated a moment before pushing the door open wider with an elbow.

The two SOCOs and Bernie, the pathologist, were standing watching the bed. Bernie still held his box of tricks held close to his chest. His assistants were standing stock still as well. They all jumped when Jim coughed to disturb the reverence. All three turned and for the first time Jim could see the body on the bed.

Stretched out on the bed was a body, tucked into the white cover of a duvet. This was the first thing that Jim noticed; the body was entombed more like you would be in a sleeping bag. A duvet would normally have its buttons or toggles at the bottom. The second thing Jim noticed was the face. It was the face of a man, aged about sixty, looking asleep. The skin held an unnatural greyish tinge. Jim could make out the forehead, most of the eyes, the nose and mouth. The eyes were apparently taped down with a thin strip of surgical tape over each eye. He realised then with a start what was more blindingly obvious. The face was peering out of the material, as if someone had cut a hole out of the material deliberately, about eighteen inches from the top edge. He moved past Bernie to look more closely, making sure that his hands were behind his back.

"Whoa wait a minute please." Bernie stepped forward but was silenced by a glance from Jim. Bernie stopped where he was, and Jim resumed his preliminary look at the man on the bed. The duvet cover was pulled over past the head Jim looked back at the cut-away part of the duvet. It was strange.

Satisfied, Jim stepped backwards to let the SOCOs carry out their work, nodding silent thanks to Bernie, who looked back at him sullenly, as if Jim had stolen the ball off him to score the winning try in a rugby match. Jim raised his eyebrows, shrugged his shoulders, and looked round the room. A cabinet was on the right-hand side of the bed, with a lamp, on top. On the other side was an old armchair. There was an old print on the wall, a scarred wardrobe against the wall. Apart from that, the room was bare apart from an old brown carpet, threadbare in parts. Jim moved to the wardrobe to open it, but a small cough from the other side of the room alerted him to Bernie, standing over the body, looking at him intently, one eyebrow raised quizzically. Jim beat a retreat to the hallway, much to the SOCOs relief and his chagrin. With one quick glance in the lounge- he couldn't risk Bernie's wrath much more- he left the flat and, once outside, took a deep breath and held onto it for a long time before exhaling slowly. His mind was spinning, he had a hundred and one things to do; but two things were the most pressing in his mind. The second was to find Rachael: the first was to have a cigarette.

The rest of the evening was like a dreamlike. He remembered the music, everything from the Thompson Twins, Paul Young, Duran Duran. Even a bit of Bucks Fizz and Odyssey, for some reason. What he couldn't remember was the conversation with Chris, however. Not that it was boring: on the contrary, it was fascinating, stimulating and joyful. It was just that there had been so much of it. They had talked for hours, at first on the stairway, then the hall, the kitchen, the garden, back into the kitchen and finally the lounge. They held hands throughout, not caring who saw them. Indeed, many people did see them but just wondered what was going on. Even John and Nicky stopped as they went past, staring at them as if they had two heads or something. He had smiled as he passed John, but he couldn't read the expression on his friend's face. As soon as they made eye contact, John looked away to look at Chris with an unreadable look on his face. At the end of the evening he had insisted on walking her home, and they had stood for ages just holding hands outside her front gate, hardly talking, but just looking at each other. After what seemed an eternity, she sighed deeply.

"I have to go. Mum and Dad will be worrying. It's been a wonderful evening. Thank you."

"You don't have to thank me for anything."

"Oh, I do. You rescued me from despair."

"I only gave you a bit of bog roll." She laughed at this, kissed him on the cheek, and opened her garden gate. She went in, closed it, and leant on it.

"I'll call you tomorrow." She smiled at him.

"You better had. Goodnight, Chris."

She smiled once more and turned to go. Halfway up the path, she turned and gave him a small wave, still smiling. He returned it and watched her until she let herself in.

Smiling, he thrust his hands deep into his pockets. This what love feels like, he chuckled. He moved off, a deep sense of warmth settling all over him, warding off the chill night air.

He smiled almost constantly the next day, the next week, the next fortnight. He was still smiling four weeks later when he went round to John's place. His mum opened the door, said hello, and told him John was 'upstairs'. She also told him she was just popping down the shops. He waved her goodbye, and bounded up the stairs, still smiling. He was still grinning to himself when he burst into John's room, and found John lifting up Chris's dress.

CHAPTER 6

Jim was fed up, unable to locate a cigarette or Rachael. The original adrenaline rush that he had felt on arrival had dissipated, to be replaced with a sense of dread. He had been on murder inquiries before, and he knew how much work they entailed. Mountains of paperwork, hours of slow-moving investigations, dozens of people involved, dead ends, lost leads. The list was virtually endless. He was wondering what to do next when Rachael came around the side of the building.

"Where have you been?" Jim asked, irritation showing.

"Canvassing." She smiled breezily. "Nothing doing though. Nobody recalls anything strange going on around here recently. No suspicious sightings." Her eyes narrowed. "No sightings of anyone living here since an elderly gentleman died six months ago. I'll get hold of the agent or the landlord in the morning."

Jim looked at his watch. "Well, I don't suppose we can do much more tonight, until the SOCOs wrap up." He spoke a little despondently, Rachael thought. Maybe calling it a night would be a good idea, so that they could refresh their batteries and attack this mystery afresh in the morning.

"I'm going to go back to the station in a while. Make a few phone calls, get the ball rolling. Early start in the morning, around seven?" He asked, an appealing look in his eyes.

"Of course," she replied, "Unless there's something else I can do tonight?" She began to turn away, but hesitated. "I could always come and keep you company."

"No, away with you to your bed. Tomorrow could be a long day; I can feel it in my water."

"Your water, Sir? Is that like a middle-aged hunch, or something?"

Jim was about to explode when he realised that Rachael was gently mocking him. Suddenly the despondency he had been feeling lifted a little, and he changed his mind. "Ok, maybe you could rustle up a little food from somewhere? I'm absolutely famished." As soon as he said this, Rachael realised that she was too. She nodded and so, the matter decided, they headed in search of a lift back to the station. A uniformed officer was unspooling a roll of police tape across the entrance to the rear of the flats. He stopped what he was doing, to let them through before finishing the job, tying the end off around a lamppost. There was one solitary patrol car. Inside were Graham and Joss. Motioning Joss to stay in the front, the inspector slid in the back behind Rachael.

As the car took off, Jim stared morosely at the flat as it passed by and said to nobody in particular," Never did get that damned cigarette."

"I thought you bought some cigars from the off licence, Sir."

"Bugger it, so I did... how could I forget that?" He looked at her, a wry look on his face. He leaned forward and spoke to Graham, "Can you drop me off at the bottom of Station Road, please?" He pulled out the packet, waving them gently in the mirror so that Graham knew his intentions.

"Of course, Sir, not a problem. Be there in a jiffy."

Jim smiled at the constable and turning to Rachael, but still speaking to Graham, said," And then can you drop Rachael off somewhere like a chippy or somewhere to get some food? The police canteen won't be open at this time. I know you two know the best places to get fast food at this time of night. Thanks." Graham nodded in reply, putting his indicators on to show he was stopping the car.

"Sorry to bugger you around and use you as a taxi." He fished in his back pocket for his wallet, and finding it, extracted a ten-pound note and handed it over to Rachael. "And try and get some coffee, too. And whatever these two want as well, nodding to the pair in the front. Joss shook her head to indicate there was no need on her account. Graham pushed out his stomach, patting it with hands whilst exhaling noisily.

"We're fine, Sir. But thank you for the offer. Very kind."

Jim grunted in reply and got out of the car. Closing the door, he waved them off whilst opening the cellophane wrapper of the cigars. He lit his one, inhaling deeply. Spluttering, he felt dizzy for a moment and reached out for the nearest wall to support him, just as a late-night dog walker walked past, giving him a filthy look as she did so. Probably thinks I'm drunk, Jim thought to himself. Luckily, the patrol car was out of sight and couldn't see him. He took another, gentler puff this time and set off in the direction of the police station, this time savouring the deep taste. He even managed a rueful smile to himself.

Meanwhile, the patrol car slowed to a stop outside a small parade of shops. Rachael got out in front of 'Oscars Grill and Burger Palace'. Thinking that 'Palace' was over-egging the point a bit, she was greeted by a blast of hot, fat-drenched air, the noise of a games machine coming from a corner, and squeals of excitement as a group of four teenagers held a mini food fight with the remnants of a chip carton. One of the teenagers looked up, leered at her and was just about to say something lewd to her when he was tugged on the arm by his mate.

"Pig, Keith, pig." The teenager called Keith turned his leer to a scowl and stared at her, but kept his mouth shut. Rachael ignored them and looked up at the menu board. An acne ridden, bespectacled youth sauntered up to the till and looked at her, saying nothing; a drinking straw hung limply from his mouth. He seemed to nod once, twice three times. Then he did it again. Rachael realised that this was some kind of nervous tic. She also realised that her need for food overcame any qualms that she held about the quality of the serving staff. As long as the food wasn't on the same level.

"Two royal deluxe and chips please."

"Drinks." This wasn't really stated as a question.

"Do you sell coffee?" The youth, whom according to a little plastic badge was called Daz, pointed up behind him to the drinks menu with one finger whilst pushing his glasses back up his nose with another. There were hoots of derision from the teenagers behind her. "Two cokes, then. Here you go." Rachael pushed the tenner across the counter rather than run the risk of touching Daz.

"Ooh, skanky pig thinks she's at the Ritz." One of the teenage girls called out to her mates. The rest of them burst out laughing again. Rachael ignored them, picked up her change and waited for her burgers to be wrapped. Only when she was sure that Daz was going to have no physical contact with her food did she turn round. She placed both palms flat on the table and leant over so that her face was about six inches from the girls' face.

"Listen up, bitch. You ever, ever, EVER, call me a pig, or a skank again, I'll be forced to tell your mates here how you use your pox ridden gob to suck off old blokes behind the Masons Arms on a Friday night." She looked round at the teenage faces one at a time, suddenly grim and silent. She looked back at the girl. "Maxine Corr, the two-pound whore. Isn't that what they call you?" Not waiting for an answer, she pushed herself up from the table, strode over to the counter, picked up the blue and white striped plastic carrier containing the food, and left the shop, oblivious of the facts that Maxine had turned a deep shade of puce, that the other three sat slack-jawed in silence, and that Daz's straw had fallen out of his mouth to lodge itself on his green nylon apron, held there by a thin line of drool.

Only when had she reached the patrol car, did Rachael allow herself a smile of satisfaction.

His neck and upper back hurt. Maybe it was tension, or stress. He ate healthily, and exercised regularly, so he knew it wasn't down to a lack of fitness on his part. He felt that he needed a massage. A proper massage by a properly qualified technician. Day after day, wherever he was, he felt that he was being constantly assailed by offers of massages, body rubs, exotic encounters- the list was virtually endless. They were on cards in phone boxes, or at the supermarket, in the back of the newspaper, in the windows of the local newsagents, even in the toilets of the pubs he had used. When he got home it was amongst the junk mail. It seemed that the whole world wanted to sell him their body.

Fortunately, amid all the detritus, he had found the one. She was called Tori, she had been a masseur and beauty therapist for ten years, and she (according to an earlier phone conversation) was willing to travel. She would be here in half an hour, time enough for a shower.

He put on some coffee. Nothing could beat the first cup of the day. Unless, of course, it was killing the bitches. But, he reflected, they deserved it almost as much as he deserved a decent cup of coffee at least once a day. Slipping beneath the scalding water of his shower, he let his mind wander in an attempt to ease the tension.

It had been a beautiful summer day. The shafts of sunlight diffused delicately through the branches overhead as they walked. The woodland smells of wild garlic, sorrel and witch-hazel assaulted their senses as they strolled hand in hand through the glades. The furtive glances they stole at each other told their own story of future promise. The coy, almost shy smiles they shared with each other betrayed a hidden passion that lurked just below the surface. They laughed at each other's jokes and listened intently when the other spoke. They had been together for only a few days but felt that they had known each for years.

"Well, here we are then," Tori said." And no-one has stolen the bikes. I told you it was perfectly safe not to lock them. You should loosen up a bit."

"Are you saying I'm locked up with a massive bicycle lock?" he replied. She giggled in return.

"Well. I don't know if the supreme being has a bike. Probably a chariot drawn by centaurs." She looked at him through long, dark lashes. Her face was dappled by the gaps in the sun hat she was wearing. She picked up a long piece of grass and stuck it between pink lips.

"The supreme being?" He coaxed, amused.

"Don't tell me that all this..." She threw arms out and pirouetted slowly," ...all this is just by chance? I'm not buying that. There has to be a higher entity, controlling everything. Mother Nature's boss, maybe."

"Tori, you are completely mad." He said, scooping up her delicate hand. She slipped away, skipping through the long meadow into which they had emerged from the wood, laughing back at him as she went.

All I ever wanted, all I ever needed is right here, he thought.

They had met quite by chance in the local record store the previous week, when he had been given a promotional poster of the latest Police single by the shops' owner, Steve. He was lucky that he had a brilliant relationship with the owner; such posters were worth a great amount of kudos. Teenagers up and down the land would gather in bedrooms to gaze at their pop idols adorning their walls. Or their friends' walls.

She had been standing right behind him in the queue and gave a little whimpered moue when she saw what he was holding. She looked at him with big, doe-like eyes, her mouth turned down in a pout. Beautiful green eyes, a tiny nose and such wondrous lips. He had no choice, and with a small sigh, he handed it to her. She took it tenderly, as it were made of vellum, not cheap printed paper. She held it front of her, gazing at it for ages. Slowly her eyes raised to search his, as if to question that this precious gift was really hers. He nodded slowly. Her face broke into the biggest smile he'd ever seen, from the little wrinkles in her forehead down to the small dimple in her chin. Reaching up, she kissed him briefly but firmly on the lips before turning quickly and skipping out of the shop. She paused on the threshold, waved, and was gone before the tingle on his lips has faded. He turned to Steve, who beamed at him and shrugged his shoulders.

"On to a winner there. After her, before she gets too far."

His assistant, Robin laughed from the back before saying, "She'll be long gone, Steve."

"Away with you, son, don't you be spoiling love's young dream before it's started." He chuckled again, and raised his eyebrows, as if to suggest that he'd better scoot along.

He had quickly left the shop, scanning both ways on the street for a sight of her. There was none, and he didn't really expect there to have been one. Taking a deep breath, he set off in the direction he'd seen her skipping, stopping briefly outside every shop window to see if she was hiding in one of them. He reached the corner, and turned a full circle, scanning the sparsely populated street. Just the normal mix of housewives, schoolchildren and business folk traipsing around on their normal Thursday routines. Not one of them clutching a poster.

He thrust his hands into his jeans disconsolately and kicked at a bit of rubbish on the ground. Suddenly somebody whistled behind him. Whirling around, there was no-one. He couldn't have imagined that, surely. He was still staring vacantly into space when her head appeared from the entrance to the bank and then just as quickly disappeared. He waited, and after half a minute or so, it reappeared, this time with a pink tongue sticking out from pink lips. An invitation, or a brush off? Plucking up his courage, he took his hands out of his pockets and walked over, taking a deep breath and saying a quick prayer as he did so.

"Thought you were NEVER coming! I almost gave up hope." Again, that little pout. "Come on, there's so much to do." And with that she was off skipping again.

And she was still skipping away from him five days later. This time she was fifty yards away in the meadow. Then she just disappeared. Concerned, he ran over to where he had last seen here. He reached the top of a small crest and looked down. There she was, sitting on the springy turf, her long, hippy skirt splayed all around her. She was looking up at him, laughing.

"Thought you were NEVER coming! I almost gave up hope!" She patted the ground beside her. He strode down the little slope and flopped down beside her. She lay back, smiling at the sky. He looked at her, lying there. She wasn't beautiful in the classical sense, but she was damned attractive and knew it. She had a look or a facial expression for every occasion, a very quick mind, a broad intelligence and a wry sense of humour. He had known her for a little over 100 hours and was totally smitten.

"You can kiss me, you know," She said, quite matter-of-factly. "You don't have to ask me."

He did. It was the latest thing to blow his mind about their relationship. It quite literally blew his mind. They kissed slowly at first, gradually growing in strength and intensity. After about five minutes, she gently pushed him away. "Let the girl breathe!" She exclaimed, almost panting. Their faces were about six inches apart, eyes locked. Staring into those beautiful pools of warmth, a man could get lost, he thought. But suddenly she was rolling away, getting firstly to her knees and then to her feet, brushing the grass from her skirt as she did so. Laughing at him, she whispered to him, "This isn't the place you know."

Before he could ask her what she meant, she was off skipping back to where they had left their bikes. He didn't catch up with her until she had climbed on her saddle and was pushing off.

"The place for what?" He managed to ask finally when they were abreast of each other.

"Later." This is all she would say until they got home.

Later came when they sitting on his bed. They were fully clothed. She looked at him enigmatically and asked in a prim voice, "Do you have any condoms?"

He nodded, and opened a drawer to find his secret, battered 'packet of three'.

When he turned back, she had already taken off her top to reveal a purple chemise bra, dark against her milky white skin. He gaped at her. My, she was forward, he thought.

"Take one out for me, will you?" He did as he was told and handed it to her. She reached out and taking it gently, started to stretch and then ping it as if it were a balloon.

"Mm. I don't imagine Alex would like it too much." She mused.

He was confused. "Alex?" was he could say.

She looked at him with a strange look in her eye before replying simply," My boyfriend. He rang earlier. We're back on."

Without another word, she put her top back on. She got up off the bed, pecked him on the cheek as she brushed past him. "Call me." And walked out, not skipping this time.

Rachael leaned back and stretched her arms, rolled her neck, and cracked her fingers. The last of these bought a disapproving stare from her superior across the office. She mimed an apology, giving a wan smile. She was bushed. She had spent over an hour typing a report about the evenings' events. Those pertaining to the case, that was. She chose to omit the events in the burger palace. The remnants of the food were scattered over her desk. She glanced over at the Inspectors' desk only to note that he had tidied his rubbish away into the bin. She suspected that he would say something to the effect of 'tidy desk, tidy mind, DC Read' and so she stood up and collected everything into the blue and white plastic bag before depositing everything in the bin. He looked up again.

"You look done in. Let's recap what we have and call it a night." He looked down at his desk and picked up a couple of sheets which had been stapled together and scanned it before speaking. "The pathologist's preliminary report is that the body is of a deceased, white male, aged about 60. Cause of death is unknown as yet, but he is heavily hinting foul play..."

"Duh. You're unlikely to put yourself in a duvet cover with only your head peering out of a small hole if its natural, Sir!" Rachael interjected.

"Doesn't mean it was an unnatural death."

"Why would anyone innocent do that though? You'd phone the police, anyone, if it was natural, surely?" The exasperation was clear; the tiredness was beginning to show. Her long hair fell forward to cover her face. "Sorry." She mumbled.

"Don't be sorry- a little passion in an officer of the law should be positively encouraged, in my view. "And this is the right time and place. Shows you're alive. All the pathologist can do now is rule things in at this stage. Ruling out comes later."

Chastened but encouraged at the same time, Rachael resumed the chair behind her desk. She looked at him expecting more, but he had stood and was putting his jacket on.

"Post-mortem at seven in the morning, if you want. Though that's only about six hours away now." He spoke ruefully, aware that the first few hours of any murder enquiry were the most crucial. However, at this stage, murder was only of the options which couldn't be ruled out. "The lads who discovered the body are downstairs, not going anywhere" he caught Rachael trying to say something and held up finger for silence. "We are unable to rule anybody out at this stage, so they are cooling their heels in a cell overnight. Free board and lodging, they can't complain."

Rachael found herself unable to disagree with him so stood up and followed him out of their office, pausing only to turn the lights off and close the door. Ten minutes later she was home, and five after that she was fast asleep, dreaming the dreams of the righteous. Jim, in his own bed, lay staring at the darkened ceiling, wondering what today's events heralded and what tomorrow what bring. His eyes closed slowly, and he drifted into a troubled sleep.

He toyed with the idea of underwear but decided against it. He went back into his kitchen, fixed himself another coffee, then turned to watch as his masseuse stepped lightly out of her car and up his garden path. He waited for her to ring the doorbell once, twice. He took a deep breath and exhaled slowly. He went to open the door, holding it wide open for her to enter. Smiling politely, she hid whatever surprise she felt at seeing him dressed only in a towel. No doubt she had seen worse. No doubt at all.

CHAPTER 7

The alarm clock woke Rachael fully. She sat bolt upright; a nice dream forgotten. She looked at the time. It was just past six; enough time for a quick shower and an even quicker breakfast. Half an hour later, she was out of the door, her hair scraped back and tied up in a simple ponytail, still slightly damp: she had run out of time and she desperately wanted to be on time for the post-mortem. As she drove into the car park, scanning for the Inspector's car, she saw he wasn't there yet. Breathing a sigh of relief, she was locking her car when the Inspector came roaring into the car park and screeched to a halt beside her.

Jim looked a complete disaster zone. His tie was askew, and there was a dollop of what looked like dried egg on his jacket lapel. Rachael also noticed that his shirt buttons weren't matched up properly. "How come you're looking so fresh and cherubic this morning, DC Read?" He said with a grimace.

"Good morning to you, too, Sir." She reached into her bag, and pulled out a tissue, moistened it with the tip of her tongue, and sponged off the errant egg. She then straightened his tie before looking him in the eye. "You can sort out those buttons yourself though."

He nodded curtly at her, embarrassed. "I can do it on the way. Don't want to miss the grisly bits, do we?" Rachael had to jog to catch up with his pace as she shook her head, stopping off to throw her tissue away in a bin.

The hospital was a fifties-built warren of pale green corridors, with unhelpful or often downright misleading signs. The pathology suite was close by the entrance, but they still had to make three turns before arriving at a white door inset with frosted glass. Someone had scraped off the grey lettering on the door so that it read 'log suit', causing Rachael to smile. Jim creased his brows at her until he saw what she was looking at. He gave a quick smirk before resuming his serious side.

"Presumably you have been to a post-mortem before?"

"Two. Sir." She looked at the door again. "But they're all the same, aren't they?" She looked at him hopefully.

A wistful look crossed his face. He looked at the ground before responding. "Not all...but this shouldn't hold too many horrors. Surprises aplenty, but hopefully no horrors." At that, he pushed open the door and entered.

Inside was a reception desk, and behind it, a dour receptionist who perked up when the pair of them entered. She gave a shuffle in her seat, patted her hair, and sat up straight.

"Well, good morning to you, Inspector Smallwood." She purred at him. "It's so nice to see you again." A heady mix of lavender scented perfume filled the room.

"Good morning to you, Lottie, I hope you're keeping fine. You're certainly look it." She positively glowed at his compliment.

"Why, thank you, kind Sir. Go on through, they are just about to begin." A perfectly manicured hand pointed to a side door.

Jim and Rachael nodded and went through the door. As he closed the door behind him, he tapped the side of his head with a finger a couple of times. "Mad as a fruit-bat."

"She likes you, though." Rachael declined to comment that it should've been as mad as a fruitcake or as a bat, but not both. They helped each other with the standard knee length green gowns and bright blue rubber boots that all visitors were expected to wear. The temperature had dropped considerably, and the lavender scent had been replaced by the altogether more sinister smell of antiseptic sterile cleaning fluid, mixed with something that Rachael couldn't quite place. She gave an involuntary shudder that Jim caught.

"Sure you're ok with this? I wouldn't think any less of you if you wanted to sit this one out."

"And listen to mindless tittle-tattle from love-struck Lottie? I rather have dinner with the Four Horsemen of the Apocalypse." She said with more bravado than she felt. She pushed at another

61

door into another corridor. Pausing briefly to take a deep breath she opened the door into the main lab.

There were four gowned people at work. In the corner was an assistant, preparing some equipment. Another stood at a long metal table, opposite the medical examiner, Bernie, with a long metal scalpel in his hand. The photographer stood to one side holding what seemed to Rachael to be a heavy camera with a huge flash attachment, waiting patiently to take images as and when required.

As they entered, Bernie looked up and raised his eyebrows. "Good of you to join us, Jim. What a find we have here." He was indicating the body stretched out on the table beneath him. His voice was remarkably clear considering his nose and mouth were covered with a surgical mask. The others carried on, barely registering their arrival. "Very interesting indeed. May I introduce you to Mr. Samuel Obadiah Taylor, not until recently a resident of this parish." The assistant moved away to reveal the body on the table. A very grey, immobile body, Rachael thought, noticing that he had his eyes taped shut. She hadn't seen him the previous evening and her breath caught in her throat. She felt the bile rising and fought it determinedly. Bernie glanced over at her and deciding that she was not going to throw up or faint, he carried on. "Mr. Taylor was 53, five foot eight in height."

"You know who he is?" Jim suddenly seemed to register what was being said. "How? Why didn't you tell me this earlier?"

"Vernon here," He said, indicating the assistant in the corner, "found his wallet about three this morning, after we submitted the initial report. It was found stuffed down the side of a sofa. We are fairly sure that it is his. The driving licence is, and another card for, Vernon?"

"The Chorley and Leyland Air Cadets."

"Thank you, Vernon. Well. These cadets have a photocard. A ten-year-old picture, but him. You can have a look at it when we have finished going through it for fingerprints and whatnot."

"Whatnot?" Enquired Rachael, keen to be involved in this discussion.

"DNA, fibres, residue, the usual."

"Ok. We know who he is then." Jim stole a glance at Rachael, as if to say some things can be ruled in, others not. "What he was doing stuffed inside a duvet cover? How he got there?"

"Inspector! Hold your horses! I have only had three hours sleep. We will get there." Bernie shot Jim a vexed look, who gave a small shrug of apology.

"As I say, the duvet was white, cotton, made in the European Union, queen size. The boffins have it now and will tell you when it yields up any of its secrets." Another nod from the Inspector. "Now, turning to the deceased. Rigor Mortis was and is still present. The liver temperature doesn't help us much, only to rule things in. Best guess would be twenty to twenty-four hours before we found him." Bernie glanced down at the body again. "And that's about all, folks. I may well be able to tell you more after I have opened him up. I'm guessing that unless you are horribly morbid, your best course of action would be a coffee in the canteen. Come back in an hour or so and I'll know more. Maybe even establish cause of death." With that. He turned to his assistant and motioned for the scalpel.

Jim thanked him and turned away. Not because he was squeamish, but that he trusted Bernie to let him know anything of importance straight away. With one hand on the door, he turned back for one last question. "Suspicious death, though, Bernie?"

The pathologist looked up, nodding. "I guess so."

After about twenty minutes of intense kneading, pummeling, stretching and rubbing, he felt as if the cares of the world had dropped from his shoulders. He felt relaxed and energised. He pushed himself up onto one elbow and looked up at the masseuse.

"That was wonderful. You have wonderful...hands." His words said one thing, but his eyes suggested that he found other things about her equally appealing. Light brown bobbed hair framed a pretty face, with nicely proportioned features. Smooth skinned, with a healthy glow from her exertions, standing about five foot six inches in her sensible flat shoes, wearing a loose-fitting t-shirt and tracksuit bottoms, her clothes tried their best to cover a sleek, lithe body. He pushed himself fully upright, well aware that in doing so, his towel slipped off, revealing his manhood to be in a state of mid-wakefulness. He noted that she didn't even look, nor bat an eyelid. Interesting, he thought. By showing no interest in him sexually whatsoever, he knew her fate was sealed. It was perverse. Had she jumped him then and there, he probably would've saved her. Her professionalism impressed him.

"Would you like some coffee before you leave? It will be freshly brewed, not instant."

"Yes, that would be lovely, thanks. Only if it's no bother, though." She spoke with a soft, Scottish lilt to her voice.

"Is that a trace of the Highlands, Tori? Can I call you Tori, or would you prefer Miss Henderson?" He was getting off the padded roll-mat that she had provided for the massage, readjusting his towel in a more decorous manner as he spoke.

"Very good. You're very good at accents."

"What can I say? It's a hobby... I'll get your coffee and put some more clothes on. Won't be a moment."

Once defrocked, they headed in search of the canteen. It proved no problem for the senior detective who had been there more times than he cared to remember. For her, this was something of a new departure. As they walked down seemingly endless corridors, she tried to digest what she'd seen and heard. A dead body turns up in suspicious circumstances. This could perhaps turn into a murder enquiry, and she hoped that she'd be right in the middle of it. This was what she had been hoping for when she had joined the police all those years ago. This, she felt, was real policing. Finding out the perpetrators of evil was better than sex, in her book. Not that she'd had much of that recently either, she reflected sadly.

The aroma of freshly cooked bacon assaulted their nostrils, and even though they had recently both eaten, they talked about it and realised that the ordeal they had witnessed warranted at least a small breakfast bap as well as coffee. Jim told her to go and grab a couple of seats whilst he paid. She insisted on it, as he'd bought the burgers the night before, and he eventually gave ground. The fact that he probably earned twice as much as she did didn't really enter the equation.

A couple of minutes later, when the breakfast baps had been eaten and the coffees half-drunk, Jim and Rachael settled for an impromptu review of what they had so far.

"It looks like murder then, Sir."

"Yes, it does, constable."

"You don't look overly enamoured with the idea, though." Jim had a far-away look on his face and Rachael had the feeling that his responses were automatic. This last question didn't even merit a reply apparently. The silence drifted until it became quite uncomfortable. Rachael was wondering what to say next when she saw Jim regain focus, finish his coffee, and stand up.

"Come on, Rachael, lots to do- "

"Sir, the pathologist said it would be at least an hour until they had anything further."

"I know that." He looked at her, now with a steely glint in his eye." We have to treat this as a murder now, and we have to duplicate, triplicate, and quadruplicate ourselves."

"Quadruplicate? Is that even a word?" Jim looked at her with his head on one side and exhaled deeply. "Ok, whatever... why are we cloning ourselves?"

"We need to find a telephone as fast as possible. We need to get a murder team together. We need to get back to the murder scene. We need to interview those two louts. Quadruplicate ourselves. It's most definitely a word." He paused to wave at a doctor he obviously knew before turning back to face her. "And no, I'm not overtly enamoured with the thought of one person taking another's life unlawfully."

"Sorry" Rachael started to apologize but he had already gone, in the direction of the doctor he'd just greeted. Rachael watched as her boss bent over the table and whispered quietly in his ear. The Inspector straightened and tapped the doctor lightly on the shoulder in appreciation. He waved her over and set off in the opposite direction from where they had entered. The doctor nodded at her when she walked past him, and she only had time to smile before she saw Jim leave. She scooted after him, nearly upsetting the fully laden tray of a porter as she went by him.

She saw him turn off halfway down a long pale green corridor and hurried off in pursuit. He'd entered the office of Mr. Andrew Budd, Ear, Nose and Throat consultant. Looking into the room, she saw her inspector standing by a desk overflowing with manila folders, dialing the telephone. He waited whilst being connected and began a rather long conversation with someone on the other end. This was obviously to a policeman more senior than Jim, because the only words she really caught were the occasional 'Yes, Sir', and 'Of course, Sir'.

Jim finished the call and depressed the bar on the telephone to get another clear line. Rachael stood there and watched. She could feel the tension palpably rising in the room but being only a constable she was unaware of the protocols. She tried to remember what Jim had said about quadruplicating themselves, even if it was only ten minutes ago.

She pretended to look in her bag as she racked her brains. She took a deep breath and let it out slowly. Think, Rachael, she told herself- if you can't remember, you'd make a great detective- and then it came to her. Go back to the murder scene and interview Seamus and Lucky. They would be really stewing but she really didn't give a damn. As she was pondering what to do, her boss put the phone down and came to stand alongside her.

"Are you OK? You a little flushed." He put his hand lightly on her arm.

"Yes, Sir, I'm fine. Just wondering where you'd like me- at the station or the crime scene." She was determined not to show any weaknesses to him. He looked concerned.

"It's fine, constable. Everything is under control. I've spoken to Superintendent Laird. He says to finish up here and then go back to the station whenever we can. We will have a stratagem meeting when everyone is assembled.

"Will you be S.I.O.?"

"I bloody hope so, Rachael. I can't see County being overly happy about it, but Laird and Nan Parker trust me well enough. They'll both be fighting my corner."

Rachael smiled but was inwardly the cogs were turning. Both the station commander and the ACC in his corner? Why? Slowly it dawned on her that politics may be playing a part. To be more precise, Masonic politics. She looked away, inadvertently biting her lip. Jim, quick as a hawk as, noticed but said nothing. A man has to have some secrets, and as long as it didn't distract Rachael from the more important matters in hand, a little wondering would do her no harm. He certainly wasn't going to reveal if the local Lodge were in control- or even if he was a member. He gave a small cough, and, checking that he hadn't left anything behind on the consultant's desk, left the office.

Neither spoke as they headed back to the pathology department- Jim deciding on how best to proceed; he wanted to wrap up any loose strands from the autopsy and get back to his meeting as soon as he could. Bernie was a pragmatist and would be well aware of the pressures on Jim and would be succinct. Any other information that wasn't crucial would be in his report, Jim was sure.

As for Rachael, she thought of the young Irishman and his mate, convinced that whilst they may not have committed the murder itself- and it was increasingly looking like murder now- they still held vital clues which had to be extracted. Anything they said or did could be the vital clue they needed to blow open this case. As she followed Jim, she started to formulate some questions for the unlucky pair still incarcerated back at the nick. She was still formulating plans when they arrived back at the lab.

A couple of minutes later and they were suited and booted once more and entered the main lab. The assistant who had been holding the scalpel was now sluicing water up and down the metal trolley, now empty. The room was otherwise empty. There was a nasty aroma in the air, which Rachael noticed even above the normal pathology smell that emanated from such places. The assistant looked up and nodded to a door on their right. They thanked him and headed through it to find themselves in a short corridor with seven or eight other doors off it. Jim knew where he was headed, the last door on the left. He knocked, waited a heartbeat, and entered.

"Ah, Inspector, do come in and take the weight off." Bernie motioned to a pair of chairs. Rachael, having never before been in a pathologist's office, looked about her with interest.

The office was not small, but every nook and cranny seemed to hold something. A shelving system ran from floor to ceiling down the entire side of one wall, containing a myriad of files- box files, Lever Arch files, smaller files, large binding files. Every kind of file that Rachael that could have conceived seemed to be there, and more besides. And then there were the textbooks. Literally hundreds of them occupied the top three shelves. Glancing round, she saw another bookcase crammed with books. Except for one shelf, that held a photograph of a woman and three children, all smiling at the camera. And there next to it, stood a small trophy in the shape of a fisherman with a long rod.

Behind the desk, which was cluttered with more files, sat the great man himself, smiling almost beatifically at them. Behind him were six great grey filing cabinets. She was impressed, although she hadn't known what to expect. She sat at and looked at her boss, who was seating himself and gazing at Bernie with an expectant look on his face.

The pathologist stared balefully at the pair of them for quite a while before making his pronouncement. Rachael squirmed in her seat, whereas Jim sat perfectly still. Bernie cleared his throat once, twice, before looking down at a sheet of paper he held in front of him. "You have a murder. Probably the most fiendish one I've seen in over thirty years in my job. Unless God is on your side, with Lady Luck trailing behind, you may never solve it."

CHAPTER 8

"I like your taste in music." Tori hadn't heard him come back into the lounge and jumped. "Thanks, it smells wonderful." She took the mug of steaming coffee. He was standing in a fresh t-shirt and crisply ironed jeans. He looked fresh and extremely fit in her eyes. It was a shame that she had a strict no dating policy for any of her clients. She would just love to explore his body with her hands more than she had already done. Definitely worth a jump, she reflected happily. What she couldn't see, was that his hands, under the coffee tray, were sheathed in blue latex gloves.

"There's a coaster there, if you want." He nodded to the cabinet next to her which held some of his precious record collection. She turned her head and set the mug down, and then traced her finger along the spines of the albums. She heard him put the tray down on a small table next to the sofa.

Maybe, just this once, I could make an exception..." She thought, as she turned back to him.

He was now only three feet from her. She suspected nothing and didn't even see the vicious punch that felled her. She was unconscious even before she hit the floor.

He looked at her prone body. She had banged her head on the cabinet as she went down. With any luck, he thought, she may be dead already. He knelt and lightly felt the side of her neck through his gloved hands. He eventually located a weak pulse. He closed both hands around her neck and squeezed. As he did so, he remembered the poster that he had given the pouting girl all those years ago; it was the Police's King of Pain.

"Maybe he was just being over dramatic, egging the point a bit too much, Sir."

"Bernie doesn't do drama. He's a fisherman. Given to patience and understanding." The inspector replied morosely. The phone rang, and Jim let it ring three times before picking up. He simply replied 'OK, Sir,' and left the handset on the desk.

Rachael stepped over and gently put it back onto the cradle. "I'm sure we will get him. He's bound to have made a mistake. They all do. At the very least we can get a description of him from Seamus or Lucky."

Jim looked up, a distant look in his eyes. Then they seemed to re-focus, he nodded, and instantly cheered up. Rachael thought it was more to do with his own thought processes than anything she had said in her attempts to cheer him.

"The boss wants to see me before we go into to meet the team. They are assembling in the conference room." He straightened himself up as he spoke. She nodded, giving him a half-smile, and left to go meet them.

She was met by a hive of activity. There were at least eight people in the room, some she knew, others that she was less sure about. Two were installing three telephones on the big mahogany table that dominated the room, two were setting up a mobile whiteboard. One was placing bottles of water and paper cups in strategic positions along the tables' length. The last person, Cheryl, one of the secretaries, was placing slim manila folders opposite each chair. Rachael counted twelve chairs, twelve folders. She stopped and whispered in her ear. "Dreadful thing, hey? I heard you were there from the outset."

They had started at the station the same week and had established an immediate bond. They were of a similar age, but Cheryl had married young and had two small children. They got on well and went out together; Rachael had even babysat on a couple of occasions.

"I'm afraid I'm not at liberty to tell you anything." She replied, a straight look on her face. "Not until you get me a large glass of wine later." Winking, she put a hand on her arm. "I'll call you later." Cheryl nodded conspiratorially and moved off.

Rachael stood, unsure of what she should be doing. A couple of the officers smiled and said hello, others who didn't know her giving her the once over. It was such a commonplace occurrence that Rachael hardly even noticed. She stopped next to one of her CID colleagues, Rick Chesterfield. He was about to speak when the door opened and in came the chiefs, Superintendent Laird, Jim and a stranger. He seemed extraordinarily tall compared to the two others. Dark features were accentuated by a sharp nose and a pair of deep, brown eyes. He was bearded and serious.

"Right, everyone, please take a seat quickly, we've got a lot to do. I'll leave the intros to Inspector Smallwood, except for this gentleman here." Laird broke off and indicated the tall Asian man they had entered with. "This is Inspector Jujara, from the Met, who joins us on secondment for the interim." He gave Jujara a quick smile, glanced at Jim and looked round the table where everyone had now seated themselves. "Inspector Smallwood will be S.I.O. He will fill you all in on what we know so far. Good luck, men, and err, woman." He blushed apologetically at Rachael and made a small goofy face, which caused a small ripple of laughter from the gathered detectives.

Jim moved round the table until he was standing next to the whiteboard. Inspector Jujara took one of the remaining seats. Rachael noticed two were still empty. Jim scanned the faces of those seated, cleared his throat, and reached into an identical folder to those on the table which.

"The body of Samuel Obadiah Taylor, aged 53 from Chorley, Lancashire was found at a flat here last night." Jim produced two sheets of paper from his folder and affixed them to the whiteboard. One of them was a picture of Sam, taken after the post-mortem. The second piece of paper was a map of the area where the flat was. "The layout of the bedroom is item three in your packs. Items four to thirty are photos of the body as it was found...and a layout of the flat, along with some photos of it. Items thirty-eight and nine are the preliminary post-mortem reports. I'll give you fifteen minutes to acquaint yourselves with them before continuing. I'm going to rustle up some coffee. Constable Read, would you give me a hand?"

Rachael stood, thinking what is he playing at, he knows I haven't seen all the photographs, especially the ones of where the body was found. She'd not even saw the corpse encased in its' shroud. He must have some plan for me, she presumed; unless he has forgotten, and he just needs a hand with the refreshments. She left the conference room first and waited for him to emerge. Taking her by the elbow, he led her to the canteen. Rachael spoke first.

"Don't you have the number of the canteen? Or is it something else?" Jim gave her a long, curious look, before stopping on the its' threshold and saying, "Look, I don't mind him joining the enquiry, if that's what you're getting at. It was me that suggested it to Nan Parker- and he readily agreed."

Rachael shook her head, worried. Jim looked defiantly at her; he was in charge. "Inspector Jujara is a fine officer. He caught the 'Hackney Harpooner' mainly by his intelligence and sheer bloody mindedness." Jim winked." And he's very good looking."

"Photogenic, for the press, you mean?" Rachael asked. "You're not too shabby, when you're not wearing your breakfast."

Jim laughed and went to organize some flasks of coffee, leaving Rachael to reflect on what he had said. It was true, she reflected; the dark-skinned Inspector might be seen as some as handsome, although she felt sure that he wasn't quite her cup of tea. Slim, tall, elegant, with a ready smile, a keen intelligence, what's not to like about him? She thought back to the previous Christmas, in Hackney. From what she had read in the newspapers, starting on Boxing Day, a madman had been going out at night and shooting people with an old, ancient maritime harpoon. Five nights, five people, spread over Hackney and Stratford. Inspector Jujara had tracked him to a shed on an allotment over in Wanstead on New Years' Eve; and with only one uniformed officer to help him, had stormed the shed, and overpowered the killer. He had received a public commendation for his bravery, Rachael recollected. And probably a private bollocking for his recklessness, she thought ruefully. When they got back, they were met by silence. Most of the officers were still engrossed in their folders, one was staring out of the window in deep thought, another sat with their hands-on top of his closed folder, head cast down as if in prayer. Jim headed back to the whiteboard and cleared his throat.

"Well now you know what we are up against." He looked round the table. "Any questions at this point?" A couple of hands shot up. Jim pointed at one of them. "Yes?" He asked.

"What about the duvet? Why? Why the head peeping out?" Asked one of the detectives.

"Who are you, sonny?"

"DC Ian Westlake. County sent me over."

"Well. Ian, welcome, but to answer your question, I haven't the foggiest. Maybe your good self and ..." Jim cast his eye over the team before resuming, "DC Russell Maitland can cover that for me. It's still with forensics at the moment but they know it's a rush job. All we know is that it's 100 percent cotton, made somewhere in Europe. There may be more now." He looked to where the other hand had been raised. "Rob? You wanted to know something?"

"Robert Franks, based... here." A small chuckle from the table. "Yes, Sir, two things really. First, what about the suspects brought in last night. And second, where are the M and M's?" Several heads shot round to look at Franks as he spoke, not least Inspector Jujara, who fixed the young detective with a suspicious glare.

"Ok, ok folks. DC Franks is referring to Mike Ballard and Mark Steyne. They are two of the detectives based here, seemingly inseparable." Nods, signifying understanding. The ghost of a smile played on the lips of Jujara. "They are at the scene, looking for clues. I will be heading over there shortly. You can come with me. Sergeant Ratcliffe and... you..."

"Ash Bradfield, Luton CID, Sir. Pleased to be with you."

"Hello, DC Bradfield. You and Sergeant Ratcliffe are to interview Lucky. Inspector Jujara will interview Lucky, along with DC Read." They all nodded.

"Moving on, then. Motive is unknown at this juncture. Why abduct an old man, and drive him 300 miles before killing him? It's a little pointless to speculate at this point without knowing more about the victim." He pointed at one of the other detectives. "That's your job, get on the blower to Lancashire and get them to start cracking heads up there." He checked his watch. Let's get on, there's a sadistic killer out there. Those who have been assigned tasks, get about them. Those without, stay here. There is something for everyone." He looked up as the coffee arrived." Even if it's only pouring coffee."

Most of the room stood up, Inspector Jujara amongst them. Rachael stayed where she was. Both inspectors noted this. "Something on your mind, Constable Read?"

"Have you told them all about how Sam died, Sir?" Jim looked at her. Everyone else stopped what they were doing, even those halfway out of the room.

"Good point. Samuel Obadiah Taylor was injected in his rectum with a mixture of Ketamine and pure grade Heroin. This is no ordinary murder."

He switched the stereo off as the last beams of sunlight slid off its gleaming lid onto the wall behind it. He looked down at the body of the masseuse, stripped down to her bra and panties. On the coffee table next to her head lay a supermarket carrier bag. Inside that, a further plastic wrapping protected a clean, white duvet cover. He varied their purchase- different shops in different towns at differing times of day. He had also ordered a couple from mail order companies to be delivered to different addresses. The same size and make, to be sure- he liked the quality feel to them- but acquired by a variety of means. He had been careful.

Next to the carrier bag were two bags, one which contained all her work stuff, the other a handbag. On top of the large bag was a diary, its page open to today. On top of the handbag was her keys. One for her car, two for her front and back door of, and another, gold Yale key for something else. This key gave him for pause for thought. From the research he had undertaken on her, he knew where she lived, knew also that she travelled to clients or they came to her house- there were no work premises. She operated from a room in her house. She lived alone. Maybe the key belonged to a friend whose house she was looking after. It was a loose end he couldn't afford. He knew he had to go there after he had disposed of the body.

Turning his attention to the diary, he looked at appointments that she had meant to have that day; his name and telephone number was second on the list of her scheduled visits. He carefully tore out the page, then the ones immediately before and after. He scanned the contacts list in the back- he was in there too. He tore all of them out. No point giving the police any pointers there. He didn't want the plod to deduce his name started with this letter or that just because he had torn only that letter out. No, he reasoned, he was cleverer than that.

Rachael and Inspector Jujara finished their coffees and went down to the interview rooms. After being introduced by Jim, and a little small talk, they hadn't spoken to each other. Inspector Jujara paused outside the interview room and turned to Rachael.

"I suspect you think that Inspector Smallwood was holding things back in that briefing." His voice was low pitched, yet mellifluous- almost hypnotic. "There's a very good reason for that." Rachael stood mute next to him, looking at him with an unreadable expression in her eyes. He cocked his head to one side and gave a small sigh. "He suspects that this is not a one-off. More bodies will follow- when, where and most importantly, why it's impossible to tell yet. He needs his team to be fresh at all times. They will be swamped with data over the next few days, and he needs them to be able to focus. By the end of three days, if we don't catch them, they will know the case backwards, forwards, sideways- any which way." Rachael still stood there impassively, noting the use of the word 'data' instead of the more widely used 'information'. She didn't know why, for the Inspector didn't seem at first glance to be the kind of person who needed to dazzle people with sophisticated language.

"However, you do need to know that he trusts everyone in that room implicitly. Those who aren't from this station were recommended by friends or colleagues he's known for years. He knows his team are bright enough to work things out for themselves. Like yourself, Rachael. May I call you Rachael?" He paused for breath, smiling a brilliantly white set of perfect teeth. She found herself gazing at him, entranced by that honeyed voice. She shook her head to clear it a little. He took that as a negative and the smile snapped shut to be replaced with a look of disdain. Rachael took a step back, shocked.

"Yes Sir. Call me whatever you like. I was just lost in your voice." She blushed a deep shade of crimson, feeling like a fourteen-year-old who had been asked out to the school prom. The inspector wore a frown of confusion which was replaced by the slowly dawning recollection of what she'd said, and he smiled again. To Rachael it was like watching the sun coming out from the clouds after a heavy storm. She looked at her shoes in an attempt to regain control of her emotions. She realised that the inspector was now talking to the top of her head, so she raised it again to look into the big brown pools that were his eyes.

"You know what you're doing, so you lead, and I'll jump in whenever I need to." He opened the door, stepping back. She entered and looked at Seamus Blockley sitting slumped in his plastic chair, staring morosely at the wall. Next to him was a duty solicitor, who half rose out of his chair to shake the hands of the police officers.

"James Locke, duty solicitor for Seamus Blockley." He sat down again. The two officers introduced themselves and took the two remaining chairs. The door was shut by a uniformed officer, who left after a nod from the inspector. Rachael slid a clean pad and her manila folder onto the desk and started to unwrap the plastic wrapper of two tapes, sliding them into the recorder when she had done. She pressed the 'record' function. A long, metallic sound reverberated around the room.

"Interview of Mr. Seamus Blockley at 11.42, Saturday the 8th of June 1996. Officers present are Detective Constable Read of the Hertfordshire and Bedfordshire constabulary..."

"Inspector Mohammed Jujara of the Metropolitan Police." At this point, all the other three turned to face him. Rachael had turned because she hadn't known his first name. The solicitor and Seamus looked at him because they didn't realise that the 'Met' was involved. There was a small silence as the two facing the police regained their composure.

"Mr. James Locke, solicitor."

"Seamus Blockley." He had sat up now, alert all of a sudden. He'd had all night to stew in his cell, planning to play it all cool and laconically like he'd seen in movies and on the TV. However, he hadn't expected the presence of the heavy-duty cops.

There was another silence as Rachael opened her folder and selected one of the photos contained within. She placed it face up on the table and slid it across to a position in front of Seamus. He looked at it briefly, then looked back at the detectives, eyes panicking. He shuffled in his seat.

"Can you tell me how you know this man, Seamus?" Rachael tapped a fingernail on the photo.

"For the tape I'm showing Mr. Blockley a photo of Samuel Taylor, discovered at 10.15 p.m on the 7th of June 1996 at 4, Harper Close, Harpenden." Rachael looked intently at Seamus. She glanced at Inspector Jujara who seemed to be studying Seamus, who for his part, kept flitting his eyes between the two detectives.

"Never seen him before, like." Seamus uttered.

"Let me tell you one thing, Seamus. Lie to us and my boss will slice your nuts off and cook them for his dinner." Rachael surprised herself at saying this and was secretly thrilled that she had found out she could play 'bad cop' so well. She saw Inspector Jujara slightly move his head round to look at her, one eyebrow raised. The solicitor was so shocked he remained quiet, especially after Rachael shot him a dark glance.

A beading of sweat had appeared on Seamus's top lip. He looked down at the photos again. He had spent a restless night, torn between anger at his liberty having been taken away, and fear about being locked away in prison for a crime he hadn't committed. His eyes flittered to the Asian again. What did the Met want with him?

"Lie to us twice and he will arrange for you to be in a cell with a hulk called Roger who just LOVES young milky white butts." She had to fight hard from smirking and pressed one foot hard on to the other under the table. Seamus crumpled completely.

"Ok, missus I'll tell you what I know, but I swear on me mam's life I never killed no-one."

Rachael smiled sweetly at him. She was just about to continue when Inspector Jujara interjected.

"If you help us with our enquiries, and tell the truth, and agree to speak up at any trial, we may be able to avoid any charges of burglary. After all, you didn't take anything did you?" Seamus glanced at the Inspector, who rewarded him with one of his smiles.

Over the course of the next hour, Seamus related all he knew about the body, why he and Lucky were there, and the mysterious strange Irishman with curly hair whom they had met in the pub just two days previously.

The light had faded almost completely as he pulled his cap further over his eyes and shivered in the cooling summer night. He eased into Tori's car and adjusted the seat a bit. Satisfied, he eased out, driving slowly to the end of the road, where he turned left, and left again, down an unmade access road, little more than a track, behind the row of houses. He left the engine idling. He stole up his rear garden soundlessly. The door to his kitchen was ajar, and Tori's body lay slumped against his fridge, still only dressed in her cotton underwear. All day he had resisted the urge to touch her, except to remove her clothing. He wasn't remotely interested in necrophilia. He picked up the carrier bag and her work bag into which he had forced her handbag. Her clothes folded neatly on the floor; he would deal with later. He retraced his steps with both bags and took them to the car, where he placed them on the front seat. He opened both of the back doors and went back inside.

In the kitchen, he took hold of both her arms and used them to swing the body. She was surprisingly light, especially semi-naked, and he was extremely fit, so it wasn't a problem for him to drag her down his garden, leaving her propped against her back wheel. He went to the back of the car and crawled onto the back seat. Just then an upstairs light showed in his neighbours house. He froze, hoping that neither Sid nor Ethel were in the habit of looking out onto their back gardens at this time of night. Fortunately, whoever it was only using the toilet. He heard it flush from thirty feet away, with him in a crouching position in the back of a car. He watched patiently as the light went out. He waited two minutes and then hauled Tori onto the back seat. He drove slowly, along the rutted track and it wasn't until he reached the end that he had realised that he'd left his kitchen door unlocked.

He cursed under his breath and hoped that he wasn't going to get burgled tonight. He was more worried about his records than the pile of female clothes piled next to it. He drove along the quiet roads, hoping that he wouldn't get stopped. But then again, he chuckled to himself, what a find it would be. Images of mad car chases reminiscent of seventies cop shows flashed through his mind just as the low pools of sodium light from the lampposts flashed past by overhead. They became less frequent as he reached the outskirts of the town. Not too far to go now.

Rachael and Inspector Jujara finished up the interview, handing a copy of the tape to the solicitor, and retaining one. It would have to be transcribed but for the moment the officers had a good mental image of their main suspect. They returned so charged with adrenaline they were buzzing. Inspector Jujara was secretly impressed with Rachael. His first impression of her had been that of a meek, mild officer beginning her career. But the way she had handled Seamus in the interview had almost taken his breath away. He made a mental note to try to not get on the wrong side of her. There was no telling what she might do.

As they entered the conference room, they heard animated voices coming from inside. Sergeant Ratcliffe and Ash Bradfield had finished with Lucky and were writing up his description of the suspect. As they wrote, Rachael compared it to their own list.

"White, male, late twenties, fair curly hair... does your witness agree with that, Sir? Ratcliffe asked Jujara, who nodded.

"Height about 5 foot 10 to 11?"

"Seamus said 5 foot 9 or thereabouts, so put the whole range down."

"Irish?"

"From a small place called Letterfrack, Galway. Check."

"Anything else? Lucky was seven sheets to the wind, and the offer of the money distracted him somewhat..." Ash Bradfield said, reading through his notes.

"Did he say how the money was given to them? By hand, or in an envelope?" Jujara asked.

"He didn't recall. Said it was there, on the table. Lucky said Seamus pocketed it and gave him slightly less than half. Reckoned that Lucky owed him." This was from Ratcliffe, who turned from writing on the whiteboard to look at the inspector.

"Are you thinking about prints, Sir?" Rachael piped up, determined to be in on the conversation. The other three looked at her, and she felt suddenly self-conscious, but carried on regardless." I mean, he wouldn't have been holding gloves in the pub, and if he took the money out of his wallet, there must be prints."

"Seamus said he spent most of his. Rent, food, cigarettes. It might be possible to track down his landlord and see if he still has the money, but the chances are slim."

"Lucky said he got a hit with his share. No chance of finding it if that's the case." Ratcliffe shrugged and turned back to the board. Jujara broke the silence.

"It's a lot of resources. We will leave it to DI Smallwood to make the final decision on it. He gave Rachael a half-smile and sat down to read a report that had just been handed to him. Rachael was left staring into the space above his head. She felt a little deflated: yes, on the one hand it was a clue, but the chances of finding anything viable on the money were minimal to say the least. She hoped to God that these weren't the fine margins that the case rested on.

Her reverie was broken by the very late arrival of lunch- a couple of platters of assorted rolls and sandwiches, a couple of large bags of crisps, something that Smallwood had organised before he'd gone out. But where was he, thought Rachael?

He turned the car of the small country road onto an even smaller farm track. Bumping along it, he thought back of all the times he had cycled all over the countryside. Back when he was becoming a teenager, he and his mates had trekked for miles, exploring everywhere they could. To his mind it had seemed like an endless summer packed with adventure after adventure; one day they would be knights in search of damsels in distress, other times they were pirates fighting across rivers for control of territory and the possibility of treasure.

But it was dark now, the tracks had become overgrown and all the treasure had long ago been lost. Edging forward, he found the place he had been looking for, and pulled over. He sat there, listening to the night-time sounds like the wind sighing through branches of unseen trees overhead, the occasional hoot of an owl, or the cry of a fox.

He went in search of Tori's last resting place and found it about twenty yards away from the car. An old dilapidated barn, with a collapsed roof at one end, the tiles having slipped off to expose old, grey wooden rafters. Satisfied that no-one was around, he went back to the car, and started to remove the articles he would need- the bag containing the duvet cover, and Tori's work bag. Balancing the latter on one knee, he searched to the bottom, where he had placed a torch beforehand. Flicking it on, he dazzled himself for a moment. Cursing, he dropped the bag, and stared out into the night for a while until the halo of light disappeared from his inner eye. When his sight had settled down again, he reached into the bag once more. This time he retrieved a flick knife, which he put in his pocket. He opened one of the rear doors and looked inside to see the inert, crumpled body of the masseuse inside. His mind registered no emotion at all. She was collateral damage; a pawn in this game of chess he was playing, an ends to a means. He couldn't even blame her parents for christening her the way they had- it was just unfortunate.

Grabbing her ankles, he pulled her out as if she was a big sack of potatoes, or an unwanted roll of carpet. Taking no particular attention to what she was being dragged through, or whether her back was scuffed or scratched on the dry mud path, he dragged her to the open doorway of the old barn. Laying her down, he switched his torch on and splayed the light around inside until he had found what he needed. A sloping shelf enabled him to place the torch adequately to illuminate where he intended to leave her. It was an old water trough, six fix long and about two feet wide. Nodding with satisfaction to himself, he opened the carrier bag containing the duvet cover, and set about his gruesome business.

CHAPTER 9

When the four detectives had gone to interview Lucky and Seamus, Smallwood was at a loss as what to do first. The conference room was a hive of activity, with everyone assigned tasks. He had a long list of things to do, which he mentally scanned down. Knowing what he wanted from his team, and them from him- strong effective management, logical decision making, and a swift conclusion to the case.

"Dave, have you got the number for Chorley station? I'm going to give their head of CID a courtesy call." DS David Tunicliffe was sweating profusely, even though it wasn't hot. It was more to do with his size. God knew how he kept passing his medical every year, but he made a wonderful administrator, which is why Jim had made him office manager for this case. Every scrap of information received would flow through him to be redistributed to whoever needed it. He was the axis of this investigation, the fulcrum which decided how successful this investigation would be; Jim placed great faith on those broad shoulders. David passed over a scrap of paper to Jim which contained the number of the station, the CID number and even the name Jim would need to speak to.

Thanking him, Jim went along the corridors of the station until he reached the relative calm of his own office and settled down behind his own desk to make the call. As he dialled the number with one hand, the other rubbed his face. When it connected, he was surprised to hear a female voice on the other end.

"DI Terry Schofield." A pleasant, warm voice, which seemed tense and annoyed.

"Good afternoon, Detective Inspector. This is D.I. James Smallwood from the Harpenden Station, in Hertfordshire." He had tried hard to keep the surprise from his voice.

"Good afternoon. What can I do for you- oh hang on a moment, please?" The phone was being held against some kind of

83

clothing whilst the Inspector obviously dealt with another pressing problem. After about half a minute, the voice came back on the line.

"Sorry about that, Smallwood. Bloody chaos here- we've got the decorators in. Only no arse upstairs told us they'd brought it forward by a week. One of my sergeants almost drank a cup of paint stripper."

"You northerners are tough enough to survive that, or so I'm told." This was met by a hearty laugh on the end of the line. "Anyway, I'm calling mainly as a courtesy about one of yours we've ended up with down here. Mr. Samuel Obadiah Taylor. Has any member of our team contacted you yet?"

"Yes- it was why Pete almost stripped his throat. Don't have many murders in this neck of the woods." She laughed again.

Jim gave a small grunt in reply. "Well, I was seeing if it wasn't too much of an imposition on your team to do some digging." He asked. He didn't really want to send two members of his team on a 500-mile round trip for what he routine background information.

"That's absolutely fine, chuck- I mean Inspector. Sorry." An embarrassed laugh this time down the line. "In fact, mebbe you can do us a favour?"

"Anything, Inspector, even it means you calling me 'chuck'."

"Well, here's the thing. My boss reckons that we should send someone down to you. Seeing as it was one of ours, and all." There was a pause, as Jim thought about it.

"I don't know how that would be a problem at all." The more the merrier, Jim thought.

"What's the price of bed and breakfasts down there, then?"

Jim thought for a moment. "I have four spare bedrooms if you're not averse to a bit of southern hospitality." I'm sure I can put up a guest for a night or two." Jim envisaged a night out with a grizzly beer swilling detective and surprised himself to find that he was enjoying the prospect.

"Good. I'll be down around eight tonight then. You won't have left by then? Not planning a night at the opera or anything? See you then. Ta-ra, chuck." The line went dead, leaving Jim open-mouthed, but with a hint of a grin forming. He replaced the line shaking his head. The inspector herself was coming down. He wondered if he was in the same boat, whether or not Laird would be so accommodating. Probably not, on balance, he reflected.

The lightness of the moment passed as Jim pulled himself out of his daydream and bustled back to the conference room. Checking in that all the team were occupied, he told David that he was off to the crime scene. He looked over to where Rick Chesterfield was finishing up a telephone call. He asked he wanted to accompany him.

"Sure, I could do with stretching my legs." He caught the look that Jim was giving him. "And also stretching my little grey brain cells." He tapped the side of his head. "Shall I drive?"

"Do you still have the old Capri?" Jim asked tentatively, unsure if he wanted to be driven to the scene as if it was a warm-up for the British Grand Prix.

"Yes, Sir. We will take it slow, Guv, I promise."

"Guv?"

"He thinks he's Dennis Waterman from the Sweeney, Sir." David interjected without looking up. Jim looked at the back of his head and nodded. He stopped in front of Rick, craning his neck to look at him. He whispered conspiratorially, "Ever call me 'Guv' again and I'll tell that nice girl in the typing pool that you've got the hots for her." He smiled sweetly as Rick looked down on him, gulping like a fish without air. "And that you wear brown nylon pants AND that you still live with your mum". With a final gulp, Rick bounded after him. He almost careered into Jim outside.

"Pick me up outside Harby's, Chesterfield. I'm going to order lunch." Jim headed to the main stairs, via Laird's office. He just wanted to give him a quick update but was informed by his ferocious secretary Pamela that the Super was attending a lunch with the local Rotary group.

Ten minutes later, they were unclipping their seat belts. Jim said, in a low voice, "My first car was one of these...in canary yellow." Rick's eyebrows rose so high they looked like they were making a dash for it into his scalp. Jim carried on, a distant look in his eye now: "Crashed her into a wall in Durham. Shame that. Come on."

After signing in with a bored looking uniformed officer, they found the M and M's, talking in the narrow hallway. They stopped and greeted the new arrivals.

"Just going out for a cigarette, Sir. Care to join us, we can tell you what we've found." One of the M and M's, Mark, said. Jim retraced his steps. Mike shared his fags around, and they all took one, no-one saying anything for a minute or so as they inhaled deeply, enjoying the moment. Jim spoke up.

"What've we got then, lads?" He looked expectantly at first Mike, then Mark. It was the latter that spoke.

"Not much, to be honest." Mark looked a little miffed. "There is virtually nothing. The place doesn't really look like anyone has been living there. Minimal furniture, very few personal effects... it's kind of like..." His voice trailed off, as he looked into the distance, searching for the right words.

"Imagine your Nan has died, Sir." Mike took over. Jim wondered where this was going but let him continue. Rick just looked confused. "And your parents have taken all the good stuff away, all the knick-knacks and such like." He looked to his partner for confirmation. Mark was pumping his head up and down enthusiastically.

"Anything else?"

"Well, there was a jacket and pair of shoes, that the SOCOs took away. They said that the body was missing both, and they didn't want to presume, so they have sent them for analysis." The two officers shared a look. Mark continued. "They found a handprint. On the carpet, in shit."

"In shit?" the Inspector looked confused.

"The SOCOs said that it was shit. He reckoned that someone wearing a glove of some sort put a hand on the carpet. A glove that was covered in shit, Sir." Mark fixed his Inspector with a stare, daring him to contradict what he was saying. Jim didn't quite know what to do with that little snippet of information.

"Anyway, they've taken a sample of it, to compare with the deceased. There is evidence of shit in the washbasin in the bathroom, and a dirty flannel on the floor."

"As if the suspect was washing his hands, eh?" The Inspector was musing out loud, but the two detectives nodded along.

Cigarettes finished, Jim thanked them and suggested that they head back to the station to make a full report, and lunch. Jim and Rich exchanged glances, and Jim asked "Nervous?"

"I'd be lying if I said I wasn't." Rick shifted his weight from one foot to the other.

"Me too. Come on." They re-entered the flat, heading straight for the bedroom. They came to a halt on the threshold. Jim handed Rick a manila folder.

"Tell me what you see. Or rather, what you don't see any more. Take your time, this isn't an exam." Rick opened the folder, licking his lips. Withdrawing a photo, he looked at it, the room, and the picture again. He cleared his throat.

"Everything, Sir?"

"Everything, Chesterfield."

"Well, the duvet cover with the body." There was a pause. "The coat on the armchair. The shoes at the bottom of the bed. Another pause, longer this time. "The curtains are open, but still there. I can't see anything else, Sir. Sorry." Rick hung his head.

Jim turned to him. "Don't worry, son. Anything else would make you a better detective than me." Rick looked up to see the inspector smiling; a kind, fatherly smile. He instantly perked up, a warm feeling in his stomach.

"Anything that is here that maybe is a bit incongruous? Remember, the decor and ... style of the furnishings suggest ...a certain age of individual lived here." Jim looked up at the young detective to see him looking past him, at the picture on the wall. He nodded in agreement. He stepped over to get a closer look, warning Rick to avoid the shit staining the carpet, nicely marked by a little piece of numbered plastic, left by the SOCOs. Rick followed him. It turned out to be a nothing more than a print of a photograph of the Empire State Building, taken, according to a small label, in

1957. There were dustings of black fingerprint powder, left by the examiners. A couple of small, smudged prints left the Inspector none the wiser.

Satisfied, the inspector looked in the wardrobe and then the bedside drawer cabinet, finding nothing of interest, apart from more black powder. Rick was on all fours to look under the bed. He waited until Rick stood up, shaking his head.

"Nothing much here then. Let's try the other bedroom." They went through and found even less in there to hold their interest, then the bathroom, and the kitchen. Rick looked under the sink while Jim looked in the cupboards in the kitchen. They shook their heads at each other when back in the hallway.

"Thoughts, Rick?" Jim intentionally used the detectives' first name, because he was impressed with his diligence and alertness. Jim had formulated the opinion that he was shaping up well, just needing a bit of encouragement. He was well aware that Rick came in for a lot of ribbing from the others back at the station, whether because of his car, his beanpole like frame, his prominent Adams' apple, or his youth and inexperience. It was Laird who had suggested that he should join the team investigating the murder, a move which Jim had initially greeted skeptically. Now he had changed his mind.

Rick exhaled noisily and shrugged. "It's like the killer just rented this place to dump the body. Doesn't even look like he lived here."

"Which means?"

"I suppose he lives somewhere else... could indicate he has a bit of money behind him. I mean didn't he offer those two lads a fair whack just to come here?"

Jim regarded him again. That was something he had already thought of himself, but he was really impressed that Chesterfield had got there as well.

"So?"

Rick, taking encouragement from the fact that the Inspector was listening to him, thought for a moment before carrying on.

Then he exhaled loudly, before saying quietly, "Not really sure, Boss." He looked at the ground, embarrassed.

"You're doing very well, I must say." Jim patted him on the arm encouragingly." How about we just finish off the lounge whilst we're on a roll, eh?"

"I guess so, Sir... do you really thing I'm doing ok?"

"I do, indeed. I wouldn't say it otherwise." Jim offered a consoling smile.

They filed into the last room that they hadn't investigated yet. "Ah. Life at last. Of a sort." Looking round the room, at first glance, things looked a bit more hopeful. There was a sofa, an armchair, a small dining table set with two chairs, a television in one corner, and next to that a big cabinet, a G-plan unit, judging by its look. He crossed over to it to investigate further, indicating that Rick could start at the mantelpiece.

"Shout out what you're finding, Chesterfield." Jim said over his shoulder.

"I've got two photos, either side of a carriage clock..."

"Photos of what, exactly?" Jim was mildly disappointed to find his cabinet only contained a couple of books. He picked one up, flicking through it. Nothing incriminating fell out of its' pages. Chesterfield kept up his running commentary, although his voice seemed to grow a bit reflective, Jim thought.

"The one on the left seems to show a girl smiling into the camera, on board a ferry, or ship." Rick was back to enjoying himself. "Shall I take it out of the frame?"

"No. We'll take it back to the station. And you'll get fingerprint powder on your hands. Devil of a job to wash it off." Jim responded, having turning his attention to the second book, a hardback that had fallen on its side. He took it out, and flicked through it, with the same negative result.

"Second photograph shows a youth the same sort of age as the girl. Giving an artful look out of a train window. Looks a bit 'arty' if you ask me."

"Like it has been staged for effect, you mean, detective?" Jim had turned to look at Chesterfield, bent over the mantelpiece. The young officer turned to look over his shoulder, a faint blush on his face.

"That's a much better way of putting it, Sir. Sorry."

Jim shrugged his shoulders as to suggest that he didn't care either way and turned to put the second book back, next to its companion. It was only after having done so that he noticed it.

"That's odd." He had said to himself, but Rick heard him anyway and echoed what he had said, looking over.

"There are only two books in this whole flat." Jim reached into the cabinet, and retrieved both of them, holding them up, one in each hand, for Rick to see. "Something called 'Good Times' by a fellow called... Andrei Birdovski". He looked at each and then at Rick.

"Is that a condom?" Jim peered at the small blue plastic packet Rick held.

"Yeah... it was just inside this cute little pot here." Rick pointed to a porcelain pot. He looked closer at a little picture painted on it. "From a place called Lijiang. Never heard of it." His brows were knitted in concentration.

"Never heard of it?" Jim put the books back in their place. "What did they teach you in school? Never mind, don't answer that." Jim was never going to admit that he had no idea of where it was either.

Neither detective found much else of interest. The cabinet drawers had nothing in them apart from dust. Jim crouched on his haunches and opened both of the lower cabinet doors at the same time, finding anything a solitary board game, also collecting dust, and the ubiquitous black fingerprinting powder. He stood up, stretching his back as he did so. He turned to see Rick peering down the gap between the sofa and the wall.

"There's something down here... no I can't quite reach it. Can you give me a hand, Sir?" the inspector crossed over to where Rick was standing at one end of the sofa. Together they heaved it away from the wall about four inches, which was enough to enable Rick to get his whole arm and shoulder in.

"Got it!" A red-faced Rick was holding a up a large piece of fluffy fur as if it was the World Cup. He was beaming.

"What IS it?" Jim was more intrigued than excited.

"It's a cuddly toy of some sort." Jim rolled his eyes. Maybe Chesterfield was going backwards after all. Not to be deterred, Rick placed it gingerly on his open palm, examining it more closely.

"It seems to be a stuffed baby kangaroo wearing a tiny t-shirt." Rick was peering at miniscule writing on the clothing. "Dunk-A-Roo's." He exclaimed excitedly, looking at his boss. Jim cocked his head slightly, a blank look on his face. "It's a clue! It has to be." There was no dampening his enthusiasm now. He handed it over to the Inspector. "Look."

Jim took the proffered soft toy, took one look at it and placed it on the sofa, shaking his head. "No." He said quietly.

"No?" A crestfallen Chesterfield enquired.

"A soft toy that has fallen down the back of an old sofa, and probably lain there for years?"

Jim stated softly. He raised an eyebrow at Rick. Then, feeling bad, he relented. He sighed.

"Right, make a note to bring it along. With the two photo frames and the pot." Out of the corner of his eye, he saw Rick smiling again, confidence restored.

"It can't have been there years. Sydney is only two or three years old."

Jim gave him a hard stare through half-closed eyelids. "It's only a toy. Definitely not real."

But Rick was adamantly shaking his head. Knowing that he was going to regret it, Jim simply asked, "What?"

Rick had bent down to retrieve the toy, putting it in his open palm again. "Dunk-A-Roo's, see? They are an American, no Canadian snack. And little Sydney here is the mascot." Rick switched his attention back from the toy to his Inspector. "And they only started making them a couple of years ago." He looked defensively at Jim. "I know biscuits."

Jim was impressed, truly so. He put out his arm and tapped Rick on the lapel with a finger. "I owe you a pint, Rick. Impressive." Rick blushed. "Come on, I think we've done here."

One of the SOCOs was just finishing up outside, checking his case. Jim put a hand up to make sure he didn't scuttle off prematurely.

"Sorry, I know you've been here for hours," The Inspector flashed one of his cheery smiles. "There's just a couple of items I need bagging up. One of the constables can make sure they reach the station- there is no need for you to make a detour." As he outlined to the SOCO which items he needed, he saw Rick furtively smoking a cigarette. He chuckled to himself, with a small shake of the head. Thanking the SOCO again with a pat on the arm, he strode off to the Capri, saying to Rick over his shoulder, "Come on."

CHAPTER 10

Fatigue overwhelmed him. He struggled as far as a sofa and gave up, sinking into its warm familiarity as if it was the arms of a long-lost lover. He drifted into a deep slumber, waking several hours later with a start, the familiar sights of his bedroom not around him, and he momentarily panicked. Where was he? He calmed down as he remembered the few hours prior to falling asleep. He'd finished with the body, cleared away any incriminating evidence before retracing his steps to the car, sighing deeply as he did so.

There was no space for feelings of remorse anywhere in his brain. No remorse meant no relief for what he had done. It wasn't relief from grief, either. He didn't grieve for those he had killed- how could he? They had made him; he had unmade them. That much was straightforward, cause and effect. If there was any relief, it was because everything had gone to plan.

He had driven carefully until he had seen the bright lights of the airport diffusing the night air with their sodium softness. He had deposited the car in a dark corner of the long-term car park, and then walked in the direction of the terminal buses. Along the way he had used one of the carrier bags to put his gloves in and tossed them into a bin, all scrunched up, with a couple of empty sandwich wrappers and a carton of drink that had been discarded on the floor. He put his hand into another carrier and used that to carry the masseuses' bag that contained her work stuff, her handbag and his tools. As he joined the back of the queue, he studied the people in front of him, trying to imagine their lives. He'd got on the bus and settled down at the back.

He got off two stops early and waited until the it had pulled away, pretending to be getting his bearings. The hill he'd had to walk up had been longer and steeper than he had anticipated. The adrenaline had long worn off, and he felt weary to his bones as he eventually reached his destination. He had fumbled a key into the lock and dragged himself into the lounge.

All this came flooding back as he had awoken. He stretched, then looked around him on the sofa. He had knocked a cushion out of place, so replaced it and stood up. He yearned for a coffee but that would have to wait. He started to search for a diary, which he guessed would be in the room at the back that Tori used for home clients. Going in, he edged around her full length, all-singing, all dancing massage table to get to a desk situated against the back wall, and on it, her day planner, open to the day before. He scanned the page, and read that Tori was meant to be having lunch with someone called Yvonne at 1pm. There was an appointment scheduled for 4pm but it had been crossed through neatly with a red pen. Underneath was written 'cancelled – holiday in Ibiza till 17th!'

He re-read the lunch date entry again. That could be a problem, he reflected. But then again, maybe not. He often thought that when one door closed, another one opened. So what if Yvonne had started to worry about her friend not showing? Maybe she had presumed another client had phoned at the last moment. Placing himself in her friends' shoes, he stared at the wall behind the desk and considered what he would do. Call round? Or simply telephone? He found a telephone on the top of the desk. It was modern, with a built-in answering machine. A small red light pulsed on the machine, next to a label entitled 'messages'. He pressed the button and a female voice came on the line; "You have two new messages. Message One..." There was a slight pause on the other end, and a male voice came on the line." Ah...yes hello, Ms. Henderson... Mr Atwood from Atwood and Son. Your essential oils will be ready for collection tomorrow. Thank you." There was a beep and the machine continued: "Message Two. "Vonney here. Sorry you missed lunch- it was fabulous, and there was a dishy new waiter who kept me occupied. Your loss! You could've called me though, although you probably had a rush-" The tape clicked off. Yvonne had probably run out of time. He deleted it.

He closed the desk planner and studied a host of little fluorescent squares of paper stuck to various parts of the desk.

He read them all, but none of them were of much importance – 'remember Auntie Audrey birthday, 7th August' read one, 'cat sitting 23-27th' was another. None of them were of any relevance to him. Satisfied that he had everything he needed, he poked his head into the kitchen briefly, checking for cat litter trays or food bowls, but there weren't any to be found. He didn't want a pesky pooch fouling his plans up. Satisfied, he let himself out, closing the door behind him softly.

An hour later, he was letting himself him into his own place. He had dropped items from her bag into various bins, leaving only his own stuff, and the work planner in it. He had a full couple of hours before the landscape gardener was coming to have a look at his neighbour's trees.

"You did well kid." Jim said when they reached the station.

"Thank you very much, Sir. Only trying to do my best and learn my craft."

"Well, keep doing as you are, and you'll go far, I'm sure. Processing a murder scene can be a quite difficult thing."

"Good thing I'm with the master then!" Rick, laughed nervously, looking at his boss, who smirked in return, slowly shaking his head.

"Glad to see you're taking this so seriously, Smallwood." The booming voice of Nan Parker echoed along the corridors from where he stood outside the conference room.

"A brief moment of levity, Sir." He came to a stop in front of the ACC. He waited for Rick to head into the conference before resuming. "Look, Sir, one thing I realise in this world of absolute horror is the humanity of us all. We are all human, with worries, hopes, fears. But keeping the morale high in my team under trying circumstances is important to me. I know that a happy team is a productive team, and a productive team is one that get results. So an occasional moment of laughter is in order, I believe." Parker blustered, but knew his junior may have a point. "Just don't let the public, let alone the press catch you doing it, or I'll have your guts for garters, understand, man?" He gave a half-smile that caused his luxurious handlebar moustache to quiver slightly. He nodded curtly and turned away, but then half turned back and said, "My opposite number in Lancashire informs me they're sending an Inspector to observe, is that right?"

"That's correct, Sir."

"Well, make he doesn't get under your feet, Jim."

"I'm sure she won't, Sir." A half smile, this time. It was met by a slight rise in Nan Parkers' bushy eyebrows, and another quiver of the moustache, as he nodded, and departed, tapping his gloves against his thighs to a military tattoo inside his head. Rachael came heading along the corridor. He noticed that she had a fading blush on her face. He enquired by inclining his head a little.

"ACC Parker, Sir. Just complimented me on my blouse, said that a looked like an English rose."

Jim took one look at the cerise silk shirt that she was wearing and inclined his head once more. "He's quite right of course, Constable. Though totally inappropriate."

Inside, Jim moved around the table, talking to each detective in turn, reading sheets of paper, looking at the whiteboards and generally taking stock. He straightened up after having a final chat with David.

"Listen up, folks, let's see where we're at. David, the floor is yours." Around the room people put pens down, finished telephone calls, stopped whatever they were reading, to give the Sergeant their full attention. David got unsteadily to his feet- he'd been sitting in the same chair, collating everything, and was stiff as a board. He cleared his throat, swallowing. "Enquiries into our victim are progressing with help from our friends in the north- "He paused, as Jim had raised his hand. "Yes Sir?"

"Just a quickie on that, Dave- sorry to interrupt- we have two of theirs coming down to observe. "Here he raised both hands to invert commas in the air, "Observe, and help if they can. I'm sure that we will offer every assistance to them. Sorry, Dave."

David nodded. "We hope to get initial reports soon on him, what he was like, where he used to go. Any interaction with the killer, that kind of thing. The police in Chorley promised an initial report before end of play today." He paused here to look at his watch and seemed surprised. Rachael looked at hers and was equally surprised that it was already 3.30.

"Toxicology results are in, and death has been confirmed as a massive injection of ketamine and heroin. Now the use of the first is interesting, if I may digress a bit, Sir?" Dave looked at his boss who shrugged and nodded at the same time. "Ketamine, used at such a high concentration as this, can cause numbness, loss of co-ordination, and most importantly, tachycardia. A doctor friend of mine assures me that its probable intended effect in this case was to speed up the rate in which the heroin was spread around. In this case the victim choked on his own vomit caused by convulsions which were in turn caused by the massive dose of the drug. The ketamine stopped him from reacting to it." David screwed up his face, looking down at his notes before resuming. "Now, getting the heroin would have been relatively simple, unfortunately. Those in the know would only have to go to Luton, say, and pick it up from the Feathers, or the Hope, for example. As far as we know, nobody is currently dealing it here." He looked around the table for DC Westlake. "Iain has been looking at the Ketamine. Please?"

Ian Westlake glanced briefly round the room. "I've been looking at thefts of Ketamine from veterinary practises in the last six months, the most likely source. Nothing in a twenty-mile radius so far so we are widening our search."

Inspector Jujara spoke up. "I can put you in touch with a mate at the Regional Crime Squad, who can tell you who to talk to at the other regional squads."

"I don't know why they don't have a national crime squad for this kind of thing." Rachael said, and was rewarded with a collective grunt of agreement from her colleagues.

"I hear it's coming, DC Read, maybe in a couple of years." She noticed that Jim was nodding silently from his perch on one of the side tables.

"Be that as it may, folks- and thanks for that Inspector, but let's get back on track here." David was saying. "Right, the duvet cover, and the tape. We are expecting the final report on the cover..." Here he tapped on the picture on the whiteboard, as if to get peoples' attention back, "...sometime tomorrow. I know, I know, but they are going as fast as they can at the lab. We discussed its provenance earlier, and we should know more soon. But for that, and the tape- which incidentally is just micropore tape and can be picked up at any chemist, I'm going to hand you over to the Inspector- Smallwood, that is." Tunicliffe stepped back against the wall so that everyone could concentrate on Jim.

"Because of the positioning of the body inside the duvet, and the use of tape over the eyes, we have decided to enlist the help of a forensic psychologist. Her name is Mary Guy and she's travelling up from Sussex University tomorrow for a consultation." He looked round at the assembled team and seemed to sense the next question and nodded. "I know we could have used someone from one of the local universities, but Superintendent Laird tells me she comes highly recommended, particularly in this field." He waved airily at the whiteboard behind him. "She will also assess the various other items we removed from the scene earlier. A copy of that report will depend on DC Chesterfield's typing speed." Rick blushed furiously. "If you're quick, you may be able to dictate it to one of the civilian staff before they go home. Go on." Rick, still blushing, excused himself and headed out.

Jim looked around the team. "Anyone got anything more to add? Rachael, are the witness statements available yet?"

"Yes, Sir. There's several copies on the side table there, and one in the folder." Rachael indicated a big folder, the 'murder' book. This one was the only blue folder, so as to signify its importance to the case.

"If I may, Rachael?" Jujara interjected, an eyebrow raised.

"Seamus folded very quickly and became quite helpful by the end." Here, Jujara flashed a quick smile in Rachael's direction. "They had obviously been duped into getting into the flat by someone they both referred to as Col." Jujara glanced at Sergeant

Ratcliffe, who had been interviewing Lucky. Ratcliffe nodded agreement. "They even agreed to giving a police artist an impression of what he looks like, to lessen any jail time."

"Although we can presume that Col isn't his real name, right?" Jim asked.

"Certainly an alias. I can't imagine someone going to the lengths that he did, just to give them his real name. He may even not be Irish, either."

Ratcliffe spoke up. "Lucky intimated that it was all down to Seamus that they went along with it at all." He looked at Jim. "although when I mentioned the money, he changed his tune."

"Good work, guys." Jim looked at all of them. "I personally think that the CPS will overlook any charges, if they're helping us now." He looked out of the window. "Well, I think that's probably all for now. Those in the middle of actions, finish up, and pick up again in the morning. Briefing at 8.15. Thank you for your hard work. We're going to catch this bastard, and hopefully really soon. Dave, you have anything urgent?"

David shook his head. "Nothing that can't wait, Sir." Jim nodded his thanks and signaled to the team that those who were to free to leave could do so. Several officers stood up, stretching stiff backs, preparing to leave. A few turned their attention to whatever had been occupying them.

"Just one last thing. DI Schofield from Chorley station will be with us this evening. I anticipate that we will find ourselves in the pub from about eight, if anyone is interested." There were several nods from the officers without girlfriends of wives. "Rachael, Inspector Jujara, a quick word in my office, please? Five minutes?" With that, he left, patting David amicably on the shoulder as he squeezed past.

Five minutes or so later, he was approaching his office, he heard laughter coming from inside. He wondered how anyone could find today amusing. He found Rachael seated at her desk, with Jujara leaning over her shoulder. They were laughing at something at the desk.

"Look, Sir, it's the Inspectors' children." She showed him the photograph. A little boy, aged about two by the look of him, stood close to the lens, and a girl, about seven, was poking her tongue out behind his shoulder. Jim smiled.

"Eshaal and Jimmy, aged six and two, last month in our back garden." Jujara was beaming with pride.

"Lovely, Mo." Jim reached over and shook him firmly by the hand. The father grinned from ear to ear, showing his perfect teeth. He nodded his thanks as he pocketed the photo. His expression changed suddenly as he focused again on why he was really here.

"What do we think, then?"

Jim sank into his chair. He puffed his cheeks out. "I really don't know. Any ideas, Rachael?" He looked across at her, swinging gently in her chair.

"Me, Sir? You're asking what I think?" Rachael asked, incredulous that both inspectors had asked her. Jujara spoke from behind her, where he was leaning against the wall.

"We value your input, DC Read. You are an integral part of this investigation. Obviously, we are asking what you think."

Rachael puffed out her cheeks, staring into space as she reflected on what she had learnt so far. "Well, we can presumably assume that the 'Col' that Seamus and Lucky met in the pub is the killer. And it's a fairly safe assumption that the killer was acting alone- "

"On what do you base that assumption?" Jim interjected.

"There was only him in the pub. There were no hints given in the pub. He said he was single."

"I'm afraid that doesn't mean anything."

"It's just..." Rachael frowned. Jujara stepped in to help.

"We need to ascertain his relationship with the deceased, if there was any." He said. "If anyone saw them together."

"Well- "

"Hunches are dangerous things, Rachael. However, in this case, I think you're right. There's something you can't always put a finger on. Maybe this forensic psychologist can confirm that." Jim said, his eyes twinkling.

"Is she a type of profiler then?" Rachael was enthused again. "I'm quite looking forward to meeting her, actually."

"I was going to do a little more on the case, just the three of us." Jim was saying." But seeing as you're right about this 'profiler' as you call her, I think it would be better to wait and hear what she has to say for herself first."

Mo made his farewells and departed. Rachael, gathering up her belongings, glanced at her boss. He was looking into space, brows furrowed, concentrating on something or other.

"Aren't you coming, Sir?"

Jim shook himself from his reverie and blinked twice before answering. "I'm just going to have forty winks or so before that Inspector Schofield shows up." The words had been spoken, but untrue, suspected Rachael. He was going to sit there and think.

"Do you want me to tag along tonight?"

"No, you're alright. Go home and disengage for a while. Recharge your batteries. Thanks for all the good work you've done today."

Rachael nodded, slung her bag over her shoulder, and left Jim to his own devices.

He was sound asleep in seconds.

CHAPTER 11

He never failed to be amazed by just how good he felt after only a couple of hours sleep. He leaped out from under his duvet and put some fresh coffee on to brew before taking a shower. Checking the time as he got out, he put on an old faded pair of jeans, a t-shirt, and old trainers. He didn't have long to wait. 'Polite, Professional and Punctual' was the logo emblazoned on the side of the flatbed truck that hove into view.

Stepping out of his front door, he watched as the tall, angular gardener jumped down from his vehicle and strode up his neighbour's garden path. He languidly walked down his own path as the gardener rang the doorbell, waited, and then tried the knocker. There was no reply. Standing with his arms on his hips the tall man looked around to see a stranger in an ancient t-shirt walking up the path, smiling at him.

"Mr. Hall? I'm Jimmy, Sid and Ethel's neighbour." He said, nodding towards his own house. "I'm sorry, but they're not in. They were called away late last night- apparently their grandson has been involved in a motorcycle accident down in Brighton. Sid called round and explained the situation. Ethel was in a bit of a state, as you can imagine."

"Oh my God!" Exclaimed Mr Hall. "Is the lad alright?" A look of concern crossed the weather-beaten face of the gardener.

He shook his head and shrugged. "I don't know, I haven't heard from them yet." His own face showed equal concern. "I sincerely hope so- they dote on little Adam." He paused, looking at the ground, chewing his lip. Actually, Adam didn't exist. Today was the day that week in, week out, Sid and Ethel went to visit her sister in Aylesbury. They wouldn't be back to early evening.

"I'd better call back then sometime." The gardener's expression was an odd mixture of vexation and sympathy. He sighed, as if weighing up how much this job was worth to him.

"Oh no, I have the spare key, and Sid explained- hurriedly, mind you- what he wanted done. But I think you know what the job

is, don't you?" He asked the gardener. "And I have the money." He said tapping a bulge in his jeans. "Shall we?"
"I'll just get my tools from the van then."
"Might be easier if you park round the rear. You know, for the branches and other rubbish." He explained how to get the van round the back and that he'd meet him round there to open the back gate. "I'll put the kettle on. Sugar in your tea?" He asked.
"Just milk. Thanks." The gardener had swung himself back into the cab of his van and he watched as it lumbered off. He let himself in, even whistling a jaunty little tune as if he hadn't a care in the world. He filled the kettle and looking out, he saw the van edging along the track. He used a tea towel to turn the back-door key. He'd been here dozens of times before, so his prints would be all over the kitchen, but no reason for them to be on any key to the back garden. He used the tea towel to open the bolt at the bottom of the garden, before nonchalantly throwing it over his shoulder as Mr. Hall appeared the other side of the gate.
"There you go, Mr .Hall. Tea won't be a minute." He said.
"Thanks once again. And call me Chris." The tall gardener said. "Alright if I leave my tools on that table?"
He nodded and turned to fetch the tea. "Chris it is then."
As if he didn't know already.

Jim dropped two Alka Seltzer into his water and groaned. His head pounded, and his eyes stared back from his bathroom mirror, blood stained and questioning him as to why he had allowed them to get in such a state.
"Where's the brown sauce?" A voice bellowed from downstairs. With a last look in the mirror, Jim downed the still fizzing water and went to meet his house guests. The smell of frying bacon threatened to turn his stomach. Standing over the cooker was DI Terry Schofield, already in her work clothes, pushing sausages round his best frying pan. His apron protected her clothes from any splashes.

103

"Tea is in the pot on the table. Took Ronnie ages to find, mind." She was watching the sausages, turned to look at him, and turned back. "By 'eck, tha's rough." Reaching under the grill, she pulled a huge glass casserole dish out that had been gently warming, piled to the brim with bacon, black pudding, mushrooms, tomatoes, and eggs, both fried and scrambled. She put it on the table and sat down, laughing again.

"Dig in, pet. I always swear by a good breakfast first thing after a little drink." She smiled, her eyes twinkling.

"Where's all this come from?" Jim sat, gesturing at the food.

"Oh, I suspected that you wouldn't have anything in. Your voice sounded thin." She winked at her sergeant, as she ladled copious amounts of food onto Jim's plate, then her own.

There was plenty left for Ronnie.

"Ronnie has cleaned up the lounge as well." She said over a mouthful of sausage. "I've got him house trained." She winked. Sergeant Ronnie Bimjano concentrated on his food.

Jim started by gingerly putting a small morsel into his mouth. Soon he was wolfing it down, as if he hadn't eaten in days. Slowly, flashback by flashback, he was putting the events of the evening before back together.

He had been dozing at his desk when he became aware of a car horn impatiently tooting outside. By the time he was fully awake, his telephone was ringing. The front desk sergeant was struggling to make himself heard over what sounded like a riot erupting in the foyer. All Jim managed to hear were the words 'loud', 'blonde' and 'help'. Shrugging himself into his jacket, Jim jogged down the stairs to find out what the ruckus was about. Reaching the front desk, he stared through the glass safety window at a large, blonde woman talking very loudly whilst throwing her arms about like a giant windmill. Behind her, a bronzed lad with short black hair stood watching her with a blank expression on his Mediterranean face. Jim was torn between letting his desk sergeant deal with it whilst making himself scarce. He was about to beat a hasty retreat when the blonde saw him and fixed him with a stare.

"...And don't think you can be sloping off, chuck. Are you in charge hereabouts?" A hand with long scarlet nails thrust itself through the gap in the window. "D.I. Terry Schofield." Jim tentatively put out his own hand and felt as if he had put it in a vice. He was sure that his bones would crack, when the grip was released as the hand withdrew to point behind the woman. "And this lummox is my bagman, Ronnie." The aforementioned Ronnie raised his eyebrows apologetically in Jim's direction in lieu of saying anything. He smiled back whilst surreptitiously trying to massage some feeling back into his other hand.

"Welcome, Inspector. You're a tad early, you made good time on the motorway..."

"The only thing I intend to be late for is my funeral, chuck," interrupted Inspector Schofield as she barged past him in a cloud of perfume that almost made Jim choke. "Oh be a good chap, bring me case, will you? This way is it?" She was off bustling up the stairs, as Jim went to pick up a suitcase heavy enough for a family of four's summer holiday.

"She always like this?" Jim looked at Ronnie, who grinned.

"She gets louder when she's had a drink, Sir. Sergeant Ronnie Bimjano." Jim mouthed 'louder? Really?' at him, noticing he was carrying a normal sized case with him.

Ronnie looked at him quizzically and said, "We can always find a bed and breakfast, Sir, if you'd prefer." His voice had a soft, Italian burr to it that Jim was sure would drive the ladies around here crazy.

"Well, to be honest, I've got more than enough room. But judging by the weight of this case, I may have to get the floorboards strengthened." He turned and heaved the case through the door and started to lug it upstairs, as Ronnie chuckled behind him. Reaching his office, Schofield was sitting in his chair, looking around her with a curious look on her face.

She had the eyes of a hawk, taking in everything and missing nothing. She smiled as Jim gratefully dropped the case by the door and started massaging his arm.

"Who's the Genesis fan? Bit poofy, aren't they?" Jim opened his mouth to protest but couldn't think of any retort, so shut it again. He felt the blood rushing back into his arm and just felt grateful for that instead. Schofield stood up.

"Let's be having a look at this incident room then, chuck. You have got an incident room, I take it?" She glared at Jim and looked around the room as if she expected it to be lurking in one of the cupboards.

"This way, Inspector." Jim indicated. He was enveloped by the fog of perfume as Terry squeezed past him. He was sure that she was brushing herself against him as she did it. She raised one eyebrow at him as if to suggest that given the chance, she'd eat him for breakfast. Jim blushed and glanced at Ronnie, who seemed to be fascinated by a spot on the ceiling above. Schofield marched along, her arms swinging and her ample buttocks swaying as she sashayed down the corridor, her surprisingly slim ankles above four-inch stilettos. Jim was flabbergasted as to what to make of her. The brief conversation he'd managed with Superintendent Laird about her hadn't revealed much beyond a lot of non-committal shrugs. He'd missed his superior's smirk when he'd left.

He'd trotted along after her until they reached the conference room. Luckily, it was deserted- all the team having departed to their families or microwave dinners or pub. Schofield went around the table, looking at everything. Pausing by the main whiteboard, studying the photo of Sam Taylor. Nothing was said. Ronnie sidled past Jim and picked up one of the manila folders containing the photos of the crime scene. Schofield was gazing at the photo with its taped shut eyes, and a sad look crossed her face. Jim was surprised- he had thought of her previously as only a loud, brash woman used to getting her own way. Now, as he looked at her looking at the victim, he saw a softer side to her. She felt his gaze and their eyes met briefly, before she turned and replaced the photo on the board. She skimmed through the murder book. She spent a couple of minutes looking at it then shut it up and looked at Jim.

"Nasty wee bugger, chuck. You'd better stop him quick."
"I thought you were here to help."
"Aye, but it's your case. We are only here to observe."
"Officially." Jim smiled and was rewarded with one in return.

"But that's for tomorrow. Tonight, I've got a fair parch on. Show me to your local watering hole." They had proceeded to the pub, and a few of the team had popped in to introduce themselves. As Jim recollected, Terry was like a flame, and all Jim's officers were like moths to it, one by one they had gotten too close and were burned. After the pub, the three of them repaired to Jim's home, where they set about his favourite malt, the two Inspectors swapping tales as if they were old army veterans. Ronnie settled into a soft snoring sleep whilst they talked deep into the night.

Which is why he found himself scoffing a hearty breakfast and drinking hot sweet tea. He pushed his plate back, fit to bursting. He felt better- his headache gone, his stomach settled, if not stretched. Ronnie got up and started the clearing away and washing up. Jim made a mental note to himself to ask him why he did all the menial tasks without even being asked to. Terry lit a cigarette and offered Jim one. He thought about it for a moment, then accepted.

"Seems bad, doesn't it, smoking, drinking tea, stuffing ourselves when that poor man is hardly cold on the slab, eh chuck?" Jim gave a shrug of his shoulders as if to agree. "Well it shouldn't!" Terry slapped the table with an upturned palm. The noise was so terrific that Ronnie even dropped one of the mugs back into the washing-up bowl with a clatter. Jim almost fell off his chair with surprise. They both stared at her.

"We're only bloody mortals, after all. We get paid to do all this dirty work, sorting out the scum of the earth and making sure they never see the light of day again! Paid, chuck- we're not angels doing this for free. We're due a break as much as the next man. Now come on, let's go and catch this snotbag." With a final emphatic snort of smoke from her nostrils, she pummeled the cigarette butt to death in the ashtray. She swept out of the room and down the hallway, where she impatiently waited for the others to catch up.

She was looking through the small stained-glass window set in the front door, her breath partially steaming it up. "Beautiful Azaleas, Jim." Her rant of two minutes previously had been supplanted by a tranquil, almost serene intonation.

"Thank you, Terry." She had insisted that they used first names out of the office, when she had been sitting in the pub the previous evening. "I must admit I have a little man come around once a week. I don't often the time to do it all myself."

"A little man? Like a hobbit?" Terry was teasing him.

"Hobbits aren't men." Ronnie and Jim said in unison and laughed as they left the house.

The kettle was boiled, the tea made. But only one mug stood steaming on Ethel's Formica top. Chris wouldn't be drinking his. He watched the gardener put on a pair of ear defenders prior to checking his electric saw. Chris had his back to the house, standing in front of a sprawling ash tree. He didn't see Jimmy dart out of the kitchen to his bag of tools. He certainly wasn't aware of him picking up a club hammer in his tea-towel wrapped hand and advance towards him. All he felt was an overwhelming feeling of pain sweep over him as the hammer connected with the back of his skull with enough force to stop an elephant. He pitched forward two of Sid's beloved roses, dead before he hit the ground.

He squatted down to check that Chris was really dead. Sightless eyes stared out point-blank at a tiny bunch of violets. Satisfied that Chris had pruned his last bush, he reached out and carefully removed the gardener's heavy work gloves, careful to avoid getting any prints on anything but the coarse fabric and leather of the gloves. He put them on and flexed his fingers inside them. Not too large. He looked at the man he had just killed. He didn't feel pity, no remorse. He was a necessary kill, a means to an end.

He yanked the body up by the collar of the polo shirt Chris was wearing. With a strength that impressed himself, he swung the larger man round and dumped him on the tarpaulin that Chris had spread out to collect his rubbish. He wrapped him in the tarp and left him, going into the kitchen and using the tea towel to lock the kitchen door, going back and through his own garden, he unlatched his gate and let himself back into Sid's garden. He straightened the rose that Chris has partially flattened in his fall. He hoped that Sid wouldn't notice. He looked around once more to ensure that nobody else was about. Mid-morning, in the back yards of suburban houses in a quiet town, nothing really happened. Only one housewife had hanging washing. The fences, mature bushes, trees and garages hid most gardens from each other. He carefully looked at the three or four of the nearest windows that afforded any view of Sid's garden. Satisfied, he unlatched one of the sides of the gardeners van. He spotted a couple of stout scaffolding boards lying in the truck bed. He hoisted himself up and manhandled them over the side, so that they formed an improvised ramp. He went around the garden, collecting up the tools that Chris had been using, throwing them all into his tool bag, and tossing that in the back.

He turned his attention back to Chris. He wrapped the sides of the tarpaulin over the body, tucking the top and bottom sides in first. When he was confident that the body was safely wrapped up like a blue nylon mummy, he hauled the package towards the van. It slid quite easily on the lawn, but the concrete path was a little trickier. He paused for breath as he reached the barge boards. He pulled with all his might as if his life depended on it. After what seemed an eternity, the tarpaulin overcame the friction and began inching up the ramp. At last the whole of the body was on the boards when it decided it really didn't want to go any further. He slumped down onto his rump, the sweat pouring off him. He sat there for a moment, pondering his options, aware that the longer he spent there, the greater his chance of being discovered. Jumping off the truck bed, and taking the feet, he swung them round with all his might. The body lurched into the bed of the truck, but not before one of the boards clattered noisily to the floor. He quickly threw it on top of the tarpaulin, and then the other one, before latching the side panel. He paused, breathing rapid shallow breaths. He looked back into the garden and spotted the mug. He drank the tepid liquid down in one long swallow.

Fear? Where the fuck had that come from? Never before, in this whole scheme of his, had such a feeling overcome him before. He was analysing his feelings as he threw the empty mug into his own garden and got in the cab. He convinced himself that it was merely a surge of adrenaline caused by his physical exertions and the sheer intensity of the situation. By the time that he'd got the van back on the road, his heart rate had returned to almost normal. Leaving the engine idling, he went up his own garden path, and leaned in through his doorway to pick up a carrier bag he left there. As he sauntered back to the van, the sun ventured from behind a cloud, shining weakly. Well, he though, it does always shines on the righteous. Grinning to himself, he found a pair of sunglasses on the dashboard and slipped them on, before pulling away.

Rachael was standing in the conference room, staring at the whiteboards, with a large takeaway coffee in her hand. Her eyes scanned the photographs one by one as she stood there, oblivious of the other members of the squad drifting into the room. She focused on one particular photo, the one of Sam's face, close up, eyes taped shut. Slowly, her gaze was diverted by a brown finger tapping lightly on another picture, one showing the face at a different angle, peering out sightlessly from the cut-out portion of duvet cover.

"What do you think's the significance of putting the body in a duvet cover, Constable?"

Rachael turned to see the deep brown eyes of Inspector Jujara looking back. A half smile played on his lips, despite the subject matter. Twinkling in his eyes matched the smile.

"I- I don't know," Rachael managed to stammer. She realised she was blushing and stared back at the board, furious with herself. Come on, girl, you're not fourteen anymore.

"Well, maybe this medium will be able to tell us, when she shows up."

"I wouldn't let Inspector Smallwood hear you call her a medium." She looked back at him, only to realise he was joking with her. Her blush deepened. They moved around the table and settled themselves close to the window. It was comfortably warm in the room already, but Rachael guessed the heat would build as the morning wore on.

The team was almost complete when Jim walked in with Inspector Schofield and Ronnie. The inspector bustled around the table, ruffling the hair of one of the detectives, winking at another one. Rachael, who hadn't been at the pub the previous evening, just stared at the brash peroxide blonde with the huge breasts as she schmoozed around the table. She'd heard the occasional whisperings of her colleagues about the sassy woman, but she was still overwhelmed by her sudden appearance and attitude.

"Close your trap, love, I can see your tonsils." A meaty fist extended itself across the table in greeting, accompanied by a big wink. Rachael giggled as they shook hands. She giggled even more when she saw that David's' face was about an inch away from her cleavage as she leant over the table. His eyes were popping out of their sockets, before the sweat started to pour into them, temporarily blinding him.

Jim clapped his hands to bring everyone into order. Inspector Schofield gave him a look and went to lean by the wall next to the whiteboards, Ronnie next to her.

"Right then, morning everyone. Let me introduce you all to Inspector Terry Schofield and-"

Terry stepped forward, cutting him off. "Just pretend I'm not here, my loves." She said, smiling all around. "Just imagine I'm a wallflower or something." She glared at Rick, who had snorted loudly at this. Rachael glanced firstly at Mo, watching impassively, and then at Jim, looking vexed. Another coquettish look from

Terry followed, and Rachael could have sworn that her boss blushed, before looking down at his feet to regain his composure.

Jim looked up. "We don't have much time before Mary Guy, the forensic psychologist, turns up. Is there anything of importance that has come up overnight?" He looked around the table at every officer in turn, before settling on Tunicliffe. "David?"

Tunicliffe, who was still recovering from his near breast experience, nodded to Robert Franks. The young man brushed his fringe away from his eyes before speaking.

"I've been speaking to Chorley, Sir." His gaze flitted nervously over to Terry; who's eyes narrowed slightly. Robert gave her a half-smile before looking carrying on with his report. "The local bobbies have seen his neighbours, who were shocked, as you can imagine. "

"Bugger." This was from Jim. All eyes turned to him.

"What is it, Sir?" Rachael asked.

"If they've told the neighbours, then we will have to bring forward the news conference. We don't want gossip and tittle-tattle whipping round everywhere."

Ronnie spoke. "You can give our officers more credit than that, Sir. The Inspector briefed the house-to-house team before she left." Terry herself suddenly found something very interesting under a fingernail, a triumphant smirk on her face. Jim just harrumphed before nodding at Robert to continue.

"The neighbours were quite shocked to hear that he had 'disappeared suddenly and mysteriously'. But the general consensus seems to be that Mr Taylor was generally a quiet soul, he would say hello, that kind of thing. Not the type to gossip on the street corner or over the back fence. One or two pubs have been mentioned that he liked to frequent. Officers are checking them out today."

"Let me guess, son... the Rose, and the George and Dragon?" Terry interposed. Robert looked down at his notes before nodding an affirmative. In response, Terry looked at the whiteboard before saying to herself, more than anyone, "I'd have guessed as much. Probably the only two he'd be allowed in, if he was stinking of shit and rats."

"He would have showered or bathed before going out, surely?" Rachael asked.

Inspector Schofield laughed out loud, a rich laugh that came from deep down inside her. "That's what he would've smelled like after his ablutions, pet." Rachael didn't reply.

"Grant and Shirley would be my best bet, at the Rose. It's nearest, and its downhill on the way home. And our Shirley is quite nice to look at, as long as Grant isn't looking."

"How do we know that he wasn't homosexual?" This was from Inspector Jujara.

"Poofs. In Chorley?" Terry gave a shorter laugh, more like a bark. "Most of them have still got outside loos." She fixed him with a steely glare. "If he was that way inclined, Inspector, believe me, we'd know."

"How?"

"Grapevine works better than the telly up there, love. Trust me."

Inspector Smallwood coughed quietly. Everyone stopped and looked at him. He was looking at the doorway. The handle was being depressed; the door was opening. Everyone turned to look.

It was Cheryl who popped her head in. "I did knock," she said shyly. "You have a visitor."

Eunice Aston-Smith strode down the track, keeping a brisk pace. She loved these mid-morning walks with the dogs. If the weather was fine, like it was today, she would always come up the lane and turn into the track leading up to Old Orchard farm. There was an abundance of wildflowers on either side of her, cranesbill, wild sorrel...she had even spotted a bunch of corncockle the previous day. She had stopped to take a photograph of it with her old trusty Leica. It was a battered old thing, but it had been her late husband's, and she cherished it almost as much as the memory of him.

She whistled as one of her dogs was lagging behind. Newton, her golden retriever, was stopping to sniff at everything interesting. Abbott, her King Charles spaniel was rooting around just ahead. She smiled at the little dog, who had turned her head to look back at her owner. The dogs, her garden, and her photography were her life. For her it was a hobby, but for her late husband it had been his job, his passion, his mistress. Since Archie had gone as well, there was a massive hole in her life, which she tried to fill as best as she could. Hence the long walks in the country.

Newton came bounding along and licked the back of her hand with a hot tongue, shaking her out of her reverie. She ruffled one of his ears and he loped off again, wagging his tail as well. Her attention was drawn by firstly Newton, and then Abbott, who had struck off the track towards a tumbledown barn. Probably a family of wood mice, or a rabbit hole, she mused, as she sauntered along. They'd soon catch up.

It wasn't for about fifty yards that she heard the barking. Newton's deep, sonorous calls intermingled with Abbott's higher but more frequent yapping. Eunice paused, leaning on her stout branch she always used in lieu of a stick, and waited for them to stop their noise and come bounding back.

Only they didn't stop. Their barking continued, louder, more insistent. Shaking her head, she stomped off to investigate what had got them so interested. Brushing an overhanging branch out of her way, she rounded the side of the dilapidated building. The noise was coming from inside. A sense of trepidation jangled her nerves. She peered inside the dim building, one hand stretching down to quieten Newton as her eyes adjusted to the gloom.

Abbott was up on two legs, her front paws leaning against the side of what looked like an old water trough, barking furiously. Eunice took a tentative step into the building, to get a better view of what seemed to be an old sheet covering something in the trough.

Seconds later she was back outside, vomiting her breakfast of porridge with banana all over a small patch of bright purple Toadflax.

Even in death, Tori hadn't stopped playing her tricks on unsuspecting victims.

CHAPTER 12

He pulled off the sunglasses as he didn't want to miss the turn-off. He had been here, once, about six months previously... in the evening, during a thunderstorm. But in the end, it didn't matter. Chris had put up a big sign over his gates. He pulled the truck into the yard and turned the van, so he ended up facing the gates again, which he closed after letting himself out. He put his hands through a little aperture in the gate and slipped the padlock shut. He pulled his cap lower and walked away- he would be coming back later, and he didn't want to arouse any suspicions. He slipped the sunglasses on and sauntered away as if he didn't have a care in the world. He fancied a pint, and he was hungry. He knew a pub up the road that served excellent roast beef sandwiches. That would hit the spot, he thought, and so he set off whistling a happy tune to himself, content.

"Err, hello... Mary?" Jim edged his way around the table, his hand extended.

"Yes, that's me. You're James Smallwood?" A woman in a tailored trouser suit extended her hand and shook Jim's.

He smiled, tilting his head, "Oh, call me Jim."

He's flirting, thought Rachael. This man is truly incorrigible. And this lady is a forensic psychologist, trained to see right through him. But then she looked at Terry and she reflected that her boss had treated her the same. Maybe he doesn't know he's doing it, she wondered. She turned her attention back to the new arrival and studied her. Long, black hair in a French plait cascaded halfway down her back; a pretty face with high cheekbones, a nice mouth over a small chin and a perfect nose. But it was her eyes that held the attention. Blue-grey, beneath full eyelashes, they never rested. They were constantly digesting every tiny piece of information they received.

Rachael noticed how Mary made full eye contact with all the team as she was introduced to them individually. They were all greeted with a full smile that included the eyes, and when it was Rachael's turn, though the eyes never left hers, Rachael was sure that if the psychologist left the room immediately, she would be able to recall what everyone was wearing, what colour eyes they had, how they styled their hair. By the time Rachael had resurfaced from her daydream, Mary had moved to the head of the table. At a nod from Jim, she laid her black attaché case on the table and extracted a slim folder. She glanced at it briefly, put it down again, and scanned the room before speaking.

"Hello, everyone, and good morning to you all. I'm aware of the time that has elapsed since the killing of this man, and I'm not going to bore you with my professional resume except to say that I have extensive expertise in this sort of case, and that I've helped out the police on at least eight other cases." She had stopped smiling. "If you want, I can bore you all with stories at lunch," she paused as the team, all hanging on every word she was saying, laughed. "However, what we have here is the first killing of what I am convinced is a serial psychopath engaged in a mission killing." Silence ruled the room as everyone took this in. Inspector Schofield was the first to react, holding up her beautifully manicured hands and waving them around.

"Whoa, whoa, lassie, we know nothing of the kind."

Mary looked at Terry, seemingly unperturbed at the interjection, or being called 'lassie'.

"Let me explain." The smile returned briefly. "I know that that is a bold statement, but there are several factors which have led me to this conclusion. Primarily, I think that this is a first killing for several reasons." She went over and tapped the photograph of the body lightly with a fingertip. "This body was meant to be discovered. These two young men..."

"Seamus and Lucky." Jim provided.

"These two young would-be burglars were not set up to retrieve anything from the place where Samuel Taylor was lying dead. They were sent there specifically to discover the body, in a specific time period. The police were meant to be informed. This isn't the action of a random killer. He wants the police to notice him. Hiding the body was never part of his plan." She looked around the room at all the faces looking back at her, rapt. She glanced at Jim and then her gaze rested on Terry, who nodded, as if to accept the point.

"This is a first killing because of the way the body was displayed. The use of a duvet, with the face uncovered... this is a sign that there may be more to come."

"How?" Rick had put his hand up like a schoolboy in class. Mary had gently tilted her chin. "How can you say that? Sorry I don't mean to be rude, it's just that I don't understand." Rick was holding his nerve well, despite everyone looking at him. Rachael was herself unsure how Mary could leap to such a bold conclusion.

"Fair question...Rick?" Mary had screwed her eyes slightly in an effort to recall his name. "It is massive overkill, the laying 'in state', the preparation of the body, the duvet, the cut away portion. I'm sure that everything was planned. Everything was intended to be there- including the items that you found in your search..."

"Even the baby stuffed Kangaroo down the back of the sofa?" Rick asked, laughing nervously, looking around at his colleagues for support.

"Even the stuffed toy. It has meaning. There was nothing there that he didn't want you to find. Let me ask you...did you find any useable prints at the scene?"

Rick was definitely out of his comfort zone now. He looked at Jim for help, gulping.

"No prints." Jim responded quietly.

Mary shook her head, her plait swinging as she did. She smiled at Rick and said. "Don't worry, constable, I'm not going to bite your head off. Questions are good. Anymore?" Rick shook his head, chastened into silence despite Mary's reassurances.

"Well then, to continue. Everything was there for a reason, which leads me onto another of my assertions. He's going to kill again, if he isn't stopped, if he hasn't already. He is acting in the most anti-social manner possible. Taking another persons' life is as bad as it gets. He acts outside the acceptable parameters of normal behaviours. He is mentally disturbed. A textbook psychopath."

Mary looked down at her notes, but Rachael was sure that this wasn't because she had forgotten what to say next. She was just letting her words sink in. The deafening silence stretched. Giving a small cough, Inspector Jujara spoke softly.

"You suggested that was a mission killing."

"Indeed it is, Inspector." Again, the sweet smile. "When taken as a whole, the body, the evidence and lack of evidence, the two men, the staging, suggests that this man is on a mission. What that is, I can't tell you yet."

"You're certain that this is a man, acting alone?" This was from Robert Franks.

"Yes, I'm 90 percent sure." She glanced at the photograph of the body again. "This is such a specific manner of killing, that I'm reasonably confident that this is the work of a male, acting alone." Jim spoke up. "What about the actual method of killing, and the eyes being taped shut?"

Mary looked at him for a while, then back at the picture. "I'm not convinced that the actual method of killing is strictly relevant. He meant the face to be unmarked. Strangulation may have sufficed. The injection in the anus, specifically, was both a forensic countermeasure and a way of the drug to enter the bloodstream quickly. The eyes being taped shut could mean anything. Guilt on the part of the killer, remorse... another pointer in the mission, perhaps. It's impossible to tell at this point." Mary reached down and put the folder back in her case, which she closed and placed under the table, before straightening up and asked if there were any other questions.

"Can I go and have a bloody fag?" Inspector Schofield asked.

"Only if you take me with you, Inspector." Mary replied, laughing. There was a general relaxing of the tension, and Jim had to raise his voice over the conversations that had broken out all around the table.

"Right, folks, take twenty minutes, no more. We have a lot more ground to cover. Mary is going to give us a profile of this madman when everyone gets back. Thanks."

Most of the team stood up and headed for the door. Rachael stayed where she was, as did Jujara, seated next to her.

"Coffee?" Inspector Jujara inclined his head, smiling.

"You can tell me what you think. Let's go next door to the cafe though, it's much nicer."

"Ok, but it's my treat." He said, as Rachael opened her mouth to protest. Only David was still in the room. Rachael asked if he wanted to come along.

"No, no, but thanks for asking, anyway." He looked up, a pained smile on his face.

"Would you like a coffee brought back?" The inspector asked, at which the pained expression gave way to a full beam.

"Ooh. We might even stretch to a donut." Rachael beamed back and the beam stretched into a full-on grin.

On the way they passed the two inspectors, swathed in smoke. They reminded Rachael of schoolchildren smoking behind the bike sheds, which she said to Inspector Jujara.

"Pointless at my school. Kid would have a bike for a week, and it'd be nicked."

"That's a shame." Rachael responded, as they went into the cafe. "Tough upbringing?"

"Inner city schooling in the late sixties. Think Quadrophenia." He turned his attention to the server behind the till as Rachael tried to compare her upbringing in her private school to his when a thought struck her.

"You would've been about six or seven when that film came out." Mo turned, handing her a bag containing three donuts.

"Precisely. Tough upbringing." Rachael pouted at him.

"But the film depicts life in the sixties, when I was starting junior school. The film didn't come out till 1979. When you were about six, I'd guess." The inspector smiled at her.

"And probably still playing with my dolls, dreaming of princes, and pretty pink dresses."

120

"Got anything for me, my lovely?" Terry Schofield called over on their way back, crushing out her cigarette with her heel.

"No, but you can have mine if you want." Mo replied. Ever the gentleman, Rachael thought.

As the two men went up the stairs, Terry looked across at Mary and Rachael, and shaking her head, mouthed "I wasn't pulling his leg!" Laughing, the three women trailed the two men into the conference room. Terry looked enviously over David's shoulder as he wolfed his donut and narrowed her eyes at the back of his head, and then at Jujara, before winking at Rachael. Jim called them all into order, making sure that they were all present, and offered the floor once more to the psychologist.

"I hope you've all managed to digest both your donuts and what I've told you so far." A ripple of laughter washed around the room. The half-smile that had been playing on her lips vanished as she resumed talking. "Now this where it gets trickier. I'm going to give you a 'profile'. It is by no means definitive- with only one dead body we can't even call him a serial killer." She paused as she noticed Ronnie had put him hand up.

"What is the body count needed to call him a serial killer?" He asked.

"The minimum is three. However, if we are lucky enough to catch him at two, or even one, we could label him as a serial, if the intention is there." Ronnie nodded, and settled back against the wall next to his boss, with whom he exchanged glances.

"Anyway, I think that you're looking for a highly educated white male, aged twenty-five to forty, with financial security. Unlikely to be in a regular, nine-to-five employment, even if he has a job at all. He may work irregular hours, or from home, allowing him time to carry out his killing. He is, however, an organised killer; this is known, and can be seen in the time taken to kill Samuel Taylor, moving him beforehand, perhaps even gaining his trust before that. He knows what he is doing. I have little doubt that Sam was intentionally targeted. For what purpose, or why, is unknown at present." Mary paused here, her eyes travelling the room. Only a couple had their heads down, making notes. They looked up at the pause.

"We do know that he is highly skilled at disguise. Admittedly he wasn't in disguise when he met Lucky and Seamus in the pub- but he will have changed his appearance significantly since then. Don't be tricked into thinking that a change of hair colour, or the removal of it, or even the growing of a beard or moustache won't fool anyone. Think spies, in all those films you watch on the television or cinema, can someone answer that?"

Mary had been distracted by the shrill tones of the telephone ringing. Although they hadn't left explicit instructions not to be interrupted, the whole station knew what they were up to, and to leave them be.

David looked up apologetically. Rachael noted the colour drain from his face as he turned to Jim, leaning by the window. "It's for you, Sir. Superintendent Laird." He held the receiver for Jim, who took it, listening intently. Rachael looked at his face and their eyes met as Jim said a quiet 'thank you', followed by 'I understand, Sir.' He looked away, as he replaced the receiver. He leant on the table with both hands, blowing out his cheeks, and said to nobody in particular, "We have another body."

He leaned back, the empty glass resting on the plate by his elbow. He felt full, even happy. He thought about Tori and wondered if she or Chris would be discovered first. Not that it mattered... but in his grand scheme, he felt it would be better if she was first. He toyed with the idea of giving the police a nudge but dismissed it. Going down that route may well complicate things, he thought. Involving Seamus and his pal had been a calculated risk. He knew their own motivating principles almost as well as he knew his own.

He wandered back to the bar to order another pint, waiting. It was a warm summer day, and the pub was fairly busy. He didn't hear the door swing open, certainly paid no heed as a man made his way to join him at the bar. He didn't bat an eyelid when the man half turned and asked his companion what they wanted. But his heart almost stopped beating when he heard a voice say, "Oh...just get me a Coke. And a packet of crisps while we decide what to eat."

He stared dead ahead, rooted to the spot, paralysed by fear. He didn't realise the barman was talking to him until the man standing next to him nudged his elbow.

With effort he managed to squeeze out 'same' as the barman became impatient. He didn't care that he received a slightly smaller measure than usual, or that the barman literally threw his change down on the bar towel next to the drink. He picked up the pint and drained it in a couple of gulps, whilst fishing out his cap from the waistband of his jeans. He took no notice even as the man called him a 'rude bastard' as he bumped into his shoulder as he left. He just knew he had to get outside, fast.

He strode over to the door and roughly barged past a group of students making their way into the pub, and when he reached the relative safety of the outdoors, he leaned against the wall, head back, breathing deeply.

Jo Holt.

Not a duplicate, not a substitute, but the real living, breathing Jo Holt. He began to shake, his breathing ragged and erratic. He screwed his eyes shut, bending over. A little old lady passed by close to him, hiking her cardigan across her chest, no doubt cursing the drunkenness and immorality of the younger generation. If only she knew, he thought as he opened his eyes again. Slowly, his breathing began to return to normal, though he could feel his heart was still racing. Pushing off from the wall he set off in the direction of the town centre. He felt the need of another drink.

Walking along the street, the sun warmed him again, chasing the chill caused by his hearing her voice. In his minds' eye, he tried to recollect when it was that he'd first heard it.

The boy they affectionately called 'Wing-nut', because of his over-sized ears, was mangling Bryan Adams to death on the karaoke machine in the pub. They may not have been able to see him, because of the press of people, the smoke, and the flashing disco lights, but they could him certainly hear him.

"Last verse, I think," Lawrence shouted in his ear, although he was standing less than a foot away from him.

"I hope so. I think my eardrums are bleeding." He laughed. Pointing to his glass, he asked, "Another?" Lawrence nodded, so he faced the bar, trying to catch the eye of the bar staff. His arm trailed in some spilt beer and soaked into his shirt. Cursing, he tried to dry it off with a bar towel, but it didn't help. Turning to his friend he handed him a note, saying "You get them, and meet me outside. I'm going to dry off and have a fag." Lawrence took the money and he headed for the toilets. Here the music was a little muted, the air less smoky, but the stench of stale piss assaulted his nostrils. His arm slowly dried off under the hot air blower. It cut off halfway through, so he put it back on again in order for it to start blowing again. It cut off a second time as he was examining his cuff. Wingnut came into the gents, sweat pouring off him and as headed for some toilet roll, he saw his mate and grinned a hello. A droplet of sweat dripped off his chin.

"Killed it tonight, Austin." He clapped his mate on the back as he went past and wished he hadn't; the t-shirt was soaked with sweat too. As soon as his friends' back was turned, he wiped his palm down his jeans. Austin stood with a fistful of toilet roll, dabbing at his face.

"You think so?" He asked.

"Well, if you'd have carried on much more, you certainly would've killed someone." They both laughed at that, and he left to find his other mate and enjoy a fag.

Lawrence was waving to him the far side of the courtyard. He'd managed to bag them a couple of places on a bench. He saw four other people sitting there as well. He perched on the end of the bench, took a swig of his drink, and lit a cigarette. A voice from the other side of the table asked politely,

"Do you have a spare cigarette, please?"

He looked up, exhaling. By his side, Lawrence offered the pack to a girl seated opposite him. Delicate fingers with pink nail varnish on carefully extracted one.

"Aren't you worried your mum will smell it, Jo?" A girl on her left said, to which another girl, on her right, laughed, "Beside the smell of cider, you mean, Caroline?" They all laughed.

"Excuse them, they don't get out much." A young man explained to the two friends.

"Only every bloody weekend." Caroline muttered, still smiling. The young man made a face at her, before extending his hand to Lawrence. "Hi I'm Dennis." Lawrence shook his hand and said. "I'm Lawrence and this is Phil. I've seen you around, though. Nice to put a name to the face at last." He smiled.

"And I'm Caroline. And the two less pretty ones are Jo and Lisa." This statement was received by protests from both friends, and a playful punch from Jo. The boys waved at the girls and the boys waved at the girls.

He thought the girls were all really attractive. Lisa, opposite him, had pink strands in her black hair which fell past her shoulders, pale make-up, except for around her eyes, heavy with Kohl and mascara accenting brown eyes beautifully. Wearing an Iron Maiden t-shirt, her arms jangled with about thirty bangles every time she moved. On the other end, Caroline had pretensions to be the most mature; her strawberry blonde hair was styled to be wilder but held in place by a whole can of hairspray. She was heavily made up, from green eyeshadow to heavily mascaraed brown eyes. A pale pink, highly glossed lipstick detracted attention from a slightly piggy nose. She was wearing an expensive white silk blouse. Obviously rich parents, he mused. His attention turned to the girl in the middle, whom he studied whilst pretending to drink his pint. She had ash blonde hair, cut in a bob style. She wore only a little eyeliner. Her bright blue eyes were what brought her face to life. Some people were like that, he mused; some had to die their hair, or used too many cosmetics. Others carried their own beauty like some carried a handbag. For a split second they eyes met, before she looked away quickly. They seemed to sparkle when she looked at him. A shiver ran down his spine.

"Mate. Wake up. Caroline asked you a question." Lawrence nudged him. Phil shook himself out of his stupor and apologized.

"I was asking what song you are going to sing." Caroline studied him from her heavily made-up eyelids, a smile playing on her glossed lips.

Lisa picked up a dog-eared pamphlet, a guide to what was available on the karaoke machine. "There's so many." Her voice drifted into silence as she looked at a page whose titles were blurred by a beer ring which had smudged the titles.

"Maybe Prince." He didn't really care what he sang, he was trying to gauge what would go down well with Jo, who was also looking at the pages. "or Status Quo." This brought a slightly wrinkled frown from her. Obviously not, then. "Bryan Adams? U2? Phil Collins?" The mention of the Canadian had smoothed her brows, the Irish rockers left her nonplussed, and the former Genesis man left her looking sick.

He ploughed on and took one last guess. "But probably something from Siouxsie and the Banshees." This bought admiring glances from both girls. Lisa kept reading through the list, but Jo asked him, "You like Siouxsie? I love 'em."

"I saw them last year in Hammersmith." He looked directly at her whilst saying this. "They were fabulous." He was rewarded with a beautiful smile.

"Were they any good?" Lisa asked. Jo was smiling at him.

"I am so jealous."

"And I'm going to sing Madonna," Caroline said, standing up, obviously bored at not being the centre of attention. "Come on, Dennis, you can be my backing singer." He grimaced, but obligingly stood up as well.

"Coming in to watch?" Dennis asked everyone, as he walked off. Lawrence nodded and struggled up from the bench. He looked down and saw that his friend and the girl with the pretty eyes sitting there, smiling at each other. He nudged his mate, and the remaining three got to their feet to follow Caroline and Dennis, Lisa muttering as she did about Dennis being a little lap dog whose sole purpose was to fulfil Caroline's every desire. Jo punched her friend playfully but was nodding in agreement as they went into the crowded bar again.

Lawrence held his mate back and whispered, "I might be wrong, but I think you're in there." He was treated to a wink from his mate swiftly followed by a cuff to the back of his head.

He reached the gardener's yard via a circuitous route. This was the time that he really could do without being seen, and as part of his preparations, he had observed a lull between mothers taking the children home from school, and the workers leaving. Working fast, he unlocked the padlock, opened and then closed the gates when he was inside. He pressed his face close to the French doors that served as an entrance to Chris's office. Not much to see, a desk with a couple of chairs; various posters advertising gardening products, a notice directing people to the workshop; an average space. Satisfied, he crossed to the cab of the truck and hauled out his bag. Donning gloves, he jumped onto the van bed. Checking to see how visible he was from the road; the gates were closed, and the new sign shielded him from inquisitive eyes. Content in his security, he resumed his work. He unwrapped the tarpaulin. The body was lying in the wrong position, so he had to move it so that the head was by the truck's cab end. He retrieved a fresh duvet, and shook it out lightly, so that the cut-out portion was facing the right way. Opening the poppers, he bent down and started to dress the corpse. The legs were easy, the rump and torso a little more difficult. He reached into the gardener's workbag and extracted the ear defenders. He looked at them, trying to figure out how they adjusted. Finally, he pushed them to the widest setting, used for larger heads. From his bag he pulled out a Walkman, with headphones. He pressed 'play' and pulled up one of the shoulders of the corpse, nestling the machine between the shoulder and the duvet cover underneath it. He put the headphones over Chris's head, and then put the ear defenders on top. It was a snug fit, even with the defenders extended to their maximum reach.

He checked his watch; a quarter to five. Everything was in order; he was back in control. After one last tug, the duvet cover completely encapsulated the body. It even fell nicely, revealing the face. Only a small adjustment was required. He smiled to himself. Some days things just went right. Except for the episode in the pub, everything had gone to plan.

Suddenly he was interrupted by a heavily rattling of the gates, and instinctively ducked down, squatting by the body. "Visitors, Chris." He whispered through clenched teeth. The rattling stopped.

"You in there, mate?" A gruff voice shouted through the gap in the gate. "I was going for a pint. Looks like you've gone on ahead already. I'll see you in there I suppose."

The thought crossed his mind as to why anyone would shout like that through an obviously closed gate. Was the man drunk, or stoned? He decided that the man rattling the chains was simply an oaf. He smiled, despite the close call and his proximity to the corpse. It was strange, but he felt alive- he was God.

Satisfied firstly that the man had wandered off, and that Chris was as he intended him to be found, he slipped over the side of the truck bed and took a final look around to make sure that he had missed nothing. Nodding to himself, he let himself out. He didn't even bother with the padlock; just slipped it into his pocket to dispose of later. A thought struck him as he walked off nonchalantly, seemingly without a care in the world. A little knowledge of Chris, his own intuition, and a little slice of good fortune meant that ten minutes later he was standing next to a man with a loud voice in the public bar of the George, drinking a Guinness. The man paid no attention to him whatsoever; instead carped on to the barman about being let down by his mate Chris. He had no idea who was standing next to him; no inkling at all that he was standing in such close proximity to God.

CHAPTER 13

The clouds rolled by and the wind threw up dust against the vehicles as they parked on the verge of a country lane. A solitary police constable waited in the mouth of the track that led up to the farm. Jim got out, wishing he had bought a coat. It had been warm, bright and sunny as they had left the station, but a sudden storm was fast approaching from over the hills to the west.

He had travelled with Rachael, Mo and Terry. Ronnie and Rick had come in Rick's Capri with Ian Westlake; Mark Steyne, Mike Ballard, and DS Ratcliffe had brought up the rear. Jim had no idea if all were needed, but he wanted them on hand. In the back of his mind he hoped that this latest finding was unrelated to Samuel Taylor, but a knot in his stomach told him that it was futile. He waited, his hands thrust deep in his pockets whilst the team gathered around him, discussing in hushed tones with one another as to what they would discover.

Rachael walked back from where she had been talking to the constable. "Seems as though we're waiting for the SOCO's Sir." A gust of wind whipped a strand of hair into her face as she spoke. She reached into a pocket and tied it up with a hair band as she waited for her boss's pronouncement.

Jim nodded, his face like stone. "Where's the witness who discovered the body?"

"She's at her home." Rachael replied, turning to point at a row of cottages down the lane. "It's the one on the far end. WPC Stafford, is having a cup of tea with her, the old lady is quite doughty, but obviously a bit shaken up."

"Ok. You get over there with Ds Ratcliffe and take a statement from her." He turned to the rest of the team. "Mark, Mike, head up to the farm at the end of this track. You'll have to go in the from the other end, I'm afraid, until the SOCO team clear this track. Ian, Ronnie, Rick, start canvassing the cottages up and down this lane." He nodded in the other direction. "You know what to ask. Anything unusual in the last few days, vehicles, strangers,

that kind of thing. Thank you." He watched them go, confident that if anybody had seen anything even remotely suspicious, they would turn it up. He looked round and saw that Terry was looking at him, one eyebrow raised.
"What?" He asked her, not too politely.
"My sergeant is here in an observer role. He's not one of your foot soldiers."
"He is when he's here." Smallwood turned his back on her and marched away to the sole constable, who was chatting to an elderly couple walking their dog. Terry looked Mo with a questioning look.
"He's worried it's a serial killer." Mo said, shrugging.
"Oh, I know pet. I'm just winding him up."
"Is that a good idea?"
"Yes, Inspector." Terry slid her arm through Mo's. "I think he's a better thinker when he's annoyed. I know I am." She gave him a conspiratorial wink. Mo gave a harsh laugh, shaking his head.
"Bitch."

In the end, they decided on Dead or Alives' 'You spin me round'. Just him and Lawrence to begin with, but about halfway through Jo and Lisa bounded up and joined in, and by the end, Dennis and even Caroline were crowded round the microphones. With jokey, camp movements, they brought the house down, the crowd gave them a raucous round of applause, cheering rowdily. They came off the little raised stage, sweating, laughing, smoke stinging their eyes. Dennis and Lawrence went to the bar to get another round in while he followed the girls outside for a breath of air. They were all talking at once, laughing till they cried. Caroline and Jo flopped down on a spare bench, still laughing. Lisa stopped, turning round, and putting one hand against his chest, whilst taking one of his with her other.
"I can see you're quite taken with Jo." She said, smiling. "But it's only fair to warn you that's she had a rough time recently. Her last boyfriend hurt her badly, mentally speaking." He had been

looking over Lisa's shoulder whilst she was talking, but now looked at her.

"And he left her... pregnant."

He looked at Lisa, at Jo, and then back at Lisa.

"Yes, she did." Lisa answered his unspoken question. "A little boy, called Harrison. Eleven months old and the apple of his mother's eye." Her eyes sparkled as she spoke of Jo's son. "He is so adorable. Crawling, pulling himself up, ever curious."

This time he did speak up. "And the father?" He was speaking to Lisa, but still looking over her shoulder. Jo was just taking a drink from Dennis. She looked up, saw Phil and smiled.

"... not on the scene. But if you pursue this and hurt her, I will kill you."

"Understood. She is very lucky to have such good friends looking after her."

Lisa chuckled. "Friend, in the singular. Caroline only looks after herself."

As they made their way over to the bench, he noticed that the friends had purposefully left a place next to Jo for him, his drink sitting on the table, fizzing away slowly. He shook his head, smiling, before settling himself onto the bench next to her. He felt her hand slip into his, squeezing it tight even though she was explaining about the cake that she had made with Harrison's assistance earlier on in the day, and not even looking his way.

Rachael knocked and waited, admiring the dog rose growing up little trellises on either side. She found herself surprised that she could be wondering at the wonders of nature at such a time and started when Joss popped her head around the frame of the door, before opening it to let her and DS Ratcliffe inside.

Rachael's senses were assaulted by freshly baked scones, pot-pourri, and dog. Her eyes took in a cosy domestic scene, a table laid out with a tea service, the scones with jam and cream. She eyed one enviously as Joss seated herself at the table again. A stout little lady appeared at the kitchen door with a teapot.

Rachael estimated her to be somewhere in her late seventies. She smiled, and was rewarded by a nod, a raising of eyebrows, and "I guess you'll be wanting a cup too, my dears."

DS Ratcliffe stepped out from behind Rachael and advanced towards the old lady. "That'd be smashing, love. I'm parched."

"Aye, then, take your jacket off, sit down, call me Mrs. Smith and I'll treat you to a scone, or would you prefer a nice slice of seed cake?"

"A scone would be perfect, lo- Mrs. Smith." Ratcliffe had corrected himself just in time. She nodded curtly at him before turning her attention on Rachael.

"Are you going to stand there, or are you going to join us?"

"Actually, Mrs. Smith, I think that under the circumstances, speed would be of the essence." Rachael was anxious to get on and back to the investigation. Instead, the little old lady seated herself at the table with the two other police officers, replying, "Well, I can still eat and talk, and I'm need of a cup." She picked up a bottle of whisky and shook it gently at Rachael, adding, "And a bit of a stiffener might help too." She gave a little laugh and wrinkled her nose in a smile at Joss. Rachael locked gazes with the uniformed constable who inclined her head to suggest that perhaps it would be quicker in the long run if Rachael joined them. Rachael took a deep breath and sat down. Eunice looked at her and smiled.

"That's better, dear. And it's not as if the poor lass up there is going anywhere fast." Her face took on a rueful expression as she concentrated on pouring the tea.

A hundred yards away, Jim stubbed out a cigarette as the van containing the SOCO team pulled up. Another patrol car pulled up, and the officers had set about putting up yellow tape across the entrance to the track. They milled around before being despatched to help in the house-to-house enquiries.

Jim approached one of the SOCOs and asked how long it would be before they could have a preliminary look at the body. One of Bernie's underlings simply known to everyone as Woody, listened to the inspector before replying "You can come with us, if you follow exactly in my footsteps." He glanced at Inspector Schofield before looking back to Jim. "As long as you're all suited and booted, Sir."

"I don't suppose you have booties that cover stilettos though?" Jim grinned. Hearing this, Terry came tottering over in her four-inch heels. "These cost me bloody near two hundred quid!" She said indignantly, hands on hips.

"I have a pair of wellingtons in the boot of my car."

"BLOODY WELLINGTONS?" Terry shrieked.

At this point Woody turned to one of his colleagues and said, "I found a ten pence piece."

"Was it shiny and new?" His colleague countered.

"It was actually..."

"What the fuck is he talking about money for?" Terry was puce, looking at Jim for answers.

"It means you're boring him." He nodded at Woody, who was retreating back to his van to get the extra suits they needed.

"What?"

"I'm afraid it's his way or the highway, for the time being."

"Bloody hell." Terry snatched a pack of overalls out of Woody's arms and stomped off to get changed. Jim and Woody exchanged winks. Mo, watching open mouthed, took his and began to change on the spot.

When they were all ready, they made their way up the track, following in the exact footsteps of the SOCO, mindful of any impressions in the mud and gravel that may have been made by vehicles. They picked their way silently, anticipating what lay ahead, but concentrating on where they were walking, all conversation stopped.

Two minutes later they approached the tumbledown barn. They stopped whilst the leading SOCO placed little metal footplates indicating that they should only step on them, nowhere else. Progress slowed as the SOCO went about his laborious task. All three inspectors knew the crucial importance of preserving any and all trace evidence. Woody shook his head

133

when Jim tried to light up. They approached the doorway of the hut with trepidation. Despite his experience, Jim's stomach was in knots. He halted about four feet short of what appeared to be an old rusting trough. He sensed Terry and Mo standing behind him, breathing through their mouths. The smell was appalling, and Jim fought an urge to gag when he glimpsed what was in it

A woman's face looked out unseeing from a rectangular hole that had been cut from what Jim knew was a duvet cover. The killer had struck again.

Rachael stowed her notebook in her bag. "Well, thank you for your time, Mrs. Smith. WPC Stafford can stay with you if you would like some company."

"Away with you, dear. I'm sure Joss here has more important things to be getting on with."

She reached down and patted the head of one of her dogs. "Besides, I've got Newton and Abbott here for company." She smiled down at them, sitting patiently by their mistress.

"Well OK, then. Thanks again." They made their way back to the cars. It started to spit, so they got in Jim's car, which Inspector Schofield had neglected to lock.

"Well, that didn't tell us much, did it?" DS Ratcliffe said.

"Expecting much, Sarge?" Joss said from the back. "She only discovered the body. What do you think, Rachael?"

"Nice seed cake." Rachael stared out of the window at the thickening rain, deep in thought.

The SOCO team had dashed outside at the first sign of rain and were spreading large clear plastic sheets around to preserve any evidence. Inside the barn, the three inspectors stood in a semi-circle around the trough, lost in their own private thoughts.

"Poor lass." Terry murmured, turning to leave. Jim looked and saw a solitary tear trickle down her face. Mo made to leave as well, a grim expression on his face, but Jim put out an arm to restrain him.

"Give her a minute, Mo." He looked at the trough again.

"We will catch him, Jim."
Smallwood shrugged, looking down at the fragile form.
"I hope so, Mo, I really do." He made his way out, oblivious of the stinging bullets of water falling on his head.
Inspector Jujara dropped his head and closed his eyes, mouthing a silent prayer.

She finished the blowjob and reached out for a tissue to spit out the warm, salty liquid. The man tossed a ten-pound note into her lap, and zipped himself up, silent in his moment of ecstasy. She scooped it up in her fist and got out of the car as quickly as she could. The car sped off almost before she had time to shut the door.
"Bastard." She shouted at the retreating vehicle. She put her hand up to her hair, where the punter had grabbed it whilst she was fellating him. She patted it, giving the sore patch a soothing rub. It was about half twelve, and she'd had three punters in the last two hours, all businessmen, two out for 'blowies', one for a hand job. Time for a kebab, and then some kip before the evening rush. Friday night was always busy- lonely old men, 'misunderstood' husbands, blokes on stag nights, they all came looking for something to enliven their mundane existences.
A sharp wind was blowing straight off the sea as she reached the front. She wrapped her thin cardigan tighter against her frame, and started to walk faster, glimpsing her reflection in the vast glass windows of the amusement arcades as she passed. She knew that she was too thin, with no breasts to speak of; in fact, she looked more like fourteen than twenty-four, which she was. At a little over five foot four, her petite frame, wavy blonde hair and pretty face appealed not only to the punters who didn't care where they got their kicks, but also the weirdo element who liked little girls. She knew it added another degree of danger to what was already a perilous occupation, but as her Gran would've said 'beggars can't be choosers, pet'. Turning off Marine Parade, she cut through Alma Road to get to the kebab shop on St. Johns Road. The

135

stiffening breeze whipped her hair across her face as she stepped off the kerb to cross the street.

She never saw the Transit. Luckily, the driver saw as she wandered right in front of him, jumping on his brakes in an attempt to stop, and almost succeeded, the front fender of the van just making contact with the bag slung over her shoulder. The nudge was enough to send her sprawling into the gutter. He stopped the van, jumping out to see how badly she was hurt. Stupid girl, he thought, as he found her trying to get up.

"Woah, there. Take it easy- you may have hit your head. Stay still." He loomed over her.

"Bastard! You almost killed me." She shouted, wincing at a sharp pain in her wrist.

"I think you were trying to kill yourself, love- here, let me help you." He put out a hand to steady her. She angrily knocked it away, but then she felt dizzy and her legs began to wobble. She started to topple over, but his big strong hands reached out and caught her, and gently lowered her to sit on the kerb.

"We should think about getting you to the hospital. Where's the nearest phone?" He straightened up, looking for a box.

"I'm fine, I'm just starving. I was just heading for a kebab." She said, tenderly prodding her wrist, trying not to cry. At least it's not my wanking hand, she thought ruefully.

"OK. First things first." He said, taking control. Let's get you up, and propped against that wall, I'll treat you to that kebab. My way of making an apology."

"You said it was my fault." She looked up at him dubiously.

"Never said that. You must be suffering from shock as well." His broke into a grin. He helped her to her feet.

At that moment two police officers rounded the corner, patrolling their beat. They knew the girl and mistook him for a punter getting violent with her. They hustled over to them.

"You ok, Olive? This man hassling you?"

"Christ. Now the police are trying to protect the whores?" The young girl spat out at them. The two officers regarded her impassively. One of them looked at the man with her, sizing him up. He was a good six inches taller than her and didn't strike the officer as looking like a typical punter. Still, you could never tell.

"I fell off the kerb, and he stopped to help me."

"Are you sure?"

"He looks like a fucking punter?" She looked at the cops.

The officers were going to point out the dangers of being drunk in the daytime, which was a civil matter, though still arrestable, when their radios crackled to life. One of the policemen peeled off to answer the call, whilst the other stood, hands on hips, and regarded them sternly. His colleague called out their presence was required at one of the nearby arcades and contented himself by silently wagging his finger at the pair of them, as if they were naughty schoolchildren. They waited by the wall until the policemen had run off.

"Wankers." Olive said, spitting on the pavement.

"Olive?" The man said.

"That's my working name." She looked at him. She wondered if he could tell what she was just by the look of her. If he didn't know before, he would surely know now. She looked into his blue-grey eyes and felt a safeness when she was with him.

He held out his hand. "Tom. Pleased to meet you, and not kill you before we'd introduced ourselves." He smiled.

"Christ. I'm the tom." She laughed. She felt better he knew; in case he got some stupid notion of asking her out. He regarded her silently, no shock showing on his handsome face. Perhaps he'd known all along. He inclined his head a touch and raised an eyebrow as if asking an unspoken question.

"I'm Mandy." She rubbed her throbbing wrist, and it reminded her how hungry she was.

No, you're not, he thought.

"Kebab, then." He said.

They reconvened in the conference room. They entered in dribs and drabs, their eyes downcast, their thoughts were of the poor girl in the trough. Rachael looked around at her colleagues. She could see the despondency written all over their faces.

The door opened and Cheryl, the secretary, struggled into the room with a whiteboard. Pete Norris sprang up and took it from her, for which she smiled at him and mouthed a silent 'thank you' before retreating once again to the typing pool. Over by the window, Terry gave a sigh, before resting her forehead on the glass, her eyes shut. Jim coughed to get everyone's attention. Everyone stopped what they were doing.

"We have a very early identification of the woman in the trough." Turning to Mo, he said in a barely audible whisper, "Do we have to keep calling it a trough?" Mo shrugged.

"Manger, crib. Take your pick." Terry, her eyes still closed, said.

"Thanks." Jim looked at her before turning back to the rest of the team. "The woman in the trough has been initially identified as Tori Henderson, aged 26 of Spring Gardens, Luton." His eyes turned to Ash Bradfield, who was Luton based. Their eyes met but no words were exchanged.

"How do we know this, Sir?" Rachael asked, wanting to break the uncomfortable silence.

"She very handily had her driving license, tucked into the back of her knickers." He replied.

"The killer intended us to find that out immediately."

"It would seem."

"He's taunting us." This was from Pete. Jim slid his gaze over to Mary Guy.

"He's showing us that he thinks he's in total control, and that he's cleverer than us."

"He is in total control." Rachael said, quietly.

"Possibly, but he's not cleverer than us." Terry had pushed herself off the windowpane and stood next to Jim, chin sticking out defiantly. "You lot will catch him, and I'm going to wrench his fucking bollocks off and fry them for me tea." She glared at everyone, and they stared back with a variety of looks of agreement, defiance, or, in David's case, plain fear. Inspector Jujara rubbed his beard, trying to hide a smile. Jim grunted.

They spent the next half hour discussing DS Ratcliffe's report, and then that of the M and M's, who had arrived quietly, and finally that of Ronnie, Rick, and Iain, who had trooped in looking like drowned rats. All five of them dourly reported that they had nothing to report. Nobody had seen anything of note apart from one of the farm workers who had thought that he may have heard a vehicle but had done nothing about it, having assumed that it was just kids or lovers.

Jim directed Ash Bradfield and Pete Norris to go off to the home of Tori Henderson, and to examine it. Or had lived, he corrected himself. Exhausted, he sat down, his head in his hands. He was due at the autopsy and was figuring who to take with him. Rachael stood up unnoticed and left, returning shortly afterwards with a cup of tea for him. He looked at her and smiled tiredly. She smiled silently back at him and resumed her seat.

"Right. I'm off to the autopsy. Hopefully they will start before too long. I would ask you to come, Rachael, but I feel the two inspectors with their experience would be of greater use" He held up both palms in a placating measure to her, as if suggesting his hands were tied.

"No problem, Sir." She was nodding but was disappointed. She noticed Terry studying her.

"Bollocks, Jimmy." Terry chortled, speaking to Jim but still watching Rachael. "How is the lass going to gain experience otherwise? Besides, I've seen enough chopping and dicing I'm sure I could open my own Chinese restaurant by now." She winked at Rachael, who looked down at the table so as to suppress a grin.

Jim looked at Terry through hooded eyes, though if this was acceptance of her offer, or annoyance at being called 'Jimmy', Rachael couldn't tell. She only felt immense gratitude to the older woman. The telephone rang again, and David picked it up, listened for a couple of seconds before replacing the receiver.

"Super wants to see you ASAP, Sir." Jim rolled his eyeballs as he got to his feet. "Wish me luck."

"And Inspector Schofield as well, Sir." David added. Mo laughed and said to her departing back as they left the room, "That'll be for calling him 'Jimmy'." Terry kept going but just flicked him a finger in silence as she left.

"You've got a bit of chili sauce on your chin," Mandy laughed, pointing at him as they sat on the low wall looking out the waves as they crashed on the beach.

"Where? Can you rub it off for me?"

"No! I'm not your mother. Here, do it yourself." She tossed him a crumpled napkin.

He regarded her as she gazed at the horizon. Damn you, bitch, you're the first girl to show me warmth in ages... shame you've got to die. He wondered for a moment if he could let this one live. Then he remembered the times that he had his heart broken, his ambitions crushed, his hopes crushed. His resolve stiffened. He threw the napkin at a nearby bin, but a gust of wind picked it up at the last moment and snatched it away. Pushing himself off the wall, he set off in pursuit. He eventually trapped it, scrunched it up and made sure it didn't miss the bin when he put it in the next time.

She shouted at a swooping seagull, who shrieked back at her. She reached into her bag to retrieve her cigarettes and winced as she knocked her wrist again. "Fuck, fuck, fuck!" She almost screamed with the pain.

"Come on, I'm taking you to the hospital to get that checked." He said, standing over her.

"I just need a drink to dumb the pain, that's all." She mumbled, brushing away a tear with the back of her good hand. He seemed to mull this over.

"Ok, just the one though."

"You can fuck off. It'll take me three to taste it." She looked up at him, attempting a smile. He rolled his eyeballs.

"Come on."

Jim went into the Superintendents' outer office and walked straight up to the desk where the secretary stopped her typing and gave him a forced smile. "He's in there, with ACC Parker."

"Oh, I'll wait then, Pam. Not like I've got much to do is it?" He snarled with frustration. Terry put a hand on his arm, and he rubbed his face. "Oh heck, I'm sorry Pam. Forgive me."

"He said to go straight in."

As they entered, they immediately saw Nan Parker, hands clasped behind him, back turned to them, staring out of the window. Laird was seated, on the telephone. He motioned them to take a seat. Nan Parker stayed where he was, immobile.

They waited quietly until Laird finished his call. He replaced the receiver softly, looking at the pair of them. He stroked his upper lip, as if mentally rehearsing what he was going to say. After what seemed an eternity, he spoke calmly and quietly.

"I'm sorry to hear that you have had another body turn up, Inspector." He gave a very slight nod backwards at the ACC in the window, a warning to Jim that this was informal, but that Jim should be circumspect in what he said here.

"Yes Sir, we are just about to go the autopsy."

"We?"

"Inspector Jujara, Constable Reed, and myself Sir."

"Very well. Anything from the first one that is of interest?"

"Enquiries are still ongoing in Chorley, Sir." Smallwood looked at Schofield, and Laird switched his attention.

"Aye, well it seems that Mr. Taylor didn't have that many friends, was a bit of a loner. That might have been something to do with his occupation."

"A rat-catcher, wasn't it?" Laird interjected. A grunt came from Nan Parker in the window.

Schofield flicked him a bemused glance before continuing. "Yes, Sir that's correct. He wasn't overly fond of bathing, unless he was planning a long session in the pub. They warned him once or twice that it was bad for business, apparently." Another grunt from Nan Parker, another glance from Terry.

"I've taken the liberty of phoning your superior at Chorley. He's willing to let you stay her for a while longer. Apparently your 'skill set' would be a huge asset in this case. He spoke highly of you, Inspector."

"More like he's glad to have me out of his hair for a couple of weeks, Sir."

"Two weeks. You think you can solve this case in that time frame?" He had turned to scrutinize the newly arrived inspector. His eyes widened as he took in the mass of blonde hair, the large breasts, the sassy styling of her clothes. Jim suddenly has a vision of Nan Parker's monocle falling out in surprise- if he had been wearing one.

"Any thoughts on a news conference?" Laird asked.

"Well, this scene was certainly more public. But there was only person who actually saw her body: an elderly lady walking her dogs. I am sure we could prevail upon her to keep her silence." Smallwood paused, scratching his stubble. "I'm in two minds about as to if a news conference would benefit us so much at this time." Laird arched a brow at this, and ACC Parker jumped in. "Keeping your powder dry, eh Inspector? Good show. But when you do have one, which at some stage I think you will have to, may I suggest that you include Inspector Schofield?"

For a fleeting moment, Jim toyed with the idea of embarrassing Parker by asking why he would want Terry at the news conference but decided against it. She, however, had no such qualms.

"And no doubt, you'd like me in a shorter skirt, and with three open buttons on me blouse, love?" She fluttered her eyelashes at one of the most senior policemen in the county, totally unabashed. Superintendent Laird almost choked himself as he sat watching. Jim squirmed uncomfortably in his chair, staring at Terry and then at the floor. Nan Parker stood there impassively. To his credit, he never even flinched.

Inclining his head, he replied. "No skirt, Inspector. Wouldn't want the media catching sight of those brass bollocks of yours."

Silence ruled throughout the room. Smallwood, still staring at the floor, could sense movement coming from the chair alongside his. He risked a sidelong glance and saw Terry heaving with silent laughter. He looked up at the ACC to see him shaking beneath his moustache. As he watched, Nan Parker began to laugh- a sound Jim had never heard before and sounded like a cross between a donkey being castrated and someone scraping their nails down a blackboard. Even Laird turned and began laughing, starting with a small chortle that soon escalated to a full-blown guffaw.

Jim didn't feel like laughing. He looked through the window at the clouds. He got up without saying a word and left the inner sanctum, ignoring the quizzical looks of Pamela. He went back to his own office and sat with his head in his hands.

CHAPTER 14

Jim was sitting in his office when Inspector Schofield popped her head around the door.

"Mo is hanging around the car park, and I said you'd go down there and drive him over to the autopsy, Constable Read." Rachael nodded and headed for the door whilst Terry slipped onto Rachael's chair. "The two gentlemen send their apologies, Jim". She tried a coquettish smile, but he stared blankly back at her. She took a deep breath and plunged on. "It's just the ACC and the super- well all of us- are under tremendous pressure, and sometimes laughter like that is some kind of perverse psychological response to the pressure." Her voice trailed away.

"I get it, inspector. I really do. It's just I don't really feel like laughing. I'm tired, there's too much to do and I don't know where to start, I don't understand what motivates this killer, and we have nothing, absolutely nothing to go on."

"Well, what we are going to do is this. Ronnie is going to take you home for a quick shower before he drives you to the autopsy. There is a little job I've given him at the hospital. I'm going to the incident room, check on how the lads are getting on with their flat search, give the other's actions to be getting on with whilst I work on a draft for the press conference."

"I thought we weren't having one yet?"

"We aren't, I'm just preparing a statement in case we have to give one in a hurry. We have to be seen to be on top of this thing. Come on, Ronnie is waiting."

Jim reluctantly got to his feet. His legs felt like lead, and he thought that a quick shower might be a good idea after all.

"Thanks for this." He said as he passed.

"No problem."

"That's one helluva laugh the ACC has." He chuckled.

"Attaboy. Don't be letting this bastard grind you down."

Forty minutes later Ronnie and Jim parted at the doors of the autopsy suite. Lottie told him that they were about to start. If he hurried, he wouldn't miss anything. He sidled up silently behind Rachael and Mo. Bernie Went was bent over the body, which was still covered by what looked like the same duvet cover that had enveloped Samuel Taylor. The pathologist gently pulled it up to reveal the body underneath.

"I thought you'd done this earlier?" Mo spoke, his voice only slightly muffled by his face mask.

"We lifted it up when we put the body in the mortuary van, yes." Bernie fixed his gaze on the inspector, stepping aside for the photographer. "But only to see if there was any identification. When we turned the body, we saw that poking out of her pants." He pointed to a tray which contained a green piece of folded paper in a plastic wallet.

The legs were revealed slowly, then the pubic area, the stomach...at which point there was a sharp intake from the three police officers. The bulbs flashed.

"There seems to considerable disturbance to the victims' chest, left hand side." Bernie intoned. He nodded to his assistant who lifted the rest of the duvet cover away from her head. The garment came free and was carefully removed for further analysis. Bernie carefully turned the face one way, then the other. "Pre-mortem blow to the left lower jaw, causing some contusions. Best guess, a punch to the face. You can just define several points of primary contact, probably caused by knuckles."

"Enough to kill her?" Asked Jujara. Bernie was feeling under the skull and remained silent. The trio waited patiently. He squatted down so that his head was the same level as the victim and examined the back of the head which was now being supported by the assistant. He prodded around for a moment or two before straightening up and regarding the three officers.

"The hair is matted, and the skull is malleable...indicating it may be broken. I stress the word 'may'. I don't want to turn the body over in case anything here..." He waved generally in the direction of the chest "...becomes...dislodged, shall we say." He turned back to his examination.

"Apart from the aforementioned injuries, what we have is a woman in her mid-to late twenties, in extremely firm condition." He drew a finger along her arm and shoulder. "Very good definition of the muscles on both arms and shoulders." He picked up one of the hands and examined the fingernails. "Well nourished, no signs of calcium deficiencies."

"Victim has what appears to be two deep penetrating cuts that converge just below the...seventh rib. The horizontal cut is... approximately four inches, the vertical one about seven. Just imagine a capital 'I'. Four of the ribs seem to have been manually broken upwards. My oh my."

"What is it?" Jim edged a little closer to the table.

"No, Jim, you don't need to see this." He took a deep breath and held his left hand up, the fingers splayed slightly. "The victim has had four ribs sawn through. Then the killer has picked up each one..." Bernie used his right hand to push each of the four fingers on the hand backwards in turn.

"Like a chicken wishbone...?" Jim asked. Rachael winced; Mo inhaled sharply.

"Precisely, Inspector. Like a chicken." Bernie inclined his head in agreement, and shut his eyes in pain. When he opened them again, Bernie had turned back to the table.

The pathologist had fallen silent again, probing and prodding. At one point he asked for some clamps, before asking for a cloth. He leant back. The photographer took more pictures.

"The pleura has been sliced in a similar manner to that of the dermis. Slightly smaller incisions. The lungs have been sliced as well." Another pause, until he turned to face the expectant trio. "It looks like he was looking for the heart."

"Is it missing?" Rachael asked, almost afraid of the answer.

Bernie shook his head. "No, it's there alright." He suddenly went silent.

"What is it then?" Jim asked impatiently.

"I've never seen anything like it." He waved at the body. "Help yourselves."

Jim edged over and peered inside the chest cavity, before letting Rachael and Mo take a look. Mo let out a low whistle.

Tori's heart had been sliced in four, neatly, like an apple.

The door opened and she was standing there, causing his heart to skip a beat like always. She beamed at him and reached up and pecked his cheek. "They're in the lounge." He went in and there he was, standing up on wobbly legs, holding on to an older woman's legs. A spool of dribble was hanging off his chin, and Jo swept past him, snatching up a tissue from a box on the sofa as she did.

"Ooh, look at you Harrison, I leave you for a minute and you're a mess!" She bent down, wiping the drool off his little chubby chin. She picked him up and held him, tickling him. He squealed with delight.

"Hi, I'm Carol, Jo's mum." The woman said, extending her hand. He shook it warmly. He couldn't help but notice how cold and bony it was, but her smile was warm and genuine. "Here, mum, take Harry while I put the kettle on. Coffee?" She asked, turning back to him.

"I'll do it." Carol said. They sat on a worn brown sofa that had seen better days.

"Nice place you have here."

"It's a dump!"

"Nothing wrong with it that I can see."

"Apart from the damp patch in the bathroom, peeling paper in my bedroom, and the doors hanging off in the kitchen."

"It's warm, and it's yours."

"The council's."

"A bit of paint, a dab of glue and a screwdriver could sort it."

She rolled her eyes, tickling her son under the chin, making him wriggle with delight. "He obviously doesn't have a toddler at home, Harry." Her eyes twinkled as she looked back at him.

"Maybe I could help."

"Maybe you could."

Carol came in with a tray of coffee, some biscuits and some sliced apple. He hoped the apple was for Harrison. The happy grandmother took her grandson and showed him a fire engine as it made way up the hill outside, its lights blazing and sirens blaring. Jo slid her hand over his and squeezed it hard.

Jim Smallwood breathed deeply as he went outside into the evening sun. The earlier rain had cleared away, giving the world that clean, scrubbed appearance and smell. To Jim, the world seemed just that bit darker, tarnished. Rachael and Mo followed Jim out squinting in the sunlight. Ronnie appeared to be enjoying the warm rays, sunglasses on, head upturned, leaning on Jim's car. He removed his sunglasses and studied them with a hard expression.

"By your faces, it must've been grim, Sir."

"Extremely." Was all that that Jim could muster in reply. Jujara had slipped on a pair of Ray-Bans and shook his head sadly. Rachael just looked pale and said nothing.

"Back to the station then?"

"Might as well. We will be going nowhere else for the foreseeable, sergeant."

Back at the station, all heads turned to Ronnie as he entered the conference room alone. He simply shook his head, shrugging. Terry furrowed her brows at her sergeant. She beckoned him over.

"Nothing about the girl, boss. They came out looking like they'd seen a ghost."

"Aye, to be suspected, I suppose. They'll tell us when they're ready. Owt else about the old man Taylor?"

Ronnie was nodding his head. "Yes. Reports of a young man supping with him several times leading right up to his disappearance." He spoke to David and returned shortly with a couple of sheets in his hand. "I spoke to a mate who drinks down

148

the pub where Sam was a regular...and it appears that the landlord..."

"Hang on, hang on, back it up a bit. Your mate drank in the same pub, and you didn't think to mention it to me?"

Ronnie put his hands up. "I didn't know myself until this morning. Another mate told me that he works round the corner and he often pops in at lunchtime for a pint. Anyway, sometimes the landlord sails close to the wind. Nothing major, the odd 'dodgy' barrel, or case of whisky off the back of a lorry. To cut a long story short, I sort of promised that we would turn a blind eye to his nefarious activities if he helped us out."

Terry grabbed his arm and hustled him out of the conference room as quickly as decency would allow. She marched him down the corridor and, finding an empty office, shoved him in before slamming the door behind him.

"WHAT THE FUCK DO YOU THINK YOU'RE DOING SERGEANT?" She hissed at him in a steely whisper.

"I thought you'd approve. It might be really helpful." Ronnie was biting his lip, anxious that he had messed up.

"It is." She gave him a bear hug.

"What is it then?" He was completely confused.

"The good news is that you're proving yourself a real sergeant, Ronnie. What's a bit of bootleg booze between friends? Bad news is that you almost blurted out back there amongst all those southern bastards."

"You're not mad then?"

"Only that you're gob's too big. What have you got then?"

"When I was at the hospital I spoke to Grant, and then his wife, Shirley. I've got a description of a man, mid-twenties, slim build, with short brown hair. Height is about 5'10" or thereabouts. The wife seems to think he was some kind of student at Edinburgh Uni."

"Different from what those Irish lads said he looked like."

Ronnie thought about this. "They were drunk, though."

"Don't go soft on those scrotes."

"I'm not- and I almost forgot something." The sergeant's eyes began to shine.
"Tell me now or I swear I'll knee you in the knackers."
He laughed and told her.

Over the previous few weeks, he had a nagging feeling that she was growing a bit distant from him. He couldn't put a finger on what it was. Sometimes when they were sitting together, just doing simple things like playing with Harrison, or watching television, he felt that she wasn't really with him. Their lovemaking was fine, and she was indeed wild with him between the sheets on the few occasions when Harrison didn't stop crying until he was nestled between them. It was during the day that he felt it. He would catch her gazing into the middle distance, lost in some kind of daydream. He struggled to forget about it, figuring if that if something was truly wrong, she would tell him.

One Thursday evening, he had popped round as he hadn't seen her for three days and had been looking forward to it. She had kissed him fiercely on the doorstep and pulled into the living room where she had put her arms round his neck and had drawn him into a passionate embrace. Harrison was banging a wooden spoon on a plastic drum, sitting on the floor. The toddler had beamed wildly for a whole ten seconds before forgetting he was there, resuming his drumming.

"Can I ask you a favour?" Jo looked at him over a steaming mug of coffee after she had put her son down again.

"Sure, honey, anything you want."

Jo looked away and wouldn't make eye contact. "Caroline has asked me out tomorrow. Apparently, she's having some trouble with her fella. She wants to have a chat."

Alarm bells started ringing. He didn't mind her seeing her friends, in fact he encouraged it. Normally they all went out as a gang, or a foursome. Carol was a most obliging babysitter, as she adored her grandson. This was something else.

"Mum is going to stay the night with her sister, and so she can't look after Harry."

"And you want me to fill the breach?" He put on his best smile, hoping it was convincing.

"Yes. If that's OK. I mean, tell me if it's not, or if you have plans or if just don't want..."

"It's fine, Jo. It really is. I'd tell you if it wasn't." He put his hand on her knee. She rested hers on his. That was the moment that he knew they were both lying to each other. She was hiding something; he was pretending he was fine when he really wasn't.

"Right, I've got to get going, there's a couple of things I was going to do tomorrow, but I should do now."

"But you've only just arrived!" She pouted. Wow, you're good, he told himself.

"I'll come around about seven, yeah?" He got up and kissed the top of her head.

"That'll be perfect." She gave him a smile, but he could tell that she was upset. You can't have it both ways, he thought. You either want me or you don't. I'm not some kind of tap that you can switch on or off at will. He scrunched down and gave Harrison a little tickle under his ear, and the youngster gave a little giggle.

"Hey, big guy. You and me tomorrow, eh? What do you say to popcorn and porn? Maybe we can hit the town and find some bitches..."

"Hey!" Jo threw a cushion at him, laughing properly now. "He isn't having any girlfriends until he's at least twenty-five!"

"Who said anything about girls, Harry? Mummy's so stupid!"

At least they parted on good terms. Maybe, he thought, things might work out after all.

"And Inspector Jujara is going to work out a press release. Smallwood finished his summation of where the investigation was up to. All of the team had been given actions. The detectives had come back from Tori Henderson's house empty handed, their main concern was that they hadn't been able to locate any diary or planner. They assumed that the masseur simply carried it round in her handbag with her, and that was still missing, presumably long gone now. There was no sign of any disturbance either, and so the thinking was that Tori had either been lured somewhere by the killer or ambushed en route.

The team had listened in silence as Mo had related the findings of the autopsy, including the post-mortem desecration of the body. There had had been no discussion as to why it had been done, what it meant, or if it was some kind of evolution in the killings. The psychologist who had been helping them, Mary Guy, was at a meeting, and had been gone for several hours, but had promised that she would be back before they all went home.

The real burning issue that confronted them- besides that of catching the killer before he did it again- was of the press conference. Jim and Mo had allowed all the team that were present to have their say. There were some, like DS Ratcliffe and Rick, who had reasoned that the last moves of Tori Henderson could only be established by an appeal for help to the general public. The naysayers, such as David and Rachael, had insisted that any such move would only serve to alert the killer as to where the police stood, and drive him further underground. A stalemate had arisen. Jim and Mo were of the same opinion; they weren't convinced by either side of the argument enough to say with certainty which way they should jump. But they were equally aware of the dangers of inaction. They felt hamstrung and frustrated in equal parts.

Terry had been uncharacteristically quiet throughout the discussions. Finally she stood up from a chair she had dragged to her favourite position by the window. She announced to the team that she had a development that would have an important bearing on the matter. "I apologise for not revealing this earlier- maybe I should've done...but I wanted to hear everyone's opinion before I said anything."

"What have you got?" He asked impatiently.

"Through some underhand dealings on the part of Sergeant Bimjano" She nodded in his direction," we have a description of the killer from when he was with Samuel Taylor."

"You have what?" Jim asked, incredulously.

"Hold you horses, Jim. Unfortunately, it's a case of two steps forward, one step back. It only serves to muddy the water. It just means the killer uses multiple disguises, if we believe the two lads, Seamus and... Lucky...are correct in their description."

"You mean it's different from theirs?" Rachael asked.

"Well yes, lady, it is." Terry fixed Rachael with a look that brooked no further questions. "But as of tomorrow morning, we will have a photo taken from a secret camera in the pub, hopefully showing the face of the killer."

The stunned silence that followed was total. Jim, though initially angry at Schofield's withholding of vital information, could see why she had done it.

"Ok, that does indeed change things. I will review the pictures and pencil in a provisional press conference for 10 AM." He thought back to the earlier meeting with ACC Parker and Laird. "I will lead, with both Inspectors." A few heads shot up that, a few quizzical looks crossed the faces of the detectives. But a glance at the boss told them that he had made his choice, and that the investigation would stand or fall on such things.

He gazed in the mirror that ran the whole length of the bar. Through the crowd, he could make her out clearly. She sat there, her hair hanging forward over her drink, obscuring her face. Although she was fairly pretty in an elfin like way, she was painfully thin, and could do with a good feed as. And a good night's sleep as well, he thought ruefully.

It was a shame she wasn't going to get any of them before she died, however.

The barman came over with their drinks, large vodka and coke for her, a pint of lager for him. This was his second, her fourth. The first one she had downed before he had even sat down, the ice cubes clinking in the empty glass as she slammed the glass down. He sighed, and wordlessly replaced the drink. She had raced most of the way through the second one as well before he had placed a restraining hand on hers and told her to slow down. She had pouted at him and was just about to complain, but something in his look had told her to be quiet. She shrugged and looked out of the window at the promenade. It was still windy, but the horizon promised a little brightness. She played with the stirrer in her drink, sulking.

He checked that the barman had his back to him, and that there was nobody at the bar near him. Satisfied, he opened his palm and poured a white powder from a little plastic sachet. He gave the glass a stir. He guessed that he had about fifteen minutes before she felt woozy, and fifteen minutes after that before she blacked out. Time for two more drinks at the speed she was downing them. He moved back to the table and she looked up and smiled as he approached, tucking an errant strand of hair behind a small ear. She absentmindedly picked up the glass with her bad hand, winced and dropped the glass. He had enough presence of mind to catch it before any of the liquid slopped out. A solitary drop splashed onto his hand. He licked it off, unable to taste anything discernibly wrong with it.

"Right, I'm taking you to the hospital to get that checked out, young lady."

"It's fine."

"It's not, and I don't want any argument about it, either. But I'll get you one for the road". In response, she tilted her head on one side, pulled a face and stuck her tongue out at him.

"I'm not staying in overnight."

"For a sprained wrist? I should hope not." He laughed at her and headed back to the bar.

"She's on a mission, isn't she?" The barman commented. He rolled his eyes in reply.

"Sisters, need I say more?"

The barman shrugged in a non-committal way that seemed to suggest understanding and switched his attention to the next customer. He picked up the drink and went back to the table. His heart was heavy, for he realised that he was actually beginning to like this girl.

"You do know I'm a whore, don't you?" She asked, surveying him over the lip of her glass.

"Really?" He regarded her sternly. "The thought never crossed my mind."

She regarded him closely for a moment before realising that he was teasing her.

"The police called you Olive, you called yourself a whore, and you look like one anyway." He remembered why, after all, he didn't like her.

"Oh yeah, I did, didn't I?" She rattled her glass, looking at it. "Must've had more than I thought." She dissolved into a fit of giggles. He decided it was time to leave, and stood up, heading round to her seat to help her.

"My gallant knight in white arm...armour." She had started to slur, and her eyes were glazing over. He pulled her towards the door slipping an arm around her waist. She nuzzled into his neck and murmured, "I really, really, really like you."

"Come on." He opened the door but couldn't get out as a group of half a dozen lads, out on a stag do, were attempting to enter the bar.

"Oi oi...someone's pulled a right slapper here." The leading man, wearing an incongruous mix of make-up with a plastic Viking helmet blocked his way.

He rested her gently on the jamb of the doorway before looking at the drunk Viking. "Look here, dickhead Davey, get out of my way and there'll be no trouble."

"Who do you think you're calling a dickhead?" The man grumbled, belching. "And how do you know my name is Davey?" His mates lined up behind him menacingly.

Just what I need, he thought. "Because all cunts are called Davey, and all people called Davey are cunts." He neglected to say that it was printed on his cheap fake army combat t-shirt. Instead, whilst Davey was trying to work out what he had said, he

pushed him in the chest strongly and quickly enough to cause him to fall backwards into the arms of his mates. Not waiting a moment, he took off with Mandy in his arms again.
"Oi! Come here, you fucker...come here." But it was Mandy who peeled round, ducking away from him, to stand in front of the lead attacker. He stopped, unsure of hitting a girl. The hesitation gave her enough time to bring her arm up and spray him full in the face with pepper spray from a small canister she had been holding in her hand. The drunk fell back, screaming in agony, his hands clawing at his face. The two mates who had come with him stopped in their tracks as Mandy waved the canister at them, a tilt of her head enough to ask them if they wanted some too. One held up his hands whilst the other reached down to help his friend. Mandy backed away, until she was sure they weren't going to pursue them any further. Turning, she simply said "You can take me to the hospital now." Needing no encouragement, he hustled her in the direction of his van.

Jim stood gazing out of the window as the shadows began to lengthen. It was turning into a fine evening, if only weather wise. His stomach rumbled, and Rachael, standing next to him laughed despite the situation.
"You have to eat, Sir. You won't be able to function for long on an empty stomach."
He turned to her, nodding vaguely. He scratched at an eyebrow. "Yes, you're right. And I've got to feed my houseguests as well, although I don't feel like cooking."
Rachael shrugged. "Let them take you out. They would be saving a lot on expenses if they've no board to pay for."
Jim looked around the room. David and a couple of the others were talking into telephones quietly, Rick was hunched up over the table trying to write some notes, but otherwise the team had been given various jobs. "Where are they, anyway?"
Rachael pressed her face against the glass and looked out at the front of the station. She could just make out one of Terrys' stilettos. And then a puff of smoke confirmed it.

"Down below, smoking." Jim nodded. He looked at his watch, thinking.

"Is there any more we can do this evening, before Mary turns up?" Rachael, keen as she was to make progress with the case, was tired and hungry too. She also had agreed to go out for a drink with Cheryl, the secretary.

"Most of the team have been given actions- background checks, trying to locate the dead girl's parents, tracking her last moves, and so on. I wish there was more we could be doing, but there you go." He sighed heavily. He followed Rachael's gaze to a new board, with Tori's photos on it. They were silent until Terry and Ronnie breezed in.

"What's happening then? Where's the 'psychobabbler'? When we going to eat something- I'm famished." The words gushed like a tidal wave out of Terry. Jim, by now scratching his five o'clock shadow, stood there, shaking his head.

"Have you seen Inspector Jujara?" Jim asked.

"He's in your office, phoning his wife, I believe." Ronnie replied. "Apparently, he likes to take a bit of time out every day to talk to his children, if he knows that he's going to be late. He says it keeps him grounded, and they like to hear his voice."

"Grounded?" Rachael asked.

"It reminds him that not all the world is evil." At this, Jim nodded thoughtfully, Terry cocked an eyebrow and Rachael stared at some point in the middle distance, lost in thought.

The hospital was shiny, large and new, but three miles out of town on a busy road. Mandy had jarred her wrist again climbing into the cab of his van, and despite the numbing effects of both the drugs and the alcohol was whining. It was getting inside his head and it was all he could do to remain quiet. He suspected that she was a bad drunk, swearing and causing trouble at every opportunity. As they crossed a series of roundabouts heading out of town, it seemed like the entire population had found some reason to be out in their cars as well, and the traffic was stop-start, crawling slowly to its destination. After about twenty minutes, he realised that she had quietened down and it looked like she was losing the battle to stay awake. As they approached the turn-off to the hospital, he felt rather than saw her head slump forward to her chest. He pulled up with a jolt. She didn't react. He reached for a bottle of water on the dashboard and opened it, resting it between his knees and dug into his pocket, pulling out another clear plastic sachet. He carefully poured the mixture into the remaining liquid and swirled the bottle round until it had dissolved. He reached over to Mandy's prone body and viciously yanked her hair back. She opened her mouth but stayed unconscious. He poured the water down her throat until the bottle was empty. Her gag reflex kicked in and she coughed once, twice, but he just pulled her head back further and placed the bottle under her chin and used it to force her mouth to close. She gave a small grunting noise through her nose but didn't wake up. He let go of her hair and her head slumped back onto her chest. A little dribble of water escaped from her lips and ran down her chin.

He watched impassively for a minute or two. Two nurses passed by about twenty yards in front of the van but didn't pay them attention. Satisfied, he turned the van around, and headed out again. But this time he was headed home. He had business with this girl who travelled with him. To some she was Olive, to her few friends she was Mandy, but he was one of the few people who knew her real name.

The girl slumped unconscious in the passenger seat of his van was called Jo Holt.

CHAPTER 15

They were on their third round of drinks, but the mood hadn't lifted. Everyone was in a sombre mood, the conversation stilted. Rachael had departed after a quick drink, citing that she had places to be. The three inspectors sat nursing their drinks, Ronnie and Rick were chatting on a settee about football, and David was feeding coins into a muted fruit machine. Joss Stafford was keeping an eye out at the station for Mary Guy, who would be redirected to the pub. There was a sudden cascade of coin from the fruit machine, and David gleefully retrieved the jackpot, grinning from ear to ear, his face bright red.

"Your round then, Davey Boy." Terry beamed from her chair. The smile disappeared quickly from David's face and he reluctantly dug his meaty fist into his pocket.

"Don't you dare, David." Ronnie had broken off from discussing Liverpool versus Chelsea to look up at him. "It's her round, and she knows it. Come on, Boss- mine's a pint."

Terry regarded him across the table. "Remind me to look at vacancies in traffic for you when we get back, sergeant." Nevertheless, she struggled to her feet and tottered off to the bar. "Same again, Love." She said to the barman even before he'd asked her what she wanted.

She was setting the tray with the drinks down when the door opened, bringing with it a gust of animated chatter. Joss, hair down and wearing a pair of tight jeans, looked really different and drew admiring glances from Ronnie and Rick.

"Might I suggest that we finish up here, and discuss things over dinner? Know anywhere where we can talk?" Mo asked, after Joss and Mary had got a drink and settled by the bar.

"San Carlo's is quite discrete, Sir."

"San Carlo's it is then. Come on let's go, I'm famished."

He made the journey back in a little over two and a half hours. Jo was still asleep, nestled in the corner. He had timed the sedative on himself, twice, and had been comatose for four hours both times. Even allowing for the fact that he was bigger than her, he figured that the four-hour limit would be about the maximum time he could safely allow. Checking his watch, he reckoned he had another hour or so.

He was aware that this was the most difficult part of the situation- getting her inside without being spotted. He had spent a considerable time in looking for this place and had been delighted when he had eventually found it- a first floor bedsit, in a large house, in a quiet area. The best part of the room was that it had a large window, looking out at the house next door. Directly opposite, less than twenty yards away was another window looking directly into his. He had sat in an old wooden chair at various times of the day, watching, waiting. Eventually, his patience had been rewarded. He returned the next day to see exactly the same thing. And then the same two days the following week, with the same result. His neighbour, whom he had christened 'Bob', arrived home from work around six, got changed, sat down to watch television for an hour whilst eating a microwave dinner. Then about seven, he put on a denim jacket and left to go down the pub, returning after closing time. He always got undressed with his main light on, before switching on a smaller, dimmer light, which stayed on for thirty minutes or so. The routine never varied. Sitting behind a pair of black curtains, with only a small chink in them, he could see perfectly, content in the knowledge that he couldn't be seen himself. The chair sometimes gave him backache, but a few moments of pain in the grand scheme of things was a sacrifice that he was willing to pay.

He undid her seatbelt and pulled her towards him, careful not to touch any of her exposed skin. He wasn't wearing gloves- carrying an unconscious girl anywhere whilst being gloved would cause suspicion in even the most trusting of minds. If he was stopped now, however, he could just claim that Jo was his girlfriend who'd simply drank too much in the pub. Lady Luck seemed to be smiling on him. He stopped by the front door and put her down gently, feet first, propped against the wall, and listened for sounds of occupation. There were three bedsits on this floor and hear the faint strains of music coming from one of the back rooms- the Rolling Stones, by the sound of it.

Picking up his human parcel once more, he put her over one shoulder in a fireman's lift and climbed the stairs, which creaked at every step under the threadbare carpet. He entered his dingy room and threw her down none too lightly onto a soiled mattress lying on the floor. She stirred but didn't wake up. Walking over to the window, he looked through it to see Bob eating his dinner, eyes glued to his television. He hadn't even noticed his neighbour enter, let alone throw down the body of a female. A slight muffled sound emanated from behind him, where Jo was regaining consciousness. He put on gloves before picking up a scrap of old material and some lengths of stout rope. He quickly tied her hands behind her back and bound her feet. Lastly, he gagged her mouth. Getting to his feet, he looked down on his handiwork, satisfying himself that she was well secured and helpless in equal measure.

Apart from the mattress and the chair, the room was completely bare. Going to a closet and selecting a tin of paint and brush, he went over to a wall where he couldn't be seen by Bob, opened the tin, dipped in a brush, oblivious to a squirming Jo behind him on the floor.

Everyone, including the rotund David and Terry, had foregone starters so that they could indulge themselves in the superb desserts that the Italian restaurant, was renowned for. They had ordered their main dishes, mainly lasagne or pizza, and a couple of bottles of wine. They had been closeted in a function room that the manager assured them was discrete and secure, the waiter leaving before Jim had let anyone discuss the case. He turned to David and asked about the latest updates.

"You have the floor, Mr. Tunicliffe."

"Do you want me to stand, Sir?"

"This isn't the bloody Masons." Terry snorted. Dave looked at her, and then at Jim, who gave him a quick shake of the head. "Well, the first body, Sam Taylor- the latest forensic results haven't given us much. Fibres taken from his coat suggest that at some time prior to his death, he was in a vehicle or room that contained chipboard panelling."

"Like half a million Transit vans, then. Great, go on." Jim sighed and looked at his napkin.

"He hadn't eaten much of interest in the hours prior to his death. Just some liquid that could be water and beer...and possibly some kind of bread product." His colleagues all seemed interested, apart from Mary, who had her head stuck in various reports. When he stopped speaking, she looked up, and smiled. David continued, "The image from the pub will be biked down overnight so we can go with it in the press conference, a copy of the statement is here." He selected a piece of paper and floated it so that it landed in front of Jim, who scanned it briefly before handing it round the table.

"There are no links of any kind that we can find between him and the second victim."

"Besides the killer." Jujara interjected.

"Besides the killer, yes. The full autopsy results are due in first thing, but stomach contents are believed to show a small amount of cereal, and coffee."

"Ah, now that's interesting." Terry interrupted David, who looked at her, as did Jim.

She looked around, willing them to make the link like she had. "It means she didn't have time for lunch. She was probably abducted before lunch on the day she was killed."

"It means no such thing." Mary looked up. "It just means that cereal and coffee were the last things she ate. A colleague always has muesli for lunch instead of a sandwich. He says it helps maintain his concentration through afternoon lectures."

The two females locked gazes for a while, before Terry conceded with a small nod.

"Anyway, as I was saying, there are no links- apart from the killer- that we have established so far, but enquiries are continuing. Apart from that, there's nothing from the vets so we still don't know where he sourced that from. It's entirely possible, according to DS Ratcliffe, that the person responsible for supplying the heroin may also have supplied the ketamine."

"Sounds like a reasonable assumption," Inspector Jujara said. "It's not unusual in London, so there's no reason why it shouldn't be the same here." David ploughed on.

"Anyway, moving on- hold on here's dinner."

"We'll leave it there for a while." Jim leaned back and tucked his napkin into his shirt, so that didn't spill any tomato sauce on it, realising how hungry he was. He was not alone.

He sat down on the sofa again, worn out.

"Come on, you must be tired, you're a tenth the size of me, and I'm bloody knackered!"

Harrison had resumed his banging on his plastic pot with his wooden spoon. Apparently, half an hour of riding 'horsey' round the lounge, the kitchen and the hallway had only been a warmup for the main event. Now he was a world class drummer embarking on a world tour. The non-stop banging was giving him a headache; getting up, he gave Harrison a quick rub on his head before going into the kitchen to get himself a glass of water.

He opened the freezer compartment in order to get a couple of ice cubes. Amongst the peas and the fish fingers was a bottle of Smirnoff. He thought this strange, as he had never known Jo to drink vodka. He lifted it out to examine it and found it was only half full. Even when they'd been out together or with their mates, and come back home to relieve Carol, or the babysitter, he had never been treated to one. The way it was positioned at the front of the freezer compartment meant that it hadn't been bought ages ago and forgotten about; it was a recent purchase. Frowning, he put it back exactly where he had found it. He rested his forehead on the fridge door, his head awash with thoughts. Slowly, he knew that something was wrong. He realised with an anguished cry that the drumming had stopped. He raced back into the lounge, stopping short when he saw Harrison slumped over his plastic pot, the wooden spoon still gripped in his little fist. He knelt by the toddler. A little string of drool escaped Harrison's lips and began to drip onto the carpet. He gave the little sniffling snort he always gave when he was falling asleep. Waves of relief washed over as he realised that the boy had worn himself out at last and dozed off. He gently reached over him and lifted him up, carrying him carefully up the stairs, sniffing his nappy as he did so. It smelled fine, and he didn't need changing.

Carrying him into the bedroom, he laid the sleeping tot in his cot, covered him up and watching the peaceful rise and fall of the youngster's chest. Satisfied that Harrison was out for the count, he retreated quietly. He was halfway down when he realised that he hadn't switched on the baby monitor. Abruptly, he turned around and retraced his steps and padded softly into the bedroom. A little electronic squawk erupted from the monitor when he switched it on, causing little Harrison to shift his position in the cot, but he didn't wake. He retreated backwards and didn't see the linen basket until it was too late. Clothes spilled out, and the lid went cartwheeling along the landing all the way into the bathroom to rest against the side of the bath with a squeak of wicker. With a sigh, he went to retrieve it.

He considered himself a fairly modern man, and he knew the sheer volume that a mother and baby could accumulate, and that Jo and Harrison went through an inordinate amount of clothing. Harrison, as a little boy who had just learnt to crawl, was forever getting dirty; Jo was always getting covered with food at mealtimes. He bent down and began scooping up handfuls of bibs, little trousers, tops, skirts, jeans, socks and the rest. He stopped when he came across a pair of silk stockings and a black silk lingerie set. Weird, he thought to himself. If it was old, he would no doubt have seen it at some point, and if it was new, and Jo had been trying it on, then there would be no need to wash it so soon.

His mind went spinning again.

The meals dispensed with, everyone except for Joss ordered the tiramisu. She claimed that she was trying to lose weight; the men scoffed that she had no need to, and she laughed.

"Right, settle down everyone." Jim spoke up, his voice cutting across the chatter. "We're not on a jolly. This is a working dinner." The conversation died down as everyone focused on their leader. He looked across at David, who shook his head to indicate that he'd finished. Jim looked at Mary, who nodded.

"Most murders are committed by someone the victim knows. There's no link whatsoever that we have established that these two were even remotely linked by blood." She paused, and glanced round. There was a general nodding of heads, so she continued. "Also, most murders are committed by people with a lower than average I.Q. level. We call them 'disorganised killers'. This can mean that they never set out to kill anyone, but were influenced by other factors, such as drink, drugs, money, sexual misadventure, anger- the list is almost endless. We haven't got that here either." More nods. Mary suddenly felt the urge to get up and walk about, so she did, walking around the dinner table.

"What we most definitely have is the much rarer, highly intelligent style of killer that we refer to as 'organised killers'. This man had planned virtually aspect of what he was going to do- from a careful choosing of the victims, to their..."

"Are we sure that they weren't chosen at random?" Inspector Jujara interrupted Mary. She regarded him coolly for a moment, her eyes narrowing as she looked at him.

"He travelled several hundred miles and befriended this man over a period of weeks, so we can safely assume that he was targeted specifically." Jim saw that Rick was preparing to ask another question, so cut in quickly instead.

"If we have any further questions for Ms. Guy, perhaps we can write them down and ask her at the end." He gave Rick a sardonic smile that left the junior officer suitably chastened.

"Thank you, Inspector." Mary gave one of her half-smiles. "As I was saying, this is a highly organised killer who specifically chose Samuel Taylor to be his first victim. The same goes for the second victim-Tori Henderson. She was found and brought to her death. The distance travelled was negligible, which maybe important, we just don't know." Mary sat down.

"Looking at the occupations of the deceased, there's no link between a rat catcher and a masseuse. Apart from the fact the victim would have minimal contact with a limited number of people in the course of their jobs. So you may be looking for someone with a bad back caused by running after mice all day."

Inspector Schofield barked out a laugh. "Very funny, miss."

Mary smiled at Terry, who winked back. There was a muted laugh from around the table.

"Seriously, though, from a psychological point of view, it may be a factor. With only limited contact with a small number or people, it could very well be argued that the killer knew that it was entirely possible for these people to go missing for a period of time without their disappearance being noted." The smile froze on her lips. "Which adds another level to this killer's level of sophistication."

He had finished one wall and half of another by the window by the time Bob switched his light off and went out. He had plenty of time. He looked down at the floor where Jo seemed to be asleep. Putting down the paint, he pulled the mattress with her on it into one of the corners of the room, away from the painted area. Picking up the brush again, he knelt and began painting the floorboards. The carpet had previously been removed. As he painted in long rhythmic strokes, he cast his mind back to the demise of his relationship with Jo.

He remembered that he'd stuffed the lingerie back into the linen basket, piling a few baby clothes on top. He went downstairs slowly, thinking of plausible reasons not only for its existence but its current location. Had she bought it to impress him, and then got it dirty somehow. An impression of mother and child sitting in the kitchen eating breakfast wearing suspenders and a Basque was as far-fetched as he could imagine.

He opened the back door of the kitchen and stepped into the unkempt garden to have a cigarette, which turned into two which then became three as his mind played scenarios which became progressively worse as they crowded into his brain. He tried to shut them out but without success as he felt himself become more upset, depressed and wound up.

Shaking his head to try and clear the negative thoughts, he entered the kitchen and opened the fridge. He found the vodka and took a long pull on it straight from the bottle.

An insistent crying broke into his thoughts and he remembered Harrison. Quickly screwing the lid back on the vodka, he replaced it before dashing upstairs. Harrison was standing inside his cot, tears streaming down his face. Rushing over, he scooped him up and cradled him. It wasn't the little chap's fault what his mother got up to, or who with.

Slowly the sobbing subsided, and Harrison began to quieten. Smelling that a nappy change was in order, he crossed to the changing mat and began to unbutton the child's clothing, talking to him all the time. Harrison seemed to be listening to him quietly, hanging onto every word he spoke. So he changed from talking gibberish to having a serious conversation instead. "No, I know you can't answer me properly, Harry, but give me a gurgle for yes and shake of your head for no." He stopped what he was doing and smoothed a lick of hair off Harrison's face. "Do you understand that? Oh well, I'll carry on then...now is your mother in love with me or is she shagging someone else behind my back? No, you can't gurgle and shake your head at the same time, that's not an option. Come on, man up, I know she's your ma and all that, but I'm a bloke and we're meant to share secrets. What do you mean by nodding? Oh you really are useless, mate. Thanks for nothing- you can do your own nappy next time!"

He walked a soothed Harrison around the bedroom until he felt the rhythmic cadence of a sleeping baby in his arms. Laying him down, he watched over him and felt an overwhelming desire to protect the little man. This must be what a father feels like, he thought. He just hoped that things would settle down with Jo and they could become a real family unit.

The floor was complete, and another wall. He had sat down an hour or so previously and waited for Bob to reappear and go through his ritual of undressing and reading for twenty minutes. He had sat on the chair, watched and waited.

Jo had woken and had started to struggle against her bonds until she had seen the strange smile playing on this madman who held her captive. She froze in abject fear of what lay ahead. The rope was tied too well to loosen, and she gave up, conserving her strength. The overwhelming stench of the paint was irritating her throat and she began to cough. He looked at her and seemed to understand, for he crossed to the window and pulled the sash up about six inches, before resuming his chair. He just stares and stares out of the window, she thought. Given half a chance, she would've thrown him out of it.

Jim checked his watch and realised that most of his team had already put in fourteen hours. Mary and Joss were developing rings under their eyes, David looked stressed. Ronnie's eyes were beginning to glaze, and he was struggling to stay awake.

The two Inspectors were alert and interested, Jujara's eyes gave no hint of tiredness, just a steely determination to see this through to the end. It was impossible to tell with Terry as her make-up was so thickly applied it looked like a mask. There seemed to be more wrinkles around her eyes, though. He hated to think what he himself looked like, as he dragged a hand through his hair and then across his stubbly chin.

"I think everybody is fit to crash. I know that I can take much more myself tonight. I want to thank Mary here for her superb help today and this evening. The only thing she hasn't done is tell us the killer's name." This feeble attempt at humour bought the tired laugh it deserved. Mary had spoken about the type of man they were looking for. If he had to put it in one sentence, Jim thought that they were looking for a criminally aware genius, who was executing a meticulously prepared plan sophisticated enough to fox the brightest police minds, a meticulous genius psychopath on a mission who was white, in his late twenties and who was showing no desire to stop. Mary had emphasised repeatedly that this man was not going to stop unless he was caught, and that the body count would surely rise.

What nobody could possibly know, however, was how quickly it would indeed rise.

CHAPTER 16

Andy Butler opened his eyes and shut them again immediately. It was far too bright for him, too early. He disliked the summer, the heat, the light, the girls in short summer dresses, all of it. Give me dark, cold, or snow anytime, he thought. Many were the hours he spent in his dull warehouse job dreaming of moving to Iceland or Siberia. Still, on his wages, a dream was what it would remain.

He forced open one eye again, blinking against the golden rays as they filtered through the dirty window. Every day he swore to himself he would go to the shops at the weekend and buy himself a curtain or large piece of material to hang up and keep out the blasted sunshine. But every evening when he stumbled home, he just wanted to sit down, eat his dinner, and go play pool with his mates. And when it came to the weekend, he always had a choice between going out with his mates or buying a curtain. His money was always that tight.

He sat up with a yawn and stretched. He poked around on the floor for a pair of underpants that weren't too dirty. He picked one pair up, sniffed them and almost retched. He threw them in the corner furthest from the bed. He supposed he'd have to go around to his mums on Sunday to use the washing machine. That meant he'd have to suffer another lunch with Reginald, her new husband. He always got the impression that Reginald looked down on him, like something he'd trodden in that offended his nostrils. Andy made a mental note to wear the underpants he'd just launched into the corner. Then he'd throw them away and buy a new pair, as well as a fucking curtain.

His back was getting hot from the sun by the time he found a pair that seemed serviceable enough, if he turned them inside out. He pulled them on and winced when he remembered the last time he'd been in this position, two weeks previously. Then, he had decided to go 'commando'. A new girl had started at work and he'd wanted to impress her. Well, not put her off to start with by smelling like a bag of rotten vegetables. Only thing was, he'd caught his foreskin in the zip of his jeans and his screams could be heard halfway down the street. He laughed ruefully at the memory.

He found a t-shirt that didn't smell too badly but couldn't find any matching socks. He wondered what James was doing next door, so he crept up to the window to spy on him. He knew James would approve, for James was a spy. No-one had sussed James out apart from him. Maybe he'd make a good spy himself.

James was the name he'd given the bloke who lived next door. Their windows looked in on each other, only twenty metres apart. He always looked smart, suave, well dressed, but occasionally changed his appearance, by changing his hair or growing a beard, or wearing different glasses or caps. This is why Andy called the man James, after James Bond. He was probably going round his normal business, but Andy imagined him going to Moscow to kill a mafia leader, or to Venice to secure some vital defence plans, or somewhere exotic to play high stakes poker. It would explain why he was gone for long periods.

He let his eyes adjust against the golden glare assaulting his eyeballs. He blinked twice, and then again. Something was wrong. As he blearily gazed across the divide it seemed to him that someone had blocked out his neighbours room with blackness. He instantly became wide awake and realised with a jolt that someone had painted the glass of the windows with black paint, so you couldn't see in. But the most alarming thing was that in big black bold lettering someone had painted a sign on what looked large pieces of paper with a simple message before painting the window.

He actually banged his head forcibly against his own windowpane to make sure that he wasn't dreaming. He winced, but the sign was still there. Grabbing a pair of beat-up trainers and his denim jacket, he bolted, and slammed his door and jumped down the stairs three at a time. Pulling open the front door of the large house, he tried to work out where the nearest phone box. He knew he passed one on the way to the bus stop. It was only about 200 yards away. Racing down the street with the laces of his trainers flapping in the breeze, and his jacket under his arm, the thoughts raced through his mind, back to the note in the black window and its startlingly simple message: HELP ME.

Tracey Vickers stepped out into the sun and breathed in deeply, admiring the perfumes of the roses in her neat front garden. Whatever his faults as a husband, Reginald certainly took a pride in his roses. Going down the path, she stopped at a beautiful reddish-yellow specimen called 'Superstar'. She inhaled its heady aroma and set off to walk the half mile or so to work.

She had two jobs, in reality; she worked two days a week at the local Marks and Spencer's; But every other Friday, like today, she worked as a bookkeeper in a small gardening firm for four hours. The books looked after themselves in the main; the rest of her time she spent cleaning, pottering around, tending plants and occasionally answering the phone if the boss was out on a job.

She reached the gates to find them locked. She rattled them but they still refused to budge. She peered through the gap and saw that the truck was in the yard, parked facing her. 'Strange' she muttered in an undertone.

She remembered that her boss had given a spare set of keys in case of emergencies. She hoped that they were still in the bottom of her handbag. She rooted around but couldn't find them. She stopped looking and tried to focus more clearly...had she taken them out and left them at home with her other keys? Then she remembered- the side pouch. Her fingers slipped around the two keys. Fishing them out, she breathed out a sigh of relief.

It took a couple of minutes and several attempts, but she managed to fit the key into the padlock, and with a little grunt, she managed to slide open the clasp. It fell to the ground as she was opening the sliding bolt, rolling unevenly into a patch of weeds. She pushed open the gates, a faint sheen of perspiration on her forehead and her top lip. Picking up her handbag, she unlocked the office, wondering where her boss was. She was unconcerned, however, thinking that he may have gone to price up a prospective job on his motorbike instead of taking the truck, an occasional, if not regular occurrence.

Switching the kettle on for a well-earned cuppa, she remembered the padlock and so she went to retrieve it. As she bent to do so, she made a note to herself to dig up the weeds when she'd finished with the books. She worked her way through the jobs that had been completed over the previous fortnight. There was nothing untoward there, the jobs tallied with the receipts, and the bills issued. Sitting back, she sipped her tea.

She dragged her thoughts back to the task in hand. Somewhere in the back of her mind, she had thought that earlier in the week he'd promised to go and do a job for an elderly couple whom lived near a friend of hers. She tried to remember their names, absentmindedly tapping her biro against her teeth as she did so. Bert? Alf? Sidney? Ah, that was it- Sid and Ethel. She searched through the planner and found that they had been scheduled in for Wednesday, two days ago. She searched through the small pile of invoices but found nothing. It had been a confirmed job, not an estimate. Odd, she thought. If the work had been completed, the invoice would be here. If there was a hold-up for some reason, like bad weather, or illness, her boss was normally efficient enough to make a note in the planner and reschedule.

The quandary was enough to give her the warning signs of an oncoming headache. Wishing to avoid this, she thought a quick stroll around outside would do her good. Making a fresh tea she smiled to herself as she spooned two sugars into a chipped mug; Reginald would never allow mugs in the house. Stepping out into the bright summer sun, she removed her cardigan to let the sun colour her arms a little. She and Reginald were due to go down to their caravan in Cornwall in a couple of weeks' time and she would've preferred a little tinge to her skin prior to their arrival. Bending down, she uprooted the trio of dandelions that had sprung up since the last time she had been here, in which the padlock had settled. This reminded her of the absence of her boss, and a little seed of worry planted itself in her mind. She wandered off in the direction of the compost heap in the corner of the yard, behind the van. Throwing them as far she could to the back, she rubbed her hands together and turned back with a sigh towards the office. She had to pass around the back of the truck to reach the office, and she casually glanced into it. She saw a large tarpaulin spread over something, sand or turf perhaps. Intrigued, she lifted a corner. Reginald always said that she was nosey. When she saw what was under the heavy blue material, she screamed.

Jim and Rachael were in their office, discussing what the psychologist had revealed about the killer in the restaurant.
"Everything alright, Sir?" She asked him. He had a faraway look in his eye.
He didn't reply instantly, but his eyes flicked in her direction before moving away again, indicating that he'd heard her.
"It's the way the bodies are displayed. It's in the back of mind, something I know I've seen before." He shook his head. "It's just I cannot remember when, where, or in what context. Maybe something I've seen on television or read in a book somewhere."
Rachael nodded sagely as if she understood, but in reality, had no idea of how his mind worked in that regard. Sometimes she felt totally inadequate in his presence.
Jim shook his head again and stood up. "Best to round up the troops, Rachael, and get them working."
"Does our psychologist reckon that there's any sexual angle here, Sir?"
Jim regarded her through narrowed eyes. "No, not in itself. There may be an angle which hasn't presented itself yet. Why do you ask?"
"I was just wondering, that's all. A man who can do this must've a pretty fucked love life."

Terry and Ronnie were in the canteen, diving into a Full English. They had both overslept and so consequently missed out earlier. Jim had wanted to be at the office early, so they only had time for a rushed cup of tea. Now they had twenty minutes to stuff themselves with bacon and sausages and they were making the best of it. In between mouthfuls, they were filling Ian Westlake and DS Ratcliffe about what Mary had said.

"Sounds like we missed quite a bit then," mused a peeved Ian. Terry, her mouth full of egg, shook her head and patted his hand. She said something about it being in the notes that David was typing up, but between the northern accent and the egg, he couldn't really understand what she was saying. Nevertheless, he nodded to give the impression that he did.

There was an eruption of crackling from the radios of two uniforms over in the corner of the canteen. Chairs were scraped back as two constables grabbed their hats and rushed out. The canteen lady pointed in vain at the sign telling people to clear up after themselves, scowled, shook her head, but moved to clear the plates away with a heavy sigh.

"Where are they headed out in such a hurry?" Rachael asked, having nearly been flattened by the constables as they rushed out. Her questions were met by a round of shrugged shoulders and shaking heads from the detectives. "A cup of coffee, please Mavis," Rachael asked the canteen lady, "I'll help you clear up."

Mavis smiled at Rachael as she walked over and helped with the mugs and the tomato ketchup bottle. It had been knocked over in the kerfuffle but none of it had spilt out. She righted the bottle, screwing the lid firmly. She even gave the table a wipe down with a napkin, before turning to Mavis for her coffee.

"No charge, dearie." Mavis curled Rachael's fingers back into the palm that held her money.

"Thanks, Mavis, you're a dear." She leaned in closer to whisper. "Do you have any idea what that shout was about?" She glanced over at the other detectives, who were finishing their breakfasts, Schofield belching her appreciation.

"All I heard Graham say was 'body'. Then they all jumped up and out they went." Mabel winked at her, and Rachael patted her arm in a silent thank you. Turning smartly on her heel, she left and collided with her boss who was running towards her.

"Another one?" Rachael asked. Jim raised an eyebrow in surprise that she somehow knew already and nodded curtly. He turned toward the stairs, shouting over his shoulder, "I'll drive." He was soon bounding down the stairs two at a time, Rachael hot on his heels. Reaching Jim's car, they dived in. Rachael reached over for the car radio.

"...31 Westfield Road. Halls Gardening Services, reports of a body of a male being found there. Further details are to follow." The voice on the radio was crackly with static.

"Roger, thanks control, and out." Jim had heard the address and was already heading in that direction. "Shouldn't we inform the rest of the team, Sir?"

"All in good time." Jim looked at her briefly before returning his full attention to the road. "COME ON!" He roared at an elderly woman trying to cross the road in front of him.

"Steady on, Sir...we don't want to cause an accident!"

"Ok, I know how to drive, thank you very much." They drove on for a minute in silence. Slowing down at a roundabout, Jim looked over. "Sorry...I want to have a look at the scene before we send the balloon up...it may be something totally unrelated."

"Yes, I'd forgotten that we're in the murder capital of England."

Jim looked at her again and actually laughed; a short harsh laugh that conveyed more than any conversation would have done. He drove on, and found two patrol cars already there, and Rachael could see an officer unwinding the blue and white barrier tape, hear the wailing siren of an approaching ambulance.

Jim was ducking under the tape. Rachael followed him and saw that they were entering some kind of builders yard. Pallets of paving stones wrapped in plastic lay next to a huge pile of sand, next to an even larger pile of soil. Planters were neatly stacked in rows, from terracotta to plastic, smaller ones slid neatly into larger ones to form neat ordered rows. Behind a slatted fence she could make out the outlines of a sizeable glasshouse. Running down one side was a single storey building- presumably the office, festooned with posters. Inside, she could make out the burly figure of PC Jake Pike, one of the officers who had rushed out of the canteen earlier. She breathed in deeply, smelling the familiar aromas of soil and creosote.

"It looks like our man again, Rachael." Jim was nodding in the direction of the truck. "There's a stepladder propped up on the other side. Look, but don't touch anything until the SOCO's have secured the scene." He turned to the constable guarding the truck. "SOCO have been called, haven't they?

The constable in question, PC Sharma, who held up his fingers to show they were five minutes away. Jim nodded, sensing that under his dark skin, Sharma was probably feeling a little bit queasy. This was his second body in a week, an almost unbearable toll for a provincial town bobby. Jim made a mental note to enquire later if the constable would need counselling, such as it was. Still, that would have to wait, for Jim had greater worries on his hands than looking out for his junior officers. He had a madman on the loose.

The paint had all but dried, at least on the rough wooden flooring. He had dragged the stained mattress back to a position in the middle of the room, then savagely picked up a quaking Jo and thrown her on top of it. Apart from a whimper, she at least had the good sense to stay quiet, even after he had removed her gag. He stood there, hands on hips. He felt tired and tried to figure how much sleep he had missed out on recently but gave up. He sighed deeply, figuring out what he was to do next, the window or the girl. He laughed harshly when he realised that he'd listed the murder of an innocent human being as just another item. "Do the hovering, hang the washing, and don't forget to kill the girl before you go out." He had begun to like her, and he would make it quick for her. If only the real Jo was there, he thought wryly...and his thought drifted back to the end again.

Harrison had settled and was fast asleep, and he had drifted downstairs, waiting for Jo to return. He switched on the television, and off again. He wandered around aimlessly, picked up a magazine on the table, threw it down. He went outside and smoked a cigarette, when he heard the raucous laughter drifting down the street. He nipped back into the lounge and threw himself on the sofa, pretending to act as nonchalantly as he could despite the turmoil of his thoughts.

The key scratched all around its lock for what seemed to an eternity before it was finally engaged and turned. The door crashed open, and a heap of bodies almost fell through it, giggling and shushing in equal measures. He felt the anger rise like bile inside him. He realised that she wasn't alone, and it wasn't just her mate Caroline with her either. She could hear the deeper tones of at least one man, telling them all to 'keep quiet' or 'ssh... you'll wake the sitter.' The door opened and Jo staggered through it, obviously very much the worse for wear. He swung his legs off the sofa and regarded her quietly. She tried to look at him seriously, but collapsed in a fit of giggles, holding onto her friend for support.

"He doesn't look very happy, does he?" Caroline frowned down at him. "Maybe he's annoyed he's missed all the fun." She staggered over to one of the armchairs and collapsed into it. Behind her, two lads came bundling in after her. One of them traipsed over to the sofa and asked him to 'budge up' in a drunken slur. The other one slouched over and sat down heavily on the arm of the chair that Caroline had collapsed in, burped, and ran a hand through a mop of unruly hair, pushing it out of his eyes. "Got any of that Vodka left, Jo?"

Jo laughed and nodded, and heading for the kitchen, saying over her shoulder, "I'll check, but you may have had it all last time." She wobbled out of sight.

His worst fears were confirmed, he thought as he stared at the carpet. A playful punch on the shoulders woke him from his reverie, and he glanced up at the lad beside him.

"You alright mate? I'm Rook, that ugly specimen over there is Paul." Paul waved at him from his position, before running his hand through his hair again. Maybe it was an affectation, he thought, but if he had to do that every thirty seconds, why not just get a fucking haircut.

Jo came back with the vodka and four glasses, which she handed round to Paul, Rook and Caroline. She held onto the last one, looking down at the sofa and swayed softly.

"I didn't get you one because you're driving." She turned away without waiting for a reply and began to fill Paul's glass, and then moved onto Caroline's. Paul held up his glass in a mock toast to him behind Jo's back before leering at her bottom stretched out suggestively in her tight jeans. Without a word to anyone, least of all Jo, he stood up and walked out.

He never heard from her again- she never called him, he didn't see her or Caroline again for a long time. He'd bumped into Lisa about six months later, when he was in the supermarket one afternoon. She let it slip inadvertently that Jo was engaged to Rook and was expecting his baby. He'd simply walked off without saying goodbye.

He stood in the dark room, his blood boiling. He yanked on his gloves and knelt down by the prostitute. Somehow it felt fitting that she was a whore. She started to struggle as his hands closed around her neck. Her whole body started to thrash as he squeezed the life out of her. He closed his eyes so he couldn't see her pain. Then he opened them again, and he saw the real Jo beneath him. Slowly, the thrashing began to subside, and then her whole body went loose and limp. A single tear rolled down his cheek and dropped into her open mouth. It was as if a little piece of his soul had left his and joined hers.

He stayed there a long time, staring at her face. He reached up and gently closed her eyelids, before wearily getting to his feet. His head fell until he was staring at the freshly painted boards. After what seemed an eternity, he dragged himself to the cupboard and extracted six pieces of paper, each printed with a big black capital letter. He arranged them face down on the floor, before retrieving tape and scissors. Peeling the end of the tape was tricky, especially with gloves on. Eventually he managed to unstick a corner, and he put the letters up in the window, one by one. When that was finished, he stooped to pick up his brush and paint and started on the windowpanes.

There was just one more job before he could go home and get some much-needed sleep.

Rachael had dismounted the stepladder, brushing her palms against her trousers, when the radios started squawking again. Jim was in the office, door shut. She was shaking slightly, and indecisive as what to do first. Her look at the body under the tarpaulin hadn't revealed much. It was the body of a man whose face was poking out of a hole cut in the middle of a white duvet cover. She hadn't touched anything, hadn't even wanted to, even if she had been allowed to. The squawking continued, with Sharma talking into it intermittently. Jake Price and Graham, two of the other constables, came rushing out of the offices, their faces drawn, and rushed past Rachael and another constable at the gate, before jumping into the patrol car and screaming off, sirens blaring. Rachael turned to Sharma; one eyebrow raised. The uniformed clipped his radio back onto his jacket before offering up any explanation.

"The station has just received one very, very weird call about a message in a window up by the old children's home. Probably a wind-up, but the Super has got everyone running around like headless chickens." Rachael raised another eyebrow, but Sharma shrugged. She heard her name being called. She turned and saw Jim urgently waving her over, and Rachael joined him.

When her eyes adjusted to the relative gloom inside, Rachael saw a pale woman sitting behind the desk, dabbing her eyes with a tissue. When she put it down, she revealed herself to be about fifty years of age, with died mousey blonde hair. Her eye make-up, just a little liner by the looks of it, was smudged from the crying, and her nose was red. She managed a little nod when Rachael smiled a silent greeting in her direction.

"This is Mrs. Vickers, a part-time bookkeeper, who is employed here." Jim had started to explain but was shut down by a vicious glare from his constable. Rachael had moved around the side of the desk and put a protective arm around the crying woman, who leant into her and started sobbing again.

"There, there, you just let it out, Mrs. Vickers. Has anyone offered you a cup of tea? Would you like a fresh one, perhaps?" Turning to her boss, she asked, "Do you think you could rustle up a really sweet mug of tea, Sir?" Jim set off for the kettle without saying anything. Rachael eased the woman off and turned, sitting on the desk, whilst still facing her. She put a supportive hand on her shoulder.

"Now, Mrs. Vickers, my name is Rachael and I really appreciate that this is very difficult, but can you explain to me and my boss what happened from when you came in this morning?" She gave one of her sweetest smiles to the distraught woman.

"Well, I just do four hours a fortnight, you know, and today was my day. But when I came in, the gates were padlocked, which is unusual, for Chris- that's Chris Halls my boss, he's usually here by seven thirty most mornings." She broke off as Jim handed her a mug of steaming, sweet tea. "Well, as I was saying the padlock was on, but the truck was here." She looked through the window and shuddered.

"Isn't the truck normally here?" Jim took the chair on the other side of the desk.

"Well, if the truck is here, the gates would be open, wouldn't they?"

"Stands to reason, Mrs. Vickers." Rachael confirmed.

"Oh, call me Tracey. Everyone does, except my husband..."

Rachael let whatever Mr. Vickers called her slip by, eager to keep her on track.

"Ok, Tracey... so the gates were shut, but the truck was here...what happened next?"

"Well, I opened them, but dropped the padlock in a patch of dandelions. I came over here and opened up and started on the books. I went for a breath of fresh air, to retrieve the padlock and pull the dandelions. They spread like wildfire if you don't get them before they seed, you know..."

Jim gave a small cough, and Mrs. Vickers looked at him. She nodded, took a sip of tea, and continued. "He sometimes goes and sizes up jobs, on his motorbike, but it would be in the diary."

"And so you weren't unduly worried by the truck being here but him not being here? What else, what did you do?"

Tracey looked back to Rachael, "I do tend to waffle on, Reginald always says that." Her eyes fixed on a stapler on the desk, and her eyes glazed over. An uncomfortable silence began to stretch, until Jim gave another little cough. Tracey instantly snapped back to the present.

"What happened next, Tracey?" He coaxed, gently.

Tracey looked out of the window, and Rachael was going to gently nudge her again, when she spoke, in a quieter voice that Jim had to strain to hear. "I threw the weeds away and looked in the truck, where I saw his body." She looked down at her hands, tears appearing in her eyes again.

"How do you know it was his body in the van? He was under a big blue tarpaulin."

Suddenly, her eyes lit up as she glanced at the Inspector. "Do you really think it's not him, Inspector? That would be so wonderful!" Her face looked totally different as she broke into a smile. Rachael squeezed her shoulder.

"We don't know who it is yet- we have to wait for a special team to come and look before we know for sure." Rachael looked sad for a moment. "But it's best not to get your hopes up before then." Tracey nodded and the sadness settled again. A solitary tear escaped her brimming eyelids and rolled down her cheek.

Jim stood and put his hands in his pockets. "Well, thank you, Mrs. Vickers... is there any one you'd like us to call for you? Your husband, perhaps?"

"No, you can't call Reginald. I'll be fine."

"Another family member, perhaps, or a friend?" Jim asked. Tracey thought about this for a moment, before shaking her head.

"You are going to have to come to the station to make a statement at some point, Tracey." Rachael had eased off the desk and taken her hand off her shoulder, but the grim smile had remained. "We will get a uniform to drop you off and get your contact details and suchlike. Thanks very much for your co-operation, I know it's been a very traumatic experience for you." Her platitudes were met by a silent nod. Both detectives shuffled out of the office.

The heat was a welcome relief as they went outside; it had been unnaturally cool in the office. Jim turned to Rachael and was about to ask her for her thoughts when Sharma came hurrying over.

"Sir, sorry to interrupt."

"Yes, PC Sharma?" The uniformed officer was suddenly finding his boots very interesting and wouldn't look up. Just as Jim was beginning to feel impatient, Sharma looked him in the face and told him with an anguished look on his face: "We have another body, Sir."

CHAPTER 17

Joss Stafford was walking her beat with PC Susan 'Momma' Holland, along one of the quiet residential streets, enjoying the early morning sunlight. Susan was the officer that all the others looked up to, and the one they went to if they needed advice on a whole range of subjects. The older lady was relaying some sage words about a lad Joss had been chatted up by in the pub the previous week. Joss was about to ask a question when her radio crackled into life, calling out her police identification number. She held up a hand to stop Susan, whilst reaching up her other to press the button on her radio to communicate with Control.

"Control, this is PC 3018, receiving."

"Joss, where exactly are you?"

Joss looked around. "Douglas Road, junction of Salisbury Avenue."

"Can you hustle on down to the phone box on the junction of Salisbury and Rothamstead? Report of a man wanting to report something mysterious on a neighbour's window."

"Can you repeat that, control? Did you say window?" Joss spoke into her radio, picking up her pace as she rounded the corner. Susan, by now behind her, closed up in order to hear what Control was saying.

"Affirmative, Joss. He sounds quite concerned."

"Roger that, Control. Got a description of the caller?"

"Negative, Joss. It was a telephone call, wasn't it?" Joss immediately felt stupid, and blushed, whilst picking up her pace again so Susan wouldn't see it.

"Have you got a name then?"

"Informant gave his name as Andy Butler. Please locate and verify as soon as you can."

Joss looked back at her colleague and gave her a head a nod to show that they needed to get to the end of the road as soon as possible. Sue gave a nod and tried to bustle along as quickly as she could, which wasn't very fast given all the equipment she was carrying and all her considerable weight as well. You're definitely built for comfort, not speed, Joss thought, but she was glad of the support of such a supportive and experienced officer such as Susan.

Joss could make out the sun glinting off the side of the silver phone box. She stopped when she realised someone was waving at her from the other side of the road. A lanky, dirty youth was sitting cross legged on a low brick wall and had languidly raised his hand in their direction. Slowing down, Joss made sure there was no traffic before crossing the road. The youth, who had been sitting on a low brick wall, unfolded his legs and revealed himself to be a lanky, dirty young man, aged probably in his early twenties. Joss slowed to a halt about six or seven yards from him, one hand reaching for her radio, and the other subconsciously reaching around her back to rest on the top of her truncheon. Susan caught up, blowing hard and removed Joss's hand, letting it swing free. She stepped past Joss, and panted out, "Andy...Butler?" She stood there, hands on hips, waiting for his response.

"Yes." The youth nodded. "I rang the police." He nodded across the street at the box.

Joss brushed past Susan. "What this is about?"

Andy looked from Joss to Susan and back again. "They didn't tell you?" He shook his head, looking at the ground.

"Why don't you just tell us again, Sir?" Joss's breathing had returned to normal. She was glad of the extra circuit sessions she did down the gym every week.

"Probably better if I show you. My room's around the corner..."

"Someone has damaged your window?" Susan was regaining control of her breathing, though she still looked red-faced.

"It's not my window...it's my neighbour's window, but with all the garden hedges, it's best seen from mine, I guess." Andy was looking from one officer to the other, giving Joss the impression that not only was he telling the truth, but that he was genuinely concerned. Either that, or he was a bloody good actor. Looking him up and down, Joss reckoned he probably wasn't very good at much, apart from lounging around.

"Lead the way then, Sir." Joss waited and turned to follow him. Passing Susan, she rolled her eyes. Susan shrugged.

They followed Andy for fifty yards back up the road and turned into a side-street. Joss noticed Susan lift her head, to scan all the windows they passed, so she did the same, but they all looked perfectly normal to her. The climbing sun obscured many of them with its blinding reflection. One made Joss start as she was temporarily blinded by one such ray of sunlight shining directly in her eye. She blinked several times and stared at the pavement instead.

Ahead, Andy had stopped outside a row of detached Victorian villas. Joss knew that most had been divided into bedsits with multiple occupancy. She looked at the house opposite, but Andy was disappearing up the short path to the door. Susan was following and Joss noted that she had undone the safety clasp on her truncheon, and she did the same.

Inside was dark, and the smell of fried food, dirty washing, and damp assaulted her nostrils as she entered. They started to mount the creaky stairs. Joss caught the whiff of cannabis on the fetid air. Reaching the first-floor landing, the smell intensified. At the end of a corridor, Andy pushed open a door and went in.

Streams of bright sunlight filtered into the untidiest room Joss had ever set foot in. Dirty clothing created a carpet, empty food cartons and cans littered a small table, the television, and every other level surface. She breathed in deeply and instantly regretted it. She stared at the room's occupant, who was pointing out of his filthy window at something outside.

Joss gingerly moved clothing aside with the tip of her boot and made her way to the side of the bed and looked out of the dirty window. Twenty yards away was the side of the next house, and Joss blinked at what she saw; Susan gave out a low whistle.

The entire window seemed to be painted black. Six sheets of white paper were posted up in it. Joss couldn't believe what she was looking at. Each of the six pieces of paper had a letter painted on them, spelling out a simple message, that Andy had seen when he had got up.

Spelled out in big black letters was the simple directive: HELP ME.

Two minutes later, and they were standing on the pavement outside Andy's house. They had debated what to do, and Susan had insisted Joss called for back-up. Joss had radioed control, who sounded veritably harassed; a body had turned up in a yard across town, and resources were stretched. Susan had taken over the radio and had reminded them that the body was dead, and could be helped no further, whereas they had no real means of forcing access into what could well be a hostage situation. Common sense prevailed and a patrol car was allocated to them. They were now discussing what secrets the darkened window with its desperate message was hiding.

"I've seen him several times, you know." Andy had come out, unknown to them, and was standing behind them. Joss started, and Susan snapped her head round to look at him.

"Step away now, son. Go back inside now." She stated, a firm edge entering her voice.

Andy didn't move.

"I said go back inside, Sir." The tone was harsher. Joss had turned around and stood facing the grimy youth. She put a placatory hand on Susan's arm.

"You said you've you seen someone in that room?

"Yeah, loads of times... I called him James." Joss looked expectantly at Susan, who looked back at her, guardedly.

"What does this James look like then?"

"Oh, I've never 'met him', if you know what I mean. Only seen him through my window."

Joss wondered whether he could see anything through that dirt-smeared piece of glass, but she wanted to hear what he had to say. "Can you give me a description?"

Andy cocked his head to one side. "Not really, no."

Joss narrowed her eyes. "Why not?"

"That's why I call him James, after James Bond. He looks different every time, or most times. Different hats or caps, different colour hair, short, long... blonde, black. Sometimes bearded, sometimes completely shaved, including his head..." Andy trailed off. He guessed that what he was saying actually sounded pretty stupid now that he'd said it out loud. He started to scuff one trainer against the other, hands thrust deeply into his jeans.

Joss was about to speak when the patrol car came tearing up. It had lights on, but no sirens. Jake Price jumped out as it skidded to a stop about a foot short of Joss's right knee. Graham, driving, held up a hand in apology as he got out.

"Sorry, Joss, the car is a lot heavier with Jake in it than when you're with me." Graham winked, and Joss couldn't help smiling. His partner, refusing to rise to the bait, turned to Sue and asked what was going on. Sue filled in him on the situation, leading him and Graham away from Joss, who was left alone with Andy.

"What I want you to do, Andy is this. Go back to your room and write it down for me. Everything you can remember, with dates if possible, and times, what this man was wearing, doing, everything. Even if this turns out to be a massive hoax, or a prank that has gone wrong- it doesn't matter- this man you've been looking at sounds like he has been up to some mischief. Now go, and thanks for all your help." She shook her head as she watched him wander back to his room. Turning around, she walked up to her colleagues who stood watching. She planted her hands on her hips, and said all of them: "What's the plan?"

Terry sought out Mo in the conference room. He was reading a report that David had handed him. It contained a couple of grainy, black-and-white photos of their suspect, taken from the secret pub camera, where Samuel Taylor was a regular. He flipped through the rest of the report and put it down when he smelled the heady perfume of Terry fill his nostrils.

"Not very good, are they?" She said, nodding at the photos.

"Not much help, I'm afraid. Must be 10,000 who dress like that just In London." He sighed.

"Is that all? I thought everyone dressed like that down there."

"Did you want something in particular, Terry?" He refused to rise to her bait.

"Two things, actually, Mo." She nodded at the door. "Come on, let's walk and talk. Sergeant, with me." She scanned the room, and her gaze alighted on Rick who seemed to be tapping his biro against his teeth. "And you, Rick." The constable snapped out of his daydream and climbed out of his chair, swinging his jacket on as he did so. All four officers trooped out and down the stairs, and out of the back door of the station.

"Let's drive."

"Where to, Ma'am?" Rick had perked up a bit. Terry opened her fist and looked at a piece of paper that had been scrunched up in it.

"Somewhere called Salisbury Avenue. Sounds posh to me, but what do I know? I'm just a wee northern lass."

With Rick explaining which way to go to Ronnie, Terry turned to Mo and spoke in a low tone. "Where are we regarding the press conference? That photo is shit and you know it. And I hear Smallwood has rushed off God knows where to another possible bloody body."

"Well, if it is another body, and one of ours, we will have to postpone the press conference for a bit." Mo added.

"A blessing in disguise, then?" Terry looked at him appraisingly.

"Not for the dead person." Mo said, apparently without a sense of irony. "Is that where we are headed now, then?"

Inspector Schofield shook her head and filled him in.

Jim and Rachael stood and watched the SOCO team going about their grisly business. Bernie stood alongside them, reluctant to clamber up onto the truck bed to examine the body. Two of the technicians had removed the tarpaulin, and placed it on a large plastic sheet, where it was carefully removed for analysis back at the lab. Bernie had climbed the stepladder, just to confirm what they all knew already - that the killer had struck again. He was relaying instructions to the two techs as they laboured over the body swaddled in its cotton cocoon. The boards and everything else lying on the truck were also being removed, piece by piece.

Jim was torn between staying here or rushing off to the other scene. Three, probably four, bodies in as many days meant that this killer was in the middle of a spree- and he and his team were nowhere. He suspected that more detectives would have to be found, the press informed, the public warned to be on the lookout for an extremely dangerous psychopath. There were no links between the first two victims that the team could find, and he fervently hoped that one would emerge when these two bodies were examined, and their lives dissected as intricately as their bodies would be. He was desolate.

"Utter madness... why is he doing this?" Rachael turned to her Inspector, and realised that he was talking to himself, completely unaware that she was next to him. She shook her head and looked to the pathologist. Bernie exhaled. He scratched his head with a gloved finger and sighed again.

"The body is of a well-developed male, aged about 30."

"How long?" Jim asked.

"Hard to be definite, but best guess is about 24 hours." The pathologist looked over the inspector's shoulder, gazing into the middle distance.

"What are you not telling me?" Jim demanded.

Bernie fixed his gaze back on the policeman. "Oh, nothing... I was just thinking about the physical endurance this man has. The adrenaline coming and going through his body would be tiring enough. Then there's the physical effort of moving the bodies. Victims one and two had been moved some distance. This man here," he pointed over his shoulder at the truck, "is probably at least fourteen stone. I think he must have been put in there post-mortem. There is simply not enough room to do what he did in that truck bed. It's just not feasible."

Jim regarded his friend thoughtfully. "What have you got, then? Cause of death?"

"I can't be sure, not yet. My technicians haven't removed the duvet cover yet, and there seems to be no facial damage. That's all I can tell you until we get him back to the lab."

Jim nodded and was about to say something when Bernie put a finger up. "But there is one interesting thing. He seems to be wearing a pair of ear defenders."

"Ear defenders?" Rachael chimed in, confused.

"Big red industrial headphone-type things. Used by gardeners to keep the noise at a minimum when they are using noisy machinery."

"Oh... like the ones my school gardener used to use when he was mowing the hockey field?"

Bernie nodded. Jim just regarded her in silence.

The pathologist cleared his throat and turned back to the truck. "We are going to take him down now and see what else we've got." He shrugged and waved farewell to them and walked over to supervise his workers.

"Come on then, Rachael, let's go see this other one."

She took one glimpse at the truck and shivered.

Joss and Graham, with Jake in tow, had got as far as the front door of the villa with the painted window when they heard the crunch of asphalt as Ronnie's car slid to a stop. They watched as the four detectives clambered out.

"FREEZE!" Inspector Schofield held a hand up just as Joss was going to ring to get access into the building. She had been going to get the attention of one of the occupants of the lower floor but had hesitated when she had heard the vehicle approach. Her hand literally was hovering next to a buzzer with a label declaring the occupant to be a 'Ms. M. Smith'.

Terry bustled up the path, followed by the others. Because of their size, and the narrowness of the path, Jake Price and Terry had to turn sideways to allow the senior officer through. As she did do, she gave the burly Price an appraisal of his body as she squeezed a little too closely to him. She greeted Joss with a raised eyebrow and a knowing look.

"Now Missy, I don't think you should be doing that." All joking gone now; she addressed the constable sternly. Joss nodded. Terry was about to push the buzzer herself when she too hesitated and gave the door a push instead. After a slight jolt, the door opened to reveal a dark, dusty hallway. Joss, peering over the inspector's shoulder, could see it was the same layout as the building they'd been in earlier. This one, however, smelled clean, with a hint of furniture polish and a delicate smell from a wilting bouquet set in a vase on a side table at the foot of the stairs.

Cautiously, all seven entered the hallway, filling it almost entirely. Terry looked around at six expectant faces.

"Rick, it's your hometown, and you're the detective. Take young Joss here with you and detect something." Her eyes indicated the stairs. Rick looked at her, at the stairs, then back at her before nodding. He crossed to the foot of the staircase, put a foot gently on the first step, then looked back. "Get a bloody move on, lad. Joss, give him a shove!" Terry hissed at him. But if the truth was to be told, she was scared as he was. Rick crept up the stairs one by one. He froze when the fifth step creaked badly, and he silently slid his front to the side of the stair and used the banister to help him ascend at the end of each new level. After what seemed an age he reached the landing.

Joss tapped his arm and pointed to the right, to the door on the end. She held a finger up to her lips, and Rick nodded. Joss caught the whiff of fresh paint. She gripped Rick's shoulder for comfort. It occurred to her that he was more scared than her.

Rick strained his ears for any sound coming from the room at the end of the short corridor. All he could hear was the occasional drip of a tap in the bathroom. There were no sounds elsewhere, apart from the muted strains of a television playing somewhere downstairs. He edged his foot forward a couple of inches, then remembered Joss still had her hand on his shoulder. Feeling bolder, he stepped forward.

Six feet, four feet, two... it was only when he was this close that he saw that the door was slightly ajar. He could see nothing in there though, it looked so dark.

He mouthed the word 'truncheon' to Joss and held out his hand. Joss fumbled around until she put it in his palm. He reached out until the point was resting against the door and held three fingers out to Joss. Then two, one, and then none.

"POLICE!" He yelled and pushed as hard as he could with his truncheon. The door swung open and revealed ...nothing.

Try as hard as he could, Rick could make absolutely nothing out in the room beyond. Everything was pitch black. He couldn't make out where the floor stopped, and the wall started or even see the windows. He leant back, blinked and tried again.

Still nothing.

He looked at Joss, whose puzzlement mirrored his own. He exhaled deeply; suddenly aware he had been holding his breath. He was heard a movement behind him, and he whirled round, truncheon aimed high.

"Put that down, you fool. Unless you want to be arrested for assaulting a police officer." Terry had crept up the stairs soundlessly and stood four feet behind him. Rick felt foolish as he lowered the truncheon. Terry was craning round him trying to see into the room.

"Constable, do you have a torch?" Terry asked Joss. She handed her one and Terry switched it on and aimed the light into the room. The stench of paint was making them feel giddy.

Terry squinted into the beam as its light revealed black painted floorboards, a black wall and... black cloth curtains. Everything was black. Then a shiny lump appeared on the floor. It seemed like someone had dumped four or five dustbin liners in a corner. Terry shined the torch over them again and swore.

"Call the SOCO team, Rick." She said, running the back of her hand against her forehead. She leaned back on the jamb of the door and stared at the ceiling. When she looked back down again, Joss inclined her head.

"Nay lass, there's now't a young lady like you needs to look at. Let Sergeant Bimjano do it. Sergeant stop hiding. I can smell your aftershave even through all these paint fumes."

Ronnie poked his head around the corner, saw the situation was safe, and ventured into the corridor. Taking a deep breath, he took Joss's torch and shined it into the room. He removed his shoes, and trod carefully onto the first paint floorboard, shining the torch around his feet for boobytraps. He crossed the room slowly and squatted near the bags. It appeared that someone had slit the seams of four dustbin liners and laid them over something. Extracting his pen, he carefully lifted the one nearest the corner.

Under the duvet cover, the unseeing face of Jo Holt stared out into her own hell.

CHAPTER 18

Neither of them said much on the journey away from the gardener's yard.

"There wouldn't BE four if I was up to the job." He sighed deeply.

"That's bollocks, Sir, and you know it. There is virtually no forensic evidence, no reliable witnesses, nothing to tie the victims together. Not even Sherlock Holmes would've solved it by now."

Jim looked over at her, still unsmiling. She could see the bags under his eyes, the worry lines etched into his face. He breathed in deeply and nodded. "I hope you're right about that. This is no time for self-pity. Let's concentrate on catching this bastard. If they bring someone in, then that's up to them."

Rachael unbuckled herself and got out. "I'll get David and the others organised. There is plenty to be getting on with."

"Maybe get the M and M's started on house-to-house back at the yard and get Franks and Westlake to go over his house." There was a spark coming back now. Rachael knew that Jim believed that good old policing, aided by modern forensics and profiling, would track down this madman and catch him. A good deal of luck wouldn't go amiss, either.

He lowered his sunglasses and looked out at the view of the mountains. He breathed in deeply, a beautiful aroma of flowers and fresh air. It really did smell differently up here. He went back into the lounge and then through into the bedroom, throwing his case on the bed. He would unpack later. He sat down on the bed and kicked off his shoes, thinking. He had caught the plane with only a couple of minutes to spare, cursing that the painting of the room had taken longer than he had anticipated. Still, he had grabbed two hours sleep on the flight, and was looking to several days of relaxation by the pool, sipping Sangria and soaking up the rays of the fierce Spanish sun. His mind recounted the events of the previous few days and smiled up at the ceiling. He deserved the rest, to recharge his batteries for the next phase of his plan. His mind wandered to the police, and he wondered how far behind him the police were. He suspected that they thought the pace of killings would go on unabated...how wrong they were. He retraced each crime scene, going over each one for the hundredth time to make sure that he had left behind exactly what he wanted them to find. It was a different matter whether or not they actually found them. He had no doubt that the police were fairly competent, and that they gobbled up the clues he'd left them like birds gobble up crumbs... but where would it lead them? No matter, he thought. He let his mind drift to the next phase, and slowly his eyelids grew heavy, and he slept, in his clothes, as the golden sun drifted across the azure sky.

Terry was leaning on the wall outside as the familiar vehicle of her colleague pulled up. She gave him a grim smile, stubbed her cigarette out under her stiletto as he approached.
"Tough one up there," She said blowing out the last of the smoke.
"And I bet yours was no better."
"Do you have another one of those?"
Terry pulled her pack open and he took one. What the heck, she thought, and lit another one. They stayed there for a moment relishing the quiet and the nicotine filling their lungs. Jim told her about what had been discovered at the gardener's yard, and she relayed what lay in wait upstairs. He'd used the car radio on the way over, informing Joss to keep the SOCO team at bay, at least until he'd had a look at the body in its surroundings.

He finished his fag and told Terry he was heading in, and she said that she was going back to the station with Rick and Ronnie. He nodded and added that he'd head back that way soon, and to round the rest of the troops up.

He passed Jake Price on the doorstep, signed in on his clipboard, and took a pair of plastic shoe covers. Susan and Graham were trying to locate all the other occupants of the villa, with varying degrees of success. One lady, Ms. Smith, seemed to be a bit of a busybody, and was filling Graham not only with information but tea and cake. Jim grunted and made his way upstairs, avoiding the SOCO who was dusting all the hallway surfaces and the banisters. At the top he encountered Ronnie and Rick, about to leave. "You alright, Constable? Inspector Schofield told me it was you who went in first."

"I'm fine now. Just these paint fumes have given me a bit of a sore throat."

"Well sit upwind of Schofield on the way back, or her perfume will finish you off." Jim clapped him on the shoulder and said he'd be back soon, and that he was a very brave lad.

Turning to face the others, he looked at who was left. As well as three SOCO's, there was Joss and Mo. One of the SOCO technicians was erecting a huge light in the room so that they could see what they were doing. Jim looked at Mo and asked him how they found the room.

"We received a tip-off about the- "He started to say, looking perplexed. Surely Jim had been appraised of this already, he thought.

"No, no, that's not what I meant at all." Jim breathed out, exasperated. "I mean, what was the state of the room? Has anything been touched?"

"Oh, right..." Mo gave a small snort. "...with you. One of the bin liners, over her face has been moved. We tweaked a curtain but put it back exactly." He regarded his colleague through narrowed eyes. "We aren't complete amateurs here, Jim."

Smallwood ignored his hurt tone and tugged him by the sleeve to the room. Turning to the SOCO, he just said, "Can you a give us a minute, please." The technician shrugged and left. When he had gone, Jim just asked his colleague to shut the door. Mo did as he was told, curious. Total blackness enveloped them. They couldn't see anything, not even each other, though they were less than two feet apart. All they could hear was muted chatter from the officers waiting in the corridor, and the call of a blackbird outside the window.

"What are you thinking, Mo?" Jim said quietly.
"That I'm glad I'm not afraid of the dark." Mo whispered.
"Precisely...that's it, I'm thinking that's precisely it. Ok, you can open the door again."

The difference was apparent immediately. Although the landing light was by no means bright, and there were four people blocking it, the light that was cast meant that they could see each other, and most of the room. Jim coughed from the paint fumes, still strong despite the door being open.

"Are you OK in there, Sirs?" A bemused looking Joss popped her head into the room but avoided looking in the direction of the body in the corner.

"Yes, I'm more than fine considering I've just been closeted in a black hole with a mad policeman and a dead body for company." Mo commented wryly, beating a hasty exit from the room, and heading for the stairs. Jim followed him, leaving Joss with instructions to close the room after the SOCO team had finished with it, and let no-one else in. He caught up with Mo on the path outside the house, removing his plastic booties.

"Come on, I'll give you a ride back to the station."

On entering, Jim vaulted up the stairs two at a time. He knew he was onto something. He could hardly wait to test out his theory on the two inspectors and Rachael. Asking Mo to wait in his office, he sped off to the conference room, stuck his head inside and asked for Terry and Rachael to come with him.

"Superintendent wants to see you immediately, Sir." David said to an already closed door.

"I think I'm onto something." He said, not waiting for them to even settle themselves.

"What's that then? I thought you looked a bit perkier."

"Phobias."

"Phobias?" Terry looked at him, blankly.

"Phobias- think what people are scared of." Jim was warming to his topic. "This last poor girl was afraid of the dark. The gardener was afraid of noise. The old man, Samuel was afraid of needles, or gay sex, or being raped, or all three."

"And the masseuse, what was she afraid of?" Terry was assessing the possibility that Jim was actually onto something.

"We must have missed something. After all, we don't know where she was killed. Find the murder scene, we find what she was scared of."

"That's easier said than done, Jim." Mo admitted to himself that it was a possible link, but that there were massive holes in his theory.

"And what is his motive, anyway?"

"Maybe he was massaged then raped in the dark by a gay gardener." Terry looked at Jim, who stared back. Terry couldn't contain herself, and stood up, laughing. "Maybe, you're onto something, Jim, but it needs a whole lot more work to it."

The door crashed open and a livid Superintendent Laird strode into the room. "My office, now!" He stormed out as he quickly as he had come in. Jim his shrugged and followed his boss. Mo raised his eyebrows, whilst Terry drew a finger across her neck in a slicing motion.

Meanwhile, Jim stood to attention whilst his boss settled himself behind his large desk. Laird took one look at him, raised an eyebrow, and carried on shuffling paperwork.

"For god's sake, man, sit down. You'll give me a crick in my neck."

Jim sat down, bolt upright. He wanted this bollocking to be over with so he could hurry back to his troops and carry on developing his theory.

"Let's get this over with; we're both busy men, and I'm sure you want to hurry back to your troops and develop any theories you've got. Have you got any at this stage?"

"We were just thrashing one about, Sir, when you came in."

Superintendent Laird had steepled his fingers and was regarding Jim through hooded eyes, nodding occasionally as Jim outlined his theory.

"Bit thin, isn't it?" Laird asked when Jim had finished. " ACC Parker has got a rocket up his backside from the Chief Constable, so he put two up mine and wanted me to put three up yours." Laird smiled, and Jim relaxed. "Consider yourself well and truly rocketed."

"Duly noted, Sir, and thank you."

Laird leaned back in his big leather chair and gripped the armrests, swiveling slowly. He kept his eyes on Jim. Laird trusted Jim, and was confident that he could catch this man, if anyone could. A sad look crossed his face. "Four is as high as they want it to get, I'm afraid."

"Four is still four too many in my book." Jim countered.

Laird nodded again and stood. He went over to a flask of coffee and poured himself one, turned and leaned on his sideboard, sighing. "If you don't wrap this up very quickly, I'm afraid the powers that be are going to send in someone more senior."

"Do you know who, yet?"

Laird nodded "DCI Carew, from Headquarters."

"Charles Carew, you mean?" Jim was incredulous.

"Yes."

"But, he's an accountant, a bean-counter, not a detective."

"He's the face of modern policing, Jim." Laird was grimacing. "I'm sure he will be able to get the maximum out of your team."

Jim shook his head. "And I can't. Is that what you're saying?"

Laird laughed. "No, no, Jim. I'm saying that the team will work harder for you because of him. Just don't tell anybody I said that, or I will put you on traffic for the rest of your days." Jim forced a smile. Didn't he have enough problems without an idiot like Carew cluttering up the office? He was so lost in his thoughts that he didn't hear Laird talking to him.

"Sorry, Sir, I was lost there for a moment." "I was just asking if you wanted any help now."

"No, thank you, I had better be getting back to the team. We know very little of the third victim and nothing at all about the last one- the girl in the dark."

"I might pop along to your briefing. I need to be kept in the loop. Reading your reports is one thing, but I'll get a better grip on things if I'm there. OK?" Laird asked, refilling his cup.

"Oh yes, by all means, Sir."

"I have every confidence you will catch him, and soon."

Jim nodded his thanks in turn and headed back to the conference room.

To help him over the shock of losing Jo in such a hard way, his mate Lawrence had suggested that they take a holiday together, just the two of them. After a bit of wrangling about where to go, they settled on Sri Lanka. They had booked it for the first two weeks of September, and as the time drew near, excitement mounted. As it was the summer holidays, he had got himself a job, helping to refurbish the local university library. The job was at times mind-numbingly tedious, just removing thousands of cards and their little holders, and sticking new labels back in the same spot, at the front of each book, one after another. There was a little group of them- some of them actual university students, and the slow monotonous work, the camaraderie, the laughter, all helped to slowly erase the pain he felt from the break-up with Jo. And there was always the holiday to look forward to.

Coming home on the bus one rainy evening at the beginning of August, a girl got on the bus and smiled at him shyly before sitting down a couple of rows in front of him. He thought nothing of it and carried on looking at the rain as it slowly ran down his window. He barely noticed the girl getting off the bus, one stop before his.

As the bus pulled away, he saw her looking his way, and as the shy smile re-emerged, it was as if the rain had stopped and the sun had started to shine. Then the bus was gone, and he had to crane his neck to see her slim figure receding in the distance. He smiled to himself, before shaking his head as he resettled himself in his seat. He wondered if the girl was a local, or just visiting a friend, or going to the dentist...or a million and one other things.

Dismounting a minute later, he was still smiling. It didn't bother him if he never saw her again. The moment that they shared would stay with him a lifetime.

Jim gathered all the team together. There were four absentees- two were doing house-to-house enquiries with the uniforms, and two were checking the dead gardeners' house. But it didn't bother Jim- the buoyant feeling he had before visiting his boss was still there. He propounded his theme to the team, and they seemed on the whole mostly supportive. All apart from Rachael, and more importantly perhaps, Mary. Jim knew that he would have to work on it more to convince the psychologist, but he was surprised at his constables' reticence to embrace the theory. He kept glancing over at her, the gleam that was in the other detectives' eyes noticeably absent.
"You're saying that the murder scene of the second victim would indicate her phobia?" DS Ratcliffe asked.
"That's exactly what I'm saying, Sergeant." He turned to Mary. "What do you think?"
Mary met and held his gaze for a full fifteen seconds before she looked down. "For what it's worth, I think you are wrong." She said simply.
The silence that ensued was total. No-one dared to speak, and the tension could be cut with a knife. Rachael had never known anyone to contradict her boss like this. "And would you like to tell me where I have gone wrong?" His eyes glittered.
"Firstly, it was only a working hypothesis, right?" Jim nodded once, but remained tight-lipped, allowing Mary to continue. "Well, you have seen something in one of the crime scenes and made the others fit it, no matter how contrived the supporting facts. Secondly, the 'm.o.' of this killer would've changed from one thing to another and back again."
David interrupted by putting his hand up like a schoolchild. "I don't understand, miss. Surely the m.o. changed with each kill- injection, a punch, and god alone knows what these last two were.

Before the post-mortem results are published, how can we know that it changed back again?" A strange look came over David's face. "That's something only the killer would know."

A snort sounded from behind David. It came from Inspector Schofield, who asked him, "So now you're saying that Mary here is the killer? Sergeant Bimjano, get your cuffs out."

Mary was shaking her head kindly in David's direction. "I wasn't referring to the killers actually method of killing, David, just the way he is operating. Of the four killing we know of, the first was found in the immediate proximity of where the death occurred. Numbers two and three, and possibly four, though I doubt it- occurred elsewhere. I think this last young girl was killed where she was found. That's what I was getting at, and I'm sorry I wasn't clearer." David was blushing, and it only intensified when Mary turned her hands up and together, as if inviting David to slap the handcuffs on her wrist. There was a muted laugh.

Mary turned her attention back to Jim and inclined her head by way of apology.

"You're saying such a change would be unusual, then?" Jim asked.

"If your theory was to stand, yes- I've never read or been involved in a case like that." Mary looked around the room at the assembled team, their faces looking intently at her, hanging on every word. "There are other reasons as well. The clues left at the first and third scene, suggest other factors at play here. It's not that you're wrong, Inspector, there is something that links these people. We just haven't looked in the right place yet."

Rachael looked over to where her boss stood, head hanging. Her heart went out to him. He'd been convinced that he had been on track, and now his dreams had been dashed.

Mary also sensed this. "Of course, having a theory like this does help focus our minds. It's just this one doesn't necessarily lead us any closer to the killer."

Mo spoke up. "How do you mean?"

Mary tilted her head to the side as she regarded him. Her long hair slid off her shoulder, to sway, gently gleaming, in a ray of sunlight. "Well, say this man hated cats, for example. We could warn cat owners to be extra vigilant as they went about their business. We could trace any acts of cruelty to cats, or even smaller animals, in the vicinity in the last year or so. With a theory based on fear, the material is so varied we wouldn't know where to start. If we went around this table, we would find a dozen things that scare people from spiders to clowns to flying." She looked back at Jim. "I'm sorry, but it just doesn't stack up."

He placed the last forkful of paella into his mouth and savoured the rich tastes and textures as much as he had relished the first. Wiping his mouth with a napkin, he picked up the wine glass and swirled the rich red Rioja around and then finished that too, loving the soft velvety feeling as it trickled down his throat. He leaned back in his chair, and looked up the bustling, narrow street. Tourists and locals mingled with each other, some heading home from the beach, others heading out for an early dinner before drinking themselves silly on cheap cocktails and beer in the numerous bars. Older couples strolled by, hand in hand, simply enjoying the sights and taking the air. Everywhere people were enjoying themselves in the last of the day's sun. And I am enjoying myself, he thought to himself. I'm sitting outside my favourite restaurant, The Yorkshire Rose, in Fuengirola on the Costa del Sol, and I've just had a great meal. He thought about what had happened. The events of the past week or so were the results of months of intricate planning; the months of intricate planning were the response to the years of suffering, rejection and humiliation he had suffered. The years of suffering, rejection and humiliation were redressed by the events of the past week. It made a lovely circle. He felt devoid of emotion when he thought of Samuel, Tori, Chris and Jo, Mandy, Olive...whatever her fucking name was. A tingle of excitement travelled the length of his spine when he thought of them. If the plods were too dumb to pick up his trail, sooner or later one of them would figure it out, and then the real fun would begin. The thought of that made him hard.

A couple of passing girls passing squealed in when they saw the bulge in his shorts. Recalled to the present, he realised he was leaning back on his chair, revealing a massive erection to the passing crowds. Blushing, he sat up. Maybe this little holiday could serve as more than a simple recharging of his batteries.

He waited a couple of minutes for normal service to be resumed down below, before throwing a couple of notes and a handful of pesetas down. Confident and happy, he strode off down the street in search of an accommodating senorita.

CHAPTER 19

Jim was getting sick of the antiseptic smell of the mortuary. Normally, he would only visit on official business two or three times a year: this was his third visit in as many days. He shuddered when he thought of the relentless nature of the job that Bernie and the other technicians had to endure day after day, sure that he wouldn't be able to do it. Suited and booted with him were Rachael and Sergeant Ratcliffe. He had insisted on Rachael coming, and suggested to the sergeant that it would be beneficial if he came along as well, and he had agreed reluctantly. He was going to bring one or other of the Inspectors, but Terry and Mo were preparing for the press conference, due in an hour or so. After a brief consultation with the Chief Super, they had decided that some sort of briefing for the press was due. Too many bodies were piling up, and eventually someone would notice what was happening in the leafy commuter town. The decision was made to head the press off at the pass, as it were, and determine what information was released, to whom, and how often. Jim wanted the public to be on the outlook for anything strange but didn't want to panic the masses or exhort the media into a feeding frenzy. Terry and Mo were two seasoned veterans when it came to dealing with reporters, and nothing would ruffle their feathers. Jim intended to join them as soon as the post-mortems on these two latest victims were over.

He was faced by two gurneys. Although he had mentally prepared himself, the two bodies lying under sheets on the metal trolleys side by side still took his breath away. It was a stark reminder that they were facing a true madman out of control, and seemingly able to pick off members of the public at random and at will. For a second, Jim's resolve almost buckled. Rachael must have sensed something because she placed a gloved hand on his shoulder to reassure him. Bernie stood between the two bodies, holding up a large saw. Jim imagined the pathologist as a modern-day Dr. Frankenstein, preparing to make himself a monster. But instead of a maniacal grin, Bernie's face was a mask of grim determination.

"I had hoped to be in a fishing competition today, Inspector." Bernie fixed his colleague with a steely glare. "But instead you bring me not one, but two bodies."

"Think of all those little fishes who get another day of freedom, Sir." Rachael made a poor attempt at levity and was rewarded with a look of scorn by the saw wielding pathologist.

"We always put the 'little fishes' as you call them back in the water, constable." He raised his eyebrows at Jim, as if to suggest that the younger generation knew nothing these days.

"To business, then," Bernie looked at the longer of the two of the bodies before him, "The first body is that of a well-nourished male, aged between 25 and 35." An assistant removed the sheet for him, and Bernie put down the saw on a small metal side table. "Height is six foot and one-half inch, weight in clothes around sixteen stones. Extremely fit, with good muscle tone. We have removed the duvet that was covering him, as well as the blue tarpaulin, although I suspect that the origin is exactly the same as the others. Tests on those will be complete in a couple of days, being near the weekend. Anything catch your eye, Inspector?"

Jim looked at the face of the gardener - and it struck him how he seemed to be just lying there asleep. The inspector's eye travelled slowly down the body and back up again, looking for anything unusual. He shook his head. "No, apart from the fact that he's still wearing his ear defenders."

"They were put back on after death, more like." Jim tilted his head, the question unasked. "If we just lift these up," Bernie continued, lifting the big red headphones. The revelation caused Jim to jolt his head back in surprise, and he heard the intake of breath from Rachael beside him.

Underneath the ear defenders were another pair of headphones, the type that were worn by people listening to a Walkman. Jim craned his neck and looked to see where the trailing wire led. Bernie lifted the shoulder and extracted a portable cassette player. It was indeed a Sony Walkman; the silver casing was smeared with something black. With a start, Jim realised it was dried blood.

"Now I know you want to know what's on this tape, and we will speed these tests through, weekend or not." Bernie looked around at the team of technicians behind him, whom just regarded him solemnly. Any of their plans for the weekend were flying out of the window.

"As you can see, if you edge round here," Bernie resumed, grunting a little as he struggled to raise up the corpse on one shoulder. Jim did as he was told and shuffled around the top edge of the gurney. He had to crouch to see what the pathologist was pointing at, with a slowly circling finger. Jim could make out a patch of blood encrusted hair, and on closer inspection, some sort of circular mark on the skull. He straightened up, and went back to the others, who had shown no interest in close examination of the skull.

"Hammer?

"Well...we will have to shave the hair off completely to have a better look, but it does look consistent with that sort of tool."

"Would death have been swift?" Rachael spoke for the first time, her voice catching.

"Pretty much so, constable." Bernie was nodding sadly. "The evil that men do." He looked down at the body of the gardener for a while, lost in his own thoughts. With a quick clearing of his throat, he whipped off his gloves and allowed a technician to remove his white plastic apron, replacing it with a fresh one. He donned a new set of gloves, snapping them on expertly. How many times has he had to do that; Jim wondered. Instantly, the answer came to him: too many. Bernie turned back and the gurney was removed into an anteroom, whilst the initial viewing of the second corpse took place. "You may want to take a deep breath before this one, folks." Ratcliffe and Rachael swopped nervous glances. Jim stood there resolutely.

When the technician removed the covering away, he revealed a completely naked young woman. But what drew Jim's immediate attention, was the proliferation of bruising all around the top of the legs. Although he couldn't see properly, he presumed that there was bruising between her legs as well, in a multitude of colours- purple, blue, brown, black.

His eyes travelled up her slender body. There were extensive bruises under her small breasts, along her shoulders, down her arms. He lets his gaze drift up to her slender neck, and sure enough, there were bruises around it.

"Now on a preliminary examination, the bruises around her neck are consistent with manual strangulation. See the three lines on either side- that's the marks made by the three largest fingers. The larger one is from the thumb. I suspect that her hyoid bone is broken, but I won't be able to confirm that until I've cut her body open." He exhaled loudly.

Jim looked round at his two colleagues. Rachael was shaking her head slowly, a tear in her eye. Ratcliffe, for his part, looked stoic but a little ashen. "Anything else you can tell us?"

Bernie gave him a look that told him to be patient. "The woman seems to be aged between eighteen and twenty-five. There was no identification on her, as her clothing and any effects were not present at the scene- or at least they haven't been found yet. We will take a cast of her teeth and send them for dental comparison...but that could take weeks, even months." Bernie paused, a frown on his face.

"What is it?" Asked Jim.

"The bruises around the neck are still forming...so they are twelve, thirteen hours old. Liver temperature indicates she was killed somewhere between three and five this morning."

"I can feel a 'but 'coming, Bernie."

"The rest of the bruising, along her shoulders here, across her chest," He lightly hovered a finger over the parts of her body as he spoke. "And here, across her legs... are at the earliest thirty-six to forty-eight hours earlier."

Ratcliffe coughed. "So you are saying the bastard held her hostage and beat her up, then?"

The pathologist looked at the sergeant with an innocent look on his face. "I am suggesting no such thing. I have seen this type of bruise patterning once or twice or before though."
"Where?" Demanded an incredulous Ratcliffe.
Bernie fixed him with his steely blue eyes and said without emotion, "On prostitutes."

The next day on his homeward journey he almost missed her. He had bought the latest Colin Dexter novel and was so deeply engrossed he was almost home when he realised that he only had a couple of stops before he had to alight. Looking around outside the bus, he looked at the familiar landmarks passing by slowly- the petrol station, the cinema, and he was relieved that he had stopped reading just in time.
As the bus slowed to let a few passengers off, he casually glanced in their direction. She was standing with her back to him. He didn't know how he recognised her, was it the luxuriant dark wavy curls that spilled out over her coat, or the way she held herself? Either way, his heart almost stopped when she gave him one final glance as she descended the steps of the bus. The look of hurt, abandonment, almost loss, gave way to the same shy smile he'd seen the day before as he had finally gotten his nose out of his paperback and noticed her.
She was lost temporarily in the melee of people getting on and off the bus but as the vehicle began to pull away he caught sight of her, looking his way. Again the shy smile lit up her face gently, as she put her hand up to her hair to smooth some errant strands away from her face. He raised his hand to the glass as if to reach out to touch her...and she was gone. He slumped back on the hard seat, tossing the book back onto the space next to him. Suddenly the complexities of the latest Inspector Morse paled into insignificance as he tried to work out what it was about her that so intrigued him.

Jim stepped into the early evening sunlight in the hospital carpark, but it seemed to him that the world was suddenly a darker place. The reflections from the windows and windscreens of a hundred cars seemed a little dimmer. Beside him, Rachael was looking for something in her bag; Sergeant Ratcliffe stood with his hands on his hips, staring at the ground, breathing deeply in and out. Jim watched them both as they stood there, wrapped up in their own thoughts. What they had learnt back in the autopsy suite had disquieted all of them.

Rachael had finished ferreting around her bag and had produced a packet of mints, which she offered to her colleagues. "What now, boss? Do we head back to the station?"

Jim sucked on his mint as the thoughts raced through his head. What was the next step? Then he remembered where he ought to be- the press conference. He pulled his keys out of his pocket and strode off towards his car, calling for the others to catch up. As the car roared across the tarmac, Jim thought back to the autopsy. That poor girl, lying cold and alone on the slab, he thought. What a life, turning tricks just to make ends meet, or feed a drug habit.

"So you think that she was a working girl, then, Sir?" Rachael asked from the back seat.

"Well, Bernie seems to think that the injuries she's suffered are consistent with that line of work, and he has over thirty years' experience in his field.".

"You reckon our killer held her and inflicted these injuries?"

Jim drew a hand across his forehead as he pondered the question. "As opposed to her actually being a prostitute, Simon?"

"Err...no... Sir."

"I was only stalling as a means of thinking of an answer as to whether you think our man is so forensically aware to make a normal person look like a prostitute."

"And what is your answer?" The sergeant asked as they entered the station.

"I don't know. I was wondering what is on the Walkman."

211

Back at the station, they wandered into the conference room with the usual hubbub of activity. David looked up; his features wore a veneer of harassed concern.

"If you're looking for the other two, Sir, they decided to hold the press conference at the town hall."

"Why?"

"Superintendent Laird was trying to hold it off until you got back but someone had obviously tipped off the nationals and the television...so it's turned into a right three ring circus."

"When did they start then?"

"About fifteen minutes ago...if you hurry you'll be able to give them the latest information."

Jim turned on his heel and charged for the door.

"Good afternoon, ladies and gentlemen. I am Superintendent George Laird of the Hertfordshire and Bedfordshire Constabulary. On my left is Inspector Mohammed Jujara of the Metropolitan Police and on my right is Inspector Terry Schofield of the Lancashire Constabulary." Laird paused and looked around the large room. Word had obviously spread that something big was going to break and he stared out at a sea of cameras, press and tv, and about forty reporters. When he had introduced his two fellow officers, the tension was electric, the room was silent. It wasn't often that such a large conference was announced in this relatively sleepy backwater of the country. Added to this was the fact that whatever was coming involved not only the 'Met' but also forces from the other end of the country.

"I am going to read a statement and then hand over the floor for a short period of time for questions. I expect you to hold your arm up if you want me to answer any of your questions. I will not let this statement descend into a frenzy. I hope we are clear on this." Laird glared defiantly around the room. It was his show and he would in no circumstances allow the press conference to become a battle of reporters all trying to scream their inane questions at him. Terry looked down at her notes and stifled a smile. Some hope, she thought.

"At around 9pm last Tuesday officers were called to attend a flat in the Southdown area. They found the body of a man in his late fifties whom officers believe to have died in suspicious circumstances." Laird looked up at the far end of the hall, willing Jim to make an appearance. Laird was no coward- he'd been awarded the Queen's Police Medal- but he still thought that this was one of the scariest things he had ever done. He gazed at the rows of reporters and he was momentarily dazzled as a couple of flashlight bulbs from cameras popped at him.

Blinking, he looked at his notes before him before resuming. "Yesterday, the body of a young woman was discovered in a barn on the outskirts of the village of Kimpton. Police have forensically linked these two killings."

An instant clamour erupted from the assembled crowd of reporters. So much for decorum, Terry thought. She stole a glance at the Chief Superintendent who was gazing out serenely at them. After about fifteen seconds he just held up a hand in an attempt to silence the crowd. Amazingly, the shouting subsided almost immediately. This man is so cool, she thought.

When he was sure that he had quiet, Laird cast another doleful gaze in the direction of the double glass doors at the front of the hall. "This morning, the bodies were recovered of a thirty-year-old male and a woman in her late teens or early twenties. Tests are ongoing, but we unfortunately believe to have died at the hands of the same perpetrator."

This time, there was stunned silence as the news sank in. Laird was aware of movement behind him and turned to look as Jim took his place at the end of the table. Mo leaned over and whispered something in his ear and Jim nodded once. "Before I open the floor to a limited amount of questioning, let me introduce the S.I.O, Inspector Smallwood, of the Hertfordshire and Bedfordshire Constabulary."

Hands shot up and questions were shouted out from across the entire huddle of press.

Laird calmly pointed at a man in the front row.

"Marcus Lacey, St. Albans Observer. Good evening Superintendent. Can you confirm that you have a serial killer running around Harpenden?"

Laird looked down at the table and raised an eyebrow at Jim, who nodded once more before clearing his throat. "I can confirm that we are looking for a person or persons unknown in relation to a series of connected killings, yes."

Marcus continued, "Do you have any leads at all?"

"Investigations are at an early stage and it would be remiss to comment further on that. Next question...yes." Jim pointed to a woman standing by a television camera near the back.

"Sophie Montgomery, BBC News... Can you give a description of this man, and are the public in danger here specifically or everywhere?" The questioner, obviously with a great deal of experience of these types of things had been able not only to ask two questions in one but had included the fact that some of the policeman at the table were from other forces.

Jim laid his head on one side laconically and looked at Terry, who seemed primed to answer the question, so with a shrug of shoulders he let have her way.

"Now just look here Missy..." Terry started off in such a way that Jim could almost hear Superintendent Laird wince, but she wasn't about to roll over at let the reporters tickle her tummy. "...I don't know about yon fancy ways 'doon ar', but 'oop narth' we wouldn't be allowed to spread such scurrilous rummers."

Superintendent Laird actually moved one of his fingers to lightly touch Terrys' hand. She looked at him before swallowing, gave a small growl and resumed. "Officers of the Lancashire Constabulary have been graciously invited down here by our hosts as the first victim was a man from our neck of the woods. Inspector Jujara here..." She airily waved a hand in his direction, "Is a highly experienced detective and any force would be proud to have him assisting."

Mo smiled at this whilst Terry paused briefly. She scanned the whole room slowly before resuming. "We are able to tell you that the public are in no danger specifically from this man- a description of whom we will circulate shortly- but is our stated intention to stop him as soon as is possible. We are working night and day to catch him and welcome any help the public and the press can give us." She nodded several times at random reporters before staring defiantly back at the lady from the BBC. There was a muted murmur from the assembled throng, but most of the reporters were digesting this and kept their hands, and heads, down for the moment. The occasional click and flash came from the cameras. A few hands started to rise cautiously.

"Yes please, Sir, you in the second row with the red tie." Jim pointed at a reporter.

"Jim Muirhead, Daily Mirror." A balding Scottish man with big glasses perched on an even bigger nose spoke up. "Do you have any motives?"

Jim chose his words carefully. In reality they had virtually nothing, but he couldn't reveal this without the whole force looking incompetent, but neither did he want to lie. "Various lines of enquiry are being pursued at the moment, but for we can't give any details just yet."

Inspector Jujara sat upright and then spoke for the first time. "Our office manager, DS David Tunicliffe, will be providing regular updates as and when they are feasible. Obviously, an operation of this size still needs to keep some avenues private." He looked at Jim, and secretly raised an eyebrow, and Jim gave him just the slightest of nods in return. "Right, we have time for two more questions. Yes, the gentleman on the right with his hand up.

"Graham Thorpe, Luton Post. What caused you to attribute these killings to the same person or persons? I mean, it can't be DNA, otherwise you'd be able to give us a name- or at the very least a description to go on."

Jim looked at the ceiling, the walls, and finally back at the reporter before committing himself to an answer. "All the bodies were concealed in a white duvet. That simple fact alone is enough to convince us that we are looking for someone in connection with all four killings. Final question please."

"Peter Trimble, the Sun...is there a sexual element to these murders?"

"No, son, there isn't." Terry was pushing herself to her feet. "So I don't expect to be reading about it your rag tomorrow. Thank you, ladies and gentlemen, and Mr. Trimble."

CHAPTER 20

The restaurant was playing 'Ain't that peculiar'- one of his favourites that always made him smile. It was still on his lips as the song faded to be replaced with something more recent.

There must have been something in the smile, as he looked up he noticed a lady looking at him. She smiled, made brief eye contact, before looking away, re-joining a conversation she was in with two female friends. Nevertheless, she was toying with her long, silky black curls, wrapping them around a long delicate finger time and again. Periodically, she looked over at him, when she thought he was looking elsewhere; it was obvious that the three were in cahoots and were discussing him. He pretended not to notice. It was all part of the game.

The sun had gone, replaced with ten thousand bulbs and neon signs, casting their glow onto the sea in front of him. It was a magical moment; it was still extremely warm, and everybody was wearing shorts and t-shirts. A few of the more elderly couples sported cardigans or shawls for the ladies, the men jumpers around their necks. There was a light breeze coming in off the Med, but it was so weak that it barely fluttered the bunting or the flags outside many of the bars. His thoughts drifted back to the trio of ladies on the other side of the restaurant. It was unusual- even in this enlightened age- for Spanish senoritas to take any notice of tourists. Usually they were like two completely different species intermingling, like cows and sheep. Both were perfectly content to be in the same space together, but with no sexual interest in each other whatsoever.

A waiter languidly strolled past. He spoke to the man in the perfectly crisp, white apron as he went past. The waiter looked at the ladies, back at him and nodded enthusiastically. Moments later the ladies had had their drinks later replenished and the waiter was politely informing them who had bought them. They turned, raising their glasses, smiling.

He was transported back to the bus, all those years ago. He slowly sipped his beer as he remembered he'd vowed to talk to the mysterious girl with the shy smile the next day. Maybe get off the bus at the same stop, or something like that.

Only she wasn't on the bus the next day. Or the one after that. And then it was the weekend. He'd gone through the normal routine things he usually did with Lawrence at weekends. Lawrence had a calendar hanging up behind his bedroom door where he was marking the days off. He'd ribbed his mate relentlessly about that, asking him if he was eight, not eighteen. However, Lawrence had noticed that his friend didn't seem as keen this week about the holiday and was only listening half-heartedly to the new A-ha track he'd just bought. Instead, his mate was staring out of the window. He'd asked him what was wrong, and slowly eased the story out of him, bit by bit.

"Let me get this straight...you've fallen in love with..."

"I never said I'd fallen in love with her!"

"Ok, so you fancy this girl, whose name you don't know. Neither do you know her name, where she lives, how old she is, what she does...school, college, work, whatever- you don't know if she's got a boyfriend who's six feet four and a Judo black belt. Wow."

"Cheers to you too."

"Come on then, we will work out a plan on the way to the pub."

Jim had asked for twenty minutes alone in his office and sat with his head in his hands. Whatever he had expected the press conference it hadn't been that. There had been a nasty undercurrent throughout, as if the media didn't trust these country bumpkins to tie their own shoelaces let alone solve a quadruple homicide. He had expected the Chief to blow his stack with Terry, but instead they had chatted amicably on the journey back to the station, as if the whole thing had been planned in advance.

There was something else playing on his mind. Something someone had said in the press conference had jarred something loose in his brain. He couldn't remember who it was, or exactly which comment had led to this thread of thinking. But it stayed deep in his thoughts, lurking somewhere under the surface, something about the ways that the bodies had been displayed. But try as he might, he couldn't mentally pick the thread. The more he tried to grasp it, the farther it slipped away. Frustrated, he kicked his chair from underneath him, stormed out of the office and went for a cigarette.

A polite cough sounded from behind him. Rick Chesterfield was also smoking a cigarette, leaning against the wall. "Mind if I join you, Sir?" He asked. Jim motioned the detective to join him. The two of them smoked in silence before Jim turned to Rick, asking, "What, no sage advice about how we're going to catch this man, and it'll be the crowning glory of my career?"

Rick emitted a long stream of smoke. Looking straight ahead, he said calmly, "Actually I thought that's what you would be saying to me, Sir." He thought he had offended Jim until he heard a small chuckle, then a bigger one, and finally a full laugh. Jim had pushed himself to his feet and was brushing dust from his behind. He extended a hand and pulled Rick to his feet, and with a wry grin, just said, "Come on, son, let's do this."

They had gone back to the conference room and had been discussing the case for half an hour or so when Mary Guy finally showed up. She had been tied up in meetings virtually all day, unable to get away sooner. "There is some good news," She added, "I've managed to pull some strings and get my colleagues to take most of my workload for a while. Thank goodness it's not term time. So at least I'm all yours for a bit." She looked around the room at the faces and saw disappointment in their faces. "Not that you looked all that pleased for me to be here."

Jim also noticed the looks from the team and interceded on their behalf. "It's not that- it's just when you said you had good news, I believe my colleagues thought you had the name of the killer for them." He gave her a forced smile.

Mary blushed, and looked down at a heap of folders on the table. "Oh, I am sorry. Give me half an hour with these photos and I'll try to give you something." Jim nodded, with a real smile this time, and turned to David.

"Sergeant Tunicliffe, tell us what we have got."

David shuffled the papers pulled out a small sheaf from his bundle. "Well, the victim in the truck, to start with."

Ian Westlake moved to a whiteboard and stuck up a photo of the face of the gardener, and stood poised, marker pen ready for David, who nodded at his colleague and read from his top-most sheet. Victims name is Christopher Halls, known as Chris. Six-foot, sixteen stone in weight, 30. He ran his own landscape garden business from Westfield Road. Lives in ..."

"Lived in... David... lived in." Terry chipped in from her usual place in the window.

David nodded without looking up and continued, "Lived in a small terraced house in Shakespeare road. Ian, Robert and the two M and M's have been around there with forensics but nothing untoward has been found there. Single, he split up from his long-term girlfriend Simone Bray six months ago. Mutual, and amicable, by all accounts. Mum deceased, dad lives in Bridport, Dorset. Locals have been around to inform him.

"Is he coming up for the identification of the body?" Asked Jim.

"No... that was done by his part time secretary... miss..."

"Mrs. Tracey Vickers." Rachael chimed in.

David nodded again "Absolutely. She's coming in at seven to give her statement. He checked his watch, as did Jim.

"Rachael and Sergeant Ratcliffe can do that. You'd better go down now, so that they're not hanging about too long. You know the drill." The two left the room.

"Whilst we were talking about witnesses, what about the young lad who saw the sign?"

"Andy Butler, and he's coming around seven forty-five, Sir."

"Well, Russell, Ronnie, Rick and Robert- "

"Russell, Ronnie, Rick and Robert? Sounds like a sixties pop combo." Terry jumped in again, chuckling. "What with Rachael, why is everybody's name begins with an 'r'?"

"Complete bloody coincidence, and absolutely irrelevant, Inspector. Can we please get on?" Jim was irritated now: it had been a long day already, a long week, and he was ravenous, and he could do without Terry right now. Behind his back, she pulled a face, but nobody noticed apart from Mo, who winked.

"Anyway, those four have been tracking down his friends down this afternoon." David paused as he looked at four sheets on his left. "They say pretty much the same thing- that he was a great bloke, they're all devastated, very generous, funny... an all-round good guy. No known enemies, no one had anything bad to say about him." He slid those notes across the table to Mary, who put them under her pile with a nod.

"Anything in his work diary for where he was meant to be yesterday or today?"

"Not a dickie bird."

"I seem to recall that the secretary, Mrs. Vickers...may have mentioned something. I'm sure Rachael will remember if it's important." Jim was still gazing at the photograph.

"Shall I continue.? There's a lot to get through, and I haven't started on the fourth victim."

"Yes, yes, carry on David."

"Anyway, as we discussed briefly earlier, cause of death was blunt force trauma. It seems that the killer sneaked up behind him and struck him with a hammer. The pathologist is adamant that death was instantaneous."

"That doesn't give us any indications about the killer whatsoever." Terry, back in serious mode walked up to the whiteboard and traced the face of the gardener with a finger. "What were you doing...where were you going, what did you see?" It was said so quietly that no one but Mo could hear her.

"Last but not least is the tape, and what was on it. Before Rick plays it, let me put it in context. The tape was a BASF C90, adapted to play on a continuous spool, over and over."

"Is that difficult to do?" Terry asked. Various comments about it being easy if you knew what you were doing came from members of the team at the same time, leaving Terry little wiser. "David, sorry to interrupt again, but I presume there were no forensics again? No sweat, stray skin cells, or the odd hair?" She smiled sweetly at him.

"None whatsoever that they've been able to find, although they are still checking the van over, and that will take time." David was about to resume when he noticed out of the corner of his eye that Mary was holding her hand up.

"Can I ask a question?"

"Of course."

"You are absolutely certain that there is no forensic evidence whatsoever from any of the first three crime scenes?"

David looked at Jim, and then back at Mary. "As far as the first two scenes of crime are concerned, no trace was found of the killer. As I've said, we've come up with nothing yet on the third body. Tests are ongoing, however."

"May I ask why, Mary?" Jim intervened.

Mary had resumed her reading of the reports and just murmured with a little hunch of her shoulders, "Just wondered."

Tracey Vickers looked drawn and tired as Rachael and Sergeant Ratcliffe met her and her husband in the car park. They exchanged greetings and introductions and Ratcliffe suggested that they use his car for the journey to the morgue to formally identify the body of Chris Halls. Once they were settled, with the Vickers in the back, Rachael turned to them and explained what they could expect.

"You will be in a side-room, with a curtain over the window into the next room. Once you are totally ready, a technician will fold down the sheet covering Mr. Hall's body- "

There was a little whimper from Tracey, and an indignant snort from her husband, Reginald. "Isn't there someone else who could have done this, Sergeant?" Reginald's voice reminded her of Basil Fawlty. Rachael softly shook her head. "Sir, your wife volunteered, and his family are a long way away. And I'm only a detective constable." She was rewarded by a raised eyebrow from Reginald as he turned to stare out of the car window, and a little apologetic smile from his wife. She smiled encouragingly back at her and settled back in her seat, after exchanging a sly glance with Sergeant Ratcliffe.

They were shown into a small, narrow room, featureless apart from a couple of chairs and a pleated orange nylon curtain, pulled out to its full extent. Rachael stood in front of it and faced the couple.

"Right, as I explained earlier, I am going to pull this curtain, and on the other side is Chris, under a sheet." Rachael used his first name to make the situation less formal, and hopefully, less tense. Reginald stood silently behind his wife, as a stiff as a board, his face showing indignation that they, the Vickers, were being forced to do this. Tracey stood with a tissue held up to her face, as if she was trying to hide behind it. Rachael turned and pulled on a cord, opening the curtain. The room next door was only slightly larger. A technician waited for Rachael's signal.

"Are you ready, Mrs. Vickers."

"Yes."

Rachael nodded to the technician, who carefully lifted the sheet to reveal Chris's head and shoulders. From behind her, Rachael heard Tracey give a small sob. She gave a virtually imperceptible signal and the technician replaced the sheet. Ratcliffe closed the curtains.

"It's him." Tracey sniffed, and rushed from the room, Reginald close on her heels.

He leaned back against the old wooden railing and looked down the road for about the twentieth time. Still no sign of the bus, but then he didn't really expect it to be early. On this day, though, maybe the gods were watching. He had left work an hour early, rushed home, changed and rushed out again. A bunch of flowers from the florists hung down by his side. They were an idea from his mate, and he hoped that she liked them. That is, if she turned up at all. He had gone through this the day before in a drizzling rain and waited there for an hour before giving up. At least his mother had appreciated the flowers, a puzzled expression on her face.

When he looked again, he saw its familiar red shape hove into view. It seemed to take an eternity at a mini roundabout before it crawled nearer, slowly gathering speed. For a scary few seconds he thought it was going to speed right past him. At the last moment, the brakes squealed in distress and the bus lurched to a stop, the doors slowly opening. Three people alighted from the bus. Then she got off the bus, thanking the driver as she did. She stood there, shaking her luxuriant wavy hair, unaware of his presence less than ten feet away. She walked towards him and was only three feet from him when she noticed who it was that was waiting. A cloud of uncertainty crossed her features before clearing away, replaced with that shy smile, and then a look of puzzlement as her eyes narrowed when she regarded him.

"Hi." Her voice was silky smooth.

"Hi." His sounded squeaky.

"You're not waiting for me, are you?" She asked, her head turning slightly. In response, he pulled the bouquet up to his chest before thrusting them towards her.

"I hope you don't mind." His voice caught and he coughed to clear his throat.

She smiled as she looked at the flowers before fading as she looked up one of the side streets, biting her lip. He took the hint and took a small step backwards. "I'm sorry, you probably already have a boyfriend- all the pretty girls do."

She shook her head. "It's not that."

"A possessive dad who doesn't like you talking to boys?"

She shook her head and gave the shy smile once more. He shrugged his shoulders. "You prefer girls?" He asked in desperation.

She laughed at that, blushing. "No."

He shook his head, searching her deep brown eyes. "I give up then."

"My gran is in the hospital and she's expecting me."

He let a sigh escape his lips. "Oh, I am sorry to hear that- I mean I'm sorry to hear that she is ill, not that she is expecting you." She nodded. "Could I walk you to the hospital then?"

She rested her head on one side as she regarded him through narrowed eyes before smiling, holding out her hand and saying, "Come on then."

He took her hand and realised that it had only taken a bunch of flowers and five minutes to fall in love.

The car journey was spent mainly in silence. Rachael could see in the mirror that every time Tracey tried to say something, her husband Reginald looked at her sternly, his moustache twitching, and she subsided into silence, looking at her hands in her lap. When they entered the car park at the back of the police station, Rachael had resolved to talk to her privately.

Sergeant Ratcliffe had picked up on the strained vibe in the car and nodded to Rachael as they all got out of the car. Rachael turned to Tracey, smiling at her kindly. "If you could just come in and sign a form for me, Tracey." She held up a hand to her husband saying, "You don't have to come Sir- your wife will literally only be two minutes." She could see his hackles rise, and Sergeant Ratcliffe sailed into the rescue the moment.

"Have you been watching the Test Match, Sir? I couldn't help noticing your tie- it's an MCC one, isn't it?" Temporarily side-tracked, Mr. Vickers looked at Ratcliffe, then his wife, and then back at the sergeant. His hand went up to check the immaculately knotted tie.

"Yes... Sergeant. And I have been watching when I can."

"Wasn't that a fine partnership between Atherton, and Hussein..." Rachael seized the initiative and taking Tracey by the arm, firmly guided her to the steps and into the station. Rachael looked back once and noticed Mr. Vickers torn between having to politely engage Ratcliffe in conversation whilst earnestly wishing he was still controlling his wife. Rachael muttered 'gotcha, bastard' under her breath. If Tracey heard her, she said nothing, but something in her eye sparked for a second, leaving Rachael to surmise that she had.

"There is no form, but I wanted to give you my card and tell you to call me anytime you wanted to chat...as a woman, not as a police officer. I guess your husband can be a little-"

Tracey was no longer listening but bending her head to try to look at a young man just entering by the front door. A uniformed constable blocked her line of sight for a moment, but then the young man was loping to the desk and was less than three feet away, with only Rachael in between them.

"Andrew?" She asked, concern and surprise managed to mix in the one word.

The young man snapped his head round at the sound of the woman's voice. "Mum?" A look of concern crossed his face, instantly replaced by suspicion. "What are you doing here?"

"Are you in trouble, dear?" Once a mum, always a mum, displaying love for her son.

"Me? Oh, not this time." Andy planted a quick kiss on his mothers' cheek, grabbing hold of her wrist. "Have you finally snapped and killed that wanker Reggie?"

"You two are mother and son?" Rachael asked incredulously. They both looked at her as if she was stupid, and she blushed.

"What are you doing here, Son?" Tracey asked, returning her attention to her son.

Andy let go of his mother, puffing out his chest. "I'm a witness to a murder, or something like that, in the house next door to mine." He gave his mother a look of self-importance. "But what about you, mum?" When asked the question, his mother cast her eyes down to the floor, unable to meet her son's gaze.

Rachael stepped in. "Your mum has been of tremendous assistance in what has been a very trying time for her. Her boss was killed." She saw Tracey shudder as she remembered discovering the body in the bed of the van.

"I'd better be getting back, Reginald will be wondering what I am getting up to," Tracey sighed. She placed her hand on Rachael's arm to express her thanks, and that done, kissed her son on his cheek. She pulled him close, and whispered in his ear, "For God's sake brush your hair and have a shower. You're a frightful sight."

Andy laughed and replied, "Love you too, mum. See you soon." Rachael told him to wait there for a minute and took Tracey back to, thanking her on the way. In the yard, Sergeant Ratcliffe seemed to have run out of conversation with Reginald. The sergeant was staring at his shoes whereas Reginald kept alternating his gaze between the back door and the road outside, as if unsure whether or not to escape on his own. The look of relief that flooded his features was there, albeit briefly, before being replaced by the more familiar scowl. He hastened his wife into their car before escaping as quickly as they could.

"Thank you for that, Sarge." Ratcliffe was shaking his head, though he did manage something resembling a smile.

"You owe me a pint, Rachael, and don't think of ever pulling a trick like that again." He ushered her back inside where Andy was still waiting for them to give his statement.

The morning sunlight played across his naked back as he lay sleeping on his front, his face turned to the open window. She eased herself gently off the bed and went to fix some coffee. She gazed out at the sea from her terrace as she waited for the coffee to percolate, a pleasant gurgle coming from the machine. The aroma of the freshly brewing coffee mingled with the scents of mimosa and jasmine from her terrace. She looked back through the door of her bedroom where she could just make out his bottom. She giggled softly to herself as she remembered the nights' lovemaking. She and her friends had spent the best part of an hour practicing their English before the two of them had been left alone by her mates. After that, there hadn't been a whole lot of conversation before they had caught a taxi back to her place, and even less when they had got there. The coffee was ready, and she poured two small cups of the steaming liquid, before padding silently back to the bedroom. She stood in front of him, blocking out the sun as it played on his face. He stirred and opened his eyes and smiled.

"Cafe negro, senor." She smiled as he turned over and propped himself up his elbows. His eyes grew wide as he gazed at her, dressed loosely in a large white shirt; the sun silhouetted her body under the shirt.

"Eres Hermosa." He began to reach for her, but she deftly avoided him, giving him her coffee instead. She picked up his and turned to the window, coquettishly looking back at him as he tried not to drop the little ceramic cup.

"You speak, Spanish?" It was the first time that a man had called her beautiful like that.

"Hablo un poco de Espanol." Which was true; he only spoke the language a little. But it seemed to work. She drained her cup and walked to the bed. She took his and set it back down on the table before putting her arms around his neck. She whooped in delight as he pulled her off her feet, and onto the bed.

CHAPTER 21

Smallwood had sent Rick to the local pizza place with orders for enough pizza, dips and fizzy drinks to feed an army. When he had returned, groaning under the weight of so much food, he had almost been lynched. Jim had grabbed a of slice for himself and retreated to his office. He had asked Mo to accompany him

"We aren't getting anywhere, are we, Mo?" He had flopped down into his chair, exhausted. It had been a very, very long day, it wasn't over, and he was dead beat. After discussing Chris Halls, they had gone over developments on the previous two bodies for the last hour or so, with precious little to show for it.

"We can't let the troops think like that though, Jim." Mo said, wiping his mouth with a napkin. He picked up his can of Fanta and took a long swig.

"I know, I know... but we have nothing."

"Something will come up, and soon, I'm sure of it."

"Like what, exactly?" Jim spat out, before holding a hand by way of an apology.

"This witness, and Mary has still to tell us what she thinks."

Jim regarded his colleague thoughtfully for a whole minute without saying anything. "Remind me how you caught that bloke in Hackney." He said finally.

"It was a mixture of luck, perseverance and solid information from the public, mainly." Mo looked back at Jim, a worried expression on his face. On the one hand, he feared the toll the case was taking on his friend; on the other was an unshakeable belief that by following solid, established policing procedures, they were going to catch this maniac. "And of course, I'm the best fucking policeman in the country." Mo sat on the edge of Rachael's desk, stroking his moustache, his dark eyes twinkling. From across the room, Jim just had to laugh at his colleague, the tension leaving him for a moment.

"There is a link, that the killer wants us to get, and it's just hidden from us...at the moment." Mo had stopped grooming

himself and was gazing absentmindedly around the room. "It's obvious to him, and only him, at the moment."
"Which means- "
Mo nodded. "Which means that he's going to kill again."
Jim had already started out of his chair and was striding towards the door. "Come on."

They lay back exhausted by the intensity of their lovemaking. He gazed across, at her beautiful face, her high cheekbones, dark eyes, full lips. He truly admired this woman. He wished that things could be different than they were. He sighed lightly, and his gaze fell to the sheets.
"You have to go, don't you?" The smile was fading from her lips. Then she pushed herself up one elbow as she saw the single tear trickle down his face. She reached up gently and wiped it away from his cheek and he caught her hand, holding it against his face, kissing it gently.
"Vuelvo ensegida," he said gently. She arched a beautifully shaped eyebrow at him, before narrowing her eyes at him. "Si tu quieres."
"Very much so. For a visit, or to ....to live here?"
"Siempre." She smiled at that, and asked gently,
"With me?"
"Si." On hearing this, she put her hand behind his neck and pulled him down onto her. If he was going, it wasn't going to be just yet.

Jim was walking back to the conference room when he saw Rachael trudge wearily up the stairs. The dark rings under her eyes told their own story.
"Get anything interesting?" He asked, more in hope than expectation.

She shook her head, glancing back down the stairs. "Sergeant Ratcliffe is just seeing him out. There is nothing much to go on, I'm afraid, but Mary may be able to do to something with it.

"We won't be much longer, Rachael. I know it's been a really long day, especially for you. Come along, there may be a slice or two of cold pizza left."

"Yummy, my favourite." She forced a sarcastic smile, and grinned when she saw Inspector Jujara laugh behind Jim. When they entered, there was not much going on. One or two of the officers were on the phones, a couple more were reading reports, and the rest of them were sitting around chatting. Mary had a group of three or four listening to her every word.

He clapped his hands for attention. "Right then, ladies and Gentlemen, one last thing before we head home." He raised his hands at the general murmur rippling around the room. "I know, I know..." he said, nodding his head at the team, "...it's been a very long day. We are going home shortly." He went to the whiteboard outlining what little they knew about the fourth victim. He tapped the photo, a close-up of the girls' face, asleep. "We were going to discuss the fourth victim...but we're all beat. I know that tomorrow is Saturday, and those who wish to can indeed stay at home, but overtime is available, and if I see any of you, your help will be greatly appreciated. That's all- apart from to say thank you for all your help. Get some sleep. You deserve it." He turned to the window and stood watching the evening as it dwindled away into the night. He checked his watch and wasn't surprised to see that it was already a quarter past nine.

"Unless you want your home to yourself this weekend, we'd like to stay." A light hand rested on his shoulder, and Jim found himself very close to Terry. She was smiling sadly.

"You don't have to stay just to keep me company, you know. I'm sure you and Sergeant Bimjano have lives up back in Lancashire that you want to get back to." He looked over to see Mary, packing numerous piles of paper into an already heavy looking case.

"I've discussed it with him, and we agreed. We came down here to help you catch a killer. We haven't done that so we're staying until we do. It's just if you'd prefer us to get a hotel...then we would understand."

Jim turned back to the window, nodding. "I need a fag, and a drink."

"Me too, honey, me too."

"Come on then."

Ten minutes later and they were ensconced with a pint each in the local pub, with Ronnie and Rachael. Inspector Jujara was intending to come but he'd been packed off by Jim with express orders to spend some time with his family. He had tried to argue but Jim was insistent, and so the inspector had reluctantly agreed.

Terry lifted her pint and drank it in one go. Rachael was amazed, Ronnie less so- he'd seen it many times before. He sipped his lemonade and looked out into the night. Jim's pint sat untouched on the table. Terry swopped her empty glass with Jim's and drank most of that as well. Ronnie got to his feet with a sigh and traipsed off to the bar to get the next round. The movement seemed to awaken Jim, who looked down at his empty glass with a puzzled expression on his face. Terry was pretending to look innocently at a painting on the wall, and Rachael had to stop herself from laughing.

"You've got froth on your moustache, Inspector. Two pints worth." Jim said, without even looking at her. Terry pretended not to hear and started to hum tunelessly to herself.

"Why didn't we discuss the fourth girl this evening?"

"Information overload, Constable." Terry replied nonchalantly, as if it was an answer any novice would know. Ronnie, returned with two new pints, tried to fill in the gaps. He sat down, gathering his thoughts before speaking.

"Remember when you were sitting your exams at school, Rachael?" She nodded, so he continued. "Well, if you had four exams on four days, say, you wouldn't revise all four on the evening before the first exam. Your brain wouldn't be able to cope with all the information. Something important would leak out, and you may not be able to answer all the questions in the first exam. It's a bit like that. By feeding your brain little bits of information at any time, over a period of time, you will have all the information you need, and remember most of it. That's when you are able to make the links and get the big answer you're looking for."

"Succinctly put." Jim was back in the room. "Sorry about that, I was away with the fairies there."

"What are you thinking, Sir?" Rachael asked.

"Many things, all at the same time, which why I'm not getting anywhere. Here, pass me that napkin." Jim took and unfolded it, then refolded it lengthways twice. He fished his pen out and started to write. Rachael saw him frowning, and he stopped. "This is a real pen with real ink, and it's just spreading into the paper." He looked at the others gathered around him. "Anyone got a biro?" Ronnie gave him one, and Jim nodded his thanks. Rachael was slightly puzzled as she watched her boss refolding a fresh napkin.

"Why don't you just use your notebook, Sir? You can use mine if- "

"All police notebooks remain the property of the police, Constable." Terry said as she tried to spy over Jim's shoulder to see what he's writing. "And we're not on the clock, and I suspect your boss is doing this unofficially." She glanced at Rachael and winked. Rachael was too far away to see what Jim was writing, and even Terry rolled her eyes and gave up after a minute or two. She surreptitiously checked her watch and was surprised to see that it was already past ten. She stifled a yawn.

"You can stop yawning now, Rachael, I've finished. He looked down at his scribbling once more and turned it round so at least she and Ronnie could see what he had written down. It seemed to be four or five columns of words, and the pair of them studied it carefully.

1. Male -Samuel Taylor - Rat-catcher - Injected/asleep - flat

2. Female - Tori Henderson – Masseur - Punched/heart ripped out - barn
3. Male - Chris Halls - Gardener - Hit from behind/earphones - truck
4. Female -? – Prostitute - ? - Strangled/ in the dark - bedsit

"Now, what I've quickly scribbled out is a comparison chart. The first column is obvious, but the second is their gender. Do you notice anything there?" Jim looked at them.
Rachael suspected that this was a trick question but her interest had been piqued and so she was willing to play along. "They are alternating."
"Correct."
"Irrelevant though." This was from Terry, and Rachael looked at her.
"Why?" Rachael asked.
"He had no way of controlling for certain if three or four was discovered first. On the probability scale, with the secretary he employed, the odds were that the gardener was going to be discovered first. But if we know one thing about this killer, it's that he doesn't deal in probabilities, only certainties. Hence, we can dismiss the sex of the victims as irrelevant." Satisfied, she stood up and loped off to the bar to get another round in.
"Is she correct, Sir?"
"Absolutely bang on- the gender is of no importance in this." Jim let this sink in for a moment or two. "Ok, so now look at the next column- profession of the victims."
Rachael looked at the list and pointed at the fourth line. "Do we know for certain that victim number four was a prostitute, Sir?" Terry was back and answered for him. "We're afraid so lovey. The number of call girls that have ended up on the slab that me and your inspector have seen...you really, really don't want to know." She set the drinks down and paused, looking down at it but seeing something else entirely.
  "The injuries are entirely consistent, I'm afraid, Rachael." Jim added softly.

"They're all customer service occupations, really, aren't they, Sir?" Ronnie said. He looked up at Jim, who motioned for him to expand. "Well, a rat-catcher comes to peoples' homes, as does a gardener, and I suppose, both a masseuse and a prostitute could too..." Ronnie stopped talking for he saw that Jim and Terry were exchanging excited glances. "What is it?" Terry sat down, her eyes sparkling. "We hadn't made that leap yet, Sergeant." She looked into space for a moment, thinking, before turning to look at Jim sat. He raised his eyebrows, nodding his head slightly from side to side in agreement.

"We will be sure to run that past Mary next time we see her."

Rachael inclined her head and asked, "She's not going to be there tomorrow?"

Jim shook his head. "Her brother is getting married in Hereford. She will be back Monday."

"Oh, right." Rachael couldn't be angry with the psychologist, and it was indeed an important family wedding, but...she just felt a little disappointed, that was all.

Jim was studying her and secretly wondering how his young protégé was faring. It was her first murder case, and it was a strain on experienced detectives, so God knew how it affected the junior ones. It felt so long since he had been one he was sure he had forgotten.

"Well, let's park that for a moment, and move on. I want you to look at the last column first- where they were found." Rachael and Ronnie both leaned forward to read what was written down on the napkin, although they both knew the facts. They looked at each other but remained quiet.

"Nothing leap out at you, grab your attention?" Terry asked, looking at both them.

Ronnie screwed up his nose, shaking his head silently. Rachael looked up at Terry, and then at her boss. "Do we know whose name the bedsit was registered in, Sir?"

Jim had to reach into his pocket to extract his notebook. He flipped through a couple of pages, tracing with his finger, before coming up with an answer. "We managed to contact the landlord, and he says the bedsit was rented to a David Court about four months ago, for an initial term of six months, at seventy-five pounds a month. No references were asked for or given. Inquiries are ongoing to see if this Mr. Court actually exists anywhere else. But that could take a while." He closed his notebook and slipped it back inside his jacket, which he then took off and threw over the back of his chair. He leant back, pint glass in hand, and took a long drink from it. He wasn't going to give them any more help.

    He left with a heavy heart but promised that he'd be back. The sun was scorching his head by the time he got back to his apartment nestled into one of the foothills that surrounded Fuengirola and the sweat was streaming down his back. He stripped off quickly and stepped into a cold shower. As he was undressing, he caught the aroma of her perfume and he smiled to himself as he remembered the events of the previous evening and night.

    As he stood under the cooling jets of the cold shower, he thought with pleasure of her body- hot, tanned, silky smooth...and suddenly he was transported back in time to the first time he had seen the girl from the bus naked. He snapped the shower off, suddenly furious. It was an image that had seared itself into his brain and always caused him anguish. He strode naked out onto the sun terrace, and the water dripped off to instantly dry on the hot stones under his feet. He hung his head and screwed his eyes shut in an attempt to rid himself of the images whirling round his brain, but it was useless. Like a dream the images unfolded, and he knew he would have to watch everything before he could think of anything else again. He lay down on a lounger in the shade, eyes staring up at the cloudless sky as his 'mind movie' played itself again.

    The rain had sluiced down as soon as they had left the gig that autumn night. By the time they had got to Hammersmith tube station they were soaked. Wet but exhilarated, they had dripped all over the tube carriage, surrounded by dozens more A-ha fans who had been at the concert with them. He himself had never been much of a fan of the group until he had seen them perform live. Then he had been converted.

They were still damp by the time they got home, but still super excited, taking it in turns to relate their favourite moments of the concert. Stepping off the train onto the platform, they hardly noticed that it was still pelting down. They peered out into the sheeting rain in a vain hope that a taxi might miraculously appear. She tapped him on the shoulder and pointed to half a dozen people huddled into raincoats underneath the sign that read: 'Taxis wait here'.

"Looks like we are going to drown then- it's a good twenty-minute walk to your home. Unless we get your dad out of bed to give us a lift."

"Can't." She replied.

"Can't or won't?"

"Can't and won't...he thinks I'm having a sleepover with Sancha."

He took her hand, and noticed it was cold as well as wet. "What are you saying, Miss Elizabeth Fairbairn?"

Smiling sweetly through the sopping strands of her hair, she said nothing.

"You think just because my folks are away that you can stay at mine?"

She stood smiling and raised her eyebrows.

Ten minutes later he was fumbling with the key with numb fingers in the dark outside his home. Eventually the key found the slot and opened the door. They tumbled in and he had hardly closed it when she was pulling his sopping t-shirt off. She placed her cold hand on his chest and leaned in for a kiss that tasted of rain and lipstick. He pulled her t-shirt off and ran his hands down her back, pulling her back to him as they stumbled into the living room. They broke apart as they struggled out of their wet jeans. He got one leg out but struggled getting the second one off and he toppled onto the sofa. She giggled at him whilst having no problems with her own, or her panties. She pushed him back against the cushions as he tried to get up, then she bent down and pulled his foot out of his crumpled jeans. This was followed quickly by his pants, and then she swung his legs round onto the sofa and literally jumped on top of him. Before he knew it he was in her warmth, and she was riding him hard, scratching his chest in her passion. Her body was supple and golden, still tanned from a recent holiday. Her breasts bounced in rhythm with her hips as she rode him. She placed her hands on his shoulders and told him she'd do all the work.

Which she did, and afterwards collapsed forward onto him, exhausted, the wetness of the rain replaced by sweat. She rolled off him and they lay for ages, he stroking her hair, she his chest. He smiled as he thought what the price of a couple of concert tickets could get you.

Ronnie checked his watch and wasn't surprised to find that it was almost eleven. He shifted in his chair, his legs and back stiff. For the last half an hour they had been discussing the places where the killer had left the bodies of his victims. They had finally come to the conclusion that it wasn't a huge factor in the case; but it did reveal important factors that the team hadn't really considered before.

"He must be rich, or fairly affluent." Rachael had. She looked at Ronnie, and then her boss. Inspector Schofield had spent the last ten minutes staring at the ceiling, and it was only when her had twitched suddenly that Rachael realised that Terry was actually asleep. Jim looked at the two junior detectives with a wry smile before placing a finger to his lips so that they should continue their discussion at a quieter level. Ronnie had shaken his head, saying that from prior experience that he'd seen the Inspector fall asleep next to an old noisy air-conditioning unit, a radiator with a rattle, and even once, a cement mixer. Jim and Rachael had both laughed at him gently.

"I'm only playing devil's advocate here-what makes you think he is rich?" Jim had asked.

Rachael had brushed an errant strand of hair out of her eyes and stared down at the napkin.

"The flat...the bedsit...and at least one place of his own," She tapped the word 'barn' on the napkin, "assuming that victim number three was killed in his own place- it all indicates money. Three places, two of them rented, maybe more. The fact that he can seemingly travel when and where he likes at will."

"He could just be on holiday." Ronnie had interjected, causing Jim to cough on his cigarette. Terry stirred but slumbered on. Jim looked at Rachael. "Carry on, Rachael."

"Well, I don't think it's the kind of holiday I've ever heard of. Besides, all this would've taken months of preparation."

"Maybe he doesn't watch television in the evenings like us mere mortals."

Suddenly the bell for 'time' rang out, Terry jolted awake with a start. "Good point." She said, as if she hadn't been asleep at all. The others all laughed, and she scowled. Jim leant back, finished his pint, and reached for his jacket. "We will finish this off in the morning, folks. But well done, you've made some great observations, especially Inspector Schofield." They laughed at this again as they struggled to their feet, stretching and yawning.

"What time do you want me to come in tomorrow morning, Sir?" Rachael had asked, holding her hand over mouth to stifle another yawn.

"You can take the day off, if you like, Rachael."

"I'd rather have Sunday off, maybe go and have a roast with my parents, if you don't mind."

Jim nodded. "Good idea. At least have a lie-in, then. Show your head about ten."

Ronnie suggested that they drop Rachael off on their way home, but she declined, saying she felt fine, and that she'd only been drinking soft drinks all evening. She turned to him, and asked quietly, "I know it's none of my business, but do you have anybody waiting for you back in Chorley?"

Ronnie chuckled at that and looked back over his shoulder to where Terry was slowly tottering up the hill. He looked back at Rachael, saying, "Between the boss and my mother, I don't think anyone would come up to scratch."

"Do you have a big family, then?"

"I'm Anglo-Italian, the third of five sons, with a little sister, Bella, the darling of the family."

"Ah, she must get spoilt rotten." Rachael smiled.

"Yes, us four boys still here in England look out for her and protect her. My eldest brother, Eduardo is in the Vatican. The second, Romero, is a doctor. The youngest two, Emilio and Giovanni, help in dad's family bakery."

"Bella...Eduardo...Emilio, Giovanni, and... Ronnie?" She laughed.

"I don't tell everyone this, Rachael...my proper name is Ronaldo."

"Don't worry, your secret is safe with me...Ronaldo." She smiled, and waved goodnight to the two senior cops who had just about made it to the car park. She got into her car, put on her seatbelt, and giving Ronnie a small wave, drove home, still smiling.

CHAPTER 22

Jim slept like a log as soon as his head hit the pillow and woke up feeling really refreshed. There was a light tap on the door, and Ronnie entered, padding in with a hot cup of tea.

"Morning, Sir. Nice hot fresh cup of tea for you."

"Oh, thank you very much- but you don't have to wait on me hand and foot, you know."

"It's nothing, Sir. We're your guests and it's such a little thing." Ronnie beamed at him.

Talking about guests, how's Inspector Schofield?" He took a sip of the scalding liquid and set it down to let it cool off a bit.

"Like a bear with a sore head." Ronnie's beam grew larger.

"Mm- she probably shouldn't have had that nightcap. Well, thanks for the drink. I'll be down for a slice of toast when I'm dressed." Jim lay back against the pillows, savouring the relative peace and quiet. An hour later, suitably fortified by tea and toast, he walked into the station and bounded up the stairs. He headed for the conference room and walked in, surprised to find Ian Westlake, David, Rick and Pete Norris already there.

"Good morning, team. Anything new, David, like fresh leads?"

"Morning, Inspector-though when I'm finished, I'll doubt you think there's anything good about it, Sir." David, normally so ebullient, wore a worried look this morning.

"Mm." Jim's upbeat mood was already dissipating. "Let me sit down first, so I'll be less tempted to kick anything." The team wore expressions that ranged from pessimism to defeat, with worry and angst thrown in. He raised an eyebrow at Rick, who gave him half a smile. He noticed that Pete Norris kept his eyes down, and that David was rearranging sheets of paper into various piles.

"Where are Inspector Schofield and Sergeant Bimjano this morning, Sir?" Rick asked, in an attempt to lighten the mood. Jim knew that all of his team had taken to the pair: Ronnie, because he was so easy-going and very much a team player; and Terry because she was something of a maverick, who always made them laugh whilst challenging them to continually up their game.

"They've nipped out to get a few more things- I think they thought everything would be sorted out by now." Jim replied. Rick nodded, at a loss as to what he should say.

"Right, in that case, Sir, do you want the good news, the bad news, or the very bad news?" David smiled ruefully at his boss.

"Oh, let's start with some good news today, David." Jim smiled, and loosened his tie. If he was going to be here for a while, he might as well make himself comfortable.

"Well, firstly, Samuel Taylor, or more specifically, the pub beforehand. We have given the image to the tech lads to see what they can do. He unclipped a photo and slid it across the desk to Jim. The Inspector picked it up and saw the killer for the first time clearly. He actually laughed out loud, causing the others in the room to look up.

"We know what his chin looks like, I suppose." Jim slid it without further comment.

"They can only do so much, Sir." David countered defensively. Jim sighed and nodded. "It ties in with what the landlady said in her statement."

"Looks like a student to me." This was from Pete Norris.

"That was his cover to the landlady, Sheila- "

"Shirley, Sir."

"Whatever, David. More good news, please."

"Twenty months ago in a small village in Dorset, a large quantity of Ketamine was stolen, from a veterinarian practice near Dorchester."

Jim just looked blankly at his office manager.

"It was the last reported theft of that drug, Sir." David noticed that Jim was no longer listening to him, so he settled down to wait.

Thirty seconds elapsed as Jim was working it out in his mind. "Rick, have you any thoughts?"

Rick was surprised to be asked but was quick to respond. "Drugs find their way up to London, then Luton, possibly to one of the pubs, Sir?" He surmised hopefully.

Jim nodded at the detective. "Sounds plausible, I suppose. You three agree with young Rick?" The others all nodded in unison.

"Good, that's a nice dead end, then. Carry on, David."

"We have received seven statements from Sam's neighbours, all saying the same thing. He was an Ok neighbour, sometimes irascible, often 'in his cups', but ultimately harmless. Nobody recalls any visitors to his place."

"In how long a time scale?"

"In ...ever." At this, Jim raised an eyebrow.

"So we can safely assume that the killer met him in the pub, befriended him, and abducted him." Jim glanced at the picture of the old man lying on the mortuary slab but said nothing more. He flicked his eyes to David, who took this as his cue to resume.

"Moving on to victim number two, the final autopsy report confirms death was instant, from a fractured skull, caused by striking something hard- a table, or wood floor. Some carpet fibres, and bleach from her underwear, consistent with being dragged through a lounge and across a kitchen floor. The knife used was a standard kitchen knife, sharp, probably new."

"Tyre prints from the crime scene?"

"Nothing useable."

Jim rubbed his forehead with the back of a hand. This is the good news, he thought.

"A thorough forensic sweep of her house revealed nothing. Even her massage table is clean. There are a couple of fingerprints that we're chasing up, but don't hold your breath."

At this point, Rachael breezed in, said good morning and sat down. She turned to Jim and gave him a bright smile, which he didn't return.

"David is updating us but has taken a lot of time to tell me nothing." Jim sighed again and stood up to look out of the window. "Sorry, David, I know it's not your fault. Please continue, if you would."

David, who had looked mortified at the inspector's rebuke, was partially pacified, and blushed when Rachael winked at him.

"Both Tori and Chris had absolutely nothing in their diaries or planners to suggest where they were meant to be. Although..." David paused, and waited for the inspector to turn round, which he did. "Although, the diary that Tori used to use, along with her handbag, is currently missing." Jim gave David one of his blank looks again and breathed in deeply, exhaling slowly.

"Is no-one else coming in today?"

"DC Maitland has gone on holiday, Ds Franks is at a wedding, Ash has to have a day off because he's worked twelve days straight..." David found another sheet and ran his finger down it. "The M and M's are playing cricket for the ACC's team...and DS Ratcliffe is in Highgate, his mother-in-law seems to have had a heart attack."

"OK...What about this last victim?" He asked.

"No identification was found, no clothing...nothing; forensics are still there, but we haven't received anything. Same goes for Chris Halls' gardening business. They are still processing the scene."

"So we are sure that she isn't one of the local 'toms' then?" Rachael piped up, anxious to get involved in the discussion.

David shook his head. "None of our lads recognised her, and the same goes for St. Albans, Luton. We have circulated the photograph nationally with an urgent flag on it, but so far there is no response." He shook his head slowly.

"There must be hundreds, if not thousands in London alone." Ian Westlake said, which drew a curious glance from the others. He held up his hands. "I'm guessing, I don't know any personally, you know." He added defensively, which made Rick and Pete chuckle.

"Ten more minutes, David, then I'll have to stop for a coffee and a fag."

The office manager nodded and looked through his sheaf of notes, before looking up at his superior. "Actually, there are only two more topics at the moment." He hesitated, as if unsure which one to reveal first.

"If they're both bad news, just go alphabetically, David."

"8.30 Monday morning DCI Charles Carew will be taking over the investigation. He will be bringing six M.I.T officers over from County." He looked at Jim fearfully.

"I had been briefed that the DCI was coming, I just didn't know when."

"Is it bad?" Asked Rachael.

"The DCI has a reputation that proceeds him, shall we say. His way is slightly authoritarian, to put it mildly." Jim stated blandly, not wishing to admonish a senior officer to his juniors.

"The man is a total asshole." Rick spoke into his lap.

"And a bully." David chimed in.

"A total slimeball." Pete Norris added to the debate. Rachael noticed that Jim was looking intently at the man from County who was here already. Ian Westlake had nodded at all the comments from around the table before adding his own. "He is all of those, true. And he's also my father in law." Everyone started to apologise at once, but Ian just laughed and smiled and told them they were right anyway. The hubbub died away and left David with all the attention again. He cleared his throat and reached under the table, pulling out a large pile of newspapers, which he slewed on the desk.

"The press are having a field day with this. Some of them are with us, but a lot of influential ones aren't exactly sympathetic." He rooted around the pile and dug out the Sun. Blazoned across the front page was a picture of Inspector Schofield pointing angrily at a reporter during the press conference. "Witless Cops Harangue Our Man." Jim held out his hand and David handed him the paper. Jim folded it up and threw it in the waste bin. "Clueless Cops" was the banner from the Mirror, over a photograph which was taken at the precise time that three of the four officers happened to be blinking. It gave the impression that they were asleep. Jim sent it the same way as the previous one. The Daily Telegraph only gave it a column on page three, but at least it was broadly sympathetic. Jim slid it along the table for Rachael to peruse and looked across at David.

"My mum used to say that all publicity is good publicity. It seems she may have been wrong after all. Has Chief Superintendent Laird seen all these?"

David shrugged. "I don't know- he's out on the golf course with the Chief Constable."

Jim sighed. "Well, I don't know if anyone else wants one, but I fancy a cappuccino and a sticky bun from Harby's, after a fag, of course." He put his hand into his jacket, extracted a twenty-pound note from his wallet and put it on the table. "Don't all jump at once!" He left the room, having left the money on the table.

Rachael, Rick and Pete came trundling down the steps at the front of the station. Rick stopped to light a fag with Jim whilst the other two went to fetch the drinks.

Rick blew out a long stream of smoke and turned to the inspector. "Rachael filled me in on the little brainstorming session last night- shame I missed it."

Jim regarded the younger man out of the corner of his eye but said nothing.

"I'm not sure that I would've been to add much to the discussion, though." Rick watched the traffic go by as he spoke. Finally Jim spoke.

"Don't keep selling yourself short, constable. You've the makings of a very fine detective. I don't know if you'll end up as Chief Constable- I doubt you went to the right schools for a start, but I can envisage you as a future DCI, if you apply yourself."

Rick turned to Jim with a shocked expression on his face. "You really think so?"

Jim pulled a face and nodded. "Come on."

He shivered involuntarily as he dismounted the steps of the plane. It was still pleasantly warm in England, but it lacked the humid heat of southern Spain, He rubbed his arms together as he headed for the terminal. An hour later and he was seated comfortably behind the wheel of his car, easing his way out of the airport long-term car park. The afternoon sun began dipping in the west and caught his eye, making him think back to the bedroom of the sultry senorita that he'd met less than twenty-four hours previously, but felt like he had known his whole life. Maybe, just maybe, he thought, she could be the key to all this. Maybe she could unlock the love that was locked deep in his heart. Her caresses and silken kisses brought a smile to his face and a stirring to his loins. Then the smile hardened along with his heart as he remembered similar feelings- such as the ones he had felt with Lizzie.

As he crossed over a roundabout in his car, so his mind crossed a threshold into his past; suddenly he was transported back ten years to the night that he had consummated his relationship. They had lain next to each other on the sofa, when Lizzie suddenly shivered. Wordlessly, she had got up off the sofa, taken his hand, and led him upstairs. He followed entranced by the way her long hair trailed down her back almost to her beautiful rear, and he felt himself hardening again.

Lizzie had paused when she reached the landing at the top of the stairs. He had pointed to the right, and she followed him into his bedroom before diving under his duvet straightaway. "Ooh, that's better!" she exclaimed. She pulled the duvet over her head whilst he just stood there, smiling. Suddenly she whipped the duvet off, laughing, "Are you getting in or do you intend to stand there all evening?"

He took one last lingering look at her golden body, from her slender shoulders, to her small, firm breasts, down to the flat stomach and the tuft of hair above her hair, Laughing, he jumped into bed beside her, and pulled the duvet above both of their heads.

Once they were all seated, and all the sticky buns had been devoured, they got back down to business. Jim fished into his jacket pocket and extracted the napkin from the night before. It was slightly crumpled but still readable. Whilst he filled in the others about what had been discussed the night before, Rachael carefully transcribed what was on the napkin to a fresh whiteboard propped up against the windowsill. When she had finished, she turned round to see that Mary Guy, the psychologist, had slipped unobtrusively into the seat next to hers, and was quietly unpacking some manila folders from her briefcase to place in front of her.

"Good morning, Mary. I wasn't sure whether to expect you or not this morning- I thought you were at a wedding or something."

"Well, I'm here, aren't I?" Mary entwined her fingers and rested them on her slim stack of folders, fully aware that her statement gave nothing away. Jim gave a look that was halfway between inquisitive and surprised, but didn't reply, just giving her a series of nods instead.

Mary pointed to the board, saying, "What's going on here then?" She looked to Rachael, who filled the psychologist in on what they had been discussing the previous evening. Listening to her, Mary alternated her glances between Jim, the board and Rachael.

When Rachael had finished, motioning to the board, she asked Jim if she could say something. Jim agreed with a simple nod of his head.

"I'm sorry to rain on your parade here, but you're not going to catch the killer like this."

Jim got to his feet and leant on the table, leaning on his knuckles. "And how did you deduce this nugget of information, may I ask?"

"Firstly, you haven't got a link between the first three victims..."

"Four, I think you'll find." Rick butted in, smiling at Pete as he did so as if to say, 'can't this woman even count?'

"Actually...Rick, it's three. You don't have the flying fuck of an idea of who this girl is in the first place, so how can you tell me if she has anything in common with the other three?"

Rick blushed at the put-down and the others blanched at the use of the rude language. Jim was secretly impressed but made a mental note not to cross Mary when she was in full flow.

Mary ran a hand through her long dark hair and looked back at the board before turning back to the group, all of whom were now hanging on every word. "Now, as I was saying, you can't find the killer like this because you have no link between the victims. They're must be one, but we haven't found it yet. Rachael, this isn't a classroom, if you want to say something just jump in. Put your hand down."

Rachael looked Mary in the eye, swallowed, and asked her question. "Could the link be that there is no link- that they are all completely randomly picked? Just being in the wrong place at the wrong time?"

Mary pointed her marker pen at the female detective and waggled it up and down. "That, if I may so is an assiduous piece of deduction. However, if that is the case, why travel 300 miles away for his first victim?" She looked around at the others, inviting replies.

"Could he have been there on business, or passing through, and the opportunity just presented itself?" Pete Norris asked tentatively.

"I think that's unlikely." Jim had intervened. "We have evidence to suggest that the killer struck up a friendship of some sort with the victim. The landlady is sketchy on the details but seems to think that Samuel told her one evening he was some sort of mature student- a lie I'm sure, by the way- but she seems to think that she saw him on at least three occasions with him over a period of a couple of weeks. She's enquiring with her bar staff if any of them recall seeing them together. David, make a note to get someone to follow that up."

Mary sensed that there was no new guesses coming from the team, so carried on. "By now you realise that this case isn't going to be solved overnight, but by putting in hundreds of hours of painstaking research, running down every lead, every clue. This isn't a police drama where the rugged male lead has a moment of inspiration after drinking a pint in the pub or reading a book." She looked at Jim. "No offence."

He responded by pulling a mock glum face. "At least you think I'm rugged." The group laughed collectively and the tension that had been building dissipated suddenly.

"Cause of death is important in most serial cases. Here, it may be the key to everything."

Jim asked, "Are you saying that there is a pattern to the manner of death as well?"

"I'm sure there is- and it's the key to everything. However, there are more problems here. Most importantly, we don't have the foggiest idea of what the pattern is. There doesn't seem to be an evolution of any kind."

Pete Norris interrupted. "What do you mean by evolution?"

"Well, let's take a simple hypothetical, who stabs people. The first victim would be expected to have hesitation marks, for example. As the killings progress, his confidence begins to grow, and you would expect more wounds and a greater precision to those wounds. We haven't got that. An injection, a blunt trauma, a strangling, and a possible accident don't show any development or consistency."

"An accident?" Jim asked, puzzled.

"I think that the punch that killed Tori Henderson probably wasn't intended to kill her, so yes I would loosely term it as an 'accident.'" There was a pause as the team digested the information that Mary was giving them. "I may have been a bit disingenuous. It's not the actual way that he killed them that's so important to him, it's how and where we found them. I don't mean 'where' as in a house, a barn, a truck or whatever- but the staging."

Rachael asked," So, finding one in darkness, one with headphones in, one with their heart cut open, and one just appearing to be asleep- they're telling a story?"

"Precisely- I couldn't have put it better myself!" Mary laughed and clapped her hands. "Well

done, Rachael, now the only thing we have to do is work out what the story is, and we will be halfway to catching him."

He sat up in his hammock as best he could so that he didn't spill any of his drink. It was a cocktail based on the local spirit, Arak. It was a sweet sickly concoction tasting of coconut, pineapples, and mangoes. He shielded his eyes from the glare of the sun even though he was in the shade of a couple of palm trees to see his friend Lawrence playing beach cricket with some of the local boys. As he watched, his mate was bowling, and the ball was smashed into the sea. He laughed with them all before holding up his hands to mime that he was thirsty. The boys all started animatedly discussing who should bowl next, seeing as their great captain had withdrawn from the game. He strode up the beach waving at them all the time, before reaching the hammocks where he toweled his face to wipe the sweat away.

"You should've joined in." Lawrence smiled at his mate, after picking up his own drink. He took a long sip and spluttered as the fierce liquid hit the back of his throat. "Wow, that one's strong." He exclaimed as he took another long swig.

"Better watch how quickly you drink it then." He watched his mate as he finished his drink. "And not too many more, either, if you intend on meeting that girl again tonight."

"That girl, as you so kindly put it, does have a name you know."

"Sukaya."

"Sukaya."

"I asked Dev if he knew what it means."

"She wouldn't tell me when I asked her," Lawrence said, smiling at his friend. "She just went all coy and changed the subject. So what does it mean then?"

He moved back a pace or two away before answering, looking out at the waves as their crashed on the shore. "It means having a beautiful body."

"You are joking, aren't you?"

He turned to face his friend again, a smile playing on his lips and a twinkle in his eyes as he shook his head. He raised an eyebrow in a silent question.

"I don't know, honestly. She lets me go so far... and then just pulls away or shakes her head..." Lawrence stared at the sand, a wistful look on his face. "You won't tell Nicky about it when we get home, will you?"

He replied by clapping him on the shoulder as he passed him to get some more drinks from the flimsy wooden bar. "What happens in Sri Lanka stays in Sri Lanka, you know that mate." Smiling to himself he moved away leaving his friend looking out to sea.

After a further hour or so of discussion, the team had decided on where they should focus for the next day or so, or at least until DCI Carew turned up with his coterie on the Monday. Pete Norris was detailed to take whoever turned in for the rest of the day and Sunday, and assign them to a victim, to discover as much as they could about each one. Rachael, Mary and Terry were going to write up a review of where they were in the case; Jim was going to write an action plan for the upcoming days. Jim had laughed at this, for when Carew turned up, he would have his own plan of attack, but it was nevertheless necessary, to demonstrate to the top brass that they hadn't just been sitting on their hands. David was to co-ordinate everything, and enter it on the computer, so it at looked least professional. Jim had a deep mistrust of such machines, but he was no fool and knew where the future was heading, at least in terms of the Police. He wished there was a reliable system already in place so that all police forces, up and down the country could simply log in and pool their resources and information. So much time was spent on the telephone, waiting for colleagues to get back to them, or hanging around the fax machine. He sometimes felt that the typical police qualities of determined sleuthing, experience and educated hunches were disappearing in the mists of time, despatched to history.

"Just two things before we go our separate ways. Firstly, I want to thank you all personally for all your exceptional hard work and dedication in what has been a truly harrowing week for all of us. I have seen several of you develop skills that you never knew you had, and that has been really, really exciting for me. Also, my thanks to Mary here." He stopped and bowed his head to the psychologist, who wrinkled her nose by way of thanks. "Secondly, if any of you want to get off this bus because it's getting too much for you, then I have no problem with that. I know DCI Carew and his crew will blow in here like a force nine gale and disrupt us all. They may make you feel small, inconsequential, and worthless, and if you want to get out now, I understand." He looked around the team and was rewarded with looks of grim determination from everyone. He stood up when Rick suddenly spoke.

"Imagine them naked."

Mary looked down at her pad, smiling, for she knew what he was talking about. The others, Jim included, stared at him. "That's what my careers teacher taught me at school, sir. If someone is trying to bully or intimidate you, she said to imagine them with no clothes on. It works for me-they suddenly seem much less scary.

"Do you imagine me with no clothes on, Rick? No- on second thoughts, don't answer that, I don't want to know the answer to that."

CHAPTER 23

Rain streamed down the windscreen as he peered out into the early evening gloom. He bent further forward in his seat to see if there were any breaks in the cloud. It had been raining on and off for the best part of two days since his return from Spain, a most unseasonal spell of weather in this English summer.

A movement in his rear-view mirror made him focus. A woman in a full-length raincoat stepped out of a doorway putting her umbrella up. A lorry drove past, driving a vast wall of rainwater up onto the pavement. The woman in the raincoat had been anticipating it and brought her umbrella down at just the right time so as to deflect the brunt of the cold, dirty water. Sitting in the warmth of his car, he was impressed by her deft movement. He raised an eyebrow and nodded in silent recognition of her skill. Bracing himself against the rain as it continued to hammer down on the road, he got out of the car. He had purposely chosen not to put on his raincoat, and the rain instantly soaked his hair, running down the inside of his shirt, making him shiver. The girl he had been observing had by now reached his car, and laughed at him whilst he was hunched over, pretending to lock it.

"You're getting soaked!" She exclaimed to his back. He turned to face her and pretended to be surprised when he saw who it was. She narrowed her eyes at him. "Hey, don't I know you?" She laughed, albeit a little nervously. "Don't tell me," she said hurriedly as he began to open his mouth. "Steve? Simon? Stephen?"

He nodded, breaking into a smile even as the rain ran in rivulets down his face. "You were right the first time." He offered up a damp hand." It's Elizabeth, isn't it? From the party in Bethnal Green?" He pretended to only vaguely recall who she was, even though he had orchestrated everything, even gate-crashing the party that he'd just mentioned.

"Yes it is, you must have a better mind for faces than me. Where's your coat?"

"It's in the boot of my car. It wasn't raining when I left home earlier." He offered up a sheepish smile as he noted her eyes taking in his muscular frame visible now that the teeming rain had turned his white shirt translucent. He started to unlock his boot, the woman following him, trying to shield him with her umbrella, the raindrops falling on her back and her hair now as the umbrella wasn't big enough for both of them.

He retrieved his jacket from the boot but made no move to put it on. Instead he turned away from her and looked over the road, before looking back at her over his shoulder. "Would you like a cup of coffee with me?" He held up his jacket. "I'll have to dry off before I put this on anyway."

She smiled at him from eyes that, though dark in colour, sparkled with vitality. "Ok then, that would be lovely." They crossed the road, both huddled under her umbrella. Elizabeth shook it out underneath the canopy of the cafe, with him waiting patiently, looking around surreptitiously to make sure that no-one was watching them. He had already noticed that the cafe only had one customer, an elderly gentleman engrossed in an edition of the Racing Post. When they entered the cafe, he didn't even bat an eyelid. They asked for two coffees to be brought over. He took a seat facing away from the counter, looking out on the dreary street, close to a decrepit, battered fan heater blowing out a weak stream of tepid air. The rest of the cafe seemed to match the efforts of the heater- no expense had been made on making the customer experience anything other than unremarkable- from a faded portrait of the queen on one wall, to a silent television high in one corner showing that afternoons' racing from a dusty screen.

Across the table, the girl had at last sorted herself out and had seated herself opposite him. Her light brown hair had been cut into a bob at some point but had been growing out for some time: it looked clean, just a little untidy. She smiled at him from dark eyes surrounded by dark brown eyeshadow and just a little too much mascara. Her little button nose had a stud in it, and perched above a small mouth supporting a shade of lipstick that was more brown than red.

The eyes narrowed and the lips pursed as she said, "Do I meet with your approval?" A small rounded chin jutted out a little in defiance.

He blushed. "I'm so sorry, it's just it was fairly dark and smoky at the party, and I couldn't really see how attractive you are." He smiled.

It was her turn to blush, and her gaze dropped to her hands, which she now brought out on top of the table, so that he could see small fingers tipped with chipped red nail varnish. "Oh look at my dreadful nails. You must be thinking I'm an awful mess really." She raised her eyes to his again, and they stayed like that, silently taking in each other. He was amused that she seemed a lot posher than she let on. It was something to do with her diction.

The coffee arrived in a pair of matching mugs, inasmuch as they had similar chips out of them by their handles.

"How did you recognise me out there, then?" He asked, aware that he was on dangerous ground here, but it was something he needed to know. If she could recognise him, then potentially anyone could, which would cause problems sooner or later.

"I didn't really, not until you were up close. I saw someone climbing out of their car without a coat on, in the pouring rain, and I just thought 'poor thing, he's going to get soaked'."

He nodded, then gazed out of the grimy window as if a though had just occurred to him.

"What is it?" She inquired, as if sensing his indecision.

"No, it's a stupid idea, and you're probably busy."

"What is it?" She repeated, raising an eyebrow quizzically. "I can't tell you if it's stupid or not if you won't tell me." She was laughing softly.

"I was meant to be going with a friend to see Gary Numan in Camden tonight, but he's had to pull out suddenly." He reached over to his jacket and pulled out a small envelope.

"I don't suppose he's your cup of tea though." He said, pulling a sad expression. He knew, however, that he was one of her favourite artists. He knew a lot about her though: that she was 28, single, lived alone with only a cat, Pandora, for company, and that she worked in the packing department of a small publishing company about a hundred yards away. He knew her favourite colour was brown, that she practiced yoga and was a struggling poet. He knew this because he had tracked her down and stalked her for quite a while. Twice he had sat in pubs just a couple of feet away from her without her realising as she chatted away to her best friends, Sadie and Chloe. He had even followed her home, been inside her small flat without her realising, snooping around without leaving any trace of having done so. Therefore, when he looked at her with little hope of success, he knew exactly what her answer was going to be.

She gave a whoop of delight, clapping her hands so that both the old man reading his paper and the cafe owner looked over before returning to their reading and cleaning. She smiled a brief apology before leaning across the table and taking his hand in hers.

"I love him! I absolutely adore him. I was going to go but I had to pay my electricity bill the day the tickets came out, and by the time I had got the money together again, they'd all sold out." She beamed across the table. "I can't believe it- what a wonderful man you are!"

She seemed so genuinely happy that he had to look down at the table as he felt a pang of guilt over deceiving her. He blinked and saw an image of his ex-girlfriend, and his resolve hardened once more. At least this one would experience some happiness before the end. Though why anyone would want to see Gary Numan escaped him. In his opinion his best work was over fifteen years previously and he couldn't even recall one single song by the artist in a decade. He looked up at her again to see her staring at the tickets like they were made of gold. He smiled and finished his coffee. His shirt dried out, and looking out of the window, he saw the rain had stopped too.

"I don't know where you live, but I could drop you off and wait for you to get changed before we head off." He checked his watch; it was fast approaching six o'clock. "We have a couple of hours before it starts- depending on how long it takes you to get yourself ready, we might even be able to get a bite to eat."

Her smile faded a little. "I'm not sure about that- funds are a little tight at the moment."

He made a deliberate show of looking up the dusty television high up on the wall. He pointed at the screen. "See that horse called Staten Island?" She nodded. "I had twenty pounds on him to win." So that's a hundred pounds coming my way." He turned back to face her again. "So we could afford to eat at the Ritz if we wanted to." His eyes narrowed as he looked at her. "Though I doubt they'd let you in if you were dressed like Gary Numan."

As they left, the cafe owner stood by the old man.

"'Ere, Bert, get that one then?"

"Staten fucking Island? Bloody nag has never won anything before. Thought he only had three fucking legs."

The owner nodded at the pair who had just left. "Nice car, nice girl. Dinner and a show- he must know something you don't."

"Fuck off, Alf."

Jim Smallwood rubbed his eyes as he sat in his office at the end of a long day. Rachael and Mo had left, leaving him with just Terry and Ronnie for company. Inspector Schofield had kicked off her stilettos and put her stockinged feet up on Rachael's desk. Ronnie perched on a corner of it, trying not to react to the smell.

Chief Inspector Charles Carew had swept in early in the morning with his six acolytes like the Horsemen of the Apocalypse and taken possession of the conference room. And then he had taken possession of the case, making Jim and David go through everything from the very beginning. There had been constant interruptions from the senior policeman, asking questions at every juncture, wondering why had Jim done this, or that- the list had been virtually endless. By the time they had finished, six hours later, both Jim and David were absolutely frazzled. They had worked through lunch, barely stopping for coffee, and not a cigarette break in sight. The other members of the team had been banished throughout the station until they had been brought in to account for their actions. Only Terry and Mo had remained throughout, as their rank befitted them.

The last hour had been the worst. Carew had blown the investigation out of the water. And then told them that he was taking absolute control of it from here onwards. At one point he had even tried to send the two northern coppers home before Ronnie had taken his life in his hands by pointing out that they were here by invitation of the ACC. He had been rewarded for his pains by one of Carew's infamous 'death stares'.

"I'm reet proud of you, Sergeant." Terry said, as she combed her hair with her fingers, trying to tame it. Ronnie looked at her, a slight smile playing on his lips. Jim had stopped rubbing his eyes but was leaning forward in his chair, staring at the floor. Terry, looking at Ronnie, stopped combing to mime having a drink, whilst nodding towards Jim. Taking the hint, Ronnie cleared his throat. "Sir, do you fancy a pint? Inspector Schofield said she's paying."

Jim didn't respond at first and Ronnie looked at his boss uncertainly. He was rewarded with an arched eyebrow and pursed lips.

"What a fucking bastard." The words escaped Jim's lips quietly, but the two detectives picked up on them nevertheless.

"I know I'm not everyone's cup of tea, but you could at least wait until I've gone till you start slagging me off." Terry said, trying to bring some happiness back into the room. Ronnie smirked and at last Jim looked up from the floor.

"What are you two still doing here?" Jim looked at the pair. "I'd have thought you two would've buggered off down the pub by now."

Terry pouted as she looked at Ronnie, who simply shrugged. "Would you like to join us, Sir?" Ronnie tried again. "Inspector Schofield said she would buy the first two rounds..." Ronnie was steadfastly ignoring the withering look he was receiving from his superior, and continued, "...and by all accounts you've had a bit of a roasting today, with all respects, Sir."

Jim gave the young policeman a shrewd look. "Yes I would care to join you, but not because the inspector is flashing her cash around. That would probably warrant another press conference. I think we need to come up with some sort of a plan on how we are going to solve this case whilst carrying the great monkey Carew on our backs." He gave the ghost of a smile, the first of the day. "And we need to see if there are any developments. Something must have happened. I mean yesterday was a complete washout... David and I hung around most of the day and it was as quiet as the grave."

"It was Sunday, Sir." Both he and Terry had attended local churches the previous day. Jim had understood that Ronnie was a Catholic, and wasn't surprised when he had slipped out to go to Mass. But he had been surprised half an hour later when Terry said she was going to a service and had asked for directions to the local Friends meeting house. He would never have put her down as a Quaker, primarily because he hadn't known her be quiet for ten minutes since he had met her.

"Policing is twenty fours a day, seven days a week. I'm surprised more than annoyed that nothing at all happened yesterday to help us." There had been a couple of responses to the appeal on the identity of the fourth victim, but these had been dismissed, as one was far too old, the other was about eight stone too heavy.

Jim scribbled on a piece of paper. "Can you ring Rachael to see if she wants to tag along too. And Ronne, go and have a quick scout around to see if any of our team is lurking in a dark corner somewhere. It's not an order but just tell them that your boss has offered to pay the first couple of rounds." He shrugged on his jacket. "I'll meet you in the car park in five." With that, he was gone even before Terry had taken her feet off the desk.

He had pleaded ignorance of her address, although he had made the trip between her flat and her place of work on at least four occasions over the course of the past year or so. She was more used to getting the bus, she explained, but the route from Stratford to Tottenham was fairly straightforward, only a couple of turns, otherwise keeping straight. Her flat was above a launderette on the busy Fore Street. And as they got nearer she explained that he could park for free in a Sainsbury's car park just a hundred yards on from her place. They had chatted easily on a variety of topics, and he was beginning to enjoy her company. Several times he had to think quite hard about what he was really doing here. Once, he was concentrating so hard he failed to hear her telling him to take a left turn. She laughed, punching him lightly on the arm. He smiled back.

"You were a bit like that at the party, I seem to recall." She looked out of the window at the evening lights just coming on as they travelled along. "You were there, but not there, if you know what I mean."

He thought fast to come up with an adequate answer. "A bit aloof, you mean?"

"Yes."

"Would you like to know the truth?" He ventured.

"A man telling me the truth? That'd be a novelty!" She gave an ironic smirk. He paused, looking straight ahead, waiting for a set of traffic lights to change. This is why, he thought, this is why. Although he suspected that she was half-joking it was precisely this kind of attitude that so completely infuriated him. He bit his lip to stop himself from screaming.

She saw the gesture and for a moment felt ashamed. She coughed, and said, "Hey, I'm sorry- I don't know you well enough to judge you like that." She laid a placatory hand on his arm. "It's just that I've met a lot of lying bastards in my life."

"If you just piped down for a second or two, I would be able to give you my answer." A half-smile played on his lips as he stole a glance at her sitting next to her. From this angle she was fairly attractive, he thought. She made a zipping motion across her lips with her fingers.

"I honestly was a bit aloof at the party because I didn't think you were attracted to me. I thought there was no point in pursuing you because you would only knock me back. Plus I'm a bit shy when I first meet people."

In response, she rocked her head with laughter, till he thought she was going to cry from laughing so much. He looked across at her with a perplexed look on his face as he turned into the entrance of the supermarket carpark, finding a space. He looked over at her again to see that she was sitting there, still convulsing with laughter. He raised his eyebrows in a silent 'what?'

She looked at him, trying to keep a straight face, but she couldn't, and the smile came again.

"You really cannot read women at all, can you?" He shook his head, as if to suggest that most men couldn't. "The way I was literally in your face, hanging off every word, playing with my hair, batting my eyelids, the touching on the arm...you're not a virgin, are you?" She bought a hand up to her mouth, her smile replaced by a look of genuine concern. This time it was his turn to laugh. He turned towards her and kissed her fully on the mouth, before pulling away again.

Elizabeth tilted her head. She ran her the tip of her tongue around her lips. "I guess not."

The mood in the pub was still subdued, even after the second round. The first round had been supped in complete silence until Terry had said 'same again then?' and heaved her heavy frame off the chair she was sitting on. A few desultory attempts at conversation were attempted, but soon petered out when people looked at Jim, staring morosely into his pint.

Suddenly a voice boomed out over the sad trio. "Has someone died, Sir?" It was Rick, a sad, confused look on his young face.

Terry burst out laughing, a strange kind of barking noise. Ronnie started chuckling, and even Jim looked up at him with the faint beginnings of a smile.

"Remind me what your job is, Rick." Jim asked. Rick, suspecting a trick question, looked around before replying. "I'm a murder detect-..." before realising what he had said. He smirked at his boss. "I didn't mean that. I meant...someone...someone you know or something." He stammered to a stop, blushing.

"Sit yourself down, constable, I'll get you a pint." Terry stood up again.

"Rachael is parking her car with Ian and David. Ash sends his apologies, and Pete and Mark will be here in half an hour, they said. Shall I put some music on? Come and help me choose, Sergeant." They wandered off to the jukebox.

Rachael slipped into the vacant chair next to her boss and put a comforting hand on his forearm as she sat down. "Not all days are going to be as tough as this, Sir."

Jim, who his glass raised halfway to his lips, waggled his little finger at her. "Thanks, but isn't that what I should say to you, not vice-versa?" Rachael smiled, but didn't have time to reply as Terry had come back from the bar and was handing her a glass of wine.

"I'm driving, Ma'am."

"One won't kill you, Rachael." Terry winked, setting down another pint in front of Jim. Eventually, after pulling over chairs from other tables, everyone was seated. Inspector Schofield breathed in deeply, and raising her glass, announced, "This is to all the downtrodden workers in the world, that they may rise up and overthrow their oppressors." There was a general cheer from the assembled group.

"Is that how you see us now, Inspector- downtrodden masses?" David asked, a light froth from his pint augmenting his wispy moustache.

"No, I remember it from a film I watched a while ago and it seemed the most appropriate thing to say in the circumstances." She winked at David, who blushing, concentrated on his pint. Indeed, he drank most of it before setting it down, which amused Jim.

"I didn't think you were much of a drinker, David." There was a general nod of assent from the rest. David was David, a sensible, hardworking individual with no outrageous opinions of anybody, a conservative attitude, a sensible approach to dress; most of the staff thought him as a large, cuddly teddy bear.

"Yeah, well, tonight I am. I'm going to get tight and if Chief Inspector Carew gives me any grief tomorrow, I'm going to give him a wedgie." He stormed off to the bar in search of another pint.

The rest of the group erupted en masse into raucous laughter. Rachael was laughing so much, she felt wetness on her cheeks. The thought of David giving the Chief Inspector a 'wedgie' made her laugh as much as David saying he was going to do it, and the language he had used to describe it. When the laughter had finally ebbed to a low stream of occasional giggling, Jim held up his hand for a little bit of quiet. "Right, team, I know I said that tonight was about formulating a plan for combating Carew and his crew. But there's been a change of plan...tonight the plan is for us all to get totally pissed!"

Everyone gathered around the table clapped and cheered except for Inspector Schofield, who sat there, stony-faced and silent. As each of them in turn noticed this, they stopped what they were doing to look at her, until at last she had all of them looking at her in silence. Looking at each one in turn, she was shaking her head sadly. She got to her feet again and just said one word.

"Seconded."

The team burst out in gales of laughter once more.

The two of them sat on a low wall, and the third stood nearby stood kicking a can against it from time to time. The noise was starting to get on Delroy's nerves.

"Stop that, bro, for fucks sake." He shouted at him. His brother, Denzil, glared at him, but did as he was told, thrusting his hands deeper into his tracksuit bottom pockets.

Delroy nodded at him to come closer. "Don't want no Feds hearing our business, man."

The other one sitting on the wall looked around the area cautiously before speaking. "So how we gonna do this grass cutting, man?"

Delroy sniffed the air around him, smelling the familiar stench of diesel, rubbish and dog shit that seemed to pervade every inch of the estate. He hawked up a big glob of phlegm and spat it over the wall behind him where it nestled between an old condom and a used syringe. He ignored both; they were common sights here.

"I say we shoot the damn nigger, right between the eyes." Delroy held up his left hand and mimicked a shooting motion with his thumb as the hammer on the gun. "Boom. He gone. No more grass on the Farm, boys."

"Nah, bro, too noisy. Big knife, right across his damn lying throat." The other occupant of the wall, Dwayne, said. He held up his hand and made a swift slashing movement and a clicking noise with his teeth.

Denzil had walked up to them and stood there shaking his head. "Too much blood, bro. How you gonna explain that to your old lady, bro?" Dwayne looked at him with contempt whilst Delroy just grinned.

"And where you gonna get the blade anyhow?" Dwayne continued, looking at Denzil. Then he looked at his older brother. "Or a shooter?"

Delroy opened up his tracksuit to reveal a pistol tucked into his waistband. Dwayne stepped back a couple of paces involuntarily, startled. Denzil opened his jacket to reveal a machete in its sheath tucked into his waistband. Dwayne whistled at the pair of them.

"You both carrying in daylight? Are you crazy, motherfuckers? What if the Feds come in?"

"Hey, chill, bro." Delroy said. "Aint no Feds coming down the Farm today, not this far in." He spat again, just missing his younger brother. Dwayne growled at him.

"What you suggest then, man?" Denzil asked him. "You the one who goes to college an' all, you must've some brain. Try using it for once." Denzil stood and tapped Dwayne on the side of his head.

"Mind the dreads, bro." He swatted Denzil's hand away. He turned round to one of the tower blocks. "We lure the fucker into one of the blocks. Maybe tell him Sherelle is giving out." He turned to face his mate and his brother. "Then we throw him off the balcony."

Denzil nodded, Delroy smiled. "Like it."

"What are we going to do with the body?" Denzil asked, cocking his head to look at the balcony and then back at his friend. In response, Dwayne reached behind his back and pulled out a rolled-up newspaper which he threw onto the top of the wall. 'Death in a Duvet' screamed the headlines.

"Wrap him in a duvet, leave him with the bins, piece of white trash."

The evening had turned into a bit of a party, with Terry, Rick and Ian even challenging a group of regulars to a game of darts. Rachael and Ronnie sat chatting amicably about music. Rachael had abandoned her plan of driving, thinking she could get a taxi home instead. She enjoyed the company of Ronnie- the dark eyes and bronzed features of those from the Med always seemed to be her preferred type- but she was fully aware that he was first and foremost a colleague, and experience had warned off work relationships. Moreover, he made her laugh, with his quick humour and sparkling, mischievous eyes that were never still, taking everything in. A friend is what she needed most, she decided. Shame, though.

"Do you think we're taking this seriously enough, Sarge?" Rachael asked, trying to look anywhere but his eyes.

"What time did you start this morning, Rach?"

"Just after seven."

"There you go. And it was a short day. Six days, say twelve hours a day, is a lot of work. Hard work. We've got to have some down time." Rachael shrugged.

Suddenly the door to the pub crashed open and a young uniformed constable burst in. A mop of curly hair bounced on top of his head, seemingly independent of its owner, as he searched for the Inspector. Finding him, he rushed up to Jim's table, where he reached into his jacket and pulled out a couple of folded pieces of paper. Jim struggled to focus on the young constable at first, but gradually realised that it was him the policeman was looking for.

"Evening, Sir- sorry to disturb you- but this came through from Great Yarmouth just now."

Jim scowled, but took the paper, still folded, anyway. "Probably another false alarm." David snorted in agreement beside him. "But thanks anyway, son. What's your name?"

The young man seemed unfazed by the inspectors' nonchalance. "Tom Handford, Sir. ".

"Well thank you, Pc Handford." Jim tossed the paper onto the bar, where a corner of it started to soak up some spilt beer.

"Thing is, Sir...just as this arrived, that pathologist bloke was dropping off a report or something at the station. He took one look at that. "Handford indicated the paper, getting damper by the second, "and he just said to find you as quickly as possible, Sir."

"Bernie was at the station?" Jim rescued the pieces of paper and tried to dry them off on his lap as best he could. By this time, the darts game had stopped, and the 'visitors' had come back to the table. Ronnie and Rachael had similarly stopped their chat and leaned in over the tabletop to see what the inspector had received.

Satisfied that it was dry enough to read, Jim unfolded the two pages and read what was inside. When he'd finished he handed it to Inspector Schofield to read next. Rachael, unable to wait her turn, asked her boss what the papers contained.

"It's her, alright- the fourth victim. It's definitely her, without a shadow of a doubt. Yes!" He punched the air. "Read it out, Terry."

Inspector Schofield shook out the sheets to separate them, cleared her throat, and began.

"To Inspector Smallwood... I'm sorry that it has taken so long to get back to you, I had a couple of days leave...I believe your body to be that of one of our local prostitutes. She went by the working name of Olive...but called herself Mandy." Terry paused, looking into space whilst her eyes narrowed for a moment. Then she refocused and continued: "Our records show that her real name, however, is Jo Susan Holt, aged 24, height ...weight...signed Constable Tim Wickham, Great Yarmouth Police.

267

Picture enclosed." P.S. our enquiries suggest that she has not been seen since last Friday. Full report will follow as soon as enquiries permit."

Quiet fell in the pub as even the regular customers realised the importance of the news. The barman reached over and muted the jukebox.

"Back to the station, Sir?" Rachael asked, though secretly she dreaded the prospect of going back into work at this time of night.

"No." Jim picked up his pint and finished it off. "I suggest we go off home now and meet early in the morning." He turned and faced the rest of the group. "CID office, seven sharp."

Terry drained her pint and went back to the bar. "Sorry to finish the party early, love."

"Just make sure you finish it off when you catch the bastard, miss."

Terry tapped the bar and nodded and headed out of the door.

They stumbled up the stairs to her flat. She fumbled with the lock, but eventually managed to open the door. She stood there and looked at him, hanging back bit a back.

"You can come in for a coffee, if you like. I won't bite." She put a finger under his chin as he crossed the threshold. "Unless you want me to." She skipped away, laughing, and threw herself down on her small sofa. He followed her into the lounge-diner. A small corridor showed three doors: bedroom, bathroom and kitchen. He knew which was which because he'd been here before but pretended he didn't know the layout.

"Where's your bathroom?"

"Second right." He padded away to the smallest room, the adrenaline pulsing through his body in waves. He took several deep breaths whilst he was standing over the toilet in an attempt to control his nerves. When he re-entered the lounge she was still sprawled on the sofa. "If you want a beer, help yourself, they're in the fridge."

"I'd love to, but if I have any more I'd have to kip on your sofa." He said, looking down on it.

"Not unless you're a midget, you won't."

He looked at her and she raised an eyebrow at him.

"If you don't want to sleep with me, we could top and tail, as long as your feet don't smell."

This time he raised an eyebrow. He found two beers in the fridge and opened a drawer in search of a bottle opener. He took it out, opened the bottles, put it back and withdrew a screwdriver that had been sitting next to it. He slid this quietly into his jacket. From the same pocket he took out a small plastic packet containing two pink tablets, which he dropped into her bottle. This will get the party started, he thought. He went back into the lounge and handed her the doctored bottle. She shuffled herself upright, allowing him just enough room to snuggle next to her before they clinked bottles and took a good long swig.

"That was a fabulous concert."

"Really? You've only said that a dozen times." She punched him on the arm, and then bent in for a kiss. They just sat there, not wildly groping each other, just kissing. After a while, they surfaced for air. He saw her eyes as they looked towards her bedroom.

"Priorities, woman. Beer, then sex." She narrowed her eyes at him, then put the bottle to her lips and finished it off in one long gulp. "That's impressive."

In response she giggled and burped. He finished his bottle off and stood up, holding his hand out to her. She took it and he pulled her up, wrapping his arm around her. He reckoned the Rohypnol would take about ten minutes to start to work, and after a quarter of an hour she would be unconscious. Time enough for a long kiss goodbye. He tenderly parted her lips with his tongue and probed inside her mouth, and she pulled him close as if she was trying to be part of him. They stood there until he felt her slightly sag in his arms and she stopped kissing him.

"You're making me feel all light-headed, you know. I think I need to lie down."

"You're such a strumpet." He laughed at her, and she smiled weakly at him as her eyelids began to flutter. He dropped her to the sofa and put on a pair of plastic gloves. He stooped down and picked her up, carrying her to the kitchen. That was where there was the most free space. Kneeling down, he gently placed her on her back. She was virtually comatose by this point, and her smile had faded to a slight frown. Backing out of the kitchen, he walked down the corridor to reach the bathroom. Withdrawing the screwdriver, he set about removing the six screws on the hinges. As each one came out, he placed it carefully in the plastic bag that had previously held the drugs.

The last screw popped out, and he put it in the bag with the others. He prised out the top hinge from the door frame using the screwdriver, then squatted down and repeated the process with the bottom one. The door suddenly came free and he stood up quickly to take its weight. He bent his knees and picked it up, steering the door carefully out of the bathroom and into the kitchen, propping it against one of the kitchen cupboards temporarily. He bent down and took her feet, positioning her body diagonally on the floor so as to maximise the room available to him. He picked the door up by the edge containing the hinges and straddled her inert body. He lined up the bottom edge of the door against her windpipe and rested it there for a couple of seconds. There was no reaction at all. Then he pushed down hard until he heard the bones snap.

CHAPTER 24

He stood by the sofa after cleaning up the flat. He had rehung the door, wiped down all the surfaces he could remember touching, from the toilet seat and handle, the bathroom door itself...the fridge door, the drawer handles, the bottle opener...he ran through the list in his head for about the tenth time to make sure everything was covered. He checked his watch and was surprised to see it was almost three in the morning. No wonder he was tired.

As his mind wandered, he thought about the original Elizabeth Fairbairn, all those years ago. He'd truly believed that they had something special between them, sensed the excitement he felt at the thought of seeing her again mount with each mile that they neared England. He'd been impatient to get through Customs, parted with his mate (whom he felt sure would understand) and raced home to see her face again. The two weeks that they had been apart felt to him like two years, and his heart ached.

They had had some real good fortune in Frankfurt. They were meant to have a four-hour stopover there, but a flight to England had been delayed by some technical fault, and there were a couple of seats still available, so they jumped on it. The result of the reduced time spent in Germany, and the fact that the pilot had obviously been trying to make up time meant they reached home soil about four and a half hours earlier than expected.

"You realise that we didn't even get any Duty Free?" Lawrence had said as they were going down an escalator. No booze, not even fags."

"I'm not fussed- in fact I've been thinking about giving up smoking." He had replied.

"Since when?" Lawrence looked at him quizzically. "Oh, don't tell me, Lizzie doesn't like you smoking." Lawrence was laughing. "Boy, you've got it bad."

"Actually, it's her mum. She's insistent that any boyfriend her daughter dates has to have the highest standards. No smoking, not getting drunk, definitely no sex before marriage."

"And I suppose Durex and Polo mints can only help so much." Lawrence chortled, and clapped him on the shoulder.

Outside they joined a mercifully short queue for taxis and were soon speeding in the direction of home. They'd arranged that he'd leave his bags with his friend, and that the taxi would drop him off at the bottom of Lizzies' road. And so it was, barely twenty minutes after getting in the taxi, he was walking up the hill towards Lizzies' house, brushing his hair with his fingers as best he could, smoothing out imaginary wrinkles from his shirt. He felt the butterflies in his stomach, and nervous, but excited, he rang her doorbell.

A minute or so went by, and he was just reaching up to ring the bell again when the door opened. A stranger with an open shirt and messed-up blonde hair stood there. He looked past him to see Lizzie at the bottom of her stair, wearing only a shirt, her legs bare, a look of shock on her face, which turned to horror when she realised who it was.

"Can I help you, buddy?" The blonde spoke again. It was then that he recognised him as the brother of one of his old school friends, who lived just a couple of doors down the road.

"I'm not your buddy, Douglas Christian." He snarled. The boy, whether taken aback at being recognised, or the tone of voice, took a step backwards. Lizzie took the opportunity to step in front of him, laying a hand on his chest to push him down the hallway a bit.

"Give us a minute, eh?" She said to Douglas, who shrugged his shoulders and padded into the kitchen to get himself a glass of water. Lizzie turned back to her boyfriend on the doorstep.

"It's not what it looks like-" She began, but he held up his hand.

"How could you?" He asked.

"It just happened. It was a mistake-"

"Don't. Just don't - I don't want to know."

"I'll get him to leave, and we will sit down and talk it through."

"Don't bother wasting your breath on more lies." He started to turn his back and walk away, but she reached out her hand to stop him.

"But I love you, Phil." She was pleading with him, and for a moment he almost turned back into her arms, but Douglas appeared in the doorway.

"Everything alright here?" He had his hand on her shoulder, smiling as if he was the cat who'd just had all the cream.

And that was all it took. He shoved Lizzie out of the way and laid Douglas out with a single punch. The glass spilled its contents down the wall before smashing itself into a thousand pieces on the parquet flooring. He ignored Lizzie and stormed off. He never saw her again.

Yet almost a decade later, he could still feel the jealousy raging through him, as if it was yesterday. Which is why I find myself here, he thought. He wandered into the bedroom where he stood and took a final look at his latest victim, sheathed in her white shroud. She looked incredibly peaceful, as if she was only sleeping. He let himself out of the flat into the fresh new morning, the sun beginning to turn the eastern sky a dark violet as it rose again over that corner of north London.

Jim woke up without any trace of a hangover. He rolled over and looked at the clock on his bedside table through one eye. It was just after five and already the sunlight was streaming in through the window where he had forgotten to pull the curtains the night before. He sat up, stretched and rubbed his eyes. He rolled out of the bed, sliding his feet into his slippers, and put on his dressing gown, deciding to brave the morning by having his first coffee of the day out in the garden, on the patio.

He felt a strange mix of emotions this morning. On the positive side of things, it looked like they did indeed have a definite identification of their fourth victim. A shiver raced down his spine as he recalled the poor girl lying in total darkness. At least they would be able to put a name to the face. The news was tempered by the arrival of Chief Inspector Carew.

Jim sighed at the thought of the unwanted wrestling of the case from his control. As he watched an early blackbird rooting for worms through one of the flowerbeds, he wondered about the best course of action to take regarding the newcomer and his team. Then he realised with a grin that it wasn't up to him to make those decisions anymore- the chain of command had had another link inserted, and it was Carew's' job to marshal everything. Good luck to him, Jim thought. The way things were nowadays, with the constant pressure from the media, it was one thing that Jim certainly wasn't going to miss.

Although the sun on his face was warm, his coffee cup was empty, and he felt a sudden chill in his bones from a deceptive little breeze blowing in from the bottom of his garden. He went back inside and fixed himself another coffee. Whilst retrieving the milk from the fridge, he noticed that it was running dangerously low on the essentials. Going back to the lounge, he hunted for a spare scrap of paper on which he scribbled a list for later on.

He checked his watch and was surprised to see it was still only ten past six. Crossing over to his stereo and found his headphones, he plugged the jack in and switched the power on and ran his finger across his extensive collection of vinyl. He got as far as 'h' and stopped there. He felt in a mood for some classic Eighties synth pop, and he thumbed through his collection of Heaven 17, then decided against them and went onto their counterparts from Sheffield, the Human League. He picked up Travelogue, then put it back, deciding its rawness didn't quite fit in with the beautifully sunny morning. He skipped past Dare, having heard it hundreds of times, and selected Hysteria instead. Soon, the opening bars of 'I'm coming back' were filtering through his headphones. Now let's do some serious thinking, he thought. The music always helped him concentrate and he knew he had a good hour before the others surfaced. He'd probably crack the case in that time.

Detective Sergeant James Drake was at his desk early. He was the kind of person who loved early mornings and he'd already gone for a long run around Trent Park, a couple of minutes from his flat. When he first started, a year or so ago, he had received a lot of quizzical looks from the early morning dog walkers. To their minds, seeing a black man running in the morning could only mean one thing. That had changed one day when he had helped an elderly man catch his errant Jack Russell, who had slipped his leash and was leading his owner a merry old dance. James had managed to corner the little four-legged rascal, and had taken it back to its owner, who was blowing heavily on a bench nearby.

"Thanks." A wary look from the old man as he re-attached the dog's collar to his lead. James stood with his hands on his hips, towering over the old man.

"Energetic wee bugger, isn't he?" James had asked, doing some warm-down stretches. The old man had barely nodded in reply. James had shrugged and reached into his tracksuit bottoms, and pulled out his warrant card, showing it to him. He always carried it- you never knew when you might be called upon to help the public. The change in demeanour on the part of the old man was instantaneous. His face brightened perceptibly as he peered at the plastic-sheathed card. "You're a copper, lad?"

"That's right." He reached down and touched the floor with his outstretched palms.

"It says 'Tottenham' 'here. Bit out of your area, son."

"The big chief says that us darkies can leave our ghetto for an hour a day if we are polite to people." James had attempted humour in attempt to break the ice further. It worked, the old man laughing, revealing more gaps than teeth. The Jack Russell looked up at his owner, not recognising the sound coming from its owner, before resuming its search of the park bench.

"So you see, we're not all muggers and rapists, Sir."

"Call me Dusty, son." And from that moment, they became friends, and James would wave at Dusty in the mornings, or stop for a chat if he was near enough. Dusty had obviously talked to the other walkers in the park, for most of them waved or nodded at him warmly when he saw them during his morning run.

Now he was seated at his desk in the Tottenham police station when a flustered looking constable dashed into the CID office. He saw James and headed over.

"Morning, Sarge."

"Good morning, Turnbull. Why are you in such a rush this morning- someone eaten all the sausages in the canteen again?"

"Body, Sir. On the Farm." James was already out of his seat and reaching for his jacket. This was more like it. He had been investigating purse snatchers in the local market all week, and the chance of looking at a suspicious death before anyone else was not something to be passed up. He knew it was suspicious, simply because it was on the Farm. Not many people lived out their full natural lifespan on the Farm. You either died or escaped from there.

"One thing, Sir." Turnbull held an old paper in his hands, folded it to the relevant page, an article on the 'duvet killer'. "The officers on the scene think it might be one of these."

James glanced down at the paper and an involuntary shiver ran down his spine.

Detective Chief Inspector Charles Carew mounted the stairs to his new fiefdom with a satisfied smirk on his face and a confidence in his step. Behind him trailed what he liked to call his 'minions'; five constables and a sergeant totally dedicated to him. They travelled with him when he was called into important cases, such as this one. Sometimes they went on before him, if Carew suspected that there may be trouble ahead, like a quarrelsome Inspector, or inadequate facilities. It was their job to sort out all the piffling problems beforehand, leaving him to swoop down like an eagle, solve the case, and move on, with an ever-heightened profile. He knew he was destined for the top. Ten, maybe fifteen years at the most, and Carew reckoned he would be Commissioner of the Met. And beware anyone who stood in his way- he (or rather his minions) would crush them like ants.

The fact that he hadn't bothered to send in his team beforehand this time was an indicator of the low regard that he had for Inspector Smallwood and his team. "Smallwood, or small fry?" he had remarked to his sergeant, Leeson, the day beforehand. The sergeant had laughed vociferously and had complimented the chief inspector on his ready wit.

Carew paused at the top of the stairs, and straightened his already immaculate tie, brushed an imaginary mote of dust from a lapel, and checked his reflection in his polished shoes. Perfect- the very definition of a modern policeman, smartly dressed, with a razor-sharp mind a quick intellect and a degree of ruthlessness seldom seen outside of the KGB. Out of the corner of his eye he saw Rachael step into Jim's office, and he turned to the only female on his team, DC Sandra Law, waiting patiently a couple of steps down with the rest of the team.

"Law, go after that dowdy female constable and tell her to get some coffee in their pokey little conference room immediately." He turned away again, confident that it was as good as done. Law set off down the corridor, Carew regarding her bottom with fondness as she strode away in her trouser suit. He turned and regarded his troops arrayed behind him, all similarly attired in black suits, with sombre ties. "Somerville, come and rescue me from that loathsome little runt, Laird, in precisely three minutes. Tell me I have an important call from London."

"Yes, Sir. Three minutes precisely, Sir."

Chief Inspector Charles Carew went into battle against the loathsome little runt.

He was sitting in the reading room of Eltham library, gazing at the photograph in the paper. He read through the article for the fourth time and became convinced that it was indeed possible. He tapped the picture and murmured softly to himself, "Now, that would hurt, Charlie boy." He smiled and lifted his gaze to look out at the trees of Eltham park outside. He rarely believed in coincidence, but this was surely a gift from God. He thought of

Mrs. Sandra Law, a nurse from Aylesbury. Maybe, she was about to be let off the hook.

He returned his gaze to the newspaper article, a report of the new policeman in charge of his case- a brash, suave moron if he'd ever seen one. "...whilst I would like to thank Inspector Smallwood and his team in all their endeavours, the powers that be have decided that a fresh approach was needed in solving these senseless killings...to catch what I believe is simply a sexual sadist killing entirely at random whenever he can... totally deranged..."

He pushed the paper away, disgusted. He may be many things, but he certainly wasn't a sexual sadist, nor totally deranged. He walked into the park, breathing in the fresh air of a beautiful summer day. The sunlight, the open air, the sounds of normal people going about their everyday business helped calmed him down. He sank down onto a bench, formulating a plan as to how he could prove Charles Carew wrong.

Superintendent Laird sat rubbing his temples. "I just wish you'd come to us first." He waved the newspaper in Carew's general direction.

"I wanted to strike while the iron was hot, Sir. Catch the killer off-guard." Carew was showing just enough contrition to his superior officer so as not to be thrown out on his ear.

"And how do you think Inspectors Smallwood, Jujara and Schofield will be feeling this morning?" Laird sighed. "This doesn't exactly cover them in glory."

"I cannot be expected to make an omelette without cracking a few eggs, can I, Sir?" Carew almost sneered. "I'm not going to apologize to a few junior officers for injuring their pride."

Laird stood up and leant on his desk. "This isn't about injured pride. You've made them out to be totally incompetent." He thundered, dangerously close to losing his temper. There was a smart rap on the door. Laird stared at it for a second or two before calling 'Come'. A smartly dressed, attractive woman poked her head around the door, surveyed the scene, and spoke to Carew.

"I'm sorry to interrupt your meeting, Sir, but the Yard are on the phone and say it's urgent." The head withdrew, and the door closed again. Carew stood and brushed down his clothes again, as if by just sitting in Laird's office they had become dirty. He raised an eyebrow but didn't offer an apology. He had yanked down the handle before Laird gave his parting shot.

"Any more press conferences come through me, Chief Inspector. Are we clear?"

"As crystal. Sir. Through you." And he was gone. Laird sat down again, running his hands through his thinning hair. This one was trouble, for sure, he thought. He'd better be right, or I'll kick him all the way back to the Yard myself.

Sergeant Drake rode with Turnbull the short distance from the station to the estate where the body had reportedly been found. The Broadwater Farm estates had seen substantial improvement from the riots 11 years previously, but it was markedly a job in progress, and police would never patrol singly, and rarely on foot, to this day. Groups of youths, both black and white, stared sullenly at them as they edged slowly deeper into the bowels of the estate, before pulling to a halt beside a police van containing three officers. Three more stood looking at something behind a big wheelie bin that had been tipped on its side and set on fire at some point.

They got out of the car and approached the three officers. Drake noted someone had set up a cordon of police tape about twenty metres away, and there were numerous locals standing next to it, all striving to get a better view. Drake paused, looking at them, thinking. Although death was not an everyday occurrence here, it was by no means unusual. There must be something extra here, he thought, bracing himself. He rounded the wheelie bin, and stopped, taking in the scene.

A body, or what he took for one, was lying under a sheet. And then he remembered what Turnbull had said about the newspaper. It wasn't a sheet; it was a duvet cover. He stepped all the way around the mess on the floor, noting that the top of the duvet had been knotted.

He crouched down and looked more closely, before a thought occurred to him. "We are sure that this person is dead, right? Did anyone think to check?"

One of the police officers who had been guarding the body stepped forward and nodded towards the van. "Pc Cockcroft noticed that there was a slight tear towards the back of the duvet, sarge. He says he was able to sneak a couple of fingers in and feel on the neck for a pulse. He says there wasn't one and so he called it in immediately, Sir."

"'Sneaked a couple of fingers in'?" Drake pulled a face at the constable. "Braver man than me." He motioned to the van. "He's in there?"

"Havin' a cuppa, sarge." The constable nodded. Drake nodded back and stepped over to the van to have a word with Cockcroft but turned back. "Constable, see if anyone one here," he pointed at the crowd, "see if anyone saw anything helpful." He grinned. The constable grinned back, knowing as well as Drake did that it was a sure-fire way of dispersing the crowd without any hassle. The two police constables also nodded conspiratorially at the sergeant before moving towards the crowd. Drake turned back and pulled back the sliding door of the police van, stopping any conversation going on in there as the three police officers looked to see who it was. Drake put one foot up in the van but stayed outside as he looked at each in turn.

"Pc Cockcroft?"

"That's me, sir."

Drake nodded at the officer. "You identified that the body was dead, right?"

"Yes, Sir. I noticed that there was a small rip in the duvet, and just snaked my hand up to find the neck..."

"Two questions, Cockcroft. I have to ask them now, because otherwise the bosses will. Ok?"

Drake thought at this point that if Cockcroft was hiding something then he would look at his two colleagues before answering. But the constable kept his eyes on Drake all the time and nodded once to say that he understood.

Drake looked back at the scene to see that the medical examiners had turned up with all their equipment and were busy setting up a plastic gazebo to shield the body from the elements and the curious stare of onlookers, which had dwindled to a solitary old man with his dog. He turned back to Cockcroft, cradling his cold tea.

"You're sure there was a hole in the duvet? You didn't make one somehow?"

Cockcroft vehemently shook his head at this. "It's quite a big tear by the looks of it, but the body is pinning it down, mostly." Drake nodded sympathetically.

"Just how much of the body did you touch before you got to the neck? The forensic guys will have to know."

Cockcroft narrowed his eyes, and his gaze slipped beyond Drake to where the gazebo was almost complete, ready to be manhandled into place. He kept his eyes on it whilst answering the sergeant, as if trying to recreate the scene in his mind.

"The top of the arm, then some material..." Cockcroft started.

"Material, like a t-shirt? What colour?"

Cockcroft shifted his gaze back to Drake. "I don't know what colour; it was under the duvet. The collar, and then the neck." Cockcroft stared defiantly at the sergeant.

Drake pulled his foot out of the van, satisfied. "Get yourself back to the nick. Good work."

"That's it, Sir?" the constable looked surprised.

"That's it, constable. If anyone asks, I'll tell them that you had to ascertain whether life was extinct. You used your intelligence in preserving as much as the evidence you could, without contaminating the scene beyond what was necessary. I wouldn't have put my hand in there without a glove on."

"If I was wearing a glove, I couldn't have felt a pulse, Sir." Cockcroft looked edgy, as if Drake was trying to catch him out somehow.

"Precisely, Cockcroft. I'll make sure that I tell your inspector that you acted by the book, and beyond." He smiled at the constable, trying to put him at ease. He nodded at the two other constables and closed the door. It was only then that he remembered something, so he re-opened the door of the van.

"...a good bloke-" One of the officers was saying, and jumped when the door slid open quickly, catching him unawares.

"One more thing, Cockcroft. Be sure to get forensics to take your fingerprints for elimination purposes. You don't want to find yourself getting nicked." Cockcroft nodded his thanks.

"You sure it's murder, Sir?" One of the other policemen asked Drake.

"Well, if not, it's the most bizarre suicide I've ever seen." And with a wink, he was gone.

Rachael sat quietly, waiting patiently for the Inspector to finish his phone call. Mo and Terry were talking quietly on the two guests chairs. Rachael was secretly impressed- she had never heard Terry speak so quietly in the week or so she had known her. She was watching them out of the corner of her eye and missed Jim replacing the receiver and steepling his fingers as he waited to them finish what they were discussing.

"Well, good news and bad news, folks. That was Great Yarmouth police, confirmation of what they told us." Jim spoke to nobody in particular but looking at them each in turn.

"Is that the good news or the bad news, Jim?" Terry asked. Jim's eyes flicked back to her before they fell to the steepled hands on his desk.

"Most of the team have been replaced. Rick, Pete, Robert and the M and M's have been sent back to CID proper. Ash has been sent back to Luton; Ian despatched back to County."

"He got rid of his own son-in-law?" Jujara asked, incredulous. Jim nodded.

"Doesn't want him claiming any of the glory?" Terry jumped in before Jim.

"And he is sending you back to the Met, Mo." Jim looked crestfallen. "I know, I know, but those were his conditions. As for the rest of us, we're at his beck and call."

Terry reached out and placed her hand on Mo's arm in a consoling gesture. He just looked over and gave Terry a sad smile and a shrug.

"How can he do this, Sir?" Rachael was indignant. "Inspector Jujara is a brilliant policeman, with a proven track record and has done some great work on this case. It's just not fair." Rachael blushed when all three had turned to look at her. "I just hope this bastard kills several more now so that they have to call him back." The outburst produced some muted laughter, before Jujara hooked his arm around the back of his chair so he could face Rachael. "Thanks for the vote of confidence, but I don't think the victims, or their families would see it that way." He smiled fondly before turning back. "When do I go back, Jim?"

"They are expecting you back as from tomorrow." Jim looked at Mo ruefully. "Still, we get to keep you for at least one more day." He looked a little brighter. "Well, the DCI wants me and you, Mo, to meet him at 10 to go over some finer details of where we are. And he wants you, Inspector Schofield, to take Rachael and go investigate the life of this last girl."

"In Great Yarmouth?" They both queried at the same time, before exchanging a look.

"The very same. They are sending an officer down, should be here any minute really..."Jim checked his watch to confirm, "...You are both to accompany him to the morgue, confirm identity, and accompany him back there to assist in their enquiries."

"Why are they sending a police officer down here to confirm identity anyway?" asked Mo.

"She was a prostitute, with apparently no family in the area, and they can hardly ask on of the local toms to do it, can they?" Apparently this officer knew her fairly well." He cast a look at Terry. "No, not like that.... but court appearances and the like." He stood up and put his jacket on. It was still the height of summer, and the

283

heat outside was building steadily, but the DCI was a stickler for appearances.

"Can I ask a question, Sir?" Rachael was still seated. "These enquiries, presumably with the other toms and suchlike, does it mean an overnight stay?"

Jim pondered for a moment and guessed Rachael's' thoughts. "Well, a lot of them will be nocturnal, so probably. Best get yourself home sharpish and get an overnight bag together." He turned back to Jujara. "Come on, and don't forget your jacket. You know what he's like."

"Should I shave my beard off?" Jujara, rising, laughed as he reached for his jacket. Jim raised an eyebrow at him and set off down the corridor to the conference room.

When they entered, the Chief Inspector was to be seen bending over the back of his young female constable, reading a report over her shoulder. Jim exchanged glances with Mo silently when he saw Carew's hand on the young officers' shoulder. He noted that the woman in question had removed her jacket and Jim snorted to himself quietly. By some sixth sense, Carew seemed to know who it was who had just entered.

"Take a seat, Inspectors. I'll be with you in a minute. I'm afraid you've just missed the coffee." Jim noted that he hadn't even turned to look at them, but he had withdrawn his hand from his constables' shoulder. But before they could even find two spare chairs, however, an excited member of Carew's team put a hand over the mouthpiece of the telephone he was holding and exclaimed excitedly, "He's struck again."

Jim, unable to control himself, blurted out: "Where's the body?" The constable holding the phone just gave him a cold look before focusing on his boss.

Carew shook his head, as if to say where, and the constable replied "Tottenham, Sir- on the Broadwater!"

Jim looked at Mo and narrowed his eyes and rewarded by the slightest shake of the other inspectors' head, as if to suggest that this wasn't one of theirs. But Jim wasn't so sure. With this guy, anything was possible.

CHAPTER 25

He left his car in the carpark of Avery Hill College, on the outskirts of Eltham; with any luck it wouldn't even be noticed for a week or so, if not longer. Although term was still out for the summer recess, there were still students always milling about- on summer courses, or those who hadn't home, working at the college or nearby. He'd even done it once, just before he'd met the girl on the bus... He had purposefully ignored the library on campus mainly because the former ballroom of Colonel Norths' mansion held especially poignant memories for him. Instead he had used the main Eltham public library, and the park afterwards before heading for the railway station, to catch the train to London Bridge, and then home. He purposefully forced himself to look at the faces of his fellow passengers as the train made its slow journey through South East London. He tried to imagine the back story of the man in the suit opposite him, and the lady seated next to him. That didn't help, so he thought back over the last week. He could hardly believe he had killed five people in the last eight or nine days. Just the very thought filled him with exhaustion. He supposed it was the adrenaline that was keeping him going; that, and the thrill of what was still to come. Five down, five to go. The excitement coursed through him like an electric shock and it was all he could do to stop himself from squirming in his seat. He forced himself to look out of the window at the roofs, industrial units and the teeming life of southern London.

"Well, we'd better dispatch a unit down there so that the local boys don't fuck up the scene too badly." DCI Charles Carew sneered out at the officers gathered in the conference room. His six chosen acolytes grinned along with him, whilst the others- Jim, Mo, and David, who had just joined them, exchanged glances with each other.

"I'm pretty sure that the lads will be able to deal with most things thrown at them, Sir." Jujara countered, his station being next to the one in question. He knew most of the officers there and had every faith in their capabilities.

"Well, if the body was found on the Broadwater Farm, they probably will be having lots of things thrown at them." Carew's sergeant, Leeson, had offered up. The team had sniggered at that, Carew included, and been rewarded by a scowl from the man from Hackney.

"Leeson, Payne, you're with me..." Carew cast a glance round the rest of them before his eyes alighted on Jujara. "I suppose you should also come along, Inspector." Jujara held his gaze, before nodding slightly.

Jim stood watching the exchange impassively. It wouldn't have been surprised him if Carew was taking him along so that he could drop him off at his own station on the way. And he wasn't unduly worried by the fact that Carew was freezing him out of his own investigation. He had more than enough to do anyway- not least of which was reviewing the forensics on the first four victims. But at last the new lead officer on the case turned to him.

"Inspector, you can mind the fort here, please. But don't make any comments to the press, they'll have their daily briefing at five, as usual." He turned away and was halfway through the door before Jim could even think of a reply. Instead he went to the window and stared out at the late morning shoppers as they went around minding their own business, thinking to himself that sooner or later Carew would screw this up. He could just feel it in his bones. Whether they'd catch the killer first or not was still up for debate though.

He sat in the library, making notes for an essay that had to be in two days later, and was still only half-written. He'd been stuck in there for almost three hours and was thinking about going for a coffee and a cigarette in the snack bar. He tried to put the thought out of his mind, but the seed was planted now, and he put the book down with a sigh. He had reached behind his chair for his pullover- it was nice and toasty here, but a biting April wind was shaking the trees outside- and was just pulling it over his head when one of his mates from the same halls wandered in, spotted him and sauntered over.

"Just leaving?" His mate, Jamie Macdonald, was eyeing his chair by the radiator with envy.

"No, just stepping out for a fag and a quick coffee, so hands off." He replied with a grin. "Coming for one?"

Jamie tapped the top of a pile of books and grimaced. "Too much to do." The grin returned. "Especially after last night." He winked.

"Do tell."

Jamie motioned him to sit down again and took a chair opposite. "Well, you know that girl Cheryl?" Jamie began, his voice sinking to a whisper.

"The one in Harper Hall?" He ought to know- he had been seeing her for a month now. They had been taking things slowly, though. Although they had spent a couple of night together, things hadn't escalated to a full-on sexual relationship. He was really fond of her though, spending lots of time thinking about her when he should've have been listening in lectures, or studying in the evening over a pile of books. She was one of those girls who demanded a lot of thinking about- from her devilish brown eyes, to her small ears, button nose, dinky chin, short curly hair. When she stood next to him the top of her head was about level with his shoulders. Small, but perfectly formed, she liked to say. He tended to agree with her.

"Are you even listening to me?" Jamie cocked his head to one side to catch his attention.

"Yeah, sorry, just trying to remember her face." He lied. He could hardly get it out of his head.

"Well, last night I was having a drink with the lads from the football team..." Jamie was a winger for the college first team. "...when up comes this Cheryl, leads me outside by the hand, takes me round the back of the bar, and gives me a fantastic blow job." Jamie raised his eyebrows at his friend, as if asking if he could believe it. "When she'd finished, swallowed and everything, she just goes back inside again. Never said a bloody word." Jamie rocked back in his chair, looking like the Cheshire cat, grinning from ear to ear.

"Wow." He really couldn't think of anything to say. He fixed a smile on his face and hoped it looked convincing. He just sat there, nodding mutely.

"Anyway, I went back to the lads, carried on drinking. At closing time, there she was again, just lurking out in the dark. So I sneaked her into my room and shagged the hell out of her."

"Was she any good?" He asked weakly.

"Banging."

"Seeing her again?"

"Probably." He paused for a moment. "She said she had been seeing someone, but that it was over between them."

He nodded again as he stood, trying to keep the bile from rising in his throat and he tapped the table lightly in appreciation. "Well done, mate. Sounds like you've got a right one there." Jamie just winked back at him as he left.

Well, she was right about one thing. It was well and truly fucking over between them.

Rachael was flicking between the pages of a magazine. They were on the A11 heading for Great Yarmouth and were twenty minutes short of Norwich. Beside her and driving fast to keep up with the car in front of her, was Inspector Schofield. The car in front contained PC Al Warren, an officer who had come down just to identify the body of Jo Holt. He was a mountain of a man, at least 6'5", seemingly all muscle. His arms-what they could see of them- were covered in tattoos. He'd taken one look at the body in the morgue and nodded to them. "Aye, it's her. Can I get a cup of tea somewhere?"

And with those eleven words, that was it. They'd had a cuppa, sitting in the hospital canteen in virtual silence. He'd nodded twice when Terry informed him of their plans, but only stood up and said 'You'd better follow me then' before heading back to his car.

Terry and Rachael had been shocked by his apparent callousness with the body, and his attitude to them. But the initial surprise had been given way to humour as Terry and Rachael had swopped ideas as to his reticence.

"Daughter."

"Client."

"Girlfriend."

"Wife." This was from Terry.

"Wife? She's got to be at least twenty years younger than him." Rachael had replied, and the conversation had lapsed into silence, which had been compounded when Inspector Schofield had turned the radio on.

"Now, what's going on here then?" Terry had said, beginning to brake and turn on her indicators. Rachael looked up from her magazine.

"Probably needs petrol."

"Maybe, maybe not. Ooh, he's pulling into a Little Chef." They cruised into a space next to the East Anglian policeman and noticed that he was already perched on his bonnet, burly arms crossed. They got out, stretching stiffened limbs.

"Not bad driving, ma'am." Alf grunted at the Inspector with a nod at her car.

"For a woman, you mean?" Terry offered her winning smile, and it seemed to melt a little of the iceberg that was called Alf.

"Come on, I'll shout you two to lunch." He strode off with barely a backward glance.

They were soon seated and agreed on burgers and chocolate milkshakes. Terry pulled out her cigarettes and offered one to Alf, who took one with another nod. "Shouldn't really, I'm trying to give up." He lit it from the Inspector's lighter, inhaled deeply and let out the smoke with a deep sigh. "I guess I should apologise for my behaviour back at the morgue." He looked at Terry, who shook her head graciously. He held up his hand. "No, I was out of order. Let me explain." He lent forward and began ticking off points with one finger against his other hand. Rachael watched the cigarette smoke as it danced around in the air.

"Firstly, I don't like morgues. Secondly, I don't like dead bodies, especially youngsters. Thirdly, I don't looking at the dead bodies of people I know."

"I don't think anyone likes looking at dead bodies, to be honest." Terry said sympathetically, leaning back as the food arrived.

"You know, the taste of milkshakes takes me back to my dad treating me at Scarborough when I was a nipper." Alf smiled sadly. "Back when the world was a happier place." He looked out of the window.

"So you're not from around here then, Sir?" Rachael piped up, more for wanting to be in the conversation, rather than wanting to know about Alf's life.

"Bradford born and bred," Alf puffed out his chest proudly. Joined the constabulary on my eighteenth birthday."

"In Bradford?" Terry had paused with a chip halfway to her mouth. Something in her tone made Rachael glance at her.

"Yes, lass." Alf looked out of the window but was only seeing the past. Terry put a hand up, warning Rachael to be quiet for a bit.

"You poor man." Terry looked fondly at Alf, who nodded once and looked down at his food.

"Did you know any of them?" Terry continued, more softly this time. Alf, still looking down at his plate, nodded once.

Alf looked up into Terrys' eyes at this and just uttered "Yvonne." Rachael, totally lost by this point, could contain herself no longer.

"Could someone fill me in here? I don't mean to be rude but I'm a bit puzzled as to what you two are referring to."

"Alf here," Terry reached her hand out to cover Alf's. "Alf was a young copper who worked on the Michael Sutcliffe case."

"The Yorkshire Ripper? God, that must've been terrible."

Alf regarded the young woman kindly. "Aye, it was, lass, and now you know why I don't like bodies of young girls." Rachael nodded her understanding.

Sergeant James Drake stood impatiently by the morgue reception desk of the North Middlesex Hospital. He had been told to stay there until the team investigating the 'Duvet Killer' case arrived, whenever that was to be. He'd been here for an hour, jumping off his seat whenever anybody arrived, to no avail. His patience was beginning to wear. He checked his watch and reckoned he'd give it another fifteen minutes before heading off in search of a sandwich. He felt ravenous.

The collection of the body had been by the book. The pathologist had confirmed life extinct; the mortuary guys had placed the body still in its' duvet carefully in the back of their van, the SOCO boys were doing their job, the uniformed officers were conducting house-to-house enquiries of the immediate vicinity. The gathered locals had been questioned- with no information forthcoming- and Drake was convinced that he had everything covered. Then he had received a call over the radio from his DI, informing him to get himself to the morgue and await the arrival of Chief Detective Carew and his team, currently up in Hertfordshire somewhere. That had been almost an hour and a half ago, and here he was, still waiting impatiently.

He tapped the top of the reception desk to get the attention of the receptionist on duty, in order to explain that he'd be back in about ten minutes, when he heard the swoosh of the doors behind him. He turned to see four officers arriving. At last, the cavalry, he thought. He stepped forward and held out his hand to the man in front, obviously the DCI.

Carew stopped, looking down at the hand. "Drake?" He asked, imperiously.

James withdrew his hand and straightened up a little. At six feet four, he had a height advantage of about six inches over the DCI. "Yes, Sir." Does this arse expect me to salute him, he wondered. Carew bent his head to look around the sergeant, searching for the door to the morgue itself.

"We will handle it from here, Sergeant. Give your report to Payne here. Leeson, Jujara, with me." Carew barked out his orders. Drake, by now thoroughly non-plussed, almost missed the last name that Carew had mentioned. He looked at the other officers, and saw two white men, almost as tall as him, standing in front of a familiar face. As Carew swept past, Mo broke into a smile and held out his hand, raising his eyebrows at Payne and Leeson.

"James." The two shook hands warmly. "Nice to see you again."

"And you, Sir. I didn't know-"

"INSPECTOR!" Yelled Carew from the mortuary doorway. Drake was sure he saw Leeson smirk before following after the DCI. Mo, shrugging his shoulders, hurried after them.

"I'll catch up with you after we're done." Jujara called back over his shoulder.

"Sure thing, Sir." Drake waved at his receding back.

A cough sounded behind him. Drake turned round and saw Payne standing there, unsmilingly staring back at him. Drake didn't bother to shake his hand. "Do you want to do this over a coffee?" He asked.

Payne look uncertainly over Drakes' s shoulder. "They won't be coming out for a while, will they, Sir?" He looked back at Drake with the doubt showing in his face.

In response, Drake just laughed and strode off to the canteen.

Jim had slouched back to his office shortly after Carew's departure, with in tow. En route, they stopped into the main CID office, where they encountered Sergeant Bimjano, who joined them. Once ensconced in there, with the new coffee machine gurgling away to itself, they made general chat before Jim suggested a comprehensive review of what they had, and where they were in relation to narrowing down the identity of the killer. David, as if from nowhere, produced a huge file of paperwork and put it on Rachael's' desk.

Ronnie gave a low whistle when he saw the pile they had accumulated. Jim, having worked on many, many cases before, didn't bat an eyelid. "Right, go back to the very first case...Sam

Taylor." David thumbed through his manilla files and extracted a couple from the pile.

"What do you want to know?"

"Start with where the body was found." David gave a concise re-cap of where Samuel was found, and of the subsequent searches undertaken by both the SOCO team, and Jim himself.

Ronnie sat deep in thought. Jim asked him what the matter was. Ronnie thought a while before saying, "If you jump forward and compare this to the fourth one... it seems like they were deliberately staged."

"In what way?" David asked him.

"Well, the fourth one seems like...like..." Ronnie sat and waved his arms around.

"A tableau?" Jim said helpfully.

"Precisely, Sir." Ronnie said, standing up. The whole room. painted black and including the body...it's a bloody big tableau, a painting. And I think that the flat in which we found the first body is as well, well parts of it."

"Which parts in particular?"

Ronnie paused. "The bedroom, and the lounge, for starters. I mean there is a rather odd picture on the wall in the bedroom of Red Square. Who has a picture of that up these days?" He looked at David, who shrugged, and at Jim, who nodded for him to continue.

"And then there's the lounge. The two copies of the same book is...odd. The board game in the drawer, the condom, even the stuffed animal. It's such a completely random range of items that maybe they aren't random at all. They were left by the killer as clues."

"I had those thoughts several days ago, but try as I might, nothing jumped out at me." Jim said from behind his desk. "But taking them with this last body... interesting." He stood up and extracted a folder from David's' pile. "Samuel Taylor's eyes were taped shut... could it not be significant of a dream, and the items be the things he was meant to be dreaming of?"

"Maybe not him, but the killers' dream." Ronnie suggested. The three of them stared into space, each of them lost in their own thoughts.

"But where do bodies two and three fit in?" David asked.

"A heart sliced apart, and a pair of headphones? I dunno..." Ronnie spread his hands apart, before letting them fall into his lap again.

"It's in here, I know it is." Jim was tapping the side of his head with a finger. He brightened as he thought of something new. "Maybe a cigarette will knock it out." He smiled at the other two. "Good work." He stood up, as did David, who pointed to the Inspector as he spoke to Ronnie:

"He does nicotine, I do sugar. I'm going to get the cakes in."

The burgers and milkshakes had been cleared and replaced with big mugs of steaming tea. The conversation had turned back to the young victim again. "She was a nice girl, quiet, but with a big smile and a wicked sense of humour." Alf had said wistfully, gazing at the traffic.

"Not your typical prostitute, then?" Terry asked softly.

"No, not really. Not brash, or pushy, like some. She seemed well liked by the other girls, mind." Alf's eyes tracked back to the inspector, before sliding past her to watch a couple as they came in for a late lunch.

"How did she end up doing it, then?" Asked Rachael. She was as aware as any of them that they knew next to nothing about Jo.

"Did well enough at school, then her parents died within months of each other. The mum of cancer, dad of a broken heart, or so they say." Alf switched his attention to Rachael. "No job, couldn't pay the mortgage, moved into a flat, got into debt, you know how it goes."

"Drugs?"

"No way, not Olive, never."

Terry looked up suddenly. "Who's Olive?" She asked, puzzled.

"Oh sorry, love-I mean ma'am- Mandy often called herself Olive." He smiled briefly

"And who on earth is Mandy? We're talking about Jo here, Jo Holt." Rachael, swopped glances with Terry, just as confused.

Alf sighed, picked up his tea, and set it down again. "We are talking about the girl that I've just identified at your place, right?" Alf looked surprised.

A look of recognition crossed Rachael's face. "It was in the report, actually. I've just remembered. You should remember, too Inspector- you read the report out yourself."

A vague look of recollection crossed Terrys' features as she nodded. "And it was only last night. Mind you, I'd had a bit to drink by then." She massaged her temples, laughing softly.

Alf laughed himself. "I've often found myself in that situation. Not in the middle of a murder enquiry, though." He cocked an eyebrow in the inspectors' direction.

"We were sort of celebrating." She filled him in with all the latest developments on the case, in relation to Carew and his crew. "Anyway, you were saying about Olive." She concluded and signaled the waitress for three more mugs of tea.

"Yeah, well she was a 'clean' kind of girl, if you know what I mean. Some of them out there are real skanks who'll do anything for a bob or two." As Alf said this, Rachael recalled the incident in the kebab shop with Maxine Corr, the two-pound whore. She smiled, and Alf saw it. "Looks like you know one or two, love." Rachael nodded, smiling again.

Alf straightened up as the fresh tea arrived. "As I was saying, she was clean, kept herself out of trouble mostly, only a couple of run-ins with us-"

"I get the impression you knew here well though?" Terry interjected.

"The boss here, Superintendent Hollows- is of a mind that as long as they are discrete, it's OK. He reckons- and I agree- that it's going to happen anyway, especially in a big seaside resort like this- and that to come down hard would just drive the situation underground." Alf looked at both female detectives, who both agreed with him.

"I know it's a radical approach, but it seems to work. Or did, until Olive got herself killed."

Jim smoked two cigarettes one after another and the nicotine rush gave him a fresh surge of energy. He bounded into his office and found only Ronnie. The adrenaline ebbed a bit as he sat down and asked, "Where's David got to?" He enquired.

"He popped into the CID room to check on the others, and then the conference room to hear whether or not we've got another body." Ronnie studied Jim for a while. "You don't think it's one of ours at all, do you?"

Jim sighed, before shaking his head silently.

"Why not?" Ronnie was intrigued.

"Don't laugh when I say this." Jim pointed a pen at him.

"What?"

"Call it a hunch." Ronnie's eyes twinkled at this but managed to maintain a straight face.

"Both Inspector Jujara and I agree on this. This killer is extremely dangerous, agreed?"

"Of course- four deaths and counting."

"Always in relatively quiet surroundings. Rented flat, room, deserted barn, own business."

Ronnie narrowed his eyes. "And you're saying that this isn't?"

"Ever been to the Broadwater Farm, Sergeant?" Ronnie shook his head. "Well, take a bit of advice from an old copper-don't." Jim leaned back in his chair. "I'm sure that the vast majority of people there are decent, law abiding citizens. But quiet is one thing that it aint."

"I've heard that."

"Anyway...if I know anything about this killer, then it's that he prefers the quiet and solitude to the hustle and bustle. Jujara knew this and went down to confirm it." Jim looked wistfully at the phone. "I just hope he'd bloody hurry up and ring me to confirm it though."

As if by magic, the phone rang.

As he waited for the phone to connect, Mo wondered where Sergeant Blake had buggered off to. He had important information to give the sergeant, and he needed to tell him now.
"Jim Smallwood speaking."
"It's not him."
"Sure?"
"Positive."
"Ok, thanks, Mo. Get back as soon as you can."
"Might be tricky, but I'll try my best."
"Bye then."
"Bye." Jujara replaced the receiver and thanked the receptionist. He turned to see Sergeant Blake return with the DC Payne. He was surprised to see them both smiling.
"You two are looking mighty friendly all of a sudden." Blake smiled whilst Payne blushed, his eyes slipping nervously to the autopsy suite. "Cheer up, Payne. I won't tell the Chief...if you pop along and get me a coffee." Payne nodded, relieved, and headed off back to the canteen. Jujara turned to Drake. "James, I've got to be quick. Carew will start wondering where I am any minute."
Drake stopped smiling and looked into Mo's eyes. "What is it?"
"This isn't one of ours- no, don't ask- but you will have to carry on your investigation on your own until they officially hand it back to you, and that may take a while."
"Are you sure?"
"I've never been more certain of anything in my life...apart from the fact that DCI Carew is an absolute prick. I'm surprised he's not wielding the bloody scalpel in there himself. "MO briefly explained as quickly as he could what had transpired in the path lab. They had all changed into their protective gear and entered into the glistening white and chrome room to see the body still wrapped in the big blue plastic body bag in which the SOCO team had placed it back on the Farm. When they were all ready, with Carew in prime viewing position, the pathologist had unzipped the

cadaver bag to reveal the body still in its protective white duvet. Two assistants wrestled the body out of the bag, and it was at this moment that Mo realised that it wasn't the fifth victim of their killer. The duvet cover had been knotted at the top but more importantly, there was no face peering out at them with features frozen at the point of death. Mo had feigned the need for an urgent toilet break and had left quietly. He could hear the cruel chuckling of Leeson and could almost feel the sneers as he left the room. He couldn't care less.

He sat in the white van and watched the house from a hundred yards away as the sun went down. Earlier, after reaching home and dozing for a couple of hours, he had made his way to his lock up, a long cardboard tube tucked under his arm. Reaching the van, he opened the tube and carefully extracted the contents. Three identical stickers popped out. He had carefully peeled away the backing tape and applied them to the sides and back of the van.

When he had finished, he stood back and admired his handywork. The legend, in writing about three feet long, was his idea of a joke. "IT'S SO SIMPLE! WASTE DISPOSAL SPECIALISTS. CALL HARPENDEN 761403 AND ASK FOR THE 'MAN IN CHARGE'".

The telephone number was that of the local police station, and the man in charge would now be Carew, not Smallwood he supposed, but the joke remained the same. He sat and chuckled to himself. If any of the neighbours happened to look out of their windows, or be taking the dog for a walk, they might remember the signs more than him. That was the plan, anyway. It was a variable he couldn't really control; however the rest of the plan was entirely of his own making and was the result of the same diligence and research that he had followed for previously.

He sat and watched as the man strolled down his garden path, through his gate and made his way to his local for a nice game of darts with his mates.

CHAPTER 26

"Inspector Smallwood, I don't like to be kept waiting." DCI Charles Carew stood in the reception of the autopsy suite, having just come from the post-mortem. He was phoning the station to see whether there had been any developments in his absence, and to tell Jim that he and his team were heading off to the Broadwater Farm estate themselves. He grunted at whatever Jim told him on the other end of the line before responding, "No, I certainly don't want you give the press briefing. Just put a statement out saying that I am chasing leads and expect an imminent arrest." He listened irritable again as Jim said something. "Of course it's one of ours- you don't really think that there are two serial murderers stuffing their victims into duvets, do you, man?" He snorted and winked at his sergeant, standing alongside him. "Just be available for a briefing when I get back." He replaced the receiver without any goodbyes and turned to his acolytes. "Come." He paused as he spotted Mo standing by a row of chairs. "Still here, Inspector? You won't catch the killer by loitering." Without waiting for a reply, he swept out.

"Who does he think he is?" The receptionist, who had heard the exchange, asked Mo.

"I don't know, but I wish he do it someplace else." Mo shrugged and smiled at the receptionist as he followed in the wake of the great Carew.

Half an hour later Inspector Jujara pulled his collar up as he stepped out onto the third-floor walkway just above where the body of Shane Butler was discovered by the burnt bin. A sudden summer storm had appeared from nowhere, and Mo looked down to see DCI Carew and his team trying to find some shelter as they made their enquiries. He was approached by a constable who paused when Mo flashed his identification card. The constable looked out at the DCI before turning back to Mo with a grim smile.

"Don't suppose you miss these." He said, touching his helmet.

"Oh, the late Eighties were a fine time for a young Asian copper fresh from university. Everyone stopping to say hello, how are you doing, officer. I've just stopped this young scallywag from stealing an apple." The constable was chuckling away. "I don't think they even noticed the colour of my skin. I even had one sergeant who kept asking the Asians how they were meant to fit their turbans under their helmets."

"Urban myth."

"It's true, the guy's a superintendent in Vice nowadays."

"Inspector?" One of the SOCO team popped his head out from a doorway halfway down the block. "Have you got a minute?"

Mo excused himself and gingerly trod on a succession of metal plates until he reached the door. "Do I need to put some booties on?"

"No need. Just thought you'd want to see this." The SOCO pointed to a bloodied handprint on the wall.

"How do you know it's not the victim's hand?"

"I've just radioed my colleague. Both the hands of the victim are blood free." The SOCO looked the wall again. "Obviously, we'll have to double check the fingerprints...but I thought you'd want to know as you're right here."

Mo thought quickly. "Can you speed it through the system?"

"Already done, Sir." Mo thanked the man and re-joined the constable at the end of the walkway. The rain was coming almost sideways at the end of the block, and the pair struggled to find some shelter.

"Can I ask a question, Sir? About the case, that is."

"Of course, constable."

"Would the fall have killed him?"

Mo was impressed that the young officer, soaked through, probably cold and certainly bored, still had the presence of mind to think about the case. "What's your name, Constable?"

"Bryan Derby, Sir. My friends call me Bry."

"Well, Brian-"

"Bry."

Mo smiled at the compliment. "Well, Bry, probably not. But the slashed throat probably wouldn't have helped." Brian nodded slowly. "But keep that under your helmet for now."

"Can't do that, Sir. It might dislodge my skull cap."

Down on the ground DCI Carew had been approached by another constable explaining that he was urgently needed on the radio. Carew looked at the constable as if he couldn't decide whether to curse the officer for disturbing him or simply ignore him.

"May be important, Sir." His sergeant, Leeson spoke quietly into his ear.

"Probably that incompetent buffoon Smallwood asking permission to go to the toilet." Carew was still staring at the constable, who seemed to have found something interesting on the floor.

"Want me to go?"

"No Sergeant, I'll do it. But make a note of this man's name and number just in case. I'll put him on traffic for the rest of his miserable life if he's wasting my time." He turned to the officer who was still waiting for the DCI. "Where's this damned radio then?"

Reaching the patrol car he sat in the drivers' seat and keyed the radio. "DCI Carew."

"Ah hello, Sir...we've been trying to reach you urgently. There's a witness who says she saw the murder, Sir, and she's given us a name."

"Well give it to me then, man."

"Dwayne Robbins. Flat 16, Hornchurch House. Not far from where you are."

"And what does he look like?"

"IC3, dreadlocks, probably in Bob Marley t-shirt and tracksuit bottoms. He associates with two brothers, Delroy and Denzil Clarke. All three have a record as long as their arms."

"Any back-up coming?" Carew was by no means a coward, but he was no fool either.

"There's a van parked around the corner from his flat. PC Bay will take you now."

"Thank you." He motioned for the constable to drive, whilst Lesson and Payne got in the back. The constable drove slowly, careful not to bring any attention to the car. Gliding to a halt behind the police van, he filled in his two officers on what was occurring. "PC Bay- take one of the men and cover the back."

"It's on the first floor, Sir."

"Never mind that. I've known criminals jump from the fourth floor straight onto concrete before."

"Really?"

"Yes- really. Stupid bastard splattered blood all over my Oxfords. Wanker."

They crept up the stairwell in single file and seven of them congregated on either side of the Flat 16. Payne closer to his boss.

"Don't we need a warrant?"

Carew shook his head. "Probable cause."

"And is the intel good?" Payne persisted.

Carew looked to one of the other officers lined up outside the door and raised his eyebrows. The officer nodded slowly. "These tossers are trouble waiting to happen. If it wasn't this, it would be something else. And it's well known they had a beef with the victim. They think he's a grass."

"Is he?"

The officer snorted. "He was."

Rachael shifted in her seat again, bored. They were parked in one of the side streets in Great Yarmouth. Alf had suggested that this was one of the likeliest places to encounter the working girls who may have known Olive. If she craned her neck, she could just make out a grey stretch of sea.

"I'm going to get a coffee."

Terry dug into her pocket and produced a tenner. "Get me some fags as well, and I'll pay for the coffees."

"On one condition."

Terry held onto the note. "What's that, Missy?"

"That I talk to any of the girls we meet."

"Why?"

Rachael breathed out. "I've not met many. I could do with the experience."

Terry nodded and let go of the money. "Ok."

Getting out of the car and rounding the corner, she almost collided with a man coming the other way. Rachael started to apologise but the man held up his hand to stop her. "Are you new around here?" The man asked with a strange kind of whiny voice.

She looked at him properly for the first time. Fortyish, with dark greasy hair in a centre parting. He heavy framed NHS-style glasses that he kept pushing up his nose when he spoke. Bad skin, bad teeth, bad breath; he was wearing a fawn coloured windcheater, dirty brown nylon trousers over dirty trainers that were straight from the seventies. As she instinctively stepped back a couple of paces, she was reaching for her warrant card.

"I'm Gavin, pleased to meet you." Rachael looked down to see that Gavin was holding out his hand, a hairy hand with very dirty fingernails.

"And I'm DC Read." Rachael shoved her warrant card two inches in front of Gavin's face. His reaction was immediate. A look of sheer terror crossed his features as he started to back away.

"D-d-don't tell Mother." Before Rachael could react, he had turned and fled, his windcheater flapping behind him as he barged shoppers and tourists out of his way. Rachael just stood there, hands on hips, feeling shocked, confused and frustrated in equal measure.

"You may be a cop, but thanks for that love, that guy is a freaking weirdo." A voice sounded behind Rachael and she turned to see a face ravaged by years of alcohol and drug misuse. The copious make-up couldn't conceal it. Rachael stood there, dumbstruck.

"Roxette. Close your gob love, you're flapping liked a fish." The prostitute smiled, a horrible rictus that didn't improve her looks. The woman was leaning against a wall, smoking a cigarette. Waves of peroxide hair cascaded over a pink bomber jacket, underneath which was only a lacy black bra. A short denim skirt, fishnets, and thigh length pink leather boots completed her looks.

"Look, you're not in any trouble, but I really need to talk to you." Rachael appealed to the prostitute, just as she felt a big fat raindrop land on her head.

"Is this about Olive.?" Roxette asked between drags on her cigarette.

"Yes- I'm one of the detectives trying to catch the bastard who killed her."

Roxette gave her a searching look before nodding up at the shy as the rain really started to fall. "Sid's cafe, next corner. Five minutes. You bring your friend, I'll bring mine." Roxette stubbed out her fag butt under her boots and strode off into the gathering gloom.

The leading police officer, wearing a sergeant's stripes, had such a look of concern on his face that Carew crept under the window and sidled up to him. He motioned for him to walk on a couple of steps until they could whisper to each other with no risk of being overheard in the flat.

"Sergeant Mayhew Sir." Carew nodded and asked him what the problem was. Mayhew sighed, craning his neck to look at the window of the flat. It seemed to be a kitchen, complete with a sink full of dirty dishes and a selection of takeaway cartons and drink cans strewn over every surface. He looked back at Carew. "I don't like it. It's too quiet."

"Are we even sure they're in?"

Mayhew nodded. "Oh they're in, alright. But they always had reggae music booming out, all hours of the day and night."

"Maybe they're asleep."

"Mm... maybe." Mayhew straightened up. "It's your call."

Carew looked at the younger man, the other officers and the flat before whispering, "Let's go. Now."

Mayhew gave the sign and the enforcer swung into action. The door gave easily and the seven of them stormed into the flat, the armed officers first, then Carew, Payne and Leeson.

The officers screamed who they were, that they were armed, and for everyone present to show themselves, but they were met by stony silence. The lounge door crashed open and three officers rushed in. They stopped short when they saw the carnage inside.

There was a body on a blood splattered sofa facing the door, half of his face shot away. There was another body face down on the floor, a large pool of blood spreading from underneath him. A third man was propped by a wall, one hand clutching his stomach, the other raised in supplication to the police, his face a mask of pain and terror.

"Don't move!" Mayhew thundered at the man, looking around him. One of the other officers seized a gun that was discarded by the man's foot and moved it out of reach.

"Call me a fucking ambulance, man. I'm dying here. That fucker Dwayne stuck us both." The man was obviously struggling for breath, bubbles of bloody froth appearing at the corner of his mouth.

Carew moved into the centre of the room. "Who shot him?"

"I did, man. C'mon, I'll fess up when you get me to the hospital man." Carew nodded to Payne, who went to call for an ambulance. He turned to the man again. "Denzil Clarke?"

"Delroy." The man shut his eyes and grimaced with pain.

Carew squatted by Delroy. "The ambulance is on its way. But tell me why he stabbed you."

Delroy was struggling to stay awake. "He wanted to tell...wanted to..."

"He wanted to what?" Carew gently shook the bleeding man by the shoulder. "Stay with us. What did he want?"

Delroy was ready to give up. "He wanted to tell the world...what he'd done." Delroy's head slumped to his chest and he lost consciousness.

CHAPTER 27

Rachael spotted the cafe first, and excitedly pulled on her colleagues arm to hurry her along. Terry had remembered to pull her umbrella from the back of her car and was extremely grateful for it, as it was really beginning to pour down. They try to peer through the window, but it was all steamed up, and they couldn't see a thing.

Pushing open the door, they hadn't realised how busy it was. Looking at the decor, it reminded Rachael of films that she had watched with her parents when she was a child. Blue and white tiles, lino on the floor, posters of circuses long packed up gone away, and the smell of chip fat. She was about to comment how wonderfully it had been renovated when she realised that this was still the original decor, even down to the dusty rubber plant perched on one of the windowsills. She scanned the crowds and spotted Roxette sitting at the table with a redhead- her friend, Rachael presumed. Terry strode over to them.

"Tea ladies?" She gave them one of her winning smiles.

"Cappuccino." The redhead was the first to speak.

"And me." This was from Roxette.

"And for me." Rachael said, catching her up and handing Terry a ten-pound note. "Here, I'll get them." It was only when Terry handed the money over at the till did she realise that Rachael had given back her own money. She was about to shout something when Rachael winked.

She started to squeeze herself into the last seat when the redhead exclaimed, "You haven't let up on the bacon butties, have you?"

Terry scowled over at her. "When you get to my age, love, you'll find that blokes prefer a little more meat on the bones."

The redhead laughed and extended her hand. "April. this is me mate, Roxette."

"Terry." She pointed at Rachael. "Rachael."

The cappuccinos were brought over and everyone was quiet for a moment as they sampled their frothy coffee. Eventually, Roxette piped up. "Can we get on? Time is money and all that."

"Don't think you'll be getting much business in this." Terry craned her neck to look out the window but couldn't see anything.

"You be surprised." Roxette arched an eyebrow that had been plucked within an inch of its life. "Haven't you ever wondered what your old man gets up to when you're at the Bingo?"

Terry looked at her, this time without smiling. In an attempt to defuse the situation, she jumped in. "So what can you tell us about Jo, or Olive, as you knew her?"

"You'll have to trade." Roxette looked at the two detectives blankly. "You answer our questions, we'll answer yours."

Terry didn't even blanch. "Shoot."

"Info. On how Olive died. If there's some nutjob going round offing us working girls. If we're next on the list."

Terry looked as if she was thinking this over when Avril piped up.

"It was bad, wasn't it?" Did he cut her up? Rape her to death? Torture her?"

"Keep your voice down. You'll get us thrown out." Warned Roxette.

"Your friend strangled, pure and simple. No torture, no rape...no sexual contact whatsoever. She wasn't cut." Terry looked from one girl to the other. "He's not targeting working girls. You're perfectly safe- at least from him. He's targeted an old man, a gardener and a masseuse so far."

Roxette and April both looked away, lost in thought about their dead friend. "Your turn now." Rachael fixed her gaze on Roxette.

Roxette rubbed her thumb and forefinger together. "It'll cost you."

Rachael stared at her. "You see that rubber plant by the window? " Rachael jerked her head behind her. Roxette glanced at it and nodded. "Well, tell us what you know, or I'll shove it so far up your fanny you won't be able to have any punters for a month."

Terry saw Roxette blanch, even under all her copious make-up. She opened her mouth but found herself unable to speak. April took over. "She was a nice girl, not really one of us. Go the extra mile, if you know what I mean." Terry and Rachael looked om impassively. "I mean we all look out for each other, but she'd bring us soup if we were poorly, patch us up if we'd been roughed up by a punter."

"You didn't see anyone following her, stalking her?" Terry watched as the pair exchanged glances and shook their heads. "And you can't think of any reason why someone would want to do away with your friend?" Again, they shook their heads. Terry pushed herself up, thanked the girls and started to walk away. Rachael gave them a sad smile.

"We will catch him for you, and for Olive." She walked away, thinking that perhaps they weren't so different from Terry and her after all.

DCI Carew looked out across the estate, at the people milling around, the ever-increasing police presence, the general hubbub. Word had spread like wildfire and the crowd was growing outside the block where the DCI was surveying the scene. Alongside him were Lesson and Payne.

"What do you think he meant, Sir? "DC Leeson was looking out at the crowds too.

Carew sighed deeply but otherwise gave no indication that he'd heard the question from his subordinate. Just when the constable was going to ask it again, Carew started to speak.

"He was admitting that his friend was the killer."

Both officers turned to look at their boss, open mouthed.

"Come again?"

Carew bristled. "That would be 'come again, Sir' if you had the temerity to question me, DC Leeson." Carew carried on looking at the crowd, impervious to the stares that both officers.

Leeson bowed his head. "I'm sorry, Sir. Of course, that's what he meant. Sir." He looked behind Carew to where Payne was standing the other side of him. They exchanged glance and Payne gave a slight shrug.

"There's no point shrugging, Payne." This time the DCI did turn slightly. "As soon as is humanly decent, we'll get out of this shithole and reveal to the press that I have solved yet another tricky murder. The country will see that I'm the best officer the force has. Come." With that, he turned on his heel and headed along the walkway and down the stairs without a backward glance.

Jim was sitting dutifully in the conference room when Carew swept in like a tsunami. He's got some colour in his cheeks, thought Jim. The DCI acknowledged his team, and pointedly ignored Jim. He nodded to Leeson who went a stuck a photo on one of the whiteboards.

"I thought our latest victim was white?" DC Sandra Law asked as she looked up at the photo.

"He was." Carew was slowly looking at the photos of the other victims. "The victim was a man called Shane Butler. However, what you are looking at is our murderer." He let his words sink in slowly. He turned to face the assembled group. "Lady and gentlemen, may I present Dwayne Robbins. Samuel Taylor, Torey Henderson, Chris Fields and Jo Holt have been avenged."

If Jim hadn't been sitting down, he would've fallen over. Did the DCI really believe that this Dwayne person had committed all these murders? Didn't the fact that they had interviewed two suspects themselves, plus all the witness statements from the pub in Chorley, all put the man as being white? Did Carew really think that the team, or the press, or even the public would swallow any of this? The thoughts swam around his head until he was feeling dizzy.

"You haven't arrested him though?" Sandra Law persisted.

"That's the brilliant thing...he's dead already. One of the other scum from the estate killed him." Carew explained what they had found when they stormed the flat on the Broadwater.

Jim finally found his voice. "It's a bit convenient, don't you think?"

Carew rounded on him, his eyes blazing. "I would've thought you would be a bit more magnanimous in defeat, DI Smallwood. I suppose it rankles a country detective like yourself when you've been struggling so badly...and a city high-flyer like me comes in and solves the case in next to no time."

" It's amazing." Jim responded with a shake of his head. Beneath the walnut table, his fists were clenched. But the irony was lost on the DCI, who, seemingly satisfied, gave a graceful nod of his head before turning back to Sandra Law. "Apparently this scum was threatening to taunt the police about being uncatchable. Two brothers, supposedly friends of this 'man'- vehemently disagreed with him. So he stabbed his two 'friends' before one of them found a gun and shot him." Carew had inverted commas with his fingers twice in this statement- another habit that infuriated Jim, but that paled into insignificance compared to his brazen arrogance. He was bewildered that a seemingly intelligent man could appear so blinkered.

"Right. I'm going to freshen up before I call a press conference."

"What a bloody waste of time that was." Rachael puffed out her cheeks as they made way back to the car.

"At least it's stopped raining." Terry unlocked the car and waited for Rachael to settle herself before resuming. "Of course, what they didn't say was more revealing."

Rachael didn't follow. "How do you mean?"

Terry smiled indulgently. "Missy, you've got such a lot to learn. These girls stuck together, right? Looked out for each other. I suppose they would have told each other about suspicious punters, people who liked it kinky, or violent for example."

Rachael suddenly understood. "So if someone was hanging around, over a period of time, let's say...she would've mentioned it to the girls."

Terry smiled. "We'll make a detective of you yet."
"So what's next then?"
"Well, we could hang around and hope to meet some more of the girls. We might have to hang around a bit. We may even have to shack up somewhere for the night."
"Really?"
"But I suppose we should phone the boss first."
"DCI Carew?"
"Fuck off. Jimmy boy."

Jim had somehow made his way back to his office and was sitting with his head in his hands when his phone rang. He was tempted to ignore it but eventually decided to answer it, on the basis that things couldn't get any worse.
"Hi Jim, it's Mo. I suppose you've heard."
Jim laughed. "Oh yes."
"Well, I've just got back from the hospital."
"Why do I get the feeling you're going to give me yet more bad news.
Mo sighed gently. "It may be. But then again it may work to our advantage."
"Spit it out then."
Jim whistled softly, trying to work out the permutations. "Ok. Thanks for letting me know. I might have to phone you this evening, at home. I hope your wife won't mind."
"I'm sure she'll understand. You don't want me to come back then?"
"Not much point tonight. Get yourself home. We've had a rough few days."
"Ok. I'm sorry."
"What are you apologising for, Mo? You should be celebrating. We've got a serial murderer."
This time Mo laughed. "Yeah, sure. See you around."
Jim replaced the receiver and felt the craving for nicotine. Checking his pocket for his cigarettes, he almost made it to the

door before the telephone rang again. He snatched up the receiver. "Yes."

"Ooh, good afternoon to you too Jimmy."

Jim rubbed his eye with his spare hand. "Sorry, Terry. Shit day."

"Well I'm not going to make it any-"

"Stop there. I've got something to tell you." Jim then filled Terry in, the cigarettes forgotten.

Terry stepped out of the phone box and swore loudly, startling a seagull sitting on a nearby wall. As it swooped away, she watched it and felt like any chance of nailing the real killer was flying away with it. How could Carew be so stupid? She was still fuming when she got in the car, and tore off, almost knocking down a cyclist as she did so.

"Woah, where's the fire?" Rachael exclaimed, as she struggled to put on her seatbelt, being thrown from side to side as Terry screeched round several corners at top speed.

"That twatting idiot Carew has closed the case."

"He's what?" Rachael thought she'd misheard.

"There was some incident down on that estate in London. Three dead, and the DC-fucking-I is claiming that one of them is our killer!"

"And I presume you think he's wrong?" Rachael was almost afraid to ask.

Terry slammed on the brakes and they screeched to a halt, the car fishtailing as it did. They were lucky that the road they were on was residential and traffic free. "The three dead were all black guys." Terry rested her head on the steering wheel, shaking with fury.

"But-"

"I KNOW!" Terry screamed and Rachael froze. There was silence in car for what seemed an eternity. Eventually Terry turned to Rachael. "Sorry, Missy, I didn't mean to shout at you."
"It's OK."

"It's not OK. It's not anything you've done, and we're friends. I shouldn't lose my shit with friends." She narrowed her eyes as Rachael looked like she wanted to speak. "What?"

"We're friends?"

"Shut yer trap, Missy, lest I change my mind." Despite her anger Terry laughed softly.

DCI Charles Xavier Livingston Horatio Carew looked out at the massed ranks of the assembled media as lightbulbs popped and camera lights switched on, bathing him in a rich golden light. This was his moment and he was reveling in it. He lived for the adoration and adulation that solving high profile cases like this bought. He was in no rush to begin, but gradually the hubbub died down and silence ruled the room.

"Good evening, ladies and gentlemen. I have a prepared statement, and I will allow for a certain period of time for questions afterwards." Carew, flanked by ACC Parker on one side, and Superintendent Laird on the other, looked down at a piece of paper in front of him. It was blank. Charles Carew did not need a crib sheet. "Early this afternoon, the murderer of Samuel Obadiah Taylor, Torey Henderson, Chris Fields, Jo Holt and Shane Butler was apprehended. He had received a wound from a gun that he was unable to survive. A confession from the shooter, Delroy Clarke, revealed that Dwayne Robbins, 24, of Hornchurch House, on the Broadwater Farm Estate in Tottenham North London was planning to reveal his meaningless crimes to the police in an attempt to provoke them, 'big himself up, and in my view, intimidate the public into paroxysm of fear." He looked up at the press as more flashbulbs popped. No further person or person are being looked for in regard to this matter." He inclined his head to show that he was finished. Pandemonium broke out as pressmen and television reporters clamoured to ask their questions at once.

Carew pointed to a pretty blonde woman sitting in the front row.

"Carina Agnew, Channel 4 News. the media were led to believe that you were looking for a white male, but you say you've arrested a black one. How is that?"

Carew gave the woman a long hard look as he considered his reply. He took a deep breath as the lightbulbs popped in his face. "At no point today have I mentioned anyone's colour." His eyes flicked away from the reporter and settled on a man in the second row.

"Nigel Aitken-Myers, The Telegraph-"

"But why can't you answer the question?"

"You had your one question, Madam."

"But-" Carina persisted.

Carew levelled a finger at her. "One more word and you will be escorted out of the premises." Lightbulbs exploded all over the place as the clamour intensified.

"Ladies and gentlemen. Please show some decorum or the press conference is over right now." ACC Parker glowered at the crowd and was rewarded with a nod from Carew. The hubbub subsided and Carew pointed to the man from the paper again. "This will be the final question."

"What was the motive for killing five innocent people?"

"That's what I want to know." Jim standing on the side-lines, whispered to Rick Chesterfield.

"I think we all do, Sir. Problem is, he can't answer the question truthfully."

"Why do you say that?"

"Two reasons mainly. First, the suspect is dead. Secondly, he didn't do it."

Jim chuckled to himself and quietly let himself and Rick out of a side door. He had seen enough. Outside, a breathless man came jogging up to them, with what looked like a microphone case tucked under his arm.

"I'm afraid you've missed the show, mate." Jim gave the man a rueful smile whilst brushing past him as he rested his case on the ground, hands on knees.

He waited until the two detectives were out of earshot until he said quietly. "I ain't missed a thing, fuckheads."

Printed in Great Britain
by Amazon